MALICE
in Memphis

MALICE
in Memphis

by
Bill Meredith

Me Me Productions
Grenada, Mississippi

ISBN: 1-886371-29-6

Cover Design: Brad Talbott

MeMe Productions
P.O. Box 5203
Grenada, MS 38901

For interviews and other information, call
1-800-396-4626

Dedication

To Billy and Barbara:
So many times I wished I had not had such a bumpy childhood. I guess I resented everything. The discipline and the country life made me a person I deemed to be "less than normal." Reflecting on my life, I wonder what you must have gone through worrying about the strange behavior of your eldest child. You could never have known you were raising a borderline autistic child with an overactive imagination. Without that imagination, there would never be *Malice in Memphis*! As I look at Emily, I see that same vivid thought pattern and I say, "I wouldn't change a thing about my life." Thanks for everything. Thank you for being there through the roughest parts. I would never have made it without you.

To Lee (my sister, that is):
I guess I'm the only person to call you by one name. I'm sorry our ages kept us from knowing each other until recently. I'm glad we do now. I'll always be there if you need me.

Jason, Robyn and Morgan:
You have such a wonderful family. Always be thankful for how lucky you are to have one another.

To Twiggy:
I think for the most part you have to say it's been a lot of fun, however rough it's been. It's been a long road, a lot of sweat and tears in getting here. I think you know how vital you were to this production. After all, you have the original, and you deserve it!

To Emily:
This book is not thick enough for me to say all I want to say to you. Through love, I hope I can show you how much you mean to me. I'm sorry it could never work for your mom and me, but we both agree on one thing—our love for you. I hope God keeps me on earth long enough to see you have children. You should know that you are the reason I cry myself to sleep after a hard day's work and then get back up to do it again the next day. I love you, and I am never more than a phone call away.

Special thanks to Jesus Christ for his "world-class" call waiting service that allows me to get through whenever I need to.

To the Reader

It started out a charmed life. At age seventeen, I was elected national president of a trade organization of nearly 300,000 students. At age twenty-two, I had a speech and drama degree, a commission as a reserve army officer, a wife and my own business. Unfortunately, I have lived more life than most people would if they had two. I never planned it that way. Sometimes life just runs people instead of people running their own lives.

In some ways I feel like General Chuck Yeager, who said, "I've been shot at, shot up and shot down." Actually, I've had less than ten bullets fired at me. Oh sure, they were all from armed robbers at close range, but getting shot might be considered just another milestone in my short life.

From abounding business growth to the brink of bankruptcy and then back to success again, I've lived it. Successful business ventures that spurred other futile failures, I've learned it. Through a failed marriage that never should have been, God granted me the honor of fathering a beautiful girl who lived the first six and a half years of her life with a part-time dad. Now I have a relationship with her that makes her thankful her parents divorced.

In order to cut the story a couple of hundred pages short, I don't know how or why I'm still alive and well, living the rest of my life. Nevertheless, someone greater than me granted me a second shot at life. Let's hope I don't screw this one up.

Bill Meredith

Roll, Tide! Roll!

Chapter 1

I f you don't stop clanging the cell door, you won't have visitation at all this week!" Deputy Burns yelled down the corridor to an irate prisoner intent on calling his wife.

"She's got to check on something for me!" the convict screamed back.

"I'll be down there in a minute! Now shut up!" Burns commanded.

Deputy Ben Seals threw down the papers he was reading in his office and got up to close the door.

"Johnny, why don't you make some more noise? I can still hear myself think."

"What do you want me to do? I'm not even supposed to be here. Mitch is suppos—" Burns was cut off by the slam of the door as Seals retook his seat and tried to concentrate on his work. He scanned a statement made in court by a public defender outlining the so-called entrapment he had used to bust a known narcotics dealer. Ben, a deputy sheriff in rural Mississippi, shook his head as he read the twisted tale of alleged entrapment supposedly rendered by himself and the rest of the sheriff's department.

There was nothing worse than spending weeks, even months, putting together a solid case against some self-proclaimed "model" citizen who had grown an entire field of pot in the hills around the Delta, only to hear some farce of how the police "planted it there" to frame the poor guy. The stories were sometimes so wild and unbelievable they were almost convincing.

The only thing worse than the accusation was when a jury was convinced there was reasonable doubt about the crime, and some punk was set free. Then he would be right back the next week selling dope and drawing his unemployment check. Ben tried not to let it bother him. He was confident in his work, and so was Sheriff McMasters.

Ben had landed this job six years ago during the sheriff's first term. Before that he had been a mere patrolman with the Greensburg Police Department. It was shortly after being elected sheriff of Green County that Gene McMasters realized the talent in this bright young twenty-two-year-old patrolman. At least that's what Ben had hoped at the time. There had been remarks, all too many, that Ben was given the job for political reasons. Ben felt sure he would never have gotten the job if he had not obtained a criminal justice degree from LSU. Surely that had to have helped, even though there was the slight possibility that the rumors were true.

The sheriff was elected at-large, so naturally he wanted to have popular deputies. Ben had been the best fullback to come through Green County...ever. Even now, ten years later, people from twenty-five to forty-five years old were still reliving tales of his high school gridiron days that he had long since forgotten. He had been everything: the first NFL prospect from the county since "Big Bob Allen" in the '50s. People liked having a "good ole boy" come home to serve the community, especially the white population. Most of the good athletes from Green County were black, no different from anywhere else. But in a town full of rednecks, it was a real ego boost to see a white kid excel in sports. It wasn't until he got to LSU that Ben discovered how good he wasn't. He may have been as good as everybody thought, but there were seventy-five other kids there who were the best in their counties, too.

None of that mattered now. He had made his mark as a detective in rural Mississippi because of his ability to sniff out growths of marijuana all over the wooded county. It seemed that the more popular pot became with the rednecks, the larger his reputation as a bloodhound became. On several occasions other counties had asked him for help in specific searches. Once he had even worked a special task force with the DEA. Deep in his heart, he knew he had earned his keep, regardless of how he might have gotten his job in the beginning.

There was only one string he wished he could cut. The fact that he and Gene McMasters went to the same church. Other deputies often commented on how nice it must be to go to church with the boss, as if he went for some motive other than worship. Ben had grown up in the First Baptist Church of Greensburg though, and even if his distaste for playing politics was as great as his desire to be a cop, he wasn't about to give up that church. First Baptist was family to him.

As for Gene McMasters, he had been in the church even longer. It was Gene, the deacon, who had held Ben's hand when he lost his parents in a car crash at the age of fourteen. Gene *was* the First Baptist Church, and everything it represented. He, like Ben, had been raised in the church and, like Ben, would be there till he died. So nothing anybody said would change that.

Julie Seals was conservative, yet breathtaking. A woman of medium stature with whom Ben felt completely secure. He met her at an LSU home basketball game where she was a cheerleader. He was in his junior year; she was a sophomore. Their courtship blossomed into a whirlwind romance. A wedding followed the next year. Ben often wondered if he would have stuck it out as a football player had he not married and subsequently taken on convenience-store jobs to support them.

He wondered, yet it did not bother him, because he knew a woman like Julie was worth more than even an NFL contract. Whenever he caught a glimpse of her getting out of the shower, he felt that he was surely the envy of every man he knew. He knew she was beautiful not only to him but to all his friends as well. He endured the constant drooling of the rednecks closest to him, those he had grown up with and been forced to call friends.

Sometimes the sexual overtures bothered him, but he would rather have a voluptuous woman like Julie than escape taking grief from his so-called friends. Her long hair and dark eyes gave her a certain look, almost if she didn't belong in the town. There was no comparison between her and the beer-drinking, hell-raising, overweight women married to people like Bob Spencer. Bob owned a package store on Highway 14 and was the obnoxious neighbor always trying to peep over the backyard fence when Julie was sunbathing.

Ben had grown up in a town full of Bob Spencers, so he knew

how to handle his sort, with their overbearing barks that carried no bite. Besides, with Julie there was never anything to be concerned about. She was faithful and honest like her husband. Julie seemed to have made the adaptation from being a New Orleans socialite to coping with day-to-day life in Greensburg. Still Ben worried that she might one day decide to go back to the fantasy life she had been raised in.

Gabriel Chapman was more than just a father to Ben's wife—he owned a conglomerate that included three major hotel casinos along the Mississippi Gulf Coast, a small fleet of charter planes in New Orleans, four tugboats and eighteen barges. But it was his part-ownership in the two floating casinos on the Mississippi River that had given Gabriel Chapman an undesirable reputation. His partners were well known as underworld figures of New Orleans.

Ben speculated that his father-in-law might be corrupt but never discussed it with Julie. He knew he could never give her the life she was accustomed to, but after eight years of marriage he felt reasonably sure she had lowered her expectations. Now that he was number three in the sheriff's office, he did have a little more to offer. His take-home pay was nearly double the money he had brought home as a rookie patrolman just out of college. But hell, who was he kidding? Julie's allowance in college was almost as much as he was making! He could do absolutely nothing about the finances, but he could love his wife the best he knew how and be proud that he was her husband.

Gabriel Chapman had tried to discourage their marriage with the argument that they were too young. Ben knew it wasn't so much the idea of marrying young as it was who she was marrying. Julie later confided that his beliefs were accurate. Her dad had been looking for wealth, or at least a driving ambition to become wealthy, in the person she married. Gabe was sure that Ben was a great kid and would do his best to take care of Julie, but he saw him as a charity case that would be best left for someone other than his daughter.

Ben's only driving ambition was to become a cop. Maybe it was because his parents were killed in a car wreck by a heroin addict stoned out of his mind. Maybe it was because that same man was out of prison before Ben was out of college. Or maybe it was because he had a hidden desire to do good for the community that had meant so much to him. Whatever it was, he was sure he didn't want to run a hotel, or a casino. He didn't know anything about airplanes or riverboats, and he for damn sure did not want to work for a father-in-law who didn't want him in the family in the first place.

So he was commissioned with the task of taking care of Julie on his salary alone. She managed to provide nice things around the house and was still able to keep a savings account. Ben had been gone so much this last year, he couldn't keep tabs on everything. He had been traipsing all over the county all hours of the day and night trying to run down and stop the influx of pot growers and crack dealers. The floating casino just two miles west of town on the Mississippi River had caused a flood of traffic into Greensburg. Drug dealers were flourishing.

As Ben sat musing at his desk, he felt the time would soon come when he would be able to slow down, spend more time with his beautiful wife and possibly plan a family. But right now, thanks to the new casino, crime was growing faster in this rural community than he and all the other cops in west Mississippi could ever curtail. There were new people moving into the area constantly looking for jobs, and with all the new faces, it was hard to tell who was there to become a productive member of society and who was there to take advantage of the latter.

It had been easy when he was growing up there. Then you knew that Leroy Williams would get drunk and beat up his wife once a month. You knew that Mike Benfield would drink a fifth of gin, smoke a couple of joints, and race his '78 Chevy truck with the loud pipes up and down the blacktop until he pissed off everybody on Carter Road.

Now things were different, drastically different. In addition to the constant problem of pot growers in the hills, crack and a variety of other street drugs new to the '90s had infiltrated Greensburg. Ben had experienced a rude awakening to the power of crack when he became a rookie deputy.

The bums would steal from their own mothers over and over just to satisfy the need for the drug. Bums. In every case—black or white, rich or poor—they were bums. Maybe not when they started out, but by the time the "rockman" had them, you could stick a fork in them, because they were done. Crack would, in every case, destroy their entire world. Automobiles, homes, jewelry—all would eventually go for crack. After all their material possessions were gone the bodies would go, partially from the use of the drug, then from the selling of the body. Women would perform illicit sex on men to get crack. Men would perform illicit sex on men just to pay for one little bitty rock of crack. It didn't matter who it was with as long as the thirst was quenched. These were problems that had been seen before only in larger towns.

The problem at times seemed overwhelming. Crack is made from cocaine, but rocked up so that it can be sold cheaper. Twenty bucks or less will get you a rock of crack that has the same effect as cocaine but is more addictive. The users were a variety of people, some rich, some poor, all colors. The small-time pot growers had turned to this affordable drug because of its availability. Now a steady stream of people from all walks of life were sending family members to rehab only to see the hold of crack drag their loved ones back into the same hell they were in before, even if rehab had proved "successful."

Ben felt a growing sensation daily that he could never have a major impact on his part of the world. Things were happening faster than he could keep up with. He had sworn to himself before he entered this line of work that he would never let that mentality take over, but it had become harder to remain vigilant. He had felt he was just treading water on the problem even before the addition of all the new faces in town. Besides, he had a loving wife at home who wanted more of his time, even though she didn't complain about his being gone so much.

Yet he knew Gene McMasters was pleased with his work because he was always put in charge of drug details, and everyone else on the force went along without any complaints. Ben guessed that this made it fairly obvious that he was doing his job, but nevertheless, it was hard to maintain enthusiasm when a major drug bust hardly dented the county drug traffic.

Ben left the office about 3:15 that afternoon, at least two hours earlier than he had any day the entire year. He had spent the previous night waiting for Tyrone Leggett, an eighteen-year-old black kid from Chicago. Tyrone was supposed to leave his aunt's house and go make a drug buy. Sheriff McMasters had been given a tip that the buy was sure to go down last night...but it never happened.

Ben had felt from the start that it might be a wasted effort. He knew Tyrone felt he was being watched, but Ben seldom disagreed with the high sheriff. He respected McMasters' wisdom as a retired highway patrolman and as a sheriff. Gene McMasters was now in his sixties and couldn't handle the overnight scenes as well. So Ben and some of the younger guys usually took the stakeouts.

He was glad to be headed home now. A quick stop at Mable Brown's to get a half-dozen roses for his neglected wife delayed him for a few minutes. After some chit-chat with the ladies in the flower shop (the same ladies who had made his corsage for his senior prom ten years earlier), he left for home. All the way along the narrow winding road off Highway 14, down past Carter's Grocery, he thought of his beautiful wife and the fact that it had been ten days since they had made love. His desire to take his wife as soon as he walked in the door became overwhelming. He hoped she would feel the same way.

As he rounded the bend over Panther Creek he could see the house. There was another patrol car in the drive. If there was one thing Ben did not want to think about the rest of the day, it was business. He couldn't imagine serving another warrant, pulling any more surveillance, or anything else related to his job. Whatever it was, it could wait! He could already envision Julie's supple buttocks and the sensuous moves that suggested that in the privacy of their own home, she was more a sex goddess than a country wife.

As he got closer, he could see that it was not just another patrol car, but that the tag was S.O.1. It was Gene himself, and it must be important for him to come all the way out here instead of phoning. He fleetingly wondered why Gene was even in town. He had left early that same morning headed to Jackson for a meeting at the Federal Building with the DEA. Ben was puzzled. One thing he had learned from Gene in six years was that time management is of the utmost importance. For Gene McMasters to drive all the way out past Panther Creek meant something urgent and probably having to do with the meeting.

Ben parked the car in front of the house and hopped up onto the old wood porch, remembering again that he had intended to paint it for over a year. As he turned the key in the front door lock, he heard someone in pain yelling for help from the rear of the house. Ben burst through the door to the back of the house where the noises were emanating from his bedroom. He ran down the hall and opened the door. For a moment he froze as his eyes took in the scene. The roses dropped from his hand as he realized the animal-like screams had come from Julie.

Julie was naked, her legs high in the air. Gene McMasters was on top of her banging her with all the force and lust that had been pent up in Ben moments ago. Julie saw Ben and screamed, "What the hell are you doing here?" Gene only grimaced as he released his tension into Julie, then cried, "Do it, baby," just as he had obviously done many times before. There was a long pause as time stood still in Ben's mind. He was reeling and profusely trying to comprehend what he was seeing. Ten seconds must have passed before his mind focused on Julie's shrieks.

"You're not going to kill him! Don't kill him!" she screamed.

"Shut up, whore!" Gene barked as he pushed Julie away from the service revolver he now clutched in his hand.

She tumbled across the bed headfirst onto the floor, her long hair falling over her head as she recovered onto her knees.

"I said don't hurt him, you bastard, or you'll never touch me again!" She dove across the bed slapping the old man's arm as he wheeled toward Ben. Her slap caused Gene's tightly squeezed trigger finger to discharge the first round diagonally across the bedroom into the wall mirror. The glass shattered into a thousand pieces, many of which found their way into Julie's naked breasts and side. Microbits of glass showered her hair. The pain of the glass cuts went momentarily unnoticed because of the severe pain in the middle of her back where Gene's toes had cut her with a swift kick.

"Stay down, you stupid slut!" he yelled.

What was this Ben was seeing? Was it real? His mind was still numb, but instincts were pulling him back into the hallway. Those same instincts had taken over for him two months earlier when he had been one-on-one with that nineteen-year-old burglar in the dark back room of Carter's Grocery. Ben and Deputy Jones had cut off the kid's escape, but Ben had gone in and taken him alone. Right now his mind was into what was happening, even though nothing seemed real except the overload of adrenaline running through his veins.

He backed into the hallway after the paralysis subsided only to catch a severe pain in his heart and abdominals. Was he having a heart attack? He reached to his side for his revolver, then didn't know why. He began to stagger down the hall bouncing twice off the walls before reaching the front door. He instinctively grabbed his keys out of the door lock. Inside the county-owned Ford Taurus, he fumbled with the keyring, going through it twice and then a third time before realizing it was a specific key for which he was searching. He fired up the eight-cylinder and then took his time backing onto the grass slowly, dazed, as if in no hurry at all.

The kids from down the street were playing baseball in the field beside his house, something he had repeatedly rebuked them for since the day they broke his bathroom window. It seemed he would never be able to break the little squirts. Maybe one day they would all grow up. In his rearview, he saw Gene appear on the front porch, trousers on, shirt on but untucked. Ben's daze carried him down the drive where Bob Spencer was getting his mail out of the rural mailbox.

"Was that gunshots?" Bob yelped as Ben pulled onto the blacktop road, not even stopping to look for traffic. Damn nosey Bob, Ben thought as he began to pick up speed. Of course it was gunshots, or at least one. Hadn't he ever heard gunfire before? Now he would want to know everything. Ben shook his head.

"What am I thinking?" Ben muttered in a voice that was not his. "My life is over and I'm worried about Bob Spencer and some kids playing ball!"

He picked up speed over the next half-mile. Panther Creek would be a good place to stop and jump off the bridge. He was still too frozen to even stop the car. If he could just get to an open stretch of road, he could drive fast, let out the anxiety, and all that he had just seen would become a dream. On the smooth blacktop road, he alternated speeding up and then slowing down, unsure of what to do. The adrenaline was resting in his stomach along with his broken heart. The weight was so heavy, he could no longer think. Ben slammed on the brakes, screeching to a stop. He opened the door as he began puking. He stared at the remnants of his afternoon snack, now splattered in the middle of the blacktop.

Slowly, he began to let his mind deal with reality. What he had seen was real, as unbelievable as it now seemed. It was real. A voice on the car radio brought him out of his fog. It was Gene McMasters'.

"Goldilocks has found the porridge!"

"Ten-four," came the reply from S.O.2.

"S.O.7, I haven't heard from ya, are ya there?" McMasters barked.

"Ugh, roger, S.O.1, this is seven. Go ahead," came the reply.

"Goldilocks has found the porridge."

"Roger that. We'll see you there."

Ben's brain cells were cloudy from all the information he was taking in in such a short time.

"What the hell.... I'm not believing.... What in God's name is happening?" he screamed to the heavens.

Ben turned back into the car, slammed the engine into overdrive, and pondered aimlessly the possibilities confronting him. The road seemed longer than normal even with his lights flashing on the top of the patrol car. He couldn't get anywhere fast enough. The biggest problem was that he had no real destination, no contingency plan. He was such a well-prepared person, but who would have considered this?

He began to blame himself. Had the signs been there? Had the signs been there all along and he was just too damn busy to notice? Finally he could see Highway 14. He breathed a small sigh of relief not even knowing why. He wondered what a reasonable man would do if he had just caught his boss screwing his wife? Probably shoot the bastard. Yeah, that's it, shoot the most beloved law enforcement officer in the history of Greensburg. After he convinced almost everybody of his story, only two or three thousand people would want to hang him down on the banks of the Mississippi. Most of them would just vandalize his home and beat the hell out of him. One or two might actually try to kill him...that is, if he wasn't sent to the gas chamber for killing a law enforcement officer.

The calls had stopped coming in for the other deputies from McMasters. Obviously, quite a few knew of this illicit affair, and Ben dwelled on how long it had been going on. How many times had he been with Julie after she had been with the old man? Carter's Grocery appeared on the left, and a patrol car marked S.O.10 was parked squarely in front. Mitch Williams. He had been on the force just as long as Ben and was still tenth in rank because he and McMasters despised each other. In fact, if Mitch weren't so skilled in managing the county jail, he would probably have been gone long before. He and Ben had always gotten along. He treated Ben with respect, and Ben returned the favor. Ben often wondered if Mitch resented his moving up so fast. Sometimes he even felt guilty about his own success. Mitch would never move any higher because Gene hated him almost as much as Mitch hated Gene.

Now Ben could explain to Mitch why he had moved up so fast. McMasters was keeping tabs on Ben for reasons other than good law enforcement. Ben wheeled into Carter's to find the only person he could go to at this time. Sprinting to the front screen door he saw Mary Carter ringing up an order of meat, cigarettes, and beer, cursing because she had forgotten to ring up the food stamp items separately. Her forty-year-old cash register would not divide the food from the nonfood.

"Where's Mitch Williams?" Ben clambered, not stopping to hear the answer.

"You know he's in the back," Mary retorted, never looking up. Almost every day, Mitch was there shooting pool on the fifty cent tables in the back of Carter's Grocery. These were the same tables that Ben had stood on recently when he pulled that burglar out of Carter's roof as he attempted to escape. Mitch shot pool for money, small money...a dollar a game, but still one more reason for McMasters to hate him. It just wasn't a good example for the public to see.

"Mitch!"

Mitch looked up from his crouched position over a two-ball.

"Grab a stick! This one's almost over."

"Mitch, I need to talk to you for a minute!" The agitation in Ben's voice went unnoticed by Williams, who was concentrating on the angle for his shot.

"Grab a seat, I'll be right there," Mitch replied.

"Now, Mitch! I need to talk to you now!"

"I'm off duty, Ben—outta uniform and everything."

"Mitch, this is personal."

"Ben, I got five bucks on this game."

Ben scrounged in his pocket and produced a ten and threw it onto the table. Mitch laid his cue to the side, picked up the ten and handed it back to Ben.

"I'm out, fellas," he proclaimed to the room. "Let's go out back, Ben."

They stepped out the back door of the grocery.

Mitch now saw the distress in Ben's face.

"What's on your mind?"

Ben took a deep breath and plunged in. "I know you're not going to believe this, but Gene has been having an affair with my wife!"

"What!" Mitch shouted, then caught himself so as not to draw attention from inside. "Are you sure?"

"I don't know how long, but I do know I caught them in my bed fifteen minutes ago."

"No!" Mitch exclaimed.

Ben relayed the whole story to Mitch just as it had happened and closed by saying, "I came to you because I knew I could count on you."

"You know it, Ben," Mitch assured him. "I've always hated the old fart anyway.... Job or no job, I'd love to burn that bastard! I can't believe he would do that to one of his own people. What are you going to do?"

"I don't know just yet.... I'm finding it hard to think. I don't know how many of 'em knew about it. The ones Gene called on the radio knew for sure, and I don't know what they could be up to either."

Mitch nodded. "One thing's for sure, you don't want them to find you before you're ready to face them! Where's your car?"

"Out front," Ben answered.

"You gotta move it! Here, gimme the keys.... I'll move it around here. You stay put."

Ben fumbled through his pocket, handed Mitch the keys and borrowed a cigarette from him. He never smoked but would light up and suck on the end a little whenever his nerves were maxed out. Ben stared into the woodline for at least five minutes before realizing that Mitch had not returned. He whipped through Carter's back door, past the pool shooters and the half-dozen shoppers in the aisles to meet Mitch coming back in the front door. Something was very wrong.... He could tell by the look on Mitch's face.

"Here...take these," Mitch shoved the keys back into Ben's hand.

Ben grasped them, then looked up to see Gene McMasters and the whole sheriff's department filing in behind him.

"You're under arrest, Officer Seals, for the illegal possession of a controlled substance!" McMasters shouted.

There was dead silence in Carter's Grocery as the tobacco chewers in rocking chairs ceased to chew or rock. The customers quit talking and everybody gawked at the scene, which though commonplace on their TV screens, had never been played out live before them.

"Cuff him and unarm him, Deputy Williams," McMasters

ordered.

Mitch Williams drew his backup .380 from his boot and told Ben to lean over the counter. Ben looked at him in disbelief.

"Not you too, Mitch...not you too," Ben sighed.

"Lean over and grab the counter, Seals," Mitch ordered.

Mitch Williams handcuffed Ben with McMasters' cuffs and removed Ben's service revolver. He led Ben outside, followed by McMasters, Mary Carter, Old Man Carter, all the deputies, the tobacco chewers, and the customers. In front of the old store, the tension could be cut with a knife as Mitch led Ben to his very own car, still parked where Ben had left it.

"Do you have in your possession anything that is illegal which you have not reported to the proper channels of command of the Green County Sheriff's Department?" Gene McMasters demanded of Ben in a voice everyone could hear.

"No. What did you have in mind?" Ben smarted back.

"Do you mind if we look in your trunk?"

"There's nothing there but my...shotgun," Ben replied as if he was unsure at this point.

"I'll take that as permission to go ahead. Get his keys and open it!"

Mitch opened the trunk of Ben's car in front of the crowd and pulled out two duffel bags. Mitch unzipped them and began to pull plastic bags of pot from each. The crowd's murmur grew louder.

"You bastard!" Ben cried as he kicked Mitch Williams in the groin and back. Mitch fell to the ground.

"All right, Mr. Seals, you just got assault on an officer and resisting arrest.... Would you like to go for more...maybe attempted murder?" McMasters taunted Ben as the other deputies wrestled him into a squad car. Someone threw a hand over his mouth just as he shouted.

"Your fine sheriff is sleeping with..."

Chapter 2

The endless throbbing in the back of Ben's head woke him. He looked around the cell he had seen everyday for the last few years, but it looked very different from this side. He remembered struggling with Mitch Williams the night before while being thrown into the cell. He felt numb from his brain to the soles of his feet. He had tried all the way into town to get straight answers from Mitch and the other deputies. He begged Mitch for answers. But so far all he had gotten from Mitch and Deputy Burns were apologies.

Johnny Burns had even gone so far as to say, "We really like you, Ben, but this is the way things have to be."

Ben had hoped that when he awoke it would all be over, just a nightmare. It now began to soak in that all of this was real, and the only explanation that he could come up with was that his devoted wife must be screwing the whole sheriff's department.

McMasters had made sure Ben was kept in the "orientation cell," as it was nicknamed. It was just inside the main populous area of the jail but far enough away from the other prisoners that you couldn't talk to anyone until you had been interrogated and put into the general population cells. It was a large facility known as the Green County Detention Center, but it housed inmates from four surrounding counties.

Ben wondered who knew of his arrest and if press or friends or even church members would be gathering to find out about him. He knew he wasn't ready to see any friends, but he was ready to see the press. Not so much Harley Roper, who ran the *Greensburg Herald*, but television, yes. Maybe all four Jackson TV stations would cover it—a deputy getting busted for drugs by his own department. He could talk to the reporters who would break the story and before sundown the attorney general would be involved. All they needed to do was find Gene's bullet hole in his house, trace the ballistics back to Gene's gun, and he would blow this whole thing apart.

First and foremost however, he had to get a lawyer. For that, he had the perfect answer, Randy Seals. Randy was a tough young lawyer from Memphis, who was not only Ben's first cousin but had spent his first couple of years working for the D.A. in Green County before returning to private practice in Memphis. Still, Randy knew Green County and he knew Green County politics. He knew Gene. He knew everybody involved, but best of all, he was family and would cost little, if anything, and yet provide some of the most valuable legal advice he could get. Ben and Randy were never close yet were always eager to help one another. Ben had helped Randy out many times when Randy worked for the Green County district attorney. Ben had often given him hot tips on things going on in and around the county so that Randy could investigate them himself and look good for his boss.

Their families had never been particularly close. Randy's parents had always shunned Ben's father somewhat and considered him the black sheep of the family. Ben's father had been content to work in the chemical factory just outside Greensburg, instead of working for his brother's shipping company in Memphis. His brother had built a huge trucking company over the years. But Ben's father had loved Greensburg and never wanted to leave. When Ben's parents were killed, his mother's sister was appointed guardian. Randy's parents never bothered to ask for custody.

Three years had passed since Randy had left Greensburg. Now he was back in Memphis practicing law and overseeing the shipping company his father had left him when he died from a stroke at the age of forty-seven. Randy's mom had blamed her husband's death on his work habits...endless hours that had built a one-man trucking company into a small empire with more than fifty trucks.

Randy and his mom loved to spend money so much they were afraid to sell the company. Together they had tried to run it. Randy was not the businessman his father was, though. He had had enormous success as a defense lawyer but often spent as much money on women in a month as Ben earned in a year. Recognizing her son's weakness for females, Mary Seals worked in the office in order to keep tabs on the business. That was fine with Randy. He was more concerned with his law practice. He loved criminal law—every facet of it. It was all a game to him and he loved to play. He was unorthodox and unpredictable. From playing blackjack at a thousand bucks a hand to volunteering his services to some poor soul who had shot his family or been caught selling crack to a narc, Randy liked the rush from the game, as he called it, and that's where Ben disagreed with Randy. Life was a game to Randy, and in most cases he finished better than odds would predict. Ben had chosen to live his life differently—conservatively, quietly—and up until now, it had worked well.

Ben waited on his bunk as the entrance to the corridor opened. He could see his cousin strolling toward the cell. "They called me for you!" Randy answered Ben's question before he asked it.

"You're not going to believe what these bastards are up to..."

Randy, in his sleek city style, merely cut Ben off with a simple pointed index finger raised to cover his lips so that Mitch could not see.

"You can use the briefing room next to the sheriff's office," Mitch advised Randy. Mitch led Ben down the hall with Randy following closely behind. Ben was bound with leg irons and his hands were cuffed in front.

"I need to go to the bathroom."

"Use the one in the briefing room. I'll take the handcuffs once another deputy secures the door behind me."

"Aw, Mitch, dammit, you know I'm not going anywhere!"

Williams stared at Ben with a sympathetic smile. "I know. All the same though, I've got orders to treat you as a hostile prisoner."

"When did you start following orders?" Ben scowled. Mitch didn't respond.

"Then tell me, how many of you are screwing Julie, and for how long?"

Mitch parted his lips as if he wanted to reply, but clammed up. "You've got thirty minutes," he snapped as he locked the door on his way out.

Ben sat across the table from his cousin and began to relay the whole gruesome story of the night before just as it had happened. Randy sat dazed as he heard the incredible tale of the night. When Ben finished his account, Randy leaned back in his chair, almost speechless. He shook his head.

"Ben, I'm sorry, truly sorry. I've always thought highly of Julie, and I can't believe this happened. Now, as your cousin, I will do anything in the world for you. As your attorney, I want you to listen and be open-minded to the things I'm about to put before you."

Ben sighed and took a deep breath, not knowing if he liked the sound of Randy's tone as his closest kin shuffled papers from a folder he had produced from his briefcase. Ben could make out his own name scribbled across the top of the folder.

"Ben, I never know where to begin on this sort of thing. I guess I should throw it right out there at you. You've been offered a deal by the prosecution."

"Deal! What deal? I'm not about to take a deal.... I haven't done a damn thing!"

"Just hear me out first," Randy interrupted him.

"Randy, I'm not dealing! Nothing! Not even a misdemeanor."

"I know you're innocent, Ben. Just listen to me! I left this hellhole because of the things that go on here!"

"Things...what things?" Ben queried.

"Well, let's just say it's a small place, small enough that justice could be bought on numerous occasions."

There was a moment of silence.

Ben took a deep breath. "Not that I'm interested...but just what are they offering?"

Randy sighed. "Well, here it is. You plead guilty to two counts of simple assault, you get six months suspended."

"No fine?" Ben asked almost laughing.

"That's it," Randy replied.

"You mean they're willing to let me walk, after all this?"

"Well, not entirely. You have to leave this county."

"Or what?" Ben knew there had to be more.

"Or the judge will invoke the sentence."

"No way...no way.... There's no way in hell I'm going to let these bastards run me out of town."

"I know how you feel, Ben, I've—"

"No you don't," Ben interrupted as he broke into tears. "You can't possibly know."

"I've got to talk to Julie." Ben's voice trembled.

"I don't think that's a good idea right now," Randy tried to soothe his cousin.

"Please!" Ben begged.

"Listen to me, I know what you're feeling."

"How could you?" Ben cried.

"Maybe, I don't, but what they're offering you is more than freedom. What do you want more than anything else? To be a cop, am I right?"

Ben nodded. "And my wife. I want my wife. I love her." Tears rolled down his cheeks.

"That's between you and her. But with this you can be a cop. If you get a felony conviction, you'll never even own a gun much less be in law enforcement! You'll do time! Hard time! You know what they do to cops in the pen!"

"But I'm innocent! I need to talk to Julie! I can't believe she did this."

"For what it's worth I'm sure that she loves you and is sorry for all this," Randy said. "But Ben, let me...let me just come straight to the point. I don't think we have a very strong case. No, let me restate that. I don't think we have a snowball's chance at this. It's you against the entire sheriff's department...and maybe your wife too. Take the deal!"

"She'd stand up for me before she'd let me rot in jail."

"Ben, I've seen these things before. No matter what she might say now, anything can happen."

Ben paused a minute before answering. "I put my faith in the system. I can't turn my back on it now.

There are so many things to consider," he started to ramble as he stared aimlessly at the wall. "So much to think about...it seems too much, not even real," he muttered almost under his breath.

"Look, while you're thinking, I'm going to let the rest of the world know we're in business, whether we like it or not," Randy broke in.

"No, I can't do that!" Ben snapped.

"What do you mean? You have no choice!"

"I mean...I've got to think...plan...I have no place to go, no job...nothing..."

"You're staying with me and Mom. We've got plenty of room and you can stay as long as you like. Besides, Mom will love having you around. You were always like another son to her."

That was news to Ben, considering the lack of effort his aunt had put forth in seeing him over the years; nevertheless, he was in no state of mind to argue.

"And," Randy continued, "as far as work goes, if you'll put down your stubborn pride and let me help, we might can fix that problem as well."

"Thanks, but no thanks. I'm a cop and always will be."

Randy laughed. "Oh, I hope you didn't think I meant at Seals Trucking!"

Suddenly, Randy's mood became serious. "A very good friend of mine was murdered last week. His name was Michael Rose."

Ben nodded, "Michael Rose...I know that name, the cop from Memphis killed in the gang bust."

"Yeah," Randy replied. "I guess every cop in the South heard about it. Well, he was a narc, shot down in a crackhouse on the west side. I feel funny talking about this, but I know his position is still vacant. I believe I've got enough clout to get you the job. You've got the experience."

"You gotta be kidding! You want me to think about taking on another job now!"

"I don't see why not. You've got to pick up the pieces. A lot of people want that job. The word is that they prefer a fresh face...an out-of-towner. They think Michael was killed because a drug dealer made him as a cop. He was undercover as a postal employee, but they spotted him and shot him when he stepped onto the front lawn of the crackhouse...shot him before the bust even had a chance to go down."

"I'd love to be the one to bust those punks inside that house!" Ben felt the true blue pride swell within himself for a moment, erasing all thoughts of his own predicament.

'Well, with a little luck, maybe you'll get that chance," Randy quipped as he snatched up his briefcase and ordered Ben to sit tight in his cell while he sprang him out of jail and into a new life.

"I can't do this!" Ben screamed. "I want to talk to Julie. You need to go out to my house and find that bullet hole before they cover it up." Ben rattled on and on before Randy got him quiet.

"They would have already covered that hole," Randy said. "And if Julie wanted to talk to you, she'd be here now! Take the deal!"

Chapter 3

Through the perilous turn of events, Ben resisted all notions of giving in. He still tried to contact Julie to no avail. Within hours the whole ordeal had come to a head. He left town with the clothes on his back and little else.

Ben felt he would go insane not being able to talk to Julie, but at Randy's insistence, he gave in and left immediately. He would send for his things after the divorce proceedings. Besides, the court order issued upon his release from jail barred his presence anywhere in the county under any circumstances. Ben wasn't sure about the legality of this small-town justice and felt sure it could be overturned somehow, but for now, the most important thing was to get free and out of town. He knew that was also what McMasters, the judge, and anybody else involved in this sham wanted as well. But he still worried that taking the deal made him look guilty and leaving town would only add fuel to the flame.

Ben woke from a foggy sleep that had done little for his weary body. Randy's Lincoln had just rolled into Tunica, Mississippi. It had been a rough ride through the Delta, and Ben was glad he had been asleep. Highway 49 wasn't the best of roads under any circumstances, and with tractors and other farm equipment constantly pulling onto the highway and slowing down traffic, it was an annoyance that Ben couldn't deal with right now.

Randy introduced Ben to his favorite "soul food" stop. Ben felt sure the food was good, but he was in no mood to enjoy anything; he didn't realize what a gloomy companion he was until one of the black ladies, the one who seemed to own the place, asked Randy what was wrong with his friend.

"Is he ill?" she asked. She was a large woman named Lou. Ben didn't realize how large until she approached him with some blackberry cobbler.

"Here, eat this honey," she demanded. "My grandkids always get cobbler and ice cream when they get down—it brings 'em right back!"

Ben managed a slight smile. It seemed the best he could do right now. Randy paid the ticket, got a carryout for the cobbler, and hurried out the door. Ben was already leaning against the dirty Lincoln, now matted with bugs from the Delta highway.

"We'll be there in forty-five minutes," Randy remarked in an effort to turn Ben's mind away from what he had left and toward what lay ahead. Ben dozed off to sleep again. When he awoke the town car was making its way along Riverside Drive into downtown Memphis. Randy and his mother shared a two-story condo overlooking the river in walking distance of Beale Street.

The Memphis sunset seemed pleasant to Ben with all the trees and the Mississippi flowing along the city's west side. The city offered a welcome change, and yet there was a certain loneliness about the change. Ben knew how lucky he was to have Randy and his aunt to lean on. Still there was no condolence for the emptiness he felt. Randy called from his cellular to let his mother know they were in town. Upon arrival, Mary Seals rushed to hug the nephew she barely knew. After offering her consolation for all that had happened, she assured Ben that things would be fine now that he was with people who loved him.

Ben, still bewildered, confused, and irritable, tried to be kind to his aunt. The sickness in his gut seemed to stand in the way of his bonding with anyone. Mary ushered "her boys" in and put on a pot of coffee. The rest of the night was given to small talk of things going on at the office where Mary occupied herself keeping the books for Seals Trucking. There was talk about a new girl in the office, her pregnancy, and the speculation about who the father of the baby might be.

Randy elected to turn in early for the evening, citing an attempt to get to the police commissioner's office extra early on Ben's behalf.

Ben followed suit, but his attempts at sleeping were futile. Two hours of tossing and turning left him staring at the river through his bedroom window. He could see the Mississippi at the bottom of the hill; it was lit up from the lights of the Mississippi-Arkansas bridge and Mud Island. A handful of tugs had inched by already, pushing barges up- and downstream. The monotony of the scene was broken by an occasional fishing boat drifting through the night or the Amtrak speeding alongside Riverside Drive some eighty feet below the Seals' home.

The night activity was soothing to Ben. He awoke at 9 a.m., not recalling how or when he went to sleep. Randy was gone. Mary was gone but had left a note behind on the sofa table relaying where everything he might need was located and instructing him to give her a call at work. An employee would pick him up and bring him to the company to spend the day. Ben stood reading the note as the phone rang. He let it ring twice and then heard the answering machine pick up. Randy Seals' voice came over the machine.

"Ben, if you're listening, pick up."

Ben grabbed the receiver.

"Hey, get dressed, you got a noon lunch date with the police commissioner."

"What?"

"I told you I would help you, if you let me," Randy retorted.

"I know, but I didn't expect this."

"Well, there's no guarantee, but it's a start."

"I'm not ready for this."

"You've got to pull yourself together, man. Don't let this slip away."

"I'll give it a try," Ben reluctantly agreed.

"Great. I'll be there in a little while."

"Oh, by the way," Randy continued, "there's a Captain Burkes who heads the task force that Michael Rose worked on. He'll meet with us. If you're hired, he'll be the one you work directly under."

The lunch meeting was to take place at Monte's, an exclusive, hidden- away diner downtown. It was a perfect gathering place for the Memphis elite, from the mayor and police commissioner to the governor, when he was in town. Even members of organized crime had been known to frequent the diner. Randy picked Ben up at 11:45. The restaurant was not far away, but it took the entire fifteen minutes to weave through the maze of cars and get to the parking lot reachable only by way of a long alley running between old abandoned warehouses. The parking lot was nearly full. Randy found a spot, stopped and slammed the car into park.

"Let's go before we're late," he ordered.

Ben hopped out, unsure even of where they were going. There were no signs, no nothing. Randy led the way up a stairwell on the side of one of the old warehouses. There was a security guard at the bottom of the stairwell, probably a necessity in this part of town, Ben thought. Inside there was an air of busyness with constant chatter occasionally interrupted by a middle-aged man of Greek descent barking instructions at busboys.

"That's Monte," Randy whispered.

Ben took note of the wall of celebrity pictures plastered with autographs. He spotted the commissioner at the same time Randy did. It wasn't hard with the dress uniform and the fact that he was motioning to them from across the room.

"Commissioner, this is Ben Seals," Randy said, shaking hands with the commissioner.

"Nice to meet you, sir," Ben quickly greeted him.

"Ben, it's nice to meet you. I've already heard good things about you and your work. Have a seat...the soup is really good today."

"Mr. Seals, you comma to see me early in the week. I'ma so honored," Monte shouted as he approached the table.

"The commissioner says the soup is good today. Is that so?" Randy smirked.

A blank look came over Monte's face.

"My soup, she's always good...very good...best in town. You know this, everyone knows this. Commissioner...he's a funny guy! I'm a gonna get you and your friend soup...you gonna see...you gonna like."

"Thanks, Monte," said the commissioner. Turning to Ben and lowering his voice somewhat, the commissioner said, "Ben, I understand you want to bring your one-man narc team to our little town."

"Well, yes sir." Ben still was unable to focus himself. He didn't want to be here or anywhere right now. His mind wandered aimlessly.

The small talk was broken by the commissioner responding to another customer coming in the door. "I want you to meet this guy coming in the door, Ben."

Ben turned to see a well-built man with a weathered face standing in the doorway.

"Over here, John." the commissioner stood as the jeans-clad man made his way across to their table and exchanged handshakes with each of them. "This is Captain Burkes of the twelfth precinct.... John, you know Randy.... This is his cousin, Ben, who I told you about this morning."

"John Burkes," the man said simply. There was an upfront gruffness about him. Ben hardly noticed. His mind drifted back to Greensburg and Julie. He fought back the tears and reconnected himself with his surroundings.

"We're having soup. You should try the soup here—it's very good," Ben's subconscious heard the commissioner say.

"Yes sir, that's fine, sir," Burkes replied.

He seemed to be a real down-to-business kind of guy...professional, not politically motivated as a police commissioner might be...probably ex-military, Ben thought.

"John, Ben here has an outstanding reputation as a real bloodhound down in the Delta. Just the kind of guy you need on your task force, especially after what happened to Lieutenant Rose." The commissioner leaned back in his chair. "I think we should consider Ben for the position on your team. You know I don't usually play a big part in the hiring of an officer in this role, but under the circumstances, I felt a need to get involved. The mayor and I want Rose's killer in custody. A massive manhunt has produced nothing!"

"We're working on it, sir!" Burkes insisted. "You know we're close."

"Well, in the meantime, we've got to think about replacing Rose, God rest his soul!" the commissioner continued. "I'd like for you to take Ben to the precinct with you and show him around."

"Well, sir..." Burkes began.

"The soup is a-goo-od," Randy mocked the Greek. "I know-a you-a like it. I make-a it extra special for you.

"That guy is so full of crap," he added with a grin.

"Monte?" The commissioner laughed. "I've known Monte for more than twenty years. He doesn't even realize how full of it he is."

John Burkes sat up in his chair. "Sir, I'd like to get a word in private with you, if you don't mind."

"Sure, Captain," the commissioner answered, and then questioned, "First, tell me what you think about my new appointment. Will you have some time to work with him this afternoon?"

"Well, sir, that's kinda what I wanted to talk to you about." He looked at Ben, who was now shifting uneasily at the hint of a problem with his soon-to-be boss. Randy Seals leaned forward with his chin resting on his hand and elbow on the table, as if to fully take in whatever was about to come from John Burkes' mouth. No offense to you, Mr. Seals, but we need experience on my team."

"Ben has experience," Randy blurted out. "Maybe he can teach you a few things."

"Hold it! Hold it!" the commissioner laughed, trying to calm everyone down. "John, I understand your concerns, but I'm comfortable with Ben. Work with him. He'll do fine." He patted John on the shoulder while standing.

"If you gentlemen will excuse me? I see Councilwoman Scott. I'll be right back. Get to know each other," the commissioner ordered as he left the table.

John Burkes sipped his water, waiting for the commissioner to get out of earshot. "You're scum!" he said, leaning over the table to speak to the defense lawyer. "And not just because of the clients you represent."

Randy laid his fork on his plate," I believe the commissioner meant for you to give Ben a fair chance."

"His getting the job is chance enough!" Burkes' face reddened.

"You might find out he's a great cop!" Randy raised his voice only to have Burkes raise his louder.

"I don't suppose you being the mayor's campaign manager had anything to do with it?" Burkes all but shouted.

Both men clammed up as the commissioner returned. Ben felt his stomach sinking, wondering if he could get any lower.

Chapter 4

Back at the Seals' Condo, Mary Seals welcomed the boys with a scotch and soda for Randy and an offer to get Ben whatever he wished.

"Mom, you know Ben's not a drinker."

"Make mine a double!" Ben spoke for the first time since leaving Monte's.

Randy gave Ben an inquisitive look. "Don't let John Burkes get to you."

"I can't take this job," Ben said.

"You forget John Burkes! You'll fit right in!"

"I can't even think about work right now!" Ben tried to fight the tears only to lose this time. "I just loved...her so much." He grimaced as the tears flowed.

"Has she called?" he asked Mary.

"No Ben, I'm sorry," she apologized. She then tried to change the subject, but Ben couldn't seem to talk about anything else.

"I tried calling her this morning—I think she's got the phone off the hook."

"You let me handle that!" Randy said. "I'll get your share of your stuff."

"I don't care about that. I don't want to think about fighting with her over that.... She can have it all as far as I'm concerned.... Anything that comes from it will just remind me of her."

"We'll see about all that later. Right now you do need to get yourself ready to meet your new co-workers."

"Oh, he got the job?" Mary asked.

"Damn right! He was great, weren't you?" Randy nudged his cousin. Ben thought to himself, Yeah I must have been great—my boss hates me.

Randy didn't give him a chance to answer. "Get your mind off Greensburg! I'll handle your divorce."

"Divorce!" Ben queried, almost as if he had some alternatives. He felt he had to talk to Julie, and he didn't want Randy making any personal decisions for him, even though he knew his cousin was just trying to help.

"Ben, let us help," his aunt pleaded. "Randy can handle the legal aspects. We have a Seals' freight truck going through Greensburg every other day. We can pick up the rest of your belongings and let you just forget that awful place.

"Speaking of trucks…why aren't you at the office?" Randy grilled his mom.

"Oh, I just came home to see if you were back yet. I wanted to know if Ben got the job."

"Yeah, they gave him the job…you can go back now," Randy replied tongue-in-cheek. "They're probably having a party down at the office without any supervision." He winked at Ben.

"Ben, he's just jealous because the people he hired for the company were for the most part…shall we say…undependable, and I have long since replaced them with my hand-picked professionals." Mary smiled as she made her statement.

"Good help will always be hard to find, though," Randy retorted. "John Burkes is lucky to be getting good help!"

"Yes! tell me about the job. When do you start?" Mary asked.

"I don't know about me getting the job," Ben mused. "Randy got it. I'm just gonna draw the paycheck for it."

Randy snapped back at Ben, "Do you think they would have given you the job if you were just some guy, or even if you were just a plain ole cop from Mississippi? No, they gave it to you because you are experienced in drug enforcement, and nobody from the DEA or the state is going to apply for a job as a cop in Memphis. They would have to take a cut in pay and prestige. Think of this as fate— Michael's death and your leaving Greensburg were simply destiny in the making.... I just hate that my best friend had to lose his life to get you a better job."

Ben looked startled.

"I'm joking...bad joke," Randy assured him.

Mary shook her head. "He's got a sick sense of humor these days...reminds me of his dad.... He was the same way, the older he got."

"Oh Mama," Randy defended himself. "Lighten up...you know how much Michael meant to me. He would have laughed."

Mary turned to Ben. "Just ignore him, honey. Now, when do you start?"

"The commissioner wants me to go on down this afternoon and get to know everybody," Ben muttered as if he didn't care or wasn't sure. "Captain Burkes is expecting me, I'm afraid."

"Oh, that's wonderful!" Mary exclaimed. "He's a good guy, I think."

"John Burkes? Do you know him?" Ben asked.

"I've spoken with him on the phone several times. He seems like a nice fellow, kinda shorttempered though," Mary observed.

"Yeah, he did come across that way," Ben said, thinking that was an understatement.

"We've delivered a number of large crates to him. I think they're antiques. They're secured with large metal straps. I believe his sister owns an antique store somewhere in Green County," Mary said.

"Chardon's antiques, on the edge of town, Ben. You passed by it everyday on the way home," Randy butted in.

"You're kidding!" Ben was amazed. "What a small world. Why didn't you say something at lunch?"

"I forgot...tension of the conversation and all," Randy responded. "There's a chance he might hear some idle gossip having a Greensburg connection and all. So watch your back."

"Great...just what I need." Ben said.

"Hey, relax, you know he's not sleeping with Julie. Oops! There I go again!" Randy punched his cousin. "You've got to lighten up, cuz. You're gonna be fine. I know Burkes well enough to know he's a fair guy, concerned about his people...that's why he was reluctant. But he'll form his own opinion of you fairly. I'm sure of it."

"Don't be so sure!" Ben exploded.

"What do you mean?" Randy asked.

"I mean, I wouldn't be surprised if he had slept with her. Everybody else has!" Ben slammed his drink on the coffee table and stood to excuse himself.

Chapter 5

Ben made his way up the concrete steps to the precinct headquarters. He scrambled up the stairwell at the end of the hall. On the second floor, he eased slowly down the hallway in search of the task force office, eager to find it but nervous as hell. There it was...207. It was a large steel door marked with a room number and a sign over a small buzzer to the right of the door. "Press buzzer for assistance," it read. There was a small intercom below the buzzer. Ben got a response almost immediately. "Yes?" came a female voice."

"Uh, I'm Ben Seals."

"I'm happy for you. Now, can I help you or am I supposed to know you?'

"I'm here to see John, uh, Captain Burkes."

"Wait one minute."

There was a long pause, then came a reply,

"Whadda say your name was?"

"Ben Seals!"

"Tell Captain Burkes, it's Ben Seals." The intercom was still on as the receptionist made her announcement.

"Mr. Seals, you can come in now."

There was a buzz as the door unlocked. Ben grabbed the knob and went in, only to enter another small area completely enclosed by 3/4-inch glass. A lady with dark, gray-streaked hair motioned at him through the glass to come through. There was another buzz as

Ben reached to open the glass door in front of him. As he appeared through the doorway, he was met by a plainclothes officer coming from an office in the rear of the room. The place was one big open conference-type room with a few offices in the rear. The rest was partitioned into many smaller sections.

"Hi, I'm Bobby Stapleton."

"Ben Seals."

"Nice to meet you, Ben, I hear you're a real bloodhound."

Ben started to reply, "Well, I don't know what all you've heard about—"

"Ben, this is Captain Crator," Stapleton cut Ben off in mid-sentence. "He's second in command of the task force headed by Captain Burkes."

"Paul Crator, good to know ya." Crator shoved his right hand forward. In his left hand he held a manila envelope and clutched a cigar between his left index and middle finger.

Ben started to speak again. "I was telling Bobby here—I don't know what you might have heard about me, but I hope you'll let me show you—" He was cut off again.

"Follow me, Ben," Stapleton advised. Ben followed him to a rear office. "This is Captain Burkes' office," Bobby said.

It seemed that Ben wasn't going to be able to get his two bits in in time to make a good first impression. Stapleton pushed the half-open door the rest of the way and led Ben into the office.

"I believe you've met Captain Burkes."

"Sergeant Stapleton, would you show Officer Seals around the precinct, please?' John Burkes asked before Ben had had time to react to seeing him again. Ben had hoped to take advantage of those first moments to set a positive attitude for Burkes to see. Burkes didn't seem interested in Ben's attitude, however—good, bad, or indifferent. Ben only hoped that Randy was right...that he would get a fair chance to prove himself. At this point, Ben began to rethink his approach. Maybe this guy was strictly a by-the-book kind of guy. Maybe Ben would be better served by keeping his mouth shut and listening for now.

"Yes sir," Stapleton snapped sharply.

Judging from the way Bobby Stapleton responded to Burkes, Ben figured he just about had this guy pegged. He was a military-style cop who ran a tight ship and didn't go in for much jovial activity among his officers. Ben knew the best way to handle this kind of guy was to be straightforward, do a good job, say "yes sir" and "no sir" often, and never go against the grain. He could adapt to that, even though it was completely different from a rural Mississippi sheriff's department, where informality was not only accepted, but expected.

"Come with me, Seals." Bobby Stapleton led the way out into the precinct area.

"Ben, let me get you to give Denise your personnel information. You met Denise when you came in."

"Denise, Officer Seals needs to get a personnel file started. Can you get him going and send it on to Division?"

"Sure, just a minute." Denise glanced up at Ben. She shuffled papers around her desk as if looking for something.

"We can come back," Bobby said.

"No, Robert, I'll get to you in a second here."

"Uh oh," Bobby laughed, "we caught her at a bad time...anytime she calls me Robert, she's either got too much to do or she needs a cigarette."

"No, dammit," Denise defended herself, "Division sent some paperwork down here for Captain Burkes to look over; now they want it back. Captain Burkes said he laid it on my desk this morning, and now I can't find it. If it gets lost, you know who gets the shaft?"

"Uh, let me see," Bobby grinned, "would it be you?"

"You got it, babe, that's the pleasure of being the only civilian on a task force. "If y'all weren't so damned top secret about everything you do down here, maybe they would trust someone else to help me."

"Why do that when we've already got superwoman on staff?" Bobby grinned.

"Kiss mine, Robert...there it is...on the computer table. I knew he didn't leave it here or I would have seen it!"

"Now, Mr. Seals, or Officer Seals, I guess it is, let's get you started."

"She'll just need your serial number, home phone, next of kin, things like that for now. I'll go to supply and get you a pager. We'll have it turned on this afternoon if we need to reach you. Be right back. He's all yours, Denise."

Bobby exited through the main entrance while Ben took a seat, uneasy about giving out too much personal information.

Denise worked fervently. "You'll have to bear with me," she said. "Around here, between people calling, coming in and out, and paperwork, I have to take advantage of every minute."

"Oh, that's fine. I understand." Ben tried to sound comfortable.

Denise went through a series of questions, pausing briefly to buzz people in and out of the door while gathering all the information she needed from Ben to start his file. She finished just as the door buzzed with Stapleton returning, pager in hand.

"It's already turned on. The number's on the back." He gave it to Ben. "If you're through here, let's start making our way around."

"Yeah, I've got all I need for now," Denise said.

"Then let's go meet the task force first," Bobby said.

Ben and Bobby weaved through people as they made their way. The precinct was a beehive of activity. To Ben it seemed as if everybody working there was almost as lost as he was. He decided to make one more stab at small talk in an effort to get to know Stapleton.

"I don't think Captain Burkes likes me very much."

Bobby Stapleton stopped in his tracks. "I'm gonna tell you about John Burkes...you have to give him time."

"Yeah, so I've heard," Ben assured him.

"He doesn't like anyone at first. He'll just have to get to know you," Stapleton continued. "He's really a good guy, doing a tough job."

"Yeah, I guess you're right," Ben agreed. He felt somewhat better about the whole situation after hearing the detective's comments.

Ben was intrigued by the look of some of the task force members. A couple of guys looked like members of a rock and roll band. They obviously spent a lot of time undercover. There were about a dozen people on the task force including several women, all of whom were very attractive (essential in undercover work). They included a redhead named Sylvia, a blonde named Judy, and Gennette, a well-built black woman with long-weave hair almost to her waist.

Gennette was currently hogging the copier. "Gennette, this is Ben Seals, our new teammate," Stapleton said, extending the formalities.

"Great, we need all the help we can get," she replied. "I have just two rules: one, don't try to set me up with any of those brothers down at Division that you may meet—be wary of their friendship because they want something to begin with—and two, don't go around staring at my butt...there's enough people doing that already."

"No problem," Ben sheepishly agreed to conform.

She smiled and moved toward the computer. Bobby laughed and led Ben back into the office area.

"She's pretty feisty," Ben observed.

"Don't take her wrong. She's not a feminist; she just has a hard time getting regular flatfoots to take her seriously. I guess because she's so good-looking. But I can assure you that everyone around here respects her for the job she does. If we need to get to some guy, especially young black pushers from up north, she can go into a club and leave with them nine out of ten times, even if they're already with another woman. She's amazing, I'm glad she is on our side."

"I've never worked with female officers before," Ben said. "This should be interesting."

"Well, get used to it quick." Bobby warned. "They're some of our best." Bobby motioned toward a tall, dark-haired man headed out the door. "Vick, hold up a sec, I want you to meet somebody. This is Ben Seals. He's going to take Michael's slot."

"Hey, Ben. Vick Killian." Vick stopped to say hello. "I'm glad you're helping us...we need all of it we can get. Sorry, but I'm in a hurry to get down to Division. Nice to meet you, Ben. I'll talk to you at the meeting."

"Great!" Ben replied.

Bobby led onward, "We've got a staff meeting this afternoon around five. I'm sure the captain will talk to you about it some more. He's gonna want to talk with you one on one first, he said. He'll kinda get you oriented and tell you what all he expects from you...that sort of garbage. Don't worry, Paul Crator runs things in the field. When we hit the streets he's in complete charge unless Burkes steps in somewhere, which he rarely does. He's usually back here monitoring things from the radio room and trying not to get too involved because he's not out there to evaluate the situation.

You just about have to have someone to take charge if things go wrong, or say, if Paul goes down. And that person needs to be in a safe, central location." Bobby paused for a moment. "Hey, I don't mean to sound like a know-it-all or to patronize you in any way...it's just that we may operate a little differently from what you're used to."

"No, no," Ben assured him, "I want to learn everything I can."

"Good! With that attitude, you'll do fine."

Ben swelled inside. Maybe he would fit in after all. He needed to win over Captain Burkes, though. That was a definite must.

"Sergeant Stapleton!"

"Speak of the devil," Bobby remarked as John Burkes' voice rang out across the precinct.

"Send Officer Seals to me, please."

"Well, so much for the tour...you're on," Bobby encouragingly whispered to Ben.

"You'd think he would just tell me to come there...after all, I am standing right beside you."

"Hey, man," Bobby grabbed his arm to stop him. "Keep a good demeanor and don't let him get you down. He really is a fair guy...he'll come around in time."

Chapter 6

O fficer Seals, you're going to be working in place of a good man. A man whose shoes are going to be hard to fill...especially for you, being from a small town and learning a whole new kind of job."

Ben didn't like the way this dialogue had started and began to feel a rush of adrenaline to his stomach. John Burkes' whole demeanor seemed that of a man who was in a room with someone he didn't want to be with. Ben tried to assure himself that it was just the way Burkes came across when first meeting someone. Surely Bobby Stapleton was right and he would come around in time.

"Captain, I'm ready to learn, and I want to be of service to you and this team."

Burkes leaned back in his chair. "That's real good. Real good. Who told you to say that...that cousin of yours?"

"Excuse me, sir?" Ben questioned, as if hard of hearing.

"All right, let's just cut to the chase," Burkes suggested. "I don't like you."

I need to forget this, Ben started thinking, before I build a resume that will never land me another job. He could see it all now: "insubordinate, untrustworthy." Maybe he should forget law enforcement altogether.

Burkes was still speaking. "...and I don't like that cousin of yours either. I'm sorry, but I'm being frank. I don't know what you two have up your sleeves, or how you got this job, even though one can easily look at the relationship of the commissioner and Mr. Big Man Around Town, Randy Seals, and see how it could happen.

Ben had always resented people saying he had gotten his first job for political reasons, and now his second job was being given to him because of pure politics and even he knew it. Ben sat quietly as Captain Burkes rambled on, hardly pausing to take a breath. "I don't think you are qualified to work on a metro task force in a city of over a million people. I've also made some calls to Greensburg. I don't know exactly why you left there, but something isn't right. Maybe you should just consider another line of work."

Ben felt at this point he could easily be persuaded to pursue another career, but then Burkes said the magic words: "I'm going to give you a fair chance just like I would anybody else. I do this because, one, I don't think you're going to leave on your own, and two, I have morals and am a fair person, unlike most people in our society...no offense intended!"

Ben did not reply. He felt it best to shut up and try not to further incriminate himself. As Burkes continued, Ben felt his own emotions beginning to harden. An inner strength began to manifest itself within him. He maintained his silence.

Burkes continued his thrashing. "I want you to know one thing...I'll be watching your every move. You start screwing up, and I'll do everything I can to get rid of you. Even if it's just a transfer, I'll find a way."

Ben sat silently.

"You have anything to say, Officer Seals?" Burkes asked.

Ben shook his head.

"Well, then, I want you in this five o'clock meeting, and I want you to know one more thing. I've been doing this city's dirty work for fourteen years, and I'm not afraid for the commissioner to find out about this conversation. I'm too valuable for them to throw away...just thought you might be wondering."

Ben offered no response.

He spent the rest of the afternoon in the precinct getting familiar with his new surroundings while trying to stay out of Burkes' way until the five o'clock staff meeting. Around four-thirty, new faces began to pile into the precinct. There was a very large black guy, named Jerome, whom Ben had heard Gennette mention earlier. Jerome seemed to command everyone's attention for the moment.

Everyone had gathered into the meeting area seemingly to laugh at him for something that had just happened involving a suspect.

Jerome's bulging arms stretched his pullover shirt. Ben's arms were not as big as when he played for LSU, but even then they were maybe half the size of this guy's. Jerome leaned back in his swivel chair, as everyone gathered around sitting on desktops, backwards in chairs, or leaning against the wall. This was either a very loose group or they were waiting for the meeting to start before getting serious. Jerome grinned, "I could have got him at anytime...but he would have had a lot more will to fight if I hadn't chased him a while first."

"Ahh...yeah...deep, deep. It's deep in here," came echoes from around the room.

Ben had grabbed a seat beside Bobby Stapleton on a desktop in the back of the conference room. "What are they talking about?" Ben quizzed Stapleton.

Stapleton tried to stop laughing with the rest of the group long enough to answer but could not resist throwing one more subtle remark at Jerome. "Maybe if he had had a Longhorn jersey on, you could have caught him faster."

Why Longhorns? Ben wondered to himself. Then he realized why Jerome looked familiar. Jerome used to be a Longhorn killer. "Jerome used to play linebacker at Texas A&M, didn't he?" Ben whispered, leaning toward Bobby.

"Yeah, are you a fan?"

"I played against him!"

"No way!" Bobby couldn't believe it.

"Yeah, I played at LSU. For a while, till I got married. I thought Jerome got drafted."

"Yeah, he did, but he only played a couple of years. I think Denver cut him, and he tried out with a couple of other teams before using his criminal justice degree to become one of Memphis's finest."

"Hey Jerome! This is Ben Seals." Bobby gathered everyone's attention. "He's part of the team now. It seems the two of you have already met."

"Is that so?" Jerome looked at Ben with interest.

"Yeah," Bobby responded. "Ben was a star at LSU."

"Oh, no...I only played a short while, and I never started." Ben tried to set the record straight. "I played in one game where I was filling in for our starting fullback some, and you tackled me twice. I still have nightmares from it." The whole room laughed. Ben felt at ease.

"Officer Seals hasn't been here one day, and he's already got war stories to tell." It was John Burkes standing in the doorway listening to everything. "Damn, no wonder you fit in so well everywhere...must be some kind of con artist." He shook his head as he entered the room.

Ben sat staring straight ahead, nonresponsive. He wasn't going to be insubordinate. He knew this would be his last job in law enforcement if he was, and if John Burkes was determined to get him fired, he was going to have to come up with a damn good reason, because Ben did not intend to give him one. So what if he got transferred? He'd just as soon work somewhere else in Memphis P.D. anyway. Sure, this job would look good on his resume if he could put in a couple of good years with the task force, but how could he put up with this kind of abuse for that long?

Tension suddenly seemed to fill the room as a number of raised eyebrows were cut in Ben's direction. Burkes strode through the room to the podium on the far side. Damn him, Ben thought. He was about to meet the team in a neutral setting without any prejudiced remarks to get them wondering about his past. Now, he thought, the whole Greensburg thing might come out, and that was something that had to be avoided at all costs.

Burkes moved quickly to the podium and fortunately, and surprisingly to Ben, turned around, looked at Jerome, and said, "So, tell us, Officer Bennett, how does it feel to realize you're old after being shown up by a young punk?" The whole room burst into laughter as Burkes cracked a smile while looking around the room at everybody but stopping short of Ben.

"Now wait a minute," Jerome tried to respond. "He ran through an alley, over cars, through a fire station, up twelve flights of stairs..."

"It was three flights of stairs," someone yelled from the back of the room.

"Well, it could have been twelve...if it was regular steps, but these went all the way up the side of the building... I'll bet no cop on the force could have caught him but this one," Jerome protested.

"Just to get everybody broken in as to what is going on," Burkes interrupted, "I'm sure all of you know, but to officially bring everyone up to speed, and for Officer Seals' Benefit (Burkes voice held sarcasm at the mention of Ben's name), I want to review the day's progress. Lieutenant Gennette Alexander and her two-man team, along with Lieutenant Rodriguez and his two-man team, which consisted of Officer Wilson and Sergeant Ex-linebacker, and I do repeat, *ex* (Burkes grinned at Jerome), Jerome Bennett, set out to serve two warrants on a Ronnie 'Pookie' Jones and his girlfriend, Tawana Griffin. As I'm sure you now know, it was quite an eventful day."

There was pushing and poking of Jerome by the people sitting closest to him as a paper airplane hit him from across the room. Jerome grabbed it looking to see who threw it.

"Hey, Jones, I don't know what's so funny to you...I heard you and Pookie Jones were cousins," he said.

More laughter filled the room. "I'm afraid not," smarted off Don Jones. "I'm like Hoppy on *Sanford and Son.* I'm of the 'Caucasian persuasion.'"

More laughter echoed around the room as Denise cracked the door open. Captain Burkes motioned for her to come on in. She handed him a file and left.

"Well, the warrants were served, nevertheless. That was the main thing," Burkes tried to squeeze in amidst the laughter. "This is the file on Pookie right here. He held the file high, then lowered it, opened it, and began to read from it. "Convictions—two counts of grand larceny, one count of possession with intent to distribute, three counts of conspiracy to solicit prostitution—he pimps out his girlfriend and some of her friends when he needs extra cash—and now he's charged with selling twelve ounces of crack cocaine to an undercover police officer."

"Yeah, go Gennette!" came the cry from another lady on the task force. She was a redhead named Sylvia who had been introduced to Ben earlier when he and Bobby made rounds.

Gennette Alexander gave herself two thumbs up for being the one to set Pookie up. She had only been in town for a year and had been instrumental in over half a dozen major busts without having to show her face in a courtroom. In almost every bust the charges had been plea bargained, or the defendants had pled guilty or helped finger somebody bigger than them. The rest of the cases had not come to trial yet. This was vital in the life of an undercover cop for the obvious reason. The more time you stayed in the street and out of the courtroom, the longer you could continue in this line of work.

Nonetheless, new task force operators had to be brought in on a regular basis for the sake of security. That made it easy for Ben to slide right into this slot. He wasn't on loan from the DEA or another city or the state. No one had to be traded for his services. He just wished he could make Burkes realize the importance of having someone like him on the team. Ben let his mind wander momentarily, reflecting on the last seventy-two hours and how his life had changed. Once again he fought back tears. Thoughts of Julie ran through his mind constantly. He felt disconnected from the real world. He was still sick in the pit of his stomach.

"Jones' girlfriend came quietly, we're happy to report," John Burkes rambled on as Ben once again tuned in to what was going on around him. "We'll be talking with him later. Hopefully we can find out what we really want, as you all know.

"We'll keep him on ice tonight, isolated with zero contact," Burkes continued. "That's gonna be it for now. Let's all meet back here at 1930 hours. Before you go, some of you, I know, have already met him, but for those who haven't, this is Officer Seals, formerly of the Green County S.O., Green County, MS. He will be joining us and working with Captain Crator."

"Whoa...talk about moving straight to the top. You're gonna team with Crator. Crator never has a partner. Specially since he runs thing out in the field. He'll probably have you giving us orders before long," Bobby buzzed.

Ben knew in his heart this was a one-time exception to the rule. He was being assigned to work with the second in command only so he could be watched closely. This was Burkes' way of "keeping his eye on him." That was fine, though. That way he could do his job knowing he had a pair of eyes watching the good stuff he did as well.

The meeting broke up, and Ben was able to meet the rest of the task force before being called aside by Crator and advised to join his new partner after work for a beer. Ben consented, made a call to Randy, and left with Crator.

Chapter 7

Paul Crator looked like the typical blue-collar guy doing a good job, not worried about promotions and things of that sort. He had wiry light brown hair and a mustache that seemed permanently dented by the unlit cigar butt gripped between his teeth. Hank's Place was the lively bar and grill frequented by Crator and some of the other team members. Today, though, it was just Crator and his new protege. Paul Crator leaned back on the bar stool beside Ben. "You don't drink much, do you, son?"

"Is it that obvious?" Ben asked.

"I can tell by the way you hold your mug, by your grip. It's not tight enough. You're not serious about your drinkin'. You should be if you're gonna do this job."

"I guess it's just never been in my nature." Ben felt a need to justify himself. "Hope it never is."

Crator shrugged his shoulders. "I dunno, you've been through an awful lot lately, couldn't hurt to drink a little."

Ben felt a chill go down his spine. "What exactly do you mean 'an awful lot'?"

"Well, with your wife...and all that."

"You know about that? How did you find out about my wife?"

"Your cousin told Burkes."

"Oh, I shoulda known," Ben grumbled. "What all did he say?"

"Just that you caught your wife screwing around, so you packed your stuff and split."

Ben changed the subject to ward off answering any more questions.

Crator dropped Ben off in front of the Seals condo around 7:30. He found Mary and Randy sitting down to a pot roast dinner prepared by the housekeeper/cook who had just left for the day. Ben joined the family as the phone rang. Randy excused himself to answer it, then walked in with the cordless receiver in his hand.

"It's for you, Ben. It's Steve Lyles."

Ben froze and began to turn pale. He took a deep breath and picked up the receiver to find out what his step-brother-in-law could possibly want.

Steve Lyles was the step-brother-in-law from hell. When Julie's mother died and Gabriel Chapman remarried, Steve Lyles came with the package. He had come from humble beginnings, but you would never know it by his grandiose attitude. He flaunted the ritzy lifestyle he had come to know since becoming involved with Gabriel Chapman Enterprises as an overseer.

Ben had always looked upon Steve as lower class...just glossed over because he had money. He had often wondered what he would have turned out to be if he had never worked for the family. Steve partied constantly to the point of almost no return. He had to continue making lots of money to support his flagrant spending. His life was one constant brush with the law. This was part of the reason he and Ben didn't like each other to begin with.

Steve thought all cops were losers and never could understand why his stepsister would be willing to settle for a cop. Ben saw Steve as obnoxious, conniving, and determined to do anything to break up the marriage to Julie in the hope that she would choose one of his friends or cohorts. Ben paused for a moment before picking up the receiver just to wonder what his life would have been like had he gone to work for Chapman. Would his marriage have been different. Maybe Julie would have been happier? Hell no, he thought, she would have just been screwing somebody richer than Gene McMasters.

"Yes?" Ben clutched the receiver firmly to his right ear.

"I don't know what your plans are, but you'd best keep your ass out of my sister's life!"

Ben had always been quick to respond when Steve had harassed him in the past. Steve was good at making fun of Ben's country life, referring to him as Barney Fife. This was different somehow.

Ben no longer felt intimidated by this loud-mouthed, over-zealous creep, and he didn't even feel the need to respond. His heart had become hardened over the things he had experienced this week, and there was nothing this high-paid high school dropout could possibly say to upset him anymore.

"Is there something I can help you with, Steve?" Ben calmly rebutted.

"You can help, all right, you useless, broke-ass hillbilly sheriff!"

Ben held the phone away from his ear. The longer Steve rambled, the louder he got, not even pausing to take breaths between sentences. "Stay yo' ass as far away from my sister and this family as you can get, or I promise you, I will kill you!"

"Why Steve, are you threatening a police officer?" Ben calmly retorted.

"You damn right! Naw, I'm not threatening...I'm warning you, you low-life, I'll kill you...I'll castrate you, then burn you at the stake! Stay away from her and this family."

Ben wondered what kind of story Julie had told her family to have made him into such a villain. He maintained his poise. "Well, as I see it, you're the one calling me. I haven't bothered you at all."

"You bother me, all right...you low-life...drag my sister off to some Godforsaken hellhole, then ruin her life. I oughta kill you anyway."

Ben moved the receiver away from his ear again and raised his eyebrows to Randy. He could obviously hear the screaming coming from the other end of the phone. Ben held the phone to its side and grinned at his cousin. "I'm not sure, but I think he's pissed."

"Screw you! You broke bastard!" Steve screamed.

"Are you through yet?" Ben asked in a sarcastic yet calm tone.

Click. There was silence. "What's his problem?" Randy asked.

"Who knows?" Ben answered. "He's always hated me...whatever she told him just gave him a reason to call me up and tell me what he thought. You're not in the book, are you?"

"No, we're unlisted," Randy answered.

"Where did he get this number?" Ben asked.

"I dunno. He probably got it from Julie, don't you think?" Randy guessed.

"Yeah, I guess."

After dinner, Ben spent most of the evening staring at the endless parade of traffic on the river. It seemed busy, yet so peaceful. There was no sleep for him in sight. He wished he could talk to Julie, but what would he say? As much as he hated her, he still loved her and wished she would come begging for forgiveness.

Paul Crator arrived at the Seals house around 7 a.m., even earlier than expected. He wanted to brief Ben on a need-to-know basis. Ben climbed into the city-owned Ford Taurus, and Crator pulled away for downtown.

"Ben, this morning we're hoping for a major breakthrough on the murder of Officer Rose. You're familiar with this case by now, I'm sure.

Ben nodded his acknowledgment.

"He and Randy were close, I understand," Ben said.

"They were, they were," Paul nodded. "In fact, they were almost always together outside of work: they were down at Hank's almost every day. They were both single and had a lot of time on their hands, so it was almost like a ritual to find those two out partying on a weeknight or weekend either one."

"Oh really?" Ben was taken aback. He knew they were close but he didn't realize just how close. Randy seemed to be doing a pretty good job of handling his friend's death and still being able to be there for Ben when his life had started falling apart. He realized for the first time how lucky he was to have a cousin who could be so supportive and was willing to help him straighten his entire life out after it had seemingly been ruined. And this guy had just lost the person who was obviously his best friend.

Ben found himself starting to daydream a little about how he had often wished he could have been more like Randy. He just seemed to have it all together. When Paul Crator's monotone voice finally sank through to Ben, he realized he was being briefed on his first day at work, and he needed to be paying attention

"This Jones kid we're going to be talking to, he knows who killed Rose, we're sure of that. We think he not only can finger the trigger man but can nail the guy who gave the order to kill in the first place. That's who we want the most anyway. We already know who he is. It's just a matter of getting someone to testify against him. I can also tell you that the one who gave the order is the one behind the drug ring we were tracking when Rose was shot. He was not in the crackhouse at the time of the shooting, but you can rest assure these street kids like Pookie Jones don't do anything without okaying it with the big dog! Now, as for Pookie, you'll meet him shortly.

Ben sat electrified by the revelations he was hearing. This was different from anything he had ever dealt with in Greensburg. This was big...huge...this was the city. The excitement of the hunt began racing through his blood. Maybe this was finally it...just what he had waited for all his life, the chance to make a difference in a big way, or at least be a part of something that had a major impact on his part of the world. Maybe that would make Julie jealous and she would realize what she had had, maybe even want him back.

"What's the deal with this drug lord? Is he just so untouchable that you can't nail him on anything else?" Ben asked without trying to pry too much. He was careful to ask enough questions to get a clear picture without pushing it at his early stage. He was sure that he was the only one on a need-to-know basis, and he hoped that would only be until Crator and Burkes were comfortable with him.

"Well, I don't know that I would call him a drug lord," Crator laughed. "He's more like a hoodlum who commands an enormous control over a number of small-time pushers, pimps, hustlers, local crap games, and just general scams around town. He is very well financed. However, he wasn't for a long time...until he became a major crack distributor in this town.

"Then he started getting financing from other places. He made a lot of money quick. Our whole investigation leading up to the day Rose was killed had centered on him and his outfit. You can't imagine the man-hours logged trying to get this one guy and bust up his operation. For a long time, Burkes and I thought he was just a middle man for somebody else, but now we feel he has become larger than that. He controls what goes in and out of at least fifty crackhouses just in Memphis alone...not to mention West Memphis, Arkansas. We have successfully raided eight houses that we believe he was behind. Naturally, he hasn't made any mistakes that would lead us directly to him."

"What makes you think that this time will be any different?" Ben asked.

Crator chuckled. "Oh, there's a lot of reasons," he said, pulling out a cigar that had been chewed on previously. "For one thing, we had tracked a shipment of dope from a lead we had to the house where Rose was shot. We were going in shortly after the dope got there. While we were waiting on the stakeout, the dope showed up in a van driven by Pookie Jones himself. We were all set and ready to go in when a black Mercedes pulls up, and it's the man himself. I guess I can go ahead and tell you his name is B.J. That's enough about him for now, other than the fact that he was once just another black kid off the streets like Pookie Jones."

Ben's curiosity was rampant now. "So what happened?"

"We didn't expect him," Crator said. "Before we could readjust our plans to make sure our people knew what was going on—and to make sure we took B.J. not only alive but with the dope—he left usually. He never came around a shipment. That was far too risky since he has become allpowerful. But wouldn't you just know it, he shows up for a brief moment! Probably checks to make sure he hasn't been stiffed by somebody, then leaves. His people stay inside to cut the dope. It can happen in less than twenty minutes. The dope will be in the house, then headed back onto the streets that quick. We have a surveillance tape of B.J. in the Mercedes just down the street after leaving the house. He's talking on what looks to be a two-way radio much like the one we found inside the house.

"Were any arrests made?" Ben asked.

"You should really go back and read some of the reports filed by other officers on the team," Paul advised. "Two suspects were shot and killed, and three others escaped during all the shooting. Of course, everyone was trying to get Rose out of there at the same time, and it was all we could do just to return the gunfire we took from them. They were well armed with fully automatic weapons, and we had lost the element of surprise, which was vital.

"Maybe we could have done things differently, and Michael would still be alive, but we never dreamed they could have made him as a cop. He was in a postal uniform. He had never really worked the streets. He was a transfer from Little Rock. In fact, your cousin helped him get that job, I think."

Ben was stunned.... He hadn't heard that before either.

Paul continued: "The only thing we can figure out is that someone inside the house recognized him from the short time he had been in town. It was a total disaster. We do know that Rose was shot with a 7.62x39 caliber shell from some type of assault rifle. Pookie was armed only with a handgun when he went in, so it's doubtful that he could be the triggerman. Whoever shot him escaped with the murder weapon—that's why we needed something better on him to make him want to talk. And that's when Jerome and his team came through with this sting. Pookie and some of the other hoods were trying to lie low for a while, hoping some of the heat would blow over. Gennette was able to take advantage of his street hustling to bring him in on a distribution charge. We should pretty much have him where we want him now.

Crator parked the Taurus in a cyclone-fenced parking lot behind the precinct. Ben could feel the stir and tension upon entering the task force room behind Crator. Something big seemed to fill the air. All this excitement over a kid named Pookie Jones. Ben couldn't wait. He hated the thought of wasting time, fooling around with personal effects, being issued a badge, locker, that sort of thing. He would be allowed to carry his own weapon. Ben had carried a Beretta 9mm as his backup weapon ever since he joined the Green County S.O. It was the most trustworthy pistol on the market as far as he was concerned. Thankfully, McMasters' boys had returned it to him when he left Greensburg.

Ben had spent an exorbitant amount of time with Denise filling out more forms, going over department policies and general rules of conduct, all the while trying to listen to the things going on all around him. There seemed to be a constant buzz around the precinct. He was eager to become a part of it all, as he thought it might help him keep his mind off his problems. The time seemed to drag as Ben stayed in the same chair beside Denise's desk. Without warning, Denise buzzed the door. Bobby Stapleton appeared through the bulletproof glass windows of the outer lobby. Denise buzzed the door again. Behind him, Bobby was pulling, almost dragging, a skinny black kid who looked to be about twenty years old. Six uniformed officers followed behind. This has to be Pookie, Ben thought. Stapleton entered first, pulling the handcuffed kid behind him.

"Man, why you draggin' me? I ain't Rodney King. I gots rights. What...you think you in L.A. or something?" The black kid barked as he twisted sideways with Bobby's tug. Denise became distracted by the commotion, Ben sneaked away to follow Bobby and the crowd that had just entered.

Bobby led his prisoner to the interrogation room. "Sit down and shut up!" he ordered.

"Well, I believe I will have a sit down. But I'll shut up when I'm damn good and ready," Jones yelped emphatically.

Bobby sat the kid down in a chair and turned to leave, instructing the uniformed officers to watch him. Bobby saw Ben standing in the doorway of the interrogation room. "He's about to drive me nuts."

"Is he that bad?" Ben laughed.

"He won't shut up," Bobby said. "He wants everything and when you don't give it to him, it's because you're prejudiced. Half the suspects I bring in say their rights have been violated. They bitch and gripe for a while, but they usually get bored and shut up. This guy doesn't stop. I oughta kick Jerome's ass. I know now why he wouldn't go down to Division and get him this morning. He didn't want to have to fool with this punk for two hours. He is worrisome as hell!"

Ben laughed as Bobby brushed pass him on his way to Burkes' office. Soon the whole team began to gather around the interrogation room. Ben stood to the side, well out of the way. He knew he wanted to be part of this, but didn't know if Burkes would let him. He hoped to stay far enough out of the way and maybe watch from behind the two-way glass.

Soon team members were assembling in the corridor to the west side of the interrogation room to observe the proceedings now only moments away. Ben slid into the corridor and found a resting place beside the coffee machine, hoping that neither Burkes nor Crator would come looking for him. All the team members were there. This was the biggest event they had been part of since the shooting itself.

All heads turned in silence as John Burkes entered the interrogation room. Ben stood on tiptoes to see over people and get a better view through the two-way window. Burkes walked to the table Pookie Jones sat behind. Pookie's mouth had not stopped running. He had been giving the uniformed officers all the earful they could stand and then some. Stapleton turned the volume up on the external speaker so everyone could listen to what was being said inside the interrogation room.

"We're waiting on your attorney," Burkes told Pookie. "He was supposed to be here by 9:30, and he hasn't shown. I just wanted you to know that we're doing everything we can to help you get things going so that you can be free as soon as possible. Too bad your lawyer doesn't want to cooperate. Maybe you can convince him it's in your best interest to help us so we can help you, Mr. Jones." Burkes looked the young man squarely in the eye.

"My man gots to take care of bidness. He checkin' on thangs and this and that, you know. I'm a very complicated man and I requires complicated procedures to make sure I gets de proper defense. You know what I mean," Jones lazily replied.

Burkes turned and headed out of the room.

Pookie Jones' attorney was a short, gray-haired, nervous man of about fifty years of age. His name was Jeffrey Perlman, and he looked as unprepared as Ben had ever seen a lawyer. Perlman was shown into the interrogation room, where he took a seat beside Pookie, slapped him gently on his back, and asked him if he had any questions about what they had gone over the night before. Pookie apparently was confident in his attorney and told him to lead the way.

Ben was amazed at Pookie's confidence in this public defender. He turned to Stapleton and said: "Pookie seems overconfident for someone whose attorney had been appointed by the court."

"Pookie probably figures B.J. will come to his rescue if he needs a really good lawyer," Bobby explained. "In the meantime, they'll ride this horse as far as they can. That's why it's so important to drive a wedge between Pookie and B.J.'s organization right now."

The corridor got quiet as John Burkes, Paul Crator, and Jerome Bennett entered the room. Bennett and Crator took seats around the table as Burkes remained standing. "Mr. Jones, you already know me and Captain Crator, and I'm sure you remember Officer Bennett, whom you gave quite a run. I can assure you he remembers you." Jerome grinned as Burkes began his question-and-answer period, which everyone watching hoped would be fruitful.

Pookie leaned back in his chair. "It's kinda hard for a brother to think with his hands all up in behind him," he said.

"Cuff one hand to the table leg," Burkes told Jerome. Jerome followed the instructions, then sat back down to take notes. He and Crator pulled out pens and small pads. Burkes also had a video recorder on. "I hope you understand that this conversation will be recorded and may be used against you in a court of law," he said. "Of course, Mr. Perlman has explained all that to you already, I'm sure."

"Man, I ain't gonna be on a recorded—" Pookie was cut off by

Perlman, who patted him on the hand and assured him everything would be fine. "We are ready to listen to what you have to offer us, Captain Burkes," Perlman began.

"Well," Burkes answered, "you'll be going before Judge Albritton here shortly to set your bail. Right now, you're looking at selling a large quantity of crack cocaine to an undercover police officer, and I don't think I have to tell you the problems you have from that already. Now, this morning the D.A. let Mr. Perlman observe the surveillance tapes of you actually selling and having your girlfriend hand the drugs to one of our undercover operatives. Would you like to see the videotape?" Burkes asked.

"Naw, I don't need to see some bullshit tapes that you made up, copper." Pookie threw his free hand up as if he didn't care.

"Well, I can assure you that it's no problem if you want to see yourself in the act. We'll be glad to show it to you." Burkes calmly responded.

Silence.

"In addition to this charge," Burkes quietly cited, "you will be charged with accessory to murdering a police officer."

"Do what!" Perlman shouted, nervously tugging at his collar. "He hasn't been charged with anything like that. What are you talking about? The D.A. never brought that up!"

"Ah, it's bullshit. Don't pay any attention to this guy. They got nothing on me. I ain't shot no cop," Pookie declared.

"I never said he was shot!" Burkes grinned. "Do you have something to tell us, Mr. Jones?"

Pookie's tone suddenly became subdued. "Naw, man, I know about that cop that gots shot, man!"

"That's enough, Pookie!" Perlman admonished. "Don't say anything else."

"Naw, man, it ain't no thang. I read 'bout that cop that gots shot." Pookie glared at Burkes. "I reads a lot, likes to keep up on my current events."

"That's enough," Perlman said to Pookie.

"When were you planning to come forward with that charge, Captain Burkes?" Perlman wanted to know.

"We intend to add that charge now, unless Mr. Jones agrees to cooperate. Maybe we can work a deal on both charges. We've already cleared it with the D.A., And he's willing to cut Mr. Jones a good deal in exchange for the information we need," Burkes coyly replied.

"Man, I ain't givin' you nuthin'!" Pookie hollered.

"That's enough, Pookie," Perlman cut him off. "Let's just listen to what the man has to say, and then we'll talk."

"I'd say that sounds like a good idea," Burkes started before being cut off by Pookie.

I'd say it sounds like dog mess!" Pookie blasted Burkes. "I'd say you sound like dog mess, cop. If you asked me, you look like dog mess too! What you lookin' at, boy?" Pookie looked at Jerome. "White man got you lookin' all crazy and shit! You need to come on back to the projects and let me hook you up with a sister that'll rock yo' world...make you forget all about these white folks."

"Kiss my ass!" Jerome was inflamed.

"Somebody needs to kiss yo' ass, as much as you been kissin' round dis joint...you need somebody too!" Pookie laughed.

"Why don't you put on the tape for Mr. Jones, Officer Bennett?" Burkes suggested.

"Gladly." Jerome smiled, got up, and exited the room.

"We'd like for you to view the following video before you make any hasty decisions about your defense." Burkes smiled at Jones and Perlman.

"Yeah, I got ya video," Pookie mumbled as Perlman tried to keep him quiet.

Jerome quickly reappeared rolling a television cart into the room. Jerome smiled frequently at Pookie while entering the room and plugging the TV and VCR into the wall socket. In his own way, he let Pookie know that they had him red-handed on the tape.

"What the hell you grinnin' 'bout, slave-boy?" Pookie started again. "You see who he asked to do the manual labor. I wouldn't be grinnin' so damn much if I was you!"

Jerome's face showed anger, but he resisted the temptation to lash out. The tape would be enough.

The tape began to roll. It showed the van parked outside the crackhouse before Michael Rose was shot. It showed Pookie getting out of the van.

"Recognize anybody so far?" Burkes asked. Perlman swallowed, thinking about the mountain of evidence his client faced. Burkes, Crator, and Jerome Bennett all smiled as the tape continued to play.

"You can kiss my black ass. I didn't have nothin' to do with that cop getting shot!" Pookie shouted.

"Who did?" Burkes shouted back.

"Man, go to hell. I ain't givin' you shit!" Pookie screamed. Perlman shook his finger at Pookie to let him know to be quiet.

"Captain Burkes, you know any response Mr. Jones makes to any of your questions will come through me," Perlman interjected. "I would appreciate it very much if you would cease your attempt to pressure my client into saying something out of emotional outrage."

"I know you're his lawyer, but if he's got something to say, we want to hear the truth," Burkes retaliated. " I know you want the same."

"You know damn well what I mean," Perlman began to shout. "Anything he might say will be said to me, and I will let you know when we are ready to respond. Now, if you have a deal for us, we want to hear it and hear it now. Otherwise stop the VCR and your recorder."

"Man, this is bullshit anyway. I ain't got nothing to say no way. They just fishin'," Pookie cursed.

The tape continued to roll until it reached the point where Michael Rose was shot. Everyone in the room cringed except Pookie. He just shrugged his shoulders and slightly chuckled under his breath.

"You find it amusing, do you Mr. Jones?" Burkes shouted at the top of his lungs. Jerome got up to pop the tape out of the VCR.

"Man, you ain't got shit!" Pookie weakly claimed as he looked away from the officers.

Perlman once again gave Pookie the signal to be quiet. "Give us the deal?" Perlman asked.

"Man, I told you, there ain't gonna be no deal!" Pookie insisted.

"There ain't gonna be no deal, huh?" Burkes slammed his fist on the table. "Well, before you get too sure of yourself, you consider what's going to happen when one of your other comrades from the crackhouse fingers you as the trigger man."

"Bullshit. I didn't kill that cop." Pookie's voice had dropped, and there was a look of fear in his eyes.

Perlman tried to quiet Pookie, to no avail.

"Look, I told you I didn't kill that cop," Pookie pleaded. "I done a lot of bad shit before, but I telling you...I didn't kill no cop!"

"Good, then," Burkes responded matter-of-factly," you have nothing to worry about. I just hope when we start bringing your buddies in, none of them finger you. Two or three point a finger at you, combined with this video, and the D.A. might make it stick. I can assure you he will try."

Perlman was busy writing, making notes to himself, acting unconcerned with the conversation, as though it was meaningless chatter. Pookie looked serious and worried at this point.

"I think I'll defer to my lawyer," Pookie said.

"What's the deal?" Perlman looked up from his notepad.

Burkes nodded and then was silent for a moment. "Captain Crator, you want to show Mr. Perlman and Mr. Jones what we have for them?" Burkes directed his first mate.

"My pleasure," Crator smiled while opening a manila folder he had brought with him. He shoved some papers across the desk to Perlman. "Basically, you I.D. the trigger man who gave the order to shoot and testify to it in court. We'll put you in a witness protection program that will take care of you." Crator spoke in a manner indicating that he knew Pookie had no choice.

"No way, baby! I ain't goin' out like that!" Pookie shouted. "You ain't movin' me and tellin' me how to live."

Perlman tried fervently to quiet the outraged young man.

"Next thing you know, y'all probably have me livin' out in Germantown amongst a bunch of white folks. No offense," he said to Perlman.

"I'm going to need some time with my client," Perlman said, ignoring Pookie's comments.

"That's fine," Burkes replied, "but you don't have a lot of time. We're afraid that once Mr. Jones is charged with accessory to murder, his life on the street won't be worth much."

"Don't you worry about me, copper!" Pookie shouted, "I'd hate for yo' white ass to lose any sleep over me!"

Settle down, settle down," Perlman interjected. "Captain, the news reports say no murder weapon was ever found in that incident."

"Oh, we'll have a murder weapon soon, you can count on that," Burkes bluffed confidently.

Perlman tried to get in a couple of questions before Pookie got started again. He wasn't quick enough. Pookie was already wound up.

"Man, you think you some bad shit, don't ya? Run around up here with all these punkie ass cops jumpin' to everything you say.

Gives you some kinda mind trip, uh?"

Perlman insisted that he be given time alone with his client and an opportunity to read the D.A. packet that was offered to them. Burkes agreed and got up to leave the room with Paul and Jerome.

Pookie couldn't resist one last shot. "Yeah, that's the ticket. Y'all go on out somewhere and eat up some donuts or somethin'. Maybe beat up on some black folks."

Jerome stared at Pookie on the way out of the interrogation room after he recuffed Pookie's hands behind his back and through the chair.

Pookie stared back. "Don't look at me. You act like you ain't never seen a black man before. You damn sho ain't one."

Jerome shook his head on his way out the door.

"Y'all come back now, ya hear!" Pookie hollered on their way out.

Perlman elected to have Pookie wait on making a deal until after his arraignment on the charge of distribution. Ben went to Pookie's arraignment. Judge Albritton seemed tough but fair. He set Pookie's bond at $50,000, of which Pookie could probably come up with 10 percent just from the gold he usually wore around his neck. The only question now was, would Pookie try to walk or would he take the D.A.'s deal?

Ben observed how Pookie never ran out of energy. In the courtroom, he gave the bailiffs hell about being dumb, fat gofers. Pookie made careful observation of the fact that one of the bailiffs would not be able to shoot him when he escaped due to his belly hanging over his gun. All the bailiffs were noticeably pissed as Pookie left the courtroom suggesting over his shoulder that the county invest in some thigh-masters and treadmills.

Back at the precinct, Ben tried to stay out of John Burkes' way. For this reason he had ridden with Jerome Bennett to Pookie's arraignment in the first place. It seemed everywhere Ben moved inside the precinct, Burkes was soon to follow.

Ben jumped at the chance to ride uptown with Bobby Stapleton and bring back a precinct car that had been repaired. Upon arriving back at the precinct, Ben and Bobby found things in a frenzy. People were piling in from everywhere. Cops were showing up from division headquarters. All the detectives assigned to the precinct were coming in one by one. Bobby grabbed Paul Crator as he rushed past. "What's going on?"

"Jones is going to take the deal! You haven't heard?"

"No! we just got back from uptown. I had no idea!"

"If you think about it, I don't see that we left him much choice," Crator seemed pleased. "He can't go to B.J. for help and run the risk of him finding out about the accessory-to-murder charge looming over his head. If B.J. thought he could be implicated, he would spring Pookie just to whack him. He would never take the chance of one of his people rolling over on him. Pookie can't take the chance that we might charge him with accessory to Michael's murder. If he is charged, he gets whacked if and when he makes bail. If he's denied bail, he sits in jail anyway, where B.J. still may get to him. It's too good to be true!"

Bobby made his way to the interrogation room while Ben tried to find a spot outside behind the two-way glass again. Inside the room Paul Crator and Jerome Bennett sat quietly waiting. Burkes entered. Crator asked where Pookie was.

"Are we gonna interrogate him?" Paul asked.

"Yeah. He's with the D.A. in the holding area signing the papers," Burkes responded. "The D.A. is going to watch the questioning but wants us to handle it since we've done so well, so far."

Soon the door opened and Pookie was led in by two uniformed officers and handcuffed to a chair. Crator and Bennett grabbed pens and pads to take notes. A video recorder had already been set up to record the entire episode.

Michael Perlman sat down beside Pookie, and Burkes began immediately.

"You do understand, Mr. Jones, that any misinformation you give us may terminate the agreement between yourself and the D.A.?"

"You mean if I lie?" Pookie cocked his head sideways when asking the question.

"Exactly." Burkes answered. "Now, let's start with you telling us who was in the house that was raided on the night Officer Rose was shot."

Paul and Jerome had pens ready and eager to get names of all individuals involved.

"Who is Officer Rose?" Pookie smarted off.

"Don't you screw around with me, boy. I'll lock you up so fast, it'll make your head spin. You don't even realize how much trouble you're in, do you? Now, either you cooperate or the deal is off!" Burkes said.

A steamed Perlman scratched his head and reassured Pookie.

"What is it you want to know?" Pookie asked.

Burkes' patience had already worn thin. "Captain Crator, tell the man what we want." Burkes leaned back as if he were through with Pookie. Pookie grinned.

Crator sighed deeply, " Mr. Jones, why don't you start by telling us who was riding in the van with you when you arrived at the house on the night in question."

Pookie sat silent for a moment. "His name is Don, man."

Jerome quickly jotted down the information, as did Crator. Burkes sat up in his chair for a moment. This is what they had been waiting for.

"Don who?" Crator prodded.

"I don't know, man. Just Don. That's all I know." Pookie answered.

"Just Don. You don't know his last name or his alias," Paul quizzed, knowing the youth was lying.

"Oh, I've seen his name written down, but I can't pronounce it. It's some weird shit," Pookie claimed.

"Can you spell it?" Paul asked.

"D-o-n-d-u-"

"Hold it." Jerome stopped him.

Bobby repeated, "D-o-n-d-u. We want to be sure we get this right. Go ahead."

"It's d-o-n-d-u-c-k." Pookie smiled.

"D-o-n-d-u-c-k. Don duck. You little shit!" Crator screamed, slamming the pen down.

Burkes jumped in, "I've heard enough. The D.A. is listening to all this. I think I'll let him come in and talk to you. Better yet, maybe we should just turn you loose and put the word on the street we're cutting a deal with you. That oughta lower your life expectancy somewhat."

Pookie sat, unfazed.

"Gentlemen, may I have a word with my client in private?" Perlman asked.

"If you think it will do any good," Burkes said.

At that moment the door flew open, as an assistant D.A. rushed into the interrogation room carrying a note pad with a scribbled message on it. Burkes acknowledged the note after reading it, then handed it back.

Chapter 8

Burkes sighed a deep breath, then leaned back in his chair. "It seems we have a new development." He was interrupted by the same assistant reentering the room with a manila folder in hand. He sat down beside Burkes.

"Is that it?" Burkes asked of the young man.

He nodded and handed Burkes the folder opened with papers folded to allow Burkes to peruse the pages toward the bottom of the stack. Perlman and Jones sat quietly waiting.

Burkes looked up from the papers. "It seems your lady friend, Tawana Griffin, who has been arrested for assisting you in the sale of narcotics, has cut a deal that implicates you in the killing of Officer Rose."

"Bullshit! She would never do that." Pookie came unglued. He looked at Perlman. "She would never do that! She knows better."

"Obviously she doesn't," Burkes argued.

"Shut up!" Pookie screamed. "You don't know a damn thang about that woman."

"I know the D.A. offered her a deal much like yours if she would sing about selling the dope for you and the murder of Officer Rose." Burkes raised his eyebrows at Pookie.

Pookie looked stunned. "She don't know shit about that cop gettin' whacked. She wasn't even there!"

"No, but you confided in her...everything we need to know, right down to the trigger man." Burkes smiled. "We don't even need you now. We can find the trigger man, give him a reduced sentence to give up B.J., and it will be over."

"The deal has already been done. Y'all can't back out now!" Perlman shouted.

"The deal was that Mr. Jones cooperate, which he has not. The deal is off," Burkes shouted back.

"Man...you ain't got nothin'," Pookie shouted the loudest.

"See for yourself." Burkes shoved a copy of a statement signed by Tawana Griffin toward Pookie. "It's several pages in length, but basically, it names a trigger man, tells of your involvement in hiding evidence after the raid on the crackhouse, and tells everything about you and her selling the mass quantity of crack cocaine to Officer Alexander." Burkes grinned. "It even goes so far as to implicate Robert "Benny" White, otherwise known on the streets of Memphis as B.J."

"Man, that crazy bitch is makin' up all that shit!" Pookie visibly upset, looked scared for the first time. Perlman begged Pookie to remain quiet until he could sort out all of this new information.

"Captain Burkes, I must insist on time to confer with my client." Perlman persisted.

Burkes stared at Pookie. "Sure, Pookie. May I call you Pookie?"

Pookie now sat with tears in his eyes, silent and motionless, staring at the table in front of him. He began to mumble. "Man, she don't know what she's doin'...she gonna get herself killed."

Burkes leaned across the table. "No, she's not. Because we are going to take care of her and keep B.J. away from her. Pookie, I still need your testimony to build a strong case. You're not the one we really want. Sure, it's hard to overlook a drug bust of this size, but we want the people responsible for killing Michael Rose. That's one crime that will not go unpunished."

"Well, she can't help you...she don't even know what happened," Pookie argued.

Perlman was nervous about what Pookie might say next but liked the way this was headed. At least Pookie seemed more cooperative.

"I know that!" Burkes responded. "But right now this is what we have to go on, and this deal will allow her to go free through the protective custody program. Unfortunately, I'm afraid this leaves you no options. You can either provide us with different or better information to dispute what she has to say, or we'll use her statement to prosecute you on the charges of drug trafficking and accessory to murder of a police officer."

There was silence for a moment.

"Pookie, you're going to jail for a long time if you don't cooperate, and we can't guarantee your safety in prison. It's a tough decision. I know about the forces working against you on the outside, but we'll protect you from all of them. This may not be the life you had in mind, but it's got to be a hell of a lot better than prison."

Pookie was so upset by the turn of events that silent tears began to roll down his cheeks. "I'll give you what you want," he stated, matter-of-factly, never looking up. Burkes glanced at Perlman. The lawyer nodded positively.

Burkes wasted no time. Pookie remained unchanged throughout the whole episode...solemn and unaffected. During the course of the questioning, Pookie named Roderick O'Bannon as the trigger man. The excitement on the outside of the room grew as Ben and the rest of the task force took notes. B.J. had just left the house on that fateful day. Seconds later he called the house on a two-way radio to say he suspected a raid. He then ordered the shooting if it became necessary. Roderick was at the door, and deemed it necessary at the time.

O'Bannon was supposed to be staying with an aunt in southwest Memphis, just a few blocks off Elvis Presley Boulevard. Immediately, the task force members in the observation area were assigned by Paul Crator to find Roderick O'Bannon. No warrants were to be issued. This would be done with as tight a lid as possible. O'Bannon would be brought in for questioning. Then when he was safely in police custody, he would be charged. There could even be federal charges depending on B.J.'s involvement in racketeering and organized crime.

After the interrogation was complete, Pookie was processed for protective custody. The Memphis P.D. would handle it until he could be transferred into a state or federal program. Ben rode to southwest Memphis with Paul Crator and Jerome Bennett to look for Roderick O'Bannon. They had already received word that Gennette Alexander and a contingent of officers had gone to O'Bannon's neighborhood and could not locate him. It was delicate work, trying not to spook Roderick or to set off any alarms with anyone in the area. They could not afford to have any word drift back to B.J. and possibly put Roderick's life in danger before he could be arrested. The D.A. had warned everybody on the task force at least once of this fact.

During the course of the interrogation, Pookie revealed some of Roderick's favorite hangouts. Crator, along with Ben and Jerome had first tried Papa Jack's Pool Hall, just off Shelby Drive. Pookie had said that Roderick could be found there in the evenings. With no luck they headed down into the projects off old Highway 61 checking out the playgrounds O'Bannon was known to frequent when playing basketball. As they passed by what Pookie had said was Roderick O'Bannon's favorite court, Jerome spotted Willie Luckett. Willie was an eighteen-year-old on probation for possession of crack. Jerome knew he was a dealer, but he had never been caught selling or with enough on him to get busted for intent to distribute.

Jerome decided to find out what he could from Willie. After all, he was the one who had busted him, so he already had a dialogue with the kid. Good or bad, he had reason to talk to him. Crator made the decision to let Jerome coax Willie into the car on the pretense of seeing how he was doing, then working the conversation around to basketball and how he had heard that some O'Bannon kid was the best on this court. If Willie mentioned anything about Roderick they would go from there.

Crator parked the car at the curb, and Jerome hopped out and strolled casually to the playground gate. The cyclone fence surrounding the basketball courts was in a state of disrepair. The gate was open and partially torn from its hinges from continuous use by the neighborhood kids.

"Hey, Mace," Jerome shouted the kid's street alias at him as he stepped onto the court. The shirtless teen backed away from the guy he was guarding to see who was calling his name.

"Let me talk to ya a minute," Jerome demanded.

Willie broke into a run away from Jerome toward the other side of the court.

"Cut him off!" Jerome shouted over his back at Paul and Ben. He started chasing Willie across the courts even though the kid had a big jump on him. Willie hit the cyclone fence on the other side of the court and scaled it like a mountain climber before leaping off on the other side, where he landed firmly on his feet. Paul and Ben rounded the corner of the fence from the outside just as Jerome jumped from the top of the fence. By now Willie had a good lead, almost twenty yards, and quite an audience watching.

"Stop! We're not here to bust you! We just want to talk to you!" Jerome shouted.

The teen never let up. Paul and Ben were gaining ground fast since they were at full speed when Willie hit the ground. Willie picked up speed as he traveled, making it harder and harder for the two to keep up. Ben, obviously faster, was pulling away from Paul somewhat. Jerome was catching up to both of them across the grassy yard east of the court.

Willie had a full head of steam when he reached pavement. In seconds, he was across the street, through a yard on the other side of the street, leaping a flower bed and disappearing behind a house and into some bushes. Ben cleared one side of the house and Jerome the other; Crator followed behind.

"Watch him! He's gonna throw something!" Jerome shouted. "He's got a score on him or he wouldn't be running," he yelled as he and Ben slashed through the bushes simultaneously. They spotted Willie again on the porch of another house, stealing a bike to try to make his getaway. He quickly realized he couldn't get going fast enough on the grass to shake the two cops so he ditched the bike and took off again, this time losing the ground that he had gained on his chasers.

He ran around to the front of the house, made a beeline toward a McDonald's across the street, and darted into the main entrance.

"He's gonna flush it!" Jerome screamed at the top of his lungs. Willie never slowed down as he nearly shattered the glass door of the hamburger hut, never stopping on his way to the rear of the restaurant. Jerome led the way with Ben on his heels. Jerome rammed the door to the men's restroom just in time to hear a flush and see Willie collapse on the wall behind the commode.

"Damn!" Jerome shouted. "I'm still takin' you in, you little shit! I got you for resisting arrest, and we'll see what your parole officer thinks about your ditching the dope. Turn around and face the wall. You know the routine!" He slapped cuffs on the teenager.

"You got him?" Ben stepped into the stall just as Paul Crator entered the restroom.

"He ain't shit!" Jerome tried to enrage the youngster, hoping he would try to resist and maybe get an assault charge added to it.

"Take it easy, Bennett!" Crator admonished. "Remember what we're doing!"

"I got him, no problem," Jerome assured.

"Man, I'm clean," Willie pleaded. "I been clean and tryin' to stay that way. I was just chunkin' somethin' somebody handed me to hold till they got back."

"Read him his rights!" Crator warned Jerome. "Let's use everything he says against him."

"Aw man, you know I ain't gonna tell nothing once you read me that shit," Willie whined.

Jerome cut his eyes toward Crator and winked. "We saw you talking to that O'Bannon kid earlier today, but we didn't see him hand you anything."

"O'Bannon? Who? Roderick O'Bannon?" Willie asked.

"Yeah," Crator said. "We saw you talking to him today."

"Bullshit," Willie laughed. "He was in the car with the guys that gave me the stuff, but I ain't talked to him today."

Bingo! The three cops exchanged silent looks. A crowd of folks began to gather around the entrance to the restroom. The trio quickly ushered Willie outside and back across the street behind some trees while Ben went ahead to get the car. Ben wheeled the car around the block, and Willie was pushed into the back seat. The three stood outside the rear of the car where they could speak in private.

"You think you can get him to find O'Bannon for us?" Crator asked Jerome while crushing out a slightly used cigar.

"Maybe, if he even knows where they are."

"O'Bannon shot Michael Rose," Crator replied. "Do whatever it takes!"

"Yes sir! Let me do all the talking," Jerome said.

The three cops got into the car.

"Yeah....on probation and resisting arrest. I wonder what the judge is gonna do. He'll have to reinstate the rest of your sentence," Jerome said with a smile as he turned toward Willie. "Especially when we tell him we were chasing you because you had a bag of dope."

"Dope! I didn't have no dope," Willie pleaded. "It was a ring."

All three officers laughed.

"It was, man," Willie repeated. "I just flushed it because I was afraid it was stolen or something. I didn't want to be caught with it. I figured that's why y'all were comin' for me, 'cause you knew I had it."

The three cops looked at each other. Then Crator shook his head at Jerome. "No way...he had a score," he said.

"Tell you what...we'll make you a deal," Jerome told Willie as he put the car in drive and pulled away from the curb, glancing in the mirror to watch the young man's reaction.

Willie rolled his eyes in disbelief. "What you got in mind?"

"You take us to the guy that gave you the ring and we don't arrest you."

"What will you do with me?"

"Just turn you loose and let you go on back home."

Willie had a look of complete astonishment, then wonder. "What if the guy says he didn't give me nothin' at all?"

Jerome thought fast. "Didn't you say he was with the O'Bannon kid?"

"Yeah, Roderick was in the ride with him."

"Well, I know Roderick O'Bannon well enough to know if he's around, there's something illegal going on. We'd rather have them than you. They'll never know you helped us, 'cause we're just gonna watch them until we can catch them doing something." Jerome eyed Crator out of the corner of his eye to make sure Crator approved of his little fibs.

"You ain't gonna mess me over if I help you?" Willie wanted to know.

He's gonna do it, Ben thought. He's too stupid to figure out they were looking for somebody else to begin with.

"Hey! We give you our word," Jerome said. "I'm gonna be watching you from now on, though...so you better stay clean."

"Deal! To North Airways Road. I think they over there." Willie sounded unsure of himself.

Jerome sped the Ford Taurus along the freeway toward Airways. Willie was nervous throughout the short trip. He was scooting around on his seat as if he wanted to say something and couldn't find the words. Soon the Ford turned down Airways Boulevard. Willie directed Jerome to the street and the house where he thought his buddies were. Jerome drove past the house. The car they were looking for, a gray Coupe de Ville, was not in the drive, so they continued driving. The plan was that once the car was spotted, they would take Willie to a nearby precinct or have a backup patrol car take him downtown while the trio went back.

Willie directed the trio to two more houses where the suspects might be. Once again both houses were deserted. Finally, Willie led the way to an obscure apartment complex, run-down and obviously drug-infested, judging from the characters roaming the grounds. There was a Memphis P.D. squad jacket lying in the floorboard of the car. Ben grabbed the jacket and covered Willie's head so he couldn't be recognized in case O'Bannon was found. As promised, no one would know Willie had helped set it up. Willie peered through the jacket to look around as the Taurus crept along the street surrounding the apartments.

People standing in small groups outside the complex began to dissipate. Two guys, one white and the other Hispanic, sat on the back of a Olds Ninety-eight. They wore "doo rag" bandannas and casually continued blowing bubblegum and staring as the car rolled by.

"There's the car!" Willie shouted.

"Where?" Crator demanded.

"On the end down there." Willie parted the jacket so he could see better. "You see it. The gray Caddy," he insisted.

"I see it," Jerome acknowledged.

"That's him!" Willie said. "That's Erik, the guy leaning up against the hood talkin' to that bitch. He gave me the stuff...I mean...the ring."

Jerome glanced at Willie in the back seat and shook his head with a frown. "Gave you the stuff, huh?"

"Never mind all that right now," Crator butted in. "Where's the guys that were with him?"

"I don't know, but they never got out of the car. It was just Erik." Willie insisted. "Erik the one you want."

"Where can we find O'Bannon?" Crator wanted to know.

"How the hell should I know!" Willie defended himself. "I hardly even know the guy. I seen him around the court before, but that's it. I'm tellin' you, Erik's the guy you want. He's a doughboy, a dealer, a high roller. He's into everything, man."

"You're sure O'Bannon was with him?" Crator asked.

"I think so," Willie replied.

"You think so, you little prick! You said back there that he was in the car. Now which is it?" Paul shouted. He was beginning to get nervous about the possibility of not finding O'Bannon or even worse, something happening to O'Bannon and his never being able to link

B.J. Now, he was also faced with the reality of Willie knowing that they were really looking for Roderick O'Bannon all along.

Willie looked scared. He wasn't sure what this crazy, stringy-haired white man was gonna do next. He didn't like riding around with three cops, especially in the neighborhoods and projects that he frequented. He just knew they were gonna beat him up. He had never been beat up by cops before but had partners who swore they had been. He knew this was his time. The car exited the projects and made its way back down Airways. Willie sat quietly in the back, afraid for his life. Little did he know that this was his lucky day. He had been arrested by good cops, and not only that, they were too busy worrying about finding a cop killer to even bother taking him downtown to book him for resisting arrest.

"Why you want that O'Bannon guy? What about Erik?" Willie began to wonder, now realizing that he had not given them what they wanted. "I took you to where you said you wanted to go. You gonna try to play that off since you didn't get what you want. What did O'Bannon do anyway?"

"We'll keep our word. You can walk, but you may have to wait a little while," Crator said.

"No man, there you go! Jankin' me around. I knew this was gonna happen."

Crator ignored him. "Pull in here...We need to talk," he told Jerome.

Jerome pulled the car into a nearby Texaco station, and the three cops got out. Crator reached into his pocket to fish out a new cigar.

"First things first," Jerome said, propping his leg up on the front bumper of the Ford. "We gotta do something with him, now that he knows we're looking for O'Bannon."

"You got that right," Crator acknowledged. "Every detective and narc in the city is looking for O'Bannon, and your patrolmen don't even know! There's no way we can turn him loose and let him run his mouth until O'Bannon is in custody."

From a pay phone, Crator called John Burkes at the precinct to tell him what was going on. Burkes said he would send someone to pick up Willie and take him downtown until O'Bannon could be found. Crator hung up the phone and walked back to the car.

"You wonder why I never want to head a team?"

"Why's that?" Jerome asked.

"Burkes is down there right now with the D.A. halfway up his ass. The D.A. wants an arrest made yesterday."

"Like we don't?" Jerome argued.

"Burkes catches the hell though. He even blew up at me," Crator said. "He never does that."

They waited about fifteen minutes before the contact showed up to get an irate Willie, who raised hell about not getting to go home.

Crator pulled Jerome to the side. "We can't hold him without a charge for more than twenty-four hours. I don't know what we're gonna do if O'Bannon doesn't turn up today or tonight."

"Maybe we can pick him up for questioning again," Jerome laughed.

Chapter 9

Back at the precinct Pookie was being processed. While he was sitting in the main precinct area cuffed to a chair, Denise was doing some paperwork along with one of the D.A.'s assistants to get Pookie ready for transfer to a secure holding place. Pookie looked over what Denise was doing, stretching his neck to try and read what she was typing.

Denise was annoyed. "I'm just getting a requisition to get you some clothes since you won't be staying in the county jail."

"Oh baby, I see, I see." Pookie relaxed back into the chair. "Just get me whatever you think I'll look good in. Pick out somethin' you'd like to see me in."

"I'm afraid you're going to be wearing county blues for a while, Mr. Jones."

"Oh baby, that's okay too. I like those loose-fittin' jail clothes. They made just right for easy access."

Denise ignored him. "You're gonna have to sign something here in a minute. I'll get an officer to come uncuff one of your hands."

"Yeah, easy access!" Pookie said. "I'll show you. Maybe they'll let you stay a night or two with me since they're supposed to be takin' care of all my needs. That way I can take care of yours while you performin' yo' duty for the state."

"Shut the hell up!" The fifty-four-year-old responded.

"What is it, baby? You don't like black men? You don't know what you're missin' till you've tried it."

"Captain Burkes!" Denise pleaded.

"Don't go callin' his ass back over here."

"Captain Burkes?" Denise pleaded.

"What, Denise?" Burkes was just down the hall.

"Could you come here a minute?" Denise was always one to bypass any chain of command structure and go straight to Burkes for everything.

Burkes approached her desk with an irritated frown on his face. "What is it, Denise? This is a bad time. The D.A. is still in my office."

"Well, I'm trying to process your subject here, but I need to get you to see if you can shut him up with his remarks and sexual innuendoes."

Burkes looked at Pookie. "Shut the hell up! As soon as we get you processed we'll get you in a hotel, and you can relax and kick back. Help us help you, okay?"

"I'm sorry, man, I'll try," Pookie agreed. "But I just got a thang for old white women."

Denise pounded her fist. "See, captain!" She looked up to see what Burkes reaction was.

He just shook his head. "Denise, can you just get the kid processed and let's get him out of here?"

One of the deputy D.A.'s at the next desk was engrossed and trying hard not to pay any attention to what was going on at the other desk. Burkes turned to walk away and then turned back upon hearing Denise plead, "But Captain!"

"Please, Denise! Just process the man!" he begged.

Enraged, she started typing furiously. Pookie just smiled and continued to flirt.

Jerome, Crator, and Ben headed back over to the apartment complexes they had just left to speak with Erik. Additional backup had already arrived from a dispatch by John Burkes. After a quick briefing by Crator, the group parked at the complex. Erik was still standing outside talking to the same girl as before. He saw Jerome headed his way and brushed the girl off, admonishing her to go back inside.

"What can I do for you?" Erik smiled in a sarcastic way. His huge grin stood out atop his thin, six-foot-plus body.

"I just want to talk to you for a minute," Jerome said.

"I don't know why. I ain't done nothin," Erik replied.

"I know. I know." Jerome assured him. "We just need some clarification. One of our detectives saw you handing something to Willie Luckett down at one of the basketball courts in south Memphis today. We were wondering if you could tell us about it."

"Am I under arrest?" Erik asked.

"No." Jerome shook his head.

"Well, I don't even know nobody named Luckett, so I don't know what you're talking about." Erik shrugged.

"Who was with you?" Jerome asked.

"Nobody," Erik replied.

"Oh really, we heard there were some other people in the car with you." Jerome had to fish harder if he was going to get something out of this guy. He had approached him alone hoping to put him at ease...black man to black man, but this wasn't working. "We heard there was a Johnson kid, a girl named Jones, a guy named O'Bannon, and somebody else in the car."

"You heard wrong." Erik was emphatic.

"I tell you what," Jerome smiled. "I can produce some pictures of you and Willie Luckett. Now, suppose you just come on downtown with me...or tell me where your friends are, and I'll have them verify your story so this thing can be over."

"I told you. I don't know nobody named Luckett. I ain't got nobody with me. I just came over to the east side to see my ole girl, and I gotta put up with all this police harassment. Man, this is bullshit!" Erik shook his head in disbelief.

"I don't have time to fool with it now, but you know I might come back and talk to some people around here. See if anybody has anything to say." Jerome smiled and walked away.

"Go ahead. I ain't got nothin' to hide!" Erik yelled as Jerome walked toward the car.

"I spooked him," Jerome whispered back in the car.

"We need to wait them out!" Crator agreed. "There's only one way into this place. You have to come down that narrow road by that store the way we came in. We need to wait down at the end across the street until we see his car leave, then stop and I.D. the people with him."

A half-hour later Ben, who had gotten all wired up from his first day of real excitement, was still waiting in the same spot. Erik was not leaving. Meanwhile, the D.A., Bob Taylor, was holding John Burkes hostage in his own office, where he raved and carried on about no arrest being made yet.

And they still had to figure out what to do with Tawana Griffin, Pookie's girlfriend, who was sitting in the main precinct area where Pookie had been earlier. He had been moved into a holding area awaiting transport to a hotel later.

There was nothing Tawana could be charged with outside of aiding Pookie in the drug sale that eventually got him arrested. Now that Pookie would not be charged with anything, it was fruitless to hold her. The only problem was that she could not be released until O'Bannon was found, since she had been questioned about Michael Rose's murder.

B.J. would be suspicious enough if she was released without Pookie and would have O'Bannon killed instantly. Tawana had somehow deduced that her boyfriend was getting a deal of some sort because of the conversations she had heard around the precinct. She was a far cry from a rocket scientist but even she had figured out that something important was going on concerning her boyfriend/ pimp. If she had figured that out, B.J. could figure the rest. To make matters worse she was constantly reminding them that she knew what was going on by asking for money. Her voice could be heard frequently saying,"When am I gonna get paid? I bet that sorry nigger Pookie done got a check. I tell you what you want to know...just get me some cash."

While Burkes and the D.A. discussed the situation, Pookie was being moved. This proved to be yet another mistake by a young assistant D.A. He carelessly had an officer lead the cuffed teenager through the main precinct area where Tawana sat. "There's that sorry nigger!" Tawana cried out at the top of her lungs.

Burkes heard the cry from his office. "What the hell is going on now?" he demanded, bursting from his office.

"Man, you can't believe nothin' this crazy bitch tells you!" Pookie shouted at the top of his lungs. "I beat da hell outta you woman!" Pookie shouted in his best macho voice.

"You look like beatin somethin' the way that white man draggin' you around," Tawana yelled back at him.

The young assistant D.A. looked bewildered. These street people were new to him. He was trying to help the officer leading Pookie, who was now kicking and screaming obscenities at his girlfriend.

Pookie shouted, "She's a crackheaded bitch, whore...dike!"

"Officer, officer...that's the man that killed that cop. He confessed it one night while he was making love to me with that little bitty growth between his legs!" Tawana yelled with a huge grin on her face.

"That's enough! Get 'em out of here!" Bob Taylor shouted.

"What do you want us to do with her?" the assistant D.A. yelled.

"Not her! You know what I mean...get him outta here." Burkes loved seeing the D.A. so flustered.

"She a whore...That's all," Pookie shouted over his shoulder while being dragged from the room.

You a faggot!" Tawana got in the last shot.

"Damn!" Bob Taylor shook his head and walked back into Burkes' office.

Ben, Crator, Jerome and the other squad car of detectives waited near a small store at the entrance leading to the apartment complex. At 4 p.m. they spotted Erik's car coming down the narrow road. The caddy bumped and rocked down along the partially paved road. A woman drove the car alone. Crator quickly ordered the other squad car to follow the caddy just in case Erik was lying down in the back. Crator, Ben, and Jerome stayed behind.

It wasn't long before the other officers came back with a negative over the radio indicating that the girl was alone in Erik's car. Crator ordered the others back. He then split up temporary shifts arming everyone with binoculars. Three would stay while the others went to eat, shower, and take a short rest. After clearing the plan with Burkes he sent Ben and Jerome home in one car with orders to return three hours later.

John Burkes wasn't at all crazy about the idea of tying up that much manpower in one place with only a chance of getting anything out of it. The only thing they really had to go on was the word of a teenage drug dealer that O'Bannon was with Erik earlier in the day and that Erik was at the apartments. But after weighing his options, he had nothing else. From Southhaven to Millington, no other detective in the city had turned up anything.

In the meantime, he had gotten a warrant for Crator and his unit to search the apartment once the girl returned. They would follow her up to the complex and watch which apartment she went into. Crator had just finished his conversation with Burkes from his cell phone when the Caddy reappeared with two women in it. Crator ordered Ben and Jerome to hold up before they left so all three of them could go in to find this guy.

The adrenaline began to flow as everybody checked their weapons, and Crator reminded them that they would go in looking for drugs. They would first give everyone a chance to flush anything they might have and open the door on their own. Then they would I.D. everyone to see if any of the guys turned out to be O'Bannon.

Crator and the team kept a safe distance from the Caddy but remained close enough for visual contact until the car parked. The two women exited the car and leisurely strolled up the stairwell to a second floor apartment. The five detectives waited a few moments, then parked in front of the complex. They took their time climbing to the second floor so that anyone looking out would see them coming and hide any dope or illegal substances they might have. As pressed for time as they were to find O'Bannon, the last thing they wanted was to get bogged down in a drug bust.

Jerome approached the apartment door from one side, followed by Ben. Crator and the other cops took the other side. Crator knocked on the door. There was no answer...just loud rhythm and blues coming from a stereo inside. Crator and Jerome started pounding on the door, as Jerome yelled, "Police! Open up!"

There was sudden silence. "Who is it?" came a voice from inside, amidst sounds of scurrying and shuffling."

Jerome grinned at Crator. "Police! We have a warrant to search the place. Open this door now!"

"It's open!" came a female voice.

Jerome looked surprised. Crator tried the door, hoping all the drugs had been flushed. The door was locked. He just smiled.

"I'm afraid the door is locked. Open it up or we'll take it down!" Crator was nearly in tears of laughter thinking about all the dope going down the drain.

Soon the door opened, revealing a smoke-filled room with the stench of pot flowing from within. The group entered the room briskly.

"Nicki!" came a cry from one of the girls. "Don't come out."

It was too late. Nicki, in her early twenties, ran naked from the shower down the hall.

"Nobody moves!" Jerome shouted. "Everybody on the floor and nobody moves!"

Crator followed. All moved in with their weapons held high in the air. The team swept through the apartment swiftly and efficiently. They rounded up three girls and four guys. All were now lying on the floor of the front room. Nicki had wrapped herself in a sheet. One by one the team members asked for everyone's I.D. under the pretense of running a "28" or a check for outstanding warrants.

Only one of the females had any I.D. on her, but that was irrelevant since they were only interested in the men. Crator and company had checked the first three guys with no luck. The fourth said his I.D. was in Erik's car.

No one asked his name. He was just jerked up and led down the stairwell to the pavement, heavily guarded. Then they had Erik open his car of his own free will after assuring him that the car would not be searched, that they only wanted this guy's I.D, which they found inside. The I.D. had the young man's picture plastered squarely in the middle of an Illinois driver's license naming him "Walter Shook," a twenty-three-year old from Peoria.

"Damn!" Jerome began to fret. "I want to know who all was with you at the park today, Erik. I want to know now, dammit!"

"Nobody, I told you," Erik pleaded. "Tell me who you're looking for...maybe I can help."

Crator jerked Jerome to the side. "It's useless. Let's get outta here!"

Chapter 10

Pookie was transferred to the Waltham Hotel. It was an old building still around from the turn of the century. It had been completely remodeled to serve as a city landmark for modern times. The old hotel lay on the riverbank downtown, less than a mile from the Seals residence. Pookie's fifth floor room overlooked the water. He immediately had a complaint to register and insisted on talking only to Burkes, who had stayed back at the precinct. A group of detectives, along with an assistant D.A., had delivered Pookie to his new address and were supposed to get him into his room and settled.

They had been told nothing about granting him phone calls but had been told to try and keep him happy and very quiet. Finally, after constant persistence, Billy Montgomery allowed him to go into the adjacent room, rented especially for police use.

Pookie had been put at the end of a hall. The two rooms across the hall were rented and left vacant. Montgomery led Pookie into the room reserved for police.

"How am I gonna talk to the man with my hands cuffed?" Pookie asked.

"I'm gonna take those off," Billy assured him. "We'll give you the other."

"Not the leg irons!" Pookie pleaded.

"Yes," Montgomery argued. "I only took them off when we came through the lobby so we wouldn't scare anyone. I know you didn't think I had that jacket over your hands just to keep you from being embarrassed."

"Yeah, I know. You don't give two cents about me and my civil rights," Pookie cried.

"Now, that's not true. When you get to your room I'm gonna let you move around freely, except for the leg irons. You'll have to use our phone since you won't have one," Montgomery reminded him.

Billy dialed the number to the precinct and held the phone while Denise got Burkes on the line.

"What's wrong?" Burkes was concerned.

"It's your boy. He insists on talking to you and only you," Montgomery informed his boss.

"Well, what the hell does he want?"

"How should I know? He won't tell us." Billy glanced at Pookie, who was trying to act as if he wasn't listening. "Here he is. You talk to him."

Billy handed Pookie the phone. Billy had neglected to take the cuffs off yet, so Pookie grabbed the phone with his hands cuffed in front of him, causing him to hold the phone with both hands. Montgomery moved behind him and out of the way. Pookie looked back at him over his shoulder as if in need of privacy. Montgomery glared at him with a look that said, "You can forget it if you think I'm leaving this room."

Clutching the phone with both hands, Pookie slowly raised it to his ear. "Big boss man," he said in a low, subdued voice as if he were a kid in trouble for breaking his mother's favorite piece of china.

"What is it?" Burkes demanded, almost shouting. "I'm very busy. I thought we had settled all our business!"

"Ah, yeah, yeah, we did," Pookie squeaked. "There's a little problem with the uh...the uh..."

"With the what?" Burkes demanded.

"With the room and everything." Pookie finally spit it out.

"Oh, did we forget the champagne or something?" Burkes blasted.

"Oh, that'd be real nice if you could do that, too," Pookie said seriously. "But I'm more worried about the room being on the backside."

"Backside of what?" Burkes queried.

"Backside of the hotel. It's overlooking the river and all that water!"

"So?"

"I don't swim," Pookie said.

"You're not leaving that room. What are you worried about?" Burkes laughed.

"Come on, boss. You know how nervous I gets around this many white folks, much less when they all cops. They might want to have an accident, or somethin'. I rather them shoot me than drown me!"

"That room is especially designed for holding key witnesses," Burkes retorted. "You will notice that the windows have bulletproof glass for your protection. Besides that, the windows in your room don't even open, so no one can push you out. Not that I would blame them if they tried."

"I just don't know if I trust these guys guarding me," Pookie rattled on.

"Look, there are going to be so many different people guarding you, you won't have time to not like them. They will be there and gone before you have a chance to worry about them." Burkes seemed annoyed by this waste of his time. He hung up the phone.

Crator sent Ben, Jerome, and the others home to rest. Ben was ordered to report back to the precinct around 9 p.m. He was to take a shift from 10 p.m. to 2 a.m. guarding Pookie's room along with other detectives.

Ben was glad to get the opportunity to do anything. He had been trying desperately to contact Julie to no avail. It was driving him crazy.

Randy picked Ben up from the precinct. He was anxious to know all about Ben's first day. Was it a good one? Was Burkes easier on him than before? Was Ben pleased with it?

"I have to go back tonight," Ben informed his cousin.

"For what?" Randy shrieked.

"I gotta guard a key witness. I guess I shouldn't be discussing it, but I do." Ben beamed with newfound confidence.

"Gosh. Sounds like you've had quite a day," Randy observed. "I thought you were working on the murder of my friend and favorite cop."

"We are," Ben assured him.

You mean you've got a witness!" Randy practically shouted.

Ben looked questioningly at Randy. He knew he shouldn't be

talking about the case. Burkes would hang him from the highest tree if he knew, but after all, Randy had gotten him this job, and Michael Rose was his best friend.

"If you've got a witness, then you have a suspect as well," Randy deduced.

Well, I'm not getting into the case, but we do have a witness. That's who I'm guarding tonight." Ben rolled up his sleeves in a matter-of-fact kind of way as if he didn't want to talk about it. He was stunned by Randy's next revelation.

"You'll be at the Waltham Hotel down by the river, then. That's where they keep witnesses," Randy remarked.

"I don't know," Ben said.

"No, I'm telling you. That's where you'll be. They have a room down there at the end of the fifth floor where they keep star witnesses. The state has the same deal at a couple of places in Nashville as well. They're just regular hotel rooms except the state paid for bulletproof glass in them, and they pay a retainer fee to the hotel. It was part of the deal when the city helped remodel the hotel."

Ben sat amazed. Again Randy knew more about his job than he did. It was kind of annoying.

At the hotel, Billy Montgomery was sitting outside Pookie's room in a chair. A detective from another precinct arrived, along with Jerome Bennett and Paul Crator. The place was heavily guarded. Jerome and Crator had strolled casually down the hall to find Montgomery sitting with a look of sarcasm on his face, his arms folded.

"What's your problem?" Jerome asked.

"Well, my problem is soon to be your problem. Sylvia went into our room for a second to get your star witness a cup of ice."

"A cup of ice," Crator repeated, not sure what the problem was. "So what's the problem?"

Billy smiled. "It's a cup of ice this time. Last time it was a turkey sandwich and a pickle. Before that it was a *Playboy* magazine, before that—"

"Hold it!" Crator barked. "Just tell him no!"

"Just tell him no," Billy repeated. "You hear that, Sylvia?" he yelled at Sylvia Burch, who was now returning with the ice.

"I heard him," she smirked.

"What's the big deal?" Crator asked.

Billy shook his head. "I tell you what. Watch this." He looked at Sylvia now holding the cup of ice she was about to give him to take into Pookie's room.

"Ronnie?" Billy called.

"You got my ice?" Pookie yelled back from inside the room.

"Naw, we ain't got no ice." Billy cracked the door as he called to the young prisoner who was lying on the bed with his feet cuffed in leg irons.

"You get me some damn ice, now!" Pookie screamed at the top of his lungs in a voice that was ear-shattering. "I needs some ice and needs it now...and have that big-butted redhead brang it to me. I'm tired of lookin' at yo' ole hard ass."

He was still screaming as Billy closed the door. Along with the screaming, he began to beat on the walls.

"I've got a chair between his legs with the irons run through it to keep him from moving around," Billy informed them.

"A chair?" Crator asked incredulously.

"We had to," Sylvia backed up Billy. "He broke the lamp the first time we refused his request. Then he smashed the clock radio."

"I get the picture." Crator laughed.

Pookie's screams were so loud they could be heard all the way down the hall.

"Should we gag him?" Billy asked, knowing Crator would never let them do something illegal.

"How long can he scream?" Crator asked. "Surely he'll tire out soon."

"He went for twenty-five minutes straight once, and then we gave in," Sylvia advised.

"Damn." Crator scratched his head in disbelief. "Well, Burkes said keep him happy. Give him his ice."

"Thank you. I will." Sylvia entered the room. "Oh yeah, baby!" Pookie started. "Come on over here and do ole Pookie some justice."

"Yeah! you just start some of that. I get to go home early if you're making lewd comments toward me," Sylvia said with her hand on the 9mm in her shoulder holster. "I oughta just shoot the little thing off," she continued, looking at his crotch with the chair spreading his legs. "If you'd be quiet Sergeant Montgomery would probably take that chair off you."

It was only a small chair from the dressing table, but nevertheless it prevented him from moving around.

"Get on out of here. I'm tired of lookin' at you now, bitch!" Pookie squealed.

"Have it your way!" Sylvia exclaimed as she left the room.

At the Seals condo Ben ran in to take a shower while Randy made some phone calls. Vick Killian was supposed to come by around 9 p.m. to pick up Ben for their shift as guards for Pookie.

"Come on and eat, boys. Supper's ready," Mary Seals called as they passed through the house.

The housekeeper had already gone for the day, having prepared dinner before she left. Ben took a quick shower and returned to the den. Randy was still on the phone. He saw Ben and hung up.

"Let's eat, cuz," Randy said.

"Don't hang up because of me. Go on about your business as usual. I don't have to have any special attention," Ben said.

"Well, I'm glad to see you pulling yourself together, but I don't get the opportunity to spend any time with you. The least I can do is have supper with you," Randy said, slapping his cousin on the back and directing him into the kitchen.

After supper, Ben, Randy, and Mary relaxed in the den until Ben had to go to work. They made small talk, mostly about Julie, until the doorbell rang around 6:45. Mary answered the door. Ben and Randy heard her ask," May I help you?"

"Is Ben Seals here?" came the response.

Mary stepped to the side in the foyer to allow the man into her home. Ben got up and walked to the foyer, where he saw Vick Killian.

"Lieutenant Killian, what are you doing here now?" Ben asked.

"Burkes wants us to come on in. Don't worry, you get all your overtime. There's been a situation," Vick said.

By now, Randy had moved into the foyer behind Ben. He had a look of concern on his face.

"Is everything alright?" Randy asked.

"Let's go," Vick said to Ben.

Ben looked at Randy. "Yeah, I just need to go on into work."

Randy had a puzzled look on his face but didn't ask any questions.

In the car Ben began to quiz Vick about what was going on. "I haven't done anything wrong, have I?" he asked.

Vick cracked a small smile. "Of course not." He glanced over at Ben, who sat beside him, worry evident on his face. "Relax, there's just been a little complication in the case." Vick stared for a moment at Ben. "Well, you're gonna find out soon enough so I might as well tell you now even though Burkes said for us not to discuss it until everybody got back to the precinct."

"What is it? Did they find O'Bannon?"

Vick had a spooked look on his face. "Yeah, they found him."

"Great!" Ben said. "Let me guess.... He has a tight alibi for the night of the murder."

"No," Vick assured him. "He doesn't have an alibi."

"Good," Ben replied. "Where did he turn up?"

Vick turned the car down the street in front of the precinct. "You'll find out soon enough, but the best I can tell from what I've been told, it was not far from here...just down by the river...well, actually, in the river!"

"In the river?" Ben echoed.

"Yep," Vick said, never taking his eyes off the street in front of him as he pulled into the precinct parking lot. "Fish food."

"You gotta be kidding me!" Ben shouted.

"Nope." Vick stated. "Some old men found a body. It was O'Bannon. That's already been confirmed."

Inside, the precinct was buzzing. Burkes was yelling at the top of his lungs, barking out orders. People were scurrying around back and forth from computers, stopping for short private conversations here and there. Burkes ordered Vick and Ben to drop Tawana Griffin off at her sister's house, then report to the hotel. That was fine with Ben. The precinct didn't look like a good place to be at the moment anyway.

After a drive across town in search of Tawana's relatives, the young girl was finally out of the way. At the hotel, Jerome Bennett and Paul Crator looked ready to leave. Billy Montgomery and Sylvia Burch were supposed to be replaced by a couple of detectives from another precinct.

"I thought y'all would never get here," Jerome smarted off as the two arrived.

"We're early," Vick informed him. "I don't think Billy and Sylvia's relief will be here until ten. We're here because Burkes wants both of you downtown now."

"I figured as much," Crator said. "Ain't that some shit about O'Bannon?"

"You think B.J. had it done?" Vick asked.

"Oh, I'm sure," Crator answered. "He probably heard Pookie had got busted and he got spooked. Decided he wouldn't take any chances. That's why we've got cops crawling all over the building just in case he's bold enough to go after Pookie. There'll be at least eight of you working on this floor alone before the night's over."

"The more the merrier!" Vick answered. "Oh, by the way," Crator turned back to Vick and Ben before leaving, "don't discuss the case with anybody outside the task force. The D.A.'s been raising hell since Pookie said B.J. tipped off the raid the night Rose was killed. He's accusing us of having a leak on the team. He's saying it's the only way B.J. could have known there was a bust going down."

"What happened to Rod? What happened to Rod, man?" came a cry from the other side of the door.

"Damn!" Crator shouted. "He must have heard me."

"Well, what the hell's he doing against the door?" Billy Montgomery said, opening the door and bumping Pookie, who was now lying on the floor with the chair between his legs. He had crawled up to the door to listen to what was being said in the hallway.

"Get him up!" Crator ordered.

"What the hell is goin' on?" Vick hollered. "What's that damn chair doing between his legs?"

"It's a long story, but I assure you it's necessary," Jerome said.

"He can't be that bad," Ben said.

"The hell he ain't," Crator defended Jerome. "He's every bit that bad...and then some."

"Oh man, what happened to Roderick?" Pookie screamed.

"Don't worry about that. Nothin's gonna happen to you as long as you testify when you're supposed to," Crator admonished him.

"He's dead! Y'all got him kilt, you bastards!" Pookie cried. "I got him kilt. I knew it. I got him kilt."

"You did not get him killed," Crator assured him. "B.J. had no way of knowing you were going to testify. He was just so scared he had him killed just in case. We'll still get him though. We can try him for conspiracy with your testimony."

"You got him kilt!" Pookie fired back. "You let word leak onto the street about me. Now they looking for me, too. You can bet that."

"We didn't leak nothing!" Crator said, setting the prisoner back up onto the bed.

After Pookie was settled down, Crator and Bennett left. Not long thereafter, the other replacements arrived. The place crawled with cops. Some in the adjacent room to Pookie...some in the hall—they were everywhere. Vick decided to talk to Pookie for a minute. He stepped inside the room where Pookie still lay on the bed with the chair between his legs.

"Crator and the others seem to think that the chair is necessary. What do you think, Mr. Jones?" Vick asked.

"I think if I try to get up and break my leg, I got me a damn good lawsuit," Pookie said with a smile.

"I've got an idea. Why don't we try and work together as a team, and everything will be fine. Otherwise, this could be a rough stay for you now that I'm here, if you catch my drift."

"Threatenin' me with violence! All you just alike. I ain't no crook compared to you. Y'all all a bunch of thugs," Pookie shouted.

"Hey, look...I'm on your side," Vick pleaded. "All I wanted to do was remove the chair and just leave you in leg irons."

"Well, do it then, dammit!" Pookie shouted.

"Can you behave?" Vick asked, pulling his keys from his pocket.

"No sweat," Pookie assured him. "I'm too upset about my buddy getting kilt to be worried about meddalin' around with you scumbags."

Vick shook his head, and with a small laugh replied, "Well, that's good...I think."

He called Ben in to stand guard with him while he removed one leg iron, removed the chair, and then replaced the iron on Pookie's leg.

"Are you sure about this?" Ben asked.

"Yeah. This is inhumane," Vick said.

"Okay," Ben replied.

Back at the precinct, B.J. had already been brought in on charges of conspiracy to kill a police officer. Since there was no Roderick O'Bannon, there was no longer a need to keep a lid on the investigation. The D.A. was hoping that B.J.'s arrest would possibly bring some of the others who were in the house on the day of the shooting out of hiding. There wasn't a strong case against B.J. yet, but with Pookie's testimony, along with the videotape, there was enough to get an indictment. With luck, the case would be a lot stronger before it came to trial.

B.J. came quietly. There was no need for force in arresting him, as Burkes had known. B.J. had learned to handle himself with class. He had an unrivaled temper but knew it was fruitless to get upset. If he had legal problems, he let his lawyers handle them. If he had problems investing his money legally, he let his accountants worry about them. If he had discipline problems among the people he controlled, he handled them.

B.J. gave orders and whatever needed to be done was taken care of. He wasn't Italian, but he had set himself up as virtually a black mafioso. He made and spent more money in six months than Burkes would see in three years. He also controlled more assets than most millionaires would ever dream of. He was careful to keep most of them out of his name. Liquor stores, strip joints, even an interest in a bowling alley were just a few of the many things the police knew he owned interests in. All of them were legitimate businesses bought into with laundered drug money.

The cops didn't care about his interests in those businesses because they were legal. B.J. did fear the I.R.S. He feared tax evasion charges worse than he feared the Memphis narcs. He was always impeccably dressed. His skin was medium brown, and he had no blemishes on his face. He was well-built and spent all his free time in a weight room. He had a suaveness when he walked that caused him to stand out in a crowd. He was usually surrounded by cronies who were too street-oriented to understand class.

John Burkes looked into the interrogation room at B.J. There was no point in trying to talk to him until his lawyer arrived. Burkes was a patrolman working at Division headquarters the first time B.J. was arrested. Even then he was smart enough to keep his mouth shut until his attorneys were present. Since then he had been arrested nine times, twice on felony charges. All the police and the D.A. had to show for their efforts was one misdemeanor conviction for simple assault on a john who had hired one of B.J.'s prostitutes and beat her up. That conviction was seven years prior. He had punched the guy in front of a police officer. The officer grabbed him and hauled him in. For the attack, B.J. paid a $257 fine, got a suspended sentence, and hit the street again.

The next month the john's house and business burned and his wife was raped. B.J. was later charged with conspiracy to commit arson, one of his two felony charges. He was acquitted when the key witness, the man who set the fires, was beaten within an inch of his life by a fellow prisoner while awaiting bail, causing him to suffer self-induced amnesia. He could not remember B.J.'s name, much less what he looked like.

Burkes remembered his name well, though. Nobody knew exactly how he had acquired the nickname B.J. All that Burkes knew was that since that acquittal almost seven years ago, the legend of B.J. had grown on the street. Talk of his power registered more fear than his actions themselves.

At the hotel, Ben sat quietly in the hallway outside Pookie's room. The excitement had subsided. His mind began to drift toward Julie. Vick was in the bathroom of the adjacent room while the other two officers sat at the entrance to the stairwell. There were more officers in the lobby. They roamed the halls and stairs. The place was well covered. The Waltham Hotel was an elegant hotel where thugs would be easily spotted should they wander into the building. In this case, however, a thug could come as the most distinguished of people. No one really knew what B.J. might be capable of doing, and now that he had been arrested, Pookie's life was sure to carry a high price.

Pookie had been led to his room using the stairs. They would take him out by the fire escape early in the morning before light. John Burkes had always been opposed to using the hotel because of civilians. There was no sense in endangering anybody's life. This had been the policy of the department for a long time, however, and it was just one night after all. Burkes would feel better when Pookie was shipped on to Nashville. In the meantime, the officers on duty, Ben included, would have to fight back the boredom to stay focused on their job. Pookie's testimony was about 80 percent of the state's case against B.J. so far, and nothing could be left to chance.

Ben was snapped away from thoughts of Julie as Pookie's door opened.

"What do you want?" Ben asked Pookie as Vick reentered the hallway.

"I want some fruit," Pookie said with a smile.

"What do you mean, fruit?" Vick asked.

"It says right here in this room service brochure they have fruit." Pookie held up a pamphlet.

Vick's temper flared. "Look, you may have given Crator and the others a hard time, but I'm gonna tell you right now, if you want to get along with me, we got to work together. Now, you're gonna be shipped out of here tomorrow and sent to a more permanent location. In the meantime, you know we can't have room service up here. It's for your safety."

"That's why one of y'all has to get it for me. I want a basket with mostly oranges and bananas."

"Hold it!" Vick cut him off. "We're on duty. We can't leave our post. You might as well go on back in there, watch TV, and just wait for dinner."

Pookie turned around with a disgruntled look on his face and went back inside, mumbling something about how the other cops did it.

"That's Crator's problem," Vick said to Ben. "He doesn't know how to handle people. Neither does Billy Montgomery. If I had been here earlier today, I would have handled it just like that. You tell them where you stand, give them a reason to want to cooperate, and they will. It's just that simple. You don't have to chain a man to a damn chair like a dog."

Whabamm! Crash! The crushing noise of glass breaking came from inside Pookie's room.

"You were saying?" Ben asked Vick, who was frozen for a moment. Ben sprung the door open and fell to the ground just in time to avoid the chair Pookie had been chained to earlier as it flew through the air, going over his head and smashing into Vick, knocking him into the room on the other side of the hall.

People opened their doors to see the commotion as the other detectives ran past them to back up Vick.

"Hotel security, folks," said the detective who had been nearest the elevator. "We've got everything under control. We just have some rowdy guests. No need to call the front desk. We're already here."

Ben had run into the room in a crouch, unaware of what might come flying through the air next. Pookie was standing in the middle of his bed about to leap onto him. He bounced one time high into the air, and Ben caught him by lunging from the side of the bed. He pulled him from midair, throwing him onto the floor as one of the other detectives pounced on him to detain him.

As all this was happening, Vick Killian hollered from the entrance, "Put that chair between his legs! Chain the little bastard back up!"

Ben looked up from where he now sat on Pookie's legs. "I thought you said that was inhumane."

"Well, if he doesn't know how good he's got it by now, we have no choice," Vick said in his own defense.

"I don't know why y'all let him go in the first place," one of the other detectives pointed out, only to have Killian turn up his nose and walk away.

He was met in the hallway by the hotel manager, who had already been informed of the incident by the other guests.

"Officer! Oh, officer," he began. "I need to speak with you, please."

"I know, I know," Vick answered. "I can assure you everything is under control."

"I'm afraid the other guests have been frightened and want to know what is going on," he said, then whispered to Killian, "Your superiors assured me everything would remain quiet. If not, I will have to ask you to leave."

"I promise you everything is under control," Vick tried to reassure the small man.

"What is that man doing with a chair between his legs?" the manager asked as he moved around Killian to peep inside the room. "He's chained to the chair!"

"Uh, we've got everything under control," Vick said.

"They're gonna rape me...hold me down and strip me!" Pookie shouted before Ben covered his mouth. Pookie bit his hand.

"Oww! you little shit!" Ben screamed in pain.

Vick slammed the door and started to walk the manager down the hall.

"Officer, I don't know if I like this."

"Look," Killian said, trying to calm him down. "We'll be out of here in the morning and out of your hair." He paused, noticing that the man was bald. "Then you can call my boss, the commissioner. Hell, call the freakin' mayor...and complain all you want!"

"I had just rather you all take your prisoner somewhere else, I think," the manager replied.

"Listen!" Vick stopped at the elevator. "That guy in there is a witness to the man that killed that cop here last month. There will be an awful lot of people pissed off if anything goes wrong."

"You're kidding!" the little man said. "You found the cop killer already!"

"I'm entrusting you with this information...that you will keep in secret," Vick warned him. "Your city is counting on you!" he added, playing to the man's pride.

"Oh, I'm glad to help under these circumstances."

"Good!" Vick said. "We'll be gone early tomorrow and we'll pay for any damage to your room."

"Okay, call me if you need me," the manager said, hopping onto the elevator and giving Killian a salute as the door closed.

Vick shook his head and made a beeline back to Pookie. "I'm gonna tell you right now..." he said, pointing his finger at Pookie, who now lay on the bed with Ben's knee in the side of his jaw to prevent him from talking. The other two detectives had rolled him onto his side and were cuffing his hands behind his back.

"We thought we could cuff him for about an hour or so...maybe give him a change of attitude," one of the detectives said.

"Well, I'm gonna tell you right now," Vick repeated, "if you can't be quiet and keep that trap of yours shut tight, I mean tight, I'll gag you with tape if I have to, and you won't even eat dinner. I mean it, dammit!"

Pookie tried to spit. "Ookkkk," he gurgled as Ben pressed his knee harder into his jaw.

At the precinct, the police had given up on interrogating B.J. On the advice of his lawyer, who felt confident that the D.A.'s case was shaky at best, B.J. had declined to say anything. He was now ready for his arraignment. He had been arrested only seven hours earlier and now he was going to make bail and be back out on the street. It really irked Burkes, but they had known before they ever picked him up that this would be the likely outcome.

In night court, B.J. sat as cool as ice. Burkes was enraged that B.J. would even be given a chance to make bail at night. A special session was being held because of the nature of the suspect. In other words, as far as Burkes was concerned, B.J. had friends downtown who had probably arranged for a judge to hear his plea. Burkes now wished they had held him longer for questioning. B.J. was smart enough to be politically involved in the city. He had helped to sponsor judges and councilmen, and he practically held the previous mayor in his back pocket. He had even received a citation from the previous mayor as a sponsor of one of the best citizen patrols in a neighborhood. That was only because he and his gang lived in the neighborhood and scared even the burglars away.

Burkes sat across the small courtroom beside the D.A., looking at B.J. Occasionally B.J. smiled at Burkes or the D.A. Burkes could tell that B.J. was awfully proud of himself for whacking O'Bannon before the cops could find him. The proceedings went quickly; for conspiracy to commit murder, B.J. was granted bail in the amount of $100,000. On the way out of the courtroom, Burkes and the D.A. passed the table where B.J. and his lawyer stood.

"Hey...Burkes!" B.J. called.

"What do you want?" Burkes asked in a voice that reflected his distaste for him.

A huge laugh bellowed from the black man. "Tell Pookie I said hello if you see him. In fact, you can tell him to come by when he gets a chance. I got something for him." The grin had turned to a cold stare.

Ben had gone downstairs for a moment to get a cup of coffee and returned quickly to his post. Vick sat outside in the hallway.

"You heard anything out of him?" Ben asked.

"Naw, he's being quiet for now," Vick frowned. "I hate to leave him chained up like an animal, but I swear, I don't know what else to do. He knows he's valuable to us, and there's not much we can do about it for now."

"Well, if it's all the same to you, I'd just as soon let him stay chained up...animal or not. That boy is crazy."

"Yeah, I guess you're right," Vick agreed as Ben took a seat on the other side of the doorway. At that very moment, the earth shook and the building moved. Vaboom! The force from an explosion knocked the detectives across the hall. The blast came from inside Pookie's room!

"Oh, my God!" Vick screamed, recovering from the floor as fast as he could.

People suddenly filled the hallway.

"Get him out!" Vick screamed to Ben, who was already slamming into Pookie's door trying to unjam it. The door was hot to the touch. The third slam, Ben crashed into the room, now devastated and burning in spots. It wasn't like a fire where the whole place was ablaze. It was more like a bomb. The destruction had already occurred, and there were remnants of fire left over.

Ben looked around for Pookie as the other detectives pushed into the door behind him, the last one trying to hold back the other guests who were crowding the doorway.

There was Pookie. Nothing more than a burnt piece of charcoal in a shell of a room whose outer wall was completely gone. The night was dark, the room was dark. Pookie's singed body was illuminated only by the scattered flames all around the room. His clothes were burnt almost completely off his body. His body was a melted skeleton. It lay motionless there on the bed. Even the chair between his legs no longer existed. The leg irons had been partially melted away.

"Dear God!" Vick uttered, standing frozen behind Ben.

The other detectives were busy pushing people away from the room when the hotel manager arrived. "I knew it! I knew something like this would happen! I told my boss I was against this sort of thing. Something finally had to go wrong before he would listen. We never made any money off this anyway. Now look what's happened. You...you've ruined our business. The place will probably close...you...you sons-of-bitches. This is awful...just awful!" The skinny little man finally broke into tears as his tirade ended.

Burkes was there before the fire department, along with a countless number of cops. He went into a rampage, yelling at everyone except Vick, Ben, and the cops who had been at the scene. He was too mad at them to yell.

During his screaming, he was interrupted by ordnance disposal. The bomb squad informed him that the room had been blown to bits by an RPG or rocket projectile, a Soviet-made light antitank weapon grenade equivalent to the U.S. Army's LAW, with a few exceptions. The Soviet RPG was more effective, larger, and had a greater range. No matter what they were called, they were used for the same thing, to kill tanks.

After he quizzed the bomb squad in intimate detail to ensure they had not been drinking or doing illicit drugs to have come up with such a farfetched notion that somebody in Memphis, Tennessee, would have access to such weaponry, Burkes strolled to the parking lot where Ben, Vick, and the other detectives stood. The group huddled on the east side of the building in disbelief, trying to take in all that had just transpired.

"Well, gentlemen, I guess I owe you an apology," Burkes said. "I really thought you had allowed someone to get a bomb in the room. It just seemed obvious when we arrived that a bomb had gone off. I had no one else to blame but you guys. I'm sorry."

"You mean it wasn't a bomb?" Ben asked in disbelief, not only at what he was hearing but also at seeing a new side of Burkes.

"I'm afraid not," Burkes replied.

"I'm sorry, but a bomb exploded in that room," Vick argued.

"No, it wasn't!" Burkes retorted. "It was a projectile from an RPG. They think it was fired from a passing boat on the river."

"An RPG?" one of the other detectives piped up. "You mean one of those hand-held rocket gizmos?"

"Yep," Burkes answered.

"How in the hell—?" the detective began to ask before Burkes cut him off.

"I don't know how."

"I thought that was just a military weapon," the detective lamely added.

"It is, Soviet at that," Burkes said.

"Well, what's it doing here?" Vick asked.

"That's the sixty-four hundred dollar question," Burkes said. "I don't know. The Soviets sold them all over the world...small Communist-backed countries, guerrillas. After the breakup of the Soviet Union, who knows how many got sold. But you tell me how in God's name B.J. got one."

Everyone looked around at one another in wonder until Vick spoke up, "I don't think so."

"You don't think what?" Burkes asked.

"I mean I don't think B.J. could be behind this. I think Pookie was involved in something else we don't know about."

What? You think the drugs he sold Gennette came from somebody else?" Burkes asked.

"Maybe," Vick said.

Burkes thought for a moment, mashed out a cigarette, and shook his head. "No way! If he had been doing business with another supplier instead of B.J., we never would have gotten him to begin with. B.J. would have whacked him way before now. I've tracked B.J. for nearly fourteen years. He keeps tabs on everybody, including me.

"Yeah, you're probably right," Vick agreed, "but how could B.J. get weaponry like that?"

Burkes shook his head. "Who knows, who knows? It's a crazy world." He looked around at all the people. "Speaking of a crazy world, it's gonna be crazy around here for a while. Why don't ya'll go home. We'll finish up. You probably don't want to be around when the mayor shows up. All our butts will be in a sling anyway. Shelby County has a massive search on already. There's nothing more you can do."

The detectives looked relieved.

"Hey, Ben, you need a ride home?" Vick asked.

"Yeah, if you don't mind," Ben answered.

The ride home was a long one. Vick drove slowly, stopping once to get gas as they tried to make sense of what had just happened.

"What did you think about how his body looked?" Ben asked as they pulled out of the convenience store where they had stopped to fill up.

"I've never seen anything like it," Vick said. "It was awful."

There was no more talk until they parked in front of the Seals' condo.

"Well, I guess I'll see you in the morning," Vick said as Ben stepped from the car.

"Yeah...see you then."

The car pulled away. Ben picked up the evening paper in the lawn. Turning around he saw Randy in the drive.

"You forgot your paper," Ben said.

"Yeah. I guess we did. It's been kinda hectic around here tonight too," Randy said.

"You mean you've already heard?" Ben asked.

"Oh yeah, the whole town knows by now," Randy replied with a worried look on his face. "It's been all over the news. We called down to the precinct to make sure you were okay."

"It was really bad," Ben said." I'm going to bed. I'm exhausted."

"Ben!" Randy called to him before he reached the front door.

"What?" Ben stopped walking, but was too tired to turn around.

"Before you go in there, I want to know how you feel," Randy said.

"I'm tired."

"Let's go for a ride. We need to talk."

"Sorry, cuz, it'll have to wait. I can't go another step. I just hope I make it to the bed." Ben walked to the door, opened it, and stepped inside. He felt his head swell, and his emotions began a rollercoaster ride...was he so tired he was imagining...there was his aunt, and on the sofa beside her sat his wife. He felt dazed. He was not only shocked and angered to see her, but in an unexplainable way, he was elated.

"Hello, Ben," Julie spoke hesitantly.

Ben could not speak. He tried, but nothing came out. He tried again...still nothing. He wanted to know what she was doing here...if Gene was with her. Still nothing came out. He finally gave up trying and just sighed.

"Please hear me out, Ben, before you tell me to leave," Julie pleaded.

Tell her to leave? Ben thought. Yeah, why hadn't he thought of that? He still could not speak. He could not understand why he hadn't immediately cursed her or shot her. He thought maybe...just maybe...he still loved her, even though he had tried to put her out of his mind by telling himself that he hated her and would never speak to her again.

Maybe it was a dream, he thought. Maybe it never happened. Then he felt the sharp reality of it again. He really had caught his wife with his boss. He had actually been set up by his comrades. He had nothing to be ashamed of. Why did this hurt so badly? None of it was his fault. The longer he stood there looking at his wife, the more he realized, as beautiful as she was, how thin she had become. She had small bags under each eye. She had obviously been in misery. Maybe she still loved him...maybe they could work things out.... What was he thinking? This was the woman who had ruined his life. It was time to have closure on this relationship. He knew it. Was he strong enough?

"Could we be alone?" Julie asked.

Ben stood there looking at her. He said nothing.

"I guess," he finally said, looking through her as if he saw nothing.

"Well…" she said.

He looked around at Randy who was standing just outside the door smoking a cigarette even though he didn't smoke, listening, almost hanging on every word. Mary had said nothing. She stood quietly.

"Let's take a walk," Ben said.

"We can leave, Ben," Mary spoke at last.

"No." Ben cut her off. "This is your home. If anybody has to leave, it should be her."

Julie's eyes filled with tears.

"He's right," Julie said, choking back the tears. Ben felt a lump in his throat. He could never bear to watch her cry. Yes, he thought, this was dangerous…he still loved her and probably always would. They walked outside, down the sidewalk side by side. Ben led the way around back of the condo, across the back yard and toward the river.

"The river is beautiful at night," Ben pointed out.

"Ben, I know you hate me."

He said nothing. He kept walking until they reached the end of the yard where the cliff that the condos sat upon overlooked the river. There were lights from the bridge in the distance: headlights and taillights twinkling as cars crossed the bridge joining Arkansas and Tennessee. There were small lights in the water shining from the boats and barges quietly sharing the water.

"Ben, I've got a lot of problems."

"I'll have to agree with you there, Julie."

"No. I mean I've got problems…that you don't even know about."

"I'm not sure I care to know," Ben replied.

"You certainly have that right. I have no right whatsoever to come to you with them either. It's not that I want help from you…I just want you to understand what was behind my ruining our marriage."

Ben rubbed his tired eyes showing no emotion, but deep inside, he had a yearning to hear this explanation. "Let's walk down to the water," he said. He led the way down the bank. They both laughed a little at her clumsiness as she nearly fell down the slope, and Ben caught her before she slipped the rest of the way.

"I wouldn't blame you if you let me fall…you should push me off anyway," Julie said, trying not to look at him.

Ben began to feel more at ease, but he was still so tired it was hard for him to concentrate on keeping his guard up. Deep inside he began to feel comfortable and happy to be with her again. The different surroundings almost made it seem as though things were normal again.

At the bottom of the bank the waves sloshed onto the rocks that jutted against the water. Ben picked up a small rock and flung it into the mighty river.

"Ben, I don't know how to tell you this. Especially since you're still a cop. By the way, congratulations on your new job. It has to be exciting. I knew you could do it...I mean make it in a big-time place like this.... You just have it in you."

Ben felt a swell of pride. "I'm a cop first. I always will be. That's the only thing that's kept me sane the last few days. Then again, if I had been less cop and more of a husband, maybe things would be different, and we wouldn't be having this conversation." Ben couldn't believe he was actually taking part of the blame for her screwing around.

"No, Ben, that's not true at all."

"Then what is it?" he flared up. "Is McMasters that good a lover? Is he so good in bed that you'd choose a sixty-year-old over me? I know it's not his looks, that's for damn sure!"

"No, no, no. That's not it at all," Julie cried.

"Then what is it, Julie? You tell me what is it that would make you screw around on me with an old man. Is it that he makes you feel good because he's my boss...was my boss, thank God.

"No!" She was in tears now. "That's not it at all!" She began to mumble.

"Well, what then?"

"I don't know how to tell you. I had it all worked out in my head and now I just can't—"

"Just spit it out!" Ben prodded.

"I don't want to hurt you anymore. I still love you," she pleaded. "I just can't bear to hurt you anymore," she sobbed.

"Talk to me." Ben put his arms around her. "There's nothing that we can't work through if we try."

"You mean that?" she shot back.

Ben realized that he may have put his foot in his mouth, speaking with his heart instead of his head. He did love her, but he didn't want to give the impression that he would take her back. The thought of her with Gene McMasters made him sick to his stomach, and he didn't know if he would ever be able to get that image out of his mind. Then suddenly—without even realizing it—he gave in. "Sure we can work it out."

"Oh, Ben, I love you," she sobbed, crushing into his chest.

He tried to hold back his anger. If she really loved him she wouldn't have screwed around on him, he thought.

"I'm sorry," she said pushing away and trying to pull herself together.

He pulled a handkerchief from his pocket to wipe her eyes. Slowly she gathered her composure.

"Ben, honey...I have a drug problem."

"A what?"

"I'm so sorry!" she cried.

He acted as though he didn't comprehend her.

"I'm addicted...I think...sometimes I don't think so, but usually I do...no...I am."

Ben could feel that lump in his throat again.

"Crack. I need crack. I don't want it. I just need it. Oh Ben, what have I done to us?" She dropped to her knees on the hard rocks and cried into her hands.

Ben stood there aghast. How could it be? His sweet and innocent wife.... He was still having trouble believing that she had had an affair, much less this.

"I have a problem that I can't handle."

"Don't say that!" Ben admonished, knowing he couldn't change things by hearing less than the truth.

"I do, Ben."

She looked so serious he knew it must be true. He just couldn't believe it.

"I'm sorry. There's nothing I can do about it. I need help."

He pulled her close. There was a long silence. The two sat together on the ground staring at the water. The longer they sat there, the more Ben's mind began to wander. He almost had to pinch himself to make himself believe everything that had happened to him just that day.

Finally he spoke. "As much as I sang the evils of crack and what it did to the people I busted for so long, why would you even consider trying it to begin with?"

She cried a little more. "It was Steve's friends. They gave me some at one of his parties when I went home to visit last summer. I was just trying to fit in. You know he and his friends party all the time."

"Your own brother? Step-brother or not, your own brother got you on drugs!"

"No. No. I asked him to let me try it since everybody else was. I'm sor-ry. Daddy thinks so much of Steve. I just wanted to be more like him. I wasn't thinking."

"I'll kill him," Ben said, glaring into the water with a growing obsession to eliminate this man whom he had hated for years.

"It's not his fault!" she sobbed. "I pleaded with him to let me try it. He didn't want me to and told me to stay away from it, but I tried it anyway. He found out and threatened to kill the girl that gave it to me." She paused to try to regain the composure she was losing again. "When I got back home, Steve was worried about me and he asked Gene to keep an eye on me in case I started fooling around with it again. He was worried that I'd become addicted. The sad part is...he was so right."

"What? Did you say Gene? When did Steve and Gene become confiding friends? When did they ever meet for that matter?"

I don't know. But I should tell you, Steve's a drug dealer. I've known it for a long time. I was afraid to tell you."

"I've known for as long as I've known you," Ben corrected her.

She looked at him quizzically. "I never knew you suspected."

"I thought maybe *you* didn't know because you've never mentioned it. If you did know, I didn't think you would condone something like that in your family," Ben answered.

"Believe me, there were times when I came close to telling Daddy, but I just couldn't," she sniffed and sobbed more.

"How did he get to know Gene?"

"I don't know, but I do know that Gene worked with him and helped him."

"To do what?" Ben's voice was almost a whisper.

"He helped him, Ben. They all did. Every last one of them—the sons of bitches.... It killed me to see you working so hard, knowing you were a good cop...and all of them, Mitch, Gene, all of them were on the take. All of them, Ben, all of them except you. You were the only good and decent one on the whole damn force. Then I betrayed you. I'm so sorry," she sobbed harder than ever.

The tale was becoming too farfetched for Ben to believe. He said nothing.

"When I found out, I was so far gone there was no coming back. Crack had me. I knew that crack was the worst, but there was nothing I could do once I tried it. I was one of the unlucky ones who got hooked the first time. I'm so sorry. I deserve everything that has happened to me."

"Help me understand. Was Gene giving you drugs?" Ben felt so naive.

"Yes...yes." She paused for a moment. "He came over one day while you were out of town. It was right after Steve had talked to him."

Ben cringed at the thought of the way this conversation was headed, but he wanted to hear it all.

"He came by to tell me that Steve had called him and confided in him, and they were both worried about me but promised to keep it from you."

I told him that I was having cravings for the drug already and didn't trust myself. I told him I was going to tell you about it." She choked up. "He told me not...to say anything to you...because you wouldn't understand. He said he did and knew I could handle the problem on my own...and he would help me anyway he could.... Then he showed me a rock of coke he had taken from a bust and said he knew the cravings would not go away until I had quenched my desire. He had a crack pipe in his pocket that he said was also from a bust, and he told me if I would promise to never touch it again, he would let me smoke the one rock he had. I knew it was wrong, but I just couldn't help myself," she cried out loud. "He knew what he was doing, Ben." Julie's ragged voice tore at Ben's heart.

"By then he had you for sure, didn't he?" Ben asked, now holding his wife against his shoulder.

"Yes!" she cried.

"So he gave you the drug for sex from then on. Am I right?

She was silent.

"It's okay," Ben gently assured her, knowing in his heart that it wasn't okay but that he had to hear all the details. He wanted to feel the pain.

"Yes," she whimpered.

"And that went on for a year?"

"I guess," she sniffed. "I wanted to stop. I love you and only you. You can't believe what that drug does to you."

"Oh, I know. I've seen it, remember, nearly every day!"

"Yeah, I guess so," she acknowledged, then added: "Ben, he was so mean to me."

Ben scoffed as if he wasn't surprised.

"I know. I deserved it! But he was just so mean, and I was under his power. I just can't quit on my own. I would never have gotten the nerve to tell you if you hadn't left me."

"Well, it's not like I was given much choice," Ben mused.

"I know," she began to cry again. "Ben, he was so-o-o mean," she mumbled.

Ben swallowed hard, "I can't believe I never knew—I never saw any signs. I was so stupid."

"Oh, Ben, no. I'm sorry."

"Well, maybe if I had been more attentive to my marriage, I could have spotted the problem."

"No, don't blame yourself. That stuff makes you do anything...I mean anything. I was very careful to make sure you never found out."

"You said he was mean to you. I never saw you bruised or beaten."

"No, no. He wouldn't have done anything to make you suspicious."

"Well, what then? Tell me," he pleaded.

"I don't want to talk about it," she squirmed.

Ben tried to be reasonable. "No, I have to know for my own self-esteem. So we can clear the air."

"No, Ben."

"If you still love me and want to work this out, you have to be completely honest with me. You owe me that much. Surely you understand that I'll never be able to rest until I know everything."

"It's just so terrible. It wasn't me. It was him using me and my body."

"I have to know!" Ben commanded.

"No!" she cried. "I won't lie to you anymore, but I won't make you hate me, either."

"Tell me and we'll go from there, I promise." He raised her head up with his hand.

"Do you promise?" she begged of him.

"What's behind us, I want to leave behind. I want to get you some help so we can start a new life. But I have to know. I can't wonder."

"Oh, Ben, I love you so much."

"Then talk to me. Let's put some closure on that part of our life."

"Oh, Ben...it's...I can't...it's so...unspeakable..."

"If we're going to go on with our lives I have to know. Now, he made you have sex, and what else?"

"Oh, Ben," she moaned.

"I can handle it. I've already thought a lot worse than what the truth probably is, I can assure you."

"He made me have sex with him. You know that. He made me have sex with other deputies too."

Ben thought he would explode. He couldn't believe the truth actually could be worse than imagined. He knew he had to stay calm if he was going to find out the whole story. He wasn't sure he really wanted the whole story now, but he knew he would have to hear it or die within. He had to work through this and somehow put it out of his mind.

"What else?" he calmly asked.

"He made me have weird sex with them," she sniffed. "That all came later...when I was nothing more than a junkie...waiting on you to leave for the day so I could get a hit to keep myself going. So much of my grouchiness that I blamed on female problems was really the drug.... He made me do it with him and two more deputies at the same time. That happened a lot."

Ben felt like he was having a heart attack. Stay calm, he told himself. He heard her still talking, but the sound seemed far away, as his mind reeled from each new revelation.

"He made me do it with one of his buddies from out of town to pay off a bet he had made.... Oh, Ben, it gets worse."

Ben just looked at her in disbelief. Nothing could be worse. How could there possibly be more?

"He's crazy. He got his kicks by doing things to me."

"What things?" Ben snapped.

"He would videotape me."

"Oh, my God!" Ben put his head in his arms.

"I'm sorry!" she cried. "I refused for a long time. But he just kept the rock away from me until he knew I couldn't take it anymore. Then I would always give in."

"What is it? Tapes of you and him?" Ben asked.

"Some. There are tapes of me and two or three guys at one time," she sobbed. "I didn't want to...I hated it...all of it!"

Ben's stomach was queasy.

"I'll leave now if you want me to."

Ben was silent. He sat quietly throwing rocks into the water for almost an hour. Julie had said nothing during this time. She knew it was best to give him time to think. Finally, Ben tried to talk, but didn't know what to say. "I just don't understand...Wasn't I enough to keep you happy?"

"Oh, yes, darling!" Julie assured him. "It's just that for so long I've watched Steve, Mr. Happy-go-lucky, and I guess I was trying to be like him, but it backfired and I found myself hooked."

Ben glared at her. "Since I left, I'd really begun to hate you...I mean really hate you!"

"I know, " she sobbed.

Suddenly, Ben was crying too, and in the midst of his sobs, his real feelings came forth. "But I still care for you.... In spite of all this, I still care..."

Now they cried together. Finally, Ben asked, "Do you really mean what you said about us?"

"What do you mean?" she replied.

"About us." He paused. "Do you still love me and only me?"

"Oh, yes, Ben. You've always been my heart, and I've never stopped loving you. I just...have this problem.... I need help."

"We can get through this, you know," Ben said.

"Oh, I love you, Ben," she gasped. "I love you so much."

He held her close.

After a while, Ben pushed her away a little as he spoke. "There are still some things I don't understand."

"What?" She never looked up.

"Steve and Gene...how did they get together? I mean, how did they meet? What could Gene possibly do for Steve?"

"I don't know how they got together. I was shocked that they even knew each other. But I do know that Steve used Gene for protection."

"What kind of protection?"

"They used Greensburg as an outlet to move their dope. Steve's people would ship drugs up the river by way of barges, then transfer them by land from Greensburg out to Shreveport, Memphis, Birmingham, God knows where."

Ben suddenly realized that he had received more education in the past two days than he had in the previous twenty years.

"Gene and all of them would protect their shipments and ensure that they were easily transferred from the barges to trucks or whatever."

Ben shook his head." I can't believe they've gotten away with this for so long."

"They'd hide it in fertilizer, ship it upriver, and unload it around the chemical plant. No one has ever suspected anything as far as I know."

"I can't believe you've known this all along."

"I didn't know a lot of it for a long time. Gene let things slip. Little things that helped me figure some of it out. Later on he talked more freely about it. I guess 'cause he knew I was under his control."

"Do you realize what you're saying?"

"Yeah, that Gene and Steve are a couple of hoods. It's true. I just hate that it took all this for me to tell you."

"No, I mean...do you realize what you're saying? If what you say is true, then Gene knows that you're a threat to him."

"He's not worried about me."

"No, but he is worried about the attorney general and the FBI. He'll panic when he realizes you're gone. The same thing just happened in the case I've been working on here. As soon as a couple of people who could bring down a major operation came up missing, they were killed."

"They wouldn't do anything to me because of Steve. I'll never turn on Steve either. You know that, don't you? That no matter what, I can't hurt my own brother."

"I understand.... I don't agree, but I do understand. But listen, honey, something is gonna happen when Gene starts looking for you. He's not gonna let this go lightly. Wouldn't you rather be the one to tell Steve first before Gene or someone tells him something different. He already blames me. He called me the other night warning me to stay away from you. I figured you had told him a lot of bad stuff about me. I'd like for him to know that I was good to you."

"I haven't talked to him!" Julie pleaded.

"Well, it must have been Gene, then. That's what I mean. There's no telling what all he's told him already. You need to set the record straight with Steve. Then we have to be careful. I don't know what Gene might do."

"No! I just can't tell Steve I'm an addict. Besides, there's nothing to worry about. Gene wouldn't come all the way here after me."

"You don't know that. They went to the trouble of setting me up.... You don't know what they might do. We just need to be careful."

"You're right, I guess. You always are, though."

Ben shook his head in disagreement. Their eyes met like new lovers. "I love you," they both said at the same time. They hugged and started to walk back up the bank toward the condo.

Mary and Randy met them at the door. They both had worried looks on their faces.

"Everything's okay," Ben announced. "You can relax now. We're gonna try to work things out. Do you mind if Julie stays a few days...until we can find a place of our own?"

"Stay forever if you want to," Mary said, ushering Julie into the kitchen to show her where everything was. "Now you just make yourself at home," she told her.

In the den, Randy pulled Ben to the side. "How goes it?"

"I think it's gonna be okay." He looked to see where Julie was. "I'll tell you all about it later."

"Yeah, go on and be with her for now. She needs you. We'll talk tomorrow. Mom isn't going into the office. She said she'd stay here with Julie if needed, so don't worry about her. Why don't you let me come get you for lunch, and we'll go to Monte's and talk for a while? You need to be with her tonight."

"Yeah," Ben rubbed his forehead, half-listening to what his cousin was saying, "that sounds good."

"Just give me a call when you're free tomorrow."

"Okay," Ben replied.

"I'm going to bed. See you in the morning." Randy went upstairs. Mary and Julie reappeared in the den.

"If there's anything you need, don't hesitate to ask, okay?" Mary pleaded.

"Thanks. I'm just glad to have my wife back." Ben looked at his wife, who was beautiful to him even with bags under her eyes from all the tears. She smiled and hung her head as if she didn't deserve his admiration.

Chapter 11

Julie fell asleep immediately that night, but Ben couldn't sleep at all. The revelations of the day were too much for him to handle. He tossed and turned...then finally sat up in the bed and watched his wife sleep. She breathed deeply, in and out. She was beautiful. Every breath she took was like a surge for him. To know that he could put his life back together was enough to keep him from going completely insane. He reasoned though that it would take a lot of work for them to put their marriage back the way it was, if that was possible. Years of therapy would definitely be needed for him to be able to deal with all he now knew about his wife's activities over the past year. He thought he must be crazy for not going on with his life without her, but she was the only love he had ever known, and he could never get over her, no matter what.

Randy drove Ben to work the next morning. He stepped out of the town car onto the pavement behind the precinct and realized that he was completely exhausted. His legs had gone to sleep on the ride to work. If he could just get through this day, he would rest tonight.

Inside the precinct he could hear John Burkes' voice booming over the rest of the noise that was filling the air. Ben wasn't geared up for Burkes' tirades this early in the morning, but he knew he had to suck it up and take whatever came his way if he were to keep this job. Even though he had lost the first witness he had ever guarded, the excitement of this job was pulsating. He was glad to be at work...he just needed a little rest before being forced to think.

It didn't take him long to find out that there was some hellacious heat coming down from City Hall over the destruction of the case, as well as the Waltham Hotel. It was going to be a long day.

"I want everybody on that video found and charged with something by the end of the day. Is that understood?" Burkes was giving Montgomery, Jerome, and Gennette two earfuls and more.

Ben stayed away from Burkes' office, where the one-way conversation was taking place. He decided to look for Paul Crator to find out what he should be doing. Damn, he thought, there was Crator in Burkes' office, behind the desk while Burkes stood in front of it addressing his squad leaders. Ben was clueless as to what he needed to be doing. He didn't want Burkes to see him doing nothing. He decided he'd take advantage of this opportunity to call Julie. He called from Denise's desk.

Julie told him there were two security guards at the condo just as he had requested. Ben had told Randy a little about McMasters and company before work that morning, and Randy had transferred the guards from the trucking company for the sole purpose of keeping an eye on Julie.

Ben explained that things would have to be this way for a little while...at least until he could get better settled into his new job and until the pace slowed down enough for them to make different arrangements. He warned her that he had already witnessed the murder of someone much more heavily guarded than she was.

Julie said she didn't believe Gene would ever do anything so drastic. She told Ben that she had called Steve right before he called. Steve was so mad he couldn't even talk and told her not to worry about Gene...that he would take care of it.

Ben was relieved to know that somebody was going to make Gene pay. He knew Steve's vengeance was something he would never want to experience, yet McMasters was deserving of every bit of it.

"Seals!" Ben heard Burkes' voice boom across the room from the doorway of his office. He cringed as he hung up the phone.

"Yes sir!" he answered.

"Go with Crator and help him."

"Yes sir!"

"Let's go," Crator told Ben.

"After you," Ben replied, eager to get out of this madhouse.

"Where are we headed?" Ben asked, as they pulled onto 240

headed east.

"We're going to find Tawana Griffin again," Crator informed him.

"Tawana Griffin?" Ben asked. "You mean Pookie's girlfriend?"

"Yeah. She's supposed to be seeing one of the other guys who was on the videotape of the house where Rose got shot. She's staying with her sister in East Memphis. If we can spot her, we'll just have to wait her out and follow her until she sees this guy." He reached in his pocket and pulled out a combination of half-chewed cigars and a black-and-white mug shot of the suspect. "His name is Malcolm Manning. I think he goes by Shorty."

"So what's the plan?" Ben asked. "Round everybody up and scare them...hoping we get the same story out of a few?"

"We want to pick up everybody who was on that videotape. If they were in that house that day, they know something. If we can get everybody's story before B.J. kills them all, maybe we'll have something."

"You really think he'd kill all those people?" Ben asked.

"No, he's got O'Bannon, the trigger man, out of the way. We have no murder weapon. The only witness we had anything big on is smoked sausage now. He knows we ain't got two cents. We gotta keep trying though. There's enough crap coming from City Hall right now that we have no choice. The freaking attorney general is sending some of his people in now that B.J. has proven he has more artillery than the Kuwaiti army. And the D.A. thinks there's a leak in the precinct.

"A leak?" Ben clambered.

"Don't say a word! To anybody, I mean it!"

"I won't," Ben assured him.

"Before he died, Pookie said B.J. tipped them off to the raid. So B.J. had to have found out about the raid right before it happened Then, to top that, Pookie gets killed. And Roderick O'Bannon."

"I thought it wasn't that big a secret where Pookie was," Ben said.

"It wasn't," Crator agreed.

"I didn't think so. My cousin knew exactly where we were keeping him."

"That's what I mean," Crator said. "We don't have any other temporary facility except for jail and our own personal homes. Who would have ever thought about a freaking rocket grenadelauncher or whatever the hell it was. We still don't have any clues as to how B.J. got one. That's a whole 'nother case unto itself."

"But the D.A. thinks there may be a leak, huh?" Ben decided to pry a little more.

"Well, he pointed out that B.J. had gotten to O'Bannon before we could. The only answer we could give him is that B.J. panicked when Pookie came up missing and figured he was cutting a deal with the cops since so many people saw Pookie get arrested. With Jerome chasing him all over a neighborhood and everything, word probably got back to B.J."

"Does the D.A. suspect any team member in particular?" Ben asked.

Crator laughed. "If he did, I'm sure he wouldn't say so. They'll probably have Internal Affairs watching all of us, if they haven't already."

"Oh, well I guess they need to consider all the possibilities in something this big," Ben said.

Crator agreed and sped along the freeway to the exit driving him northbound on Sumner Avenue. Crator soon found the house where Tawana's sister lived. They watched the house all morning, but no one went in or out. They were finally relieved at lunch when two more officers arrived to give them a break. Ben called Randy and told him he would be back at the precinct shortly. Randy picked Ben up there, and they headed for Monte's.

Inside the restaurant, Monte's voice boomed over all the noise of dishes rattling, pots clanging, patrons jabbering, and busboys scurrying around to avoid Monte's wrath.

"You-a too-a slow. Move, move!" he ordered a fair-skinned kid with freckles who looked like he was at his first job.

"Over here, Randy!" came the commissioner's voice.

"We're eating with the commissioner again?" Ben whispered in Randy's ear.

"Enjoy the prestige," Randy answered.

"Hey, boss. How you doin'?" Randy grabbed the commissioner's hand. "I know you're not by yourself."

"No, no. John Burkes is here. He went to the restroom. I asked him to lunch to discuss the case they're working on that got the Waltham blown up. Ben, Randy says you were there."

"Yes sir!"

"I guess it's been a rather eventful week for you already."

"Yes sir, you could say that again!"

"Have a seat. Burkes will be back in a second."

They took their seats. Ben was perusing the menu when Burkes walked up to the table.

"Damn, Seals," Burkes exclaimed. "You've eaten with the commissioner more this week than I have all year. I have to do something wrong before I get to eat lunch with the commissioner."

The commissioner laughed. "If you gentlemen will excuse me for a second, the mayor just sat down over there. I think I'll go kiss up a little bit."

He grinned and left the table. Ben's eyes followed him to where the mayor was. He wanted to see what he looked like. Before he could get a look at him, he was startled by Burkes.

"Showing your clout, Seals?" He was glaring at Ben. "Get him and the D.A. and everybody else in this Godforsaken town off my back. Then I'll be impressed."

"Now just hold on there, Officer Burkes." Randy interrupted.

Ben was frozen. He shouldn't be here. Burkes was pissed and Randy was going to keep him in trouble just when Burkes was starting to tolerate him.

"There's no reason to take this out on Ben. Hasn't he done a good job for you?" Randy asked.

"Yeah, but I'm still getting my butt chewed twenty times a day for this case getting blown to hell and back." Burkes glanced to make sure the commissioner wasn't coming back.

"I've got to go to the bathroom," Ben announced. He didn't want to listen to Burkes' rantings, so he decided to leave until the commissioner got back.

When Ben left for the restroom, Randy turned to Burkes and said, "Look, John. May I call you John?"

Burkes just glared at the attorney.

"This boy is trying to do his job," Randy said.

"Oh, he's done fine. I've got no problem with him so far. It's just that I'm under pressure that you would not believe," Burkes said.

"Well, I hate to be the one to ask for favors from you right now, but I think it would be for your own good..."

"What?" Burkes cocked his head curiously.

"Ben would be able to perform better if he could have the rest of the day off," Randy said.

"No way! Forget it! I need every man I've got on the street today."

"He's worked unbelievable hours the last two days after coming here from Greensburg. To make matters worse, his wife came back to him last night, after he thought they were divorcing."

"Really?" Burkes had a mildly sympathetic tone.

"Really!" Randy continued. "She was there after he came in from the explosion. He's worried to death about her and his home situation. I'll guarantee you that if you let him have the afternoon off, he'll be twice as good tomorrow and from then on."

"Well, I'm sure this job was probably quite a culture shock coming from Green County, Mississippi," Burkes said, only half-interested.

"I hate to put it like this, but I don't think you have a choice," Randy said.

"What do you mean by that?" Burkes asked.

"I'm worried about him," Randy said. "All he's been through...and then his wife confessed to sleeping with a bunch of other men."

"Good grief!" Burkes said.

"You and I are the only ones who know that though. He told me about it on the way to work this morning. I'm afraid he might snap...do something crazy...if he doesn't get a break."

"You don't think he's suicidal, do you?" Burkes asked.

"No, but anybody could get crazy after all he's been through. If it were me, I'd kill the bitch. If he doesn't get a break and a chance to relax a little, who knows?"

"Point taken," Burkes agreed.

When Ben returned to the table, Burkes told him he had the rest of the day off. Ben thanked his boss at least four times before lunch was over.

The afternoon proved to be a very productive one for him and Julie. They walked downtown and tried to just enjoy themselves. They strolled down Beale Street and took a horse-drawn carriage ride around downtown, laughing and playing like two children. That evening they caught the local news, which was still dominated by the explosion at the Waltham Hotel. It was quite an ego trip for Ben, who felt he had impressed his wife by leaving little Greensburg and becoming involved in something so big his first day on the job in the city. She smiled at him when they saw him in the background of a camera shot...the same one they had been showing all day on every station.

In bed, Julie again fell asleep quickly. Ben was still awake trying to find something on the tube. Finally, he gave up. He looked to his side at his beautiful wife under the covers fast asleep. They had decided to wait a while before making love. They wanted to reacquaint themselves with one another all over again. Ben laid his Beretta on the dresser. He had carried it with him all day. The fear of Gene was what had kept him on his toes. He was probably back in Greensburg, but one of those bogus deputies may have been sent up here to do God knows what to him and Julie. Just in case, he stayed prepared. He fell asleep almost at once after turning out the light.

Chapter 12

en was awakened around 2:00 a.m. by a blunt thumping noise and a soft shriek from his wife...then silence. He saw a couple of silhouettes in the dark hovering over his bed. Before he could react, he was struck on the side of the head and knocked unconscious. He lay there motionless. Julie lay beside him, dead.

Ben awoke within the hour, aching and throbbing, clutching the side of his head, now riddled with pain. What had happened? Then, as the pain became even more excruciating, it came to him. Julie! His right eye was swollen almost completely shut. The glimmer of the moonlight through the second-floor window shed enough light for him to see his wife lying still on the bed in a pool of blood.

"Julie! Oh, Julie! Dear God! Help! Help! Oh-h-h God! Why? Why? I didn't think they would really.... Why?" he screamed.

"Ben! Ben!" came the shouts of Randy and Mary Seals from their first-floor bedrooms.

"Help!" Ben cried at the top of his lungs. "Help us, please! Call 911!

There was no phone in the guest bedroom. He laid Julie's body back on the bed and sprinted downstairs to call; his sobs made his broken sentences incoherent.

The stairwell consisted of nothing more than two short flights of steps at the end of a hall that ran between Randy and Mary's bedrooms. Ben bounded off the steps into the dark hall. Halfway down the hall he ran into something and was knocked to the floor. He didn't see anything. He reached up to feel his obstruction. It felt like a rope...whatever it was had caught him in the midsection.

"My door is jammed!" Randy shouted from his room.

Ben reached for the hall light, flicked it on and found a piece of cable. Simple hardware-store cable strung from Randy's doorknob to Mary's doorknob directly across the hall. The cable had been pulled tight to prevent either door from opening, as the pressure from either knob would pull against the opposite door. Ben yanked the cable off Randy's doorknob.

"Julie's been shot! Call 911!" Ben screamed and headed back upstairs to be with his wife.

"Julie's been shot?" Mary screamed. "Dear God!"

Randy grabbed the phone and somehow made the dispatcher understand their plea, then ran upstairs with his own shotgun.

There was no need for CPR. That was obvious. But Ben continued breathing into Julie's mouth pausing to scream: "Why? Why?"

Randy stuttered, "I should have had security here at night too! I didn't realize what kind of trouble she might be in."

"Why didn't I just forget my pride and tell her outright that I forgave her? She knew I loved her, but I never told her that I had forgiven her," Ben mumbled to himself.

"They may still be in the house!" Randy cautioned.

"No," Ben yelled back as Randy started to leave the room. "They knocked me out! I've been out for a while! They've been gone!"

"What did they look like?"

Ben was crying too hard to answer. He was still slumped over his wife's body, crying, when the paramedics arrived. Randy and one of the medics had to drag him away and downstairs, kicking and crying.

"Why? Why?" he screamed. "I just don't understand. Why does God hate me so much?" His eyes met his cousin's through the tears.

"Ben." Randy tried to calm him only to be ignored.

Randy managed to get Ben outside in the night air and sit him down against the side of the house just as the first police car arrived.

"Ben, listen," Randy began, "the cops will be here asking questions about Julie. They're gonna want to know why she was killed.... When you tell them why, everything that happened in Greensburg is going to come out. Are you ready for this?"

Ben looked at him with the blankest of stares.

"It's okay," Randy assured his cousin. "I'll just tell them you can't talk now."

"No. No. I want them to catch these bastards tonight!" Ben cried. "I'll talk to them."

"Well, here's your first chance." Randy said. "That's Terry Mills, Homicide." He pointed to a white car now parking in front of the condo.

"You certainly made it here fast, Officer Mills," Randy said as Terry Mills approached them. Mills busied himself directing patrolmen arriving on the scene about searching the grounds.

"I was in the coffee shop around the corner when the call came in," Mills said, searching his pocket for a notepad. Randy met him halfway across the grass. Mills peered over Randy's shoulder. "Is that the husband, boyfriend or whatever?" he asked, looking at Ben sitting against the wall crying.

"Yes, he is. He's also my cousin," Randy let him know quickly. "It was his wife who was killed," Randy said. "He's one of you people."

"Whatta ya mean?" Mills asked.

"Memphis' finest. He works on John Burkes' team," Randy said.

"Huh. I've never seen him before." Mills pushed his way past Randy and walked toward the house. He strolled past Ben sitting off to the right of the front door on the grass. Mills said nothing to Ben as he disappeared into the house. More police cars began arriving. Mills came from upstairs to meet the arriving officers and brief them on securing the area. He then pulled Randy to the side. "What's your cousin's name?"

"Ben Seals."

"I'll need to call Burkes."

"Fine," Randy replied.

Mills went to his car. Randy walked over to Ben to fill him in on what was going on. Ben was unresponsive. Randy finally coaxed Ben inside to the dining room. Ben's demeanor was that of a zombie, starting straight ahead and saying nothing. Randy sat with Ben for a while. People were in and out of the condo in droves. Mary Seals went over to stay at a neighbor's.

"Captain Burkes." Terry Mills met Burkes coming across the grass. The scene now looked like a movie set. Neighbors, TV cameras, and curious passersby were gathered all around the patrolmen who were trying to keep them back off the grounds for fear they might hinder the gathering of evidence.

"Captain, sorry to get you out so late," Mills said in a mildly sarcastic tone. On the surface the two appeared to like each other, but they had competed many times for promotions and so on. They had joined the force at the same time and had worked their ways through the ranks.

"Yeah," Burkes replied. "I hope you don't lose too much sleep worrying about me," he added without a smile.

"Well, Captain, there's no need to get testy. Is this one of your boys?" He showed Burkes a notepad with Ben's name on it.

"New man. Just got him. He was working at the Waltham last night when it blew," Burkes said to the homicide cop, who seemed a bit taken aback by this revelation.

"Well, I guess he's having a bad week. It's his wife who got hit here. Some burglars or something is what we assume, but we haven't talked to your boy yet. I thought I might wait till you got here for that."

"Damn," Burkes said, "that guy had been through enough as it was. I gave him this afternoon off so he could relax. His cousin said he had been under a lot of stress. This may put him over the edge, though." Burkes stepped on a cigarette he had just thrown down.

"You don't say?" Mills pondered. "So he's been under a lot of stress?"

"Yeah, why?" Burkes asked.

"Well, we assumed it was burglars, but we're waiting on you to question your man. The only thing is...we found no evidence of forced entry or anything. We're not finding fingerprints as of yet."

Burkes looked at Mills with a cold stare. "What are you trying to say?"

"Oh, nothing. I just thought I'd point that out before we start questioning him. I talked to his cousin to get as much as I could while we were searching the neighborhood, but he was in his room during the shooting and didn't hear anything. No one has seen anybody suspicious hanging around either. Of course from what his cousin said, it happened a while ago. They supposedly knocked Ben out and killed his wife using a silencer. No one knew about it until Ben woke up a good while later." Mills' voice echoed doubt as he spoke.

"Knocked out?" Burkes asked.

"Yeah. They hit him and knocked him unconscious." He smiled at Burkes. "I know, why didn't they just shoot him as well? I'll let you be here for that part. He's your man, after all."

"Fine," Burkes said.

"Oh, one more thing," Mills remarked as Burkes started toward the door.

"What?" Burkes snapped.

"You might want to read him his Miranda's before you talk to him," Mills said.

Burkes pretended to ignore Mills as he entered the Seals' home. Burkes of all people knew better than to judge somebody from such little evidence, but there was cause to be alarmed. Burkes was under the gun, not Terry Mills. It was his team that had let an officer and a star witness get killed. It was his team that had watched a hole the size of a moon crater be blown in the side of a Memphis landmark. Now his newest team member was a possible murder suspect.

Ben was sitting in a chair staring at the dining room table.

Burkes looked at Ben,then glanced at Randy as if to ask what to do.

"Ben," Randy spoke in a low voice. "Captain Burkes is gonna have to know all about what has happened if they're gonna get these guys!"

Ben stared straight ahead. Burkes sat down. Mills moved around the kitchen to lean against a counter, out of the way but very intent on what was to be said.

"Ben!" Burkes spoke harshly. Ben's eyes rose slowly to meet Burkes'.

"Ben, we've got to know what happened here if we're gonna help."

Ben nodded slowly.

"Talk to us, then." Burkes seemed impatient. "Did someone try to rob you?"

Ben shook his head in the negative.

"What happened?"

Ben shook his head again as if he couldn't talk about it yet. There was silence, everyone staring at each other. Finally, Burkes' patience wore out.

"Ben, did you kill your wife?"

Ben's look turned to one of sheer horror. He didn't have time to react to the blunt question because his cousin beat him to it.

"You son of a bitch! You would have to come with up some crap like that. Just when I think you may be halfway okay, you turn back into a lowlife! You are disgusting, and I can't believe you would stoop so low. I refuse to pay one more cent of taxes to this freakin' city as long as part of it is going to pay your salary." Randy was breathless, but he continued, "Where did you go to detective school? Disneyworld?"

Burkes leaned back against the counter and looked at Mills for help. Terry Mills appeared amused by the directness of Burkes' question. He let Randy yell for a few moments, then stepped in to help.

"Mr. Seals!" he addressed Randy. "We only know that this lady was with her husband when she was killed. You said you didn't see anything. Nobody else in the neighborhood has seen anything. We've found no evidence of anybody else being in the house. Your cousin isn't talking, and he's a cop. He of all people knows how important it is that we find out as much as we can as quickly as we can. We just need to know what happened. Help us help you." He looked at Ben, hoping that his speech had spurred Ben to talk.

Ben breathed in deeply and tried to talk without choking up.

"I woke to the noise of her getting shot." He had to stop as he started crying again.

Mills looked at Randy. "You heard the shots?

"No, they used a silencer or something," he said.

Ben nodded in agreement.

Burkes was shifting uneasily. "But you heard the shots?" he asked Ben.

Ben nodded.

"They were kind of muffled, I take it?"

Mills gave Burkes a dirty look for putting words in Ben's mouth.

"Yeah. You know how they sound. I've only seen them at the Academy, but it was a typical silencer, I guess," Ben mumbled in a low, strained voice. It was the best he could do under the circumstances. He laid his head back in the chair. "Oh, man, I can't believe this," he mumbled to himself.

Ben felt the sharp pain on the side of his head where he had been slugged coming back. It had been hurting all along, but he had been too dazed to feel it. While Ben rubbed his head, Randy went to the cabinet and got some aspirin. He laid them on the table in front of Ben.

"Here, take these. You must have two headaches. One from the lick, the other from these two clowns."

John Burkes interrupted Terry Mills just as he said "Kiss my—" to Randy. Burkes wanted to avoid any sideshows with Randy Seals.

"Ben, I'm sorry for accusing you, but there's no evidence, and your cousin here said that your wife had just come back to you and that's why he thought you needed the day off. That's why I gave you yesterday off, and well…" He looked at Randy. "You tell him what you told me."

Randy looked at him quizzically. "What?"

"Tell him why you thought he should have the day off yesterday. Tell him what you said you would do under his circumstances with all he had been through."

Randy had a stunned look on his face. "I didn't mean literally!"

Ben looked confused. Randy shrugged his shoulders. "It was nothing, Ben. I just told him that you had been through a lot, and your wife had confessed a lot of bad things to you, and I didn't know how I could keep from killing her if I were in your shoes."

Ben sank back in his chair.

"When were you going to share this information with me?" Mills peered at Burkes.

"Kiss off!" Randy barked at the homicide cop.

"It's not important," Burkes said.

"Then why mention it at all?" Mills asked.

Ben spoke up. "I told you…I woke up…there were two men standing over my bed. They were sent here by Gene McMasters. He's the sheriff of Green County, Mississippi."

Mills was caught off guard. "You mean…you know who did this?"

Ben was becoming choked up again.

Randy took over. "What he's saying is that McMasters was the one he worked for in Green County. He was involved with Ben's wife."

Ben had started crying again. "Ben, can I tell them everything so they can find these guys?" Randy asked.

Ben nodded.

Randy briefly relayed the story to the two detectives, telling them everything that had happened to Ben in Greensburg.

John Burkes was all ears. Mills still had a look of obvious disbelief on his face.

"You're telling us they killed your wife to keep her quiet, but they let you live?" Mills asked sarcastically.

Randy glared at him. "Well, I think that's obvious."

"But why kill your wife and not you too?" Mills asked, looking Ben straight in the eye.

Everybody stared at Ben, waiting for a response.

Randy spoke up. "They probably thought they did.... Look at that whelp on the side of his face.... He probably should be dead."

The bruise had begun to swell and was plainly going to cover the right side of his face.

"Nice try, boys, but a bad bruise hardly qualifies as attempted murder," Mills said.

"Well, just maybe," Randy said in his most sarcastic voice, "they did it like this to set Ben up. You ever think of that? They probably know how gullible you idiots are and figured you wouldn't be able to figure out what happened so you'd blame Ben. Yeah...that's it. That way no one would come talk to them because Ben's story would be unbelievable."

Mills had had enough of Randy. "I think it's time we spoke to Ben alone, Officer Burkes, don't you?"

"Screw you!" Randy smarted off. "I'm Ben's lawyer. Right, Ben?"

Ben looked dazed again, then nodded more out of fear than understanding.

"So," Randy continued, "you're not asking crap without me. You got that?"

"Why is it you hate cops so much anyway?" Mills asked Randy. "You're always defending the lowest thugs you can find."

"Are you calling a fellow officer a thug?" Randy asked.

"Not him," Mills said looking at Ben and at Burkes. "I'm talking about the trash you're usually getting off the hook."

"Gentlemen, please!" Burkes interrupted. "Back to the business at hand."

"Yeah, you're right," Mills said. "About this Greensburg incident. You're saying that an entire sheriff's office, from what it sounds like, is on the take from drug dealers?"

"I don't really want to get into what's wrong in Green County," Burkes said. "If you don't mind, we probably should save that for later, Captain Mills. I think we'd probably be better served by gathering everything we can about what happened here. This other stuff is going to take far greater attention than we can give it tonight, don't you think?"

"You're probably right," Mills agreed. "Ben, there's no chance you could I.D. these guys since it was dark, I presume?" he asked in a skeptical manner.

Ben shook his head no.

"That's funny," Randy said.

"What?" Mills asked.

"You wait until now to ask what the murder suspects look like. You didn't ask because you already had your mind made up that Ben was guilty, and nobody did this but him."

"Well...no," Mills stuttered, "but since you brought it up again about Ben's guilt...clarify in my mind how they got in here. We saw no evidence of any break-in."

Randy looked at Ben and back at Mills. "I don't know, and I don't doubt that with your incompetence you can't figure it out either, but I can assure you these people are not stupid and you..."

"You smartass..." Mills fired back before being cut off by Burkes.

"Hold it!" Burkes shouted.

"I just want an explanation for all this evidence that we're not finding.... I think I'm entitled to that," Mills said.

"I can tell you what you're entitled to," Randy said.

"See, John," Mills said, referring to Randy, "this is what makes him so successful in the courtroom. He wins half his cases before he gets there. He lives by intimidation. He's a pro. I like to watch him work. I just hate when he's working on me."

"Do you have anything else to ask?" Randy said.

"I'd still like to know how somebody got in without breaking in. Did you leave some windows open or a door unlocked?" Mills asked.

"Maybe we did," Randy said.

"Well, we haven't found any open windows, and I'm sure the front door was locked, wasn't it?" Mills continued.

"Obviously not," Randy said.

"No, I checked it before I went to bed," Ben said.

"Ben, you stay out of this," Randy said. "Better yet, why don't you advise him of his rights if you want to question him."

"Ben's not a suspect," Burkes assured them.

Mills rolled his eyes as if to differ.

"So you don't have any idea how anybody could have gotten in? Did anyone else have access to a key...a housekeeper...anybody at all?" Burkes asked.

"Yeah. I have a maid who comes three times a week. She has a key," Randy said. "Ben, has anybody had access to that key I gave you? Anybody? Try to think of anything you can remember."

"Only when we were at the Waltham," Ben said. "All the cops put their stuff inside the room adjacent to the one we were guarding...the one designated for us. We left our stuff...like keys, snacks, even our wallets in there...so we wouldn't be carrying any excess baggage in case we had trouble. It was Vick Killian's idea." Ben thought for a moment. "There were a lot of people in and out of there, but they were all officers."

"See, there were any number of people who could have had a key," Randy said.

Mills rolled his eyes at Randy as if he were listening to a preacher begging for money.

"This is my third housekeeper this year. There are a number of keys out there, or there's the possibility someone could have gotten Ben's keys and in the time it takes to go somewhere for a cup of coffee, had a key made," Randy said.

"Maybe one of your cops, Burkes?"

"Ben, do you still have your key?" Mills asked.

"Yes," Ben replied.

"We know these guys back in Greensburg are involved in drug trafficking. We know a lot of the drugs coming up the river to them go to places like Memphis and Birmingham.... Maybe they bought some cops in some other towns too. Like Memphis," Randy suggested.

"Now, hold on right there!" Burkes was pissed now.

"No, you hold on, Captain," Randy fired back. "There are some things I've been wondering about anyway. Michael Rose told me he was working on a detail with Captain Crator and you weren't even involved. Maybe you learned of Rose and Crator and the rest about to bust B.J.'s boys and you tipped him off. The way Michael told it you always had your head so far up the commissioner's ass you didn't know anything till the last minute, anyway. Then your star witness got killed in your custody. Maybe you're working with the drug lords. Huh?"

Burkes was squirming now. First the D.A. suggesting a leak on his team and now this.

"By the way, Captain," Randy said, "you have an awful lot of contacts in Greensburg yourself. Say, don't you have a sister in Greensburg?"

Burkes didn't respond.

Mills took over the questioning. "Tell us about the blow to your head, Ben."

Ben didn't hear the question Mills posed to him.

"Ben," Burkes said, "the blow to your head, tell us about it."

"They hit me. What's there to tell?" Ben smarted off. "They hit me with the butt of the pistol."

Mills interrupted. "The wound to your wife looked large, like a 9mm or 40-caliber."

Ben thought for a moment and then started to cry again. "Hard to say..." he mumbled. "It was too dark.... I could only make out shadows.... Those bastards..."

Mills seemed to be becoming increasingly impatient with Ben. "So they hit you with the gun?" Mills asked.

Ben nodded.

"Your wife was on the left side of the bed as you face the bed from the foot?"

"So?" Randy asked.

"Well, it's just that Ben's bruises are on the right side of his head. That's the side where his wife was. Did you turn sideways or something that would have caused you to get the lick on that side? Or maybe they reached all the way across you to hit you.?"

"You don't have to talk," Randy advised Ben. "Is he being questioned as a suspect yet?" He looked at Mills.

"Of course not. I just want to get to the bottom of this. I'm looking to find out as much as I can."

Ben spoke up, " I think they gave me a backhand with the butt of the pistol."

Mills wrote down some quick notes to himself. "The bullet entered your wife from the other side of the bed. The one who hit you must have been on your side of the bed."

Ben looked confused. "There was one on my side. One on hers' too."

"You say a backhand?" Mills asked.

"That's right!"

"You would think you might have yelled for help as soon as you saw them." Mills smiled.

Ben just looked at him."There was no time."

"Or maybe," Mills continued, "it was a self-inflicted wound, and you made a mistake in remembering the way in which you got this lick...when you made up this whole story?"

"That's enough!" Randy shouted.

"Tell the truth, Seals!" Mills shouted. "Why did you kill her? You certainly had every reason to, and she deserved it. Just tell the truth so we can all get some rest."

"Get outta here, you son of a bitch!" Randy shouted.

Just then another detective appeared in the doorway to the kitchen. "Captain Mills, I think you'd better come look at this."

"Take them away—both of them—you bastards!" Randy shouted.

Randy turned to Ben after watching the two leave. When he was sure they were out of earshot, he turned to Ben. "Try to remember who else could have had access to your keys."

Ben, still in a daze, looked at his cousin. He thought for a moment. "Nobody but Vick and the others while we were at the hotel."

Randy looked at him with sympathy. "Then don't you see what I've been saying to these clowns?"

Ben looked confused. "What?"

"I got you a job up here. Who was against you?"

Ben still looked confused.

"Think, Ben. Even though the commissioner was all for it. Who was against you?"

Ben thought for a moment. "Well, the only one I know of was Burkes," he said.

Randy nodded. "He didn't want you up here because he's probably on the take. Maybe he's hooked up with McMasters. He could be their Memphis connection."

"He does have a sister there."

"That might explain why he gets all those shipments from Greensburg. They may be antiques from his sister's store, but I'll bet the farm that those crates are full of dope as well."

Ben was stunned. "You're serious!"

"Damn right!" Randy snarled. "This may be a conspiracy. You said yourself they ship drugs from New Orleans to here and Birmingham. You know they have to have an inside person here to help them. Somebody on a narcotics task force would be perfect!"

"I don't believe Burkes would..." Ben paused to think.

"Would you please explain to me how somebody broke into this place when the only person with access to your key is with the police department?" Randy demanded.

"You said your housekeeper has a key—maybe they bought her off," Ben suggested.

"They would never approach my housekeeper. She might come to me or to the cops. They had somebody inside—I can feel it, Ben. Burkes is dirty."

Ben was in tears again. "I don't care!" he screamed. "Don't you understand? I just lost m-my wife."

Randy extended a sympathetic hand toward Ben's shoulder. "I understand perfectly, cuz. I also understand that there are two cops in there who are acting like they want to pin this on you."

"Maybe somebody copied your key...or Aunt Mary's key," Ben suggested, wiping away his tears.

"Maybe so," Randy agreed. "But why haven't they made a big deal about that possibility?"

Ben looked puzzled. "I don't know.

Randy nodded, "I know exactly why. Somebody's got it in for you."

Ben looked scared now. Randy's tone became more comforting. "Look, you know what happened in Greensburg. We don't know what's going on here. I'm just trying to keep you out of the pen. I don't mind telling you I don't like the way any of this is going so far. They don't have any evidence at all, and yet they're suggesting that you may have killed Julie."

Ben looked as if he had just remembered something important. "Well, maybe if you hadn't said all that to Burkes about me having reason to kill her, this wouldn't have been brought up."

Randy changed the subject. "That's no reason for him to suggest you really did. This could get stickier before it gets better."

Burkes reentered the room alone. "Randy, tell us where you were again."

"When?"

Burkes looked perturbed. "When this happened!"

"Unknowingly, locked in my room. My room and my mother's room are directly across the hall from each other. There was a cable running from my doorknob to her's. Neither door would open because they both open inward and the cable was pulled tight."

Burkes raised his eyebrows as if to question the story.

"You can ask Ben," Randy continued.

Ben was nodding in agreement.

"He's the one who let us out of our rooms," Randy continued.

"I see," Burkes said, scratching his head.

"You see what, Captain? Please tell us 'cause so far it doesn't seem as though you can see a damn thing."

"Don't abuse me!" Burkes shouted.

"If you can't see that this was a setup to make it look like Ben is guilty, then I don't know what to think about you," Randy lashed back.

Terry Mills reentered the room holding a black pistol by a piece of string that he had tied around the trigger guard. "They found this under a rock down by the river. I guess this gets you off the hook. No cop would be dumb enough to leave a weapon anywhere on the premises. We comb every inch."

Randy sighed. "Well, thank God for that! Now we're getting somewhere."

Ben stared straight ahead, back in his zombie mode.

"Ben, are you okay?" Randy asked.

"May I be excused?" Ben asked.

"Sure," Mills replied. "We're gonna run this for prints. We couldn't find the silencer." He smiled.

Ben went upstairs while Randy stayed to badger the detectives. "Well, why don't you get that on downtown and run some prints, and let's see if we can get these guys," he said.

Mills laughed under his breath at the young lawyer telling him his job. "It's not always that simple," he informed Randy.

"I know that," Randy said. "I was the assistant D.A. in Greensburg when I got out of law school. I'm well aware of that, but I'm also aware of the fact that you can't get shit done standing around runnin' your flap in my kitchen."

Mills turned and left in a huff.

John Burkes stayed behind in the kitchen for a moment.

"Well, I guess this is quite a relief, huh?" Randy asked Burkes.

"What is?" Burkes asked.

"To know that you don't have a murderer on your team," Randy said.

"Yeah, right," Burkes said. "Well, I'd better go call the commissioner. He'll want to know about all this."

Chapter 13

Randy ran upstairs to check on his cousin who was in the bedroom across the hall from the murder scene. That room had been roped off with police tape, as investigators were still combing it. Randy found his cousin sitting on the guest bed crying. He sat on the bed beside him and started to speak but was interrupted by Ben's uttering, "It's my gun."

"What?"

"It's my gun they found," Ben muttered, clutching his hands to his face and propping his elbows onto his knees to hold his head up. He was confused and exhausted.

"What do you mean?" Randy asked.

"My gun is missing. I came up here to check. It was on the dresser in our bedroom where they're searching right now. The door is slightly open over there.... You can see from the hall that my gun is gone."

Randy grimaced. "This is not good. That's why you came up here?"

"Yeah," Ben sniffed. "That pistol looked like mine. I thought I'd see if mine was missing."

"But isn't that a standard gun for most detectives?" Randy asked.

"Yeah, but they found one here, and mine is missing. You know it's mine. It's got to be. You were right all along. It's a setup."

"Yeah, I guess so, Ben," Randy said.

"Oh, my God!" Ben stuttered suddenly. "You don't think I really did it, do you?"

Randy looked at Ben and said, "Of course not.... I'm just trying to think through everything that has happened, so maybe I can come up with some idea, or something. I don't know.... We gotta get you outta here," he concluded.

"We can't do that," Ben argued. "They'll know something is wrong."

"They'll know soon enough if that gun really is yours," Randy said. "We still don't know for sure. If it isn't yours, you have nothing to worry about anyway. If it is, then you can't help me get to the bottom of this if you're sitting behind bars."

Ben started to cry. " I can't believe this!" he cried, running into the bathroom.

Randy heard the sound of his vomiting. "Are you okay?" He followed Ben into the bathroom and found him hovering over the toilet.

Ben nodded.

"Just nerves?" Randy asked.

"I guess," Ben mumbled as he tried to compose himself.

John Burkes met them in the hallway as Randy helped his cousin back to the bedroom and onto the bed. Burkes stood in the hallway outside the door.

"Ben?" Ben was lying motionless on the bed. Burkes looked at Randy. "Is there someplace he can go for the time being where he can try to get some rest?"

Ben perked up a little, realizing that this might be a chance to get away from this place and clear his head.

Randy stuttered a little and then spoke. "Yeah, he can go down to the trucking company. I've got an office with a couch. Or we may just get him a room at a hotel. We'll do something."

"He needs to be where somebody can help him if he needs anything," Burkes said. "I'll ask if one of the other officers has a place for him tonight."

"No! That's all right," Randy headed Burkes off before he left the room. "We've got it under control." He winked at Ben. "Don't we?"

"Yeah," Ben said. "I'll be fine."

"You sure?" Burkes asked.

"Yeah, I'm fine," Ben assured his boss.

"Okay, then." Burkes left the room.

"Why is this happening to me?" Ben cried to Randy.

"Shhh," Randy admonished him. "Everything's gonna be fine."

"Easy for you to say," Ben replied.

"You gotta listen to me and do as I say if we're gonna get to the bottom of this," Randy harped.

"If I run, they'll think I'm guilty," Ben said.

"Not if they find out the murder weapon was somebody else's gun," Randy said. "And if it's your gun, you'll go to jail without bail, period."

"Maybe that's best." Ben spoke solemnly now, full of self-pity.

"Well, you'll really be doing yourself a hell of a lot of good locked up. Besides the fact that you need to help me get to the bottom of this and figure out how McMasters pulled this off, you'd go crazy sitting in jail."

"I guess you're right," Ben said.

"Damn right I am!" Randy said. "I'm gonna take you to the freight line. I'll call Henry—he's working security tonight—and tell him we're coming. There's about three or four hundred dollars petty cash in my desk drawer that you can use."

"Thanks."

"No problem."

Ben stood there looking at Randy as if he were drunk and unable to follow through with the plan.

"Well, go on," Randy urged him.

"I don't know," Ben said. "This may not be wise.... It's gonna make me look pretty guilty."

"Don't worry about how you look. If that gun turns out to be yours, you can think about it on death row!"

Ben continued to stand still with a lost look on his face.

"Come on, dammit!" Randy said. "I'll drive you down to the freight line. You can go from there."

They raced downstairs, Ben wobbling behind and trying to keep up but not really paying attention to what he was doing or where he was going.

Burkes stood in the den talking with Terry Mills. "Can I get my car out?" Randy asked. "It's parked on the street and blocked in by squad cars."

"Yeah, we'll move 'em," Burkes said.

"Where are you going?" Mills flared up.

"They're going to take Ben somewhere for the night," Burkes answered.

"Oh, you're going to be somewhere you can be reached, I presume?" Mills said to Ben, who looked as though he had not heard a word of what had just transpired. Mills glared at him.

"I'm taking him down to get some rest," Randy said. "He'll be available if you need him."

Mills clearly wasn't happy with Ben's lack of response. "You're not gonna leave town or anything like that, are you?" Mills asked.

"Screw you!" Randy said.

"Hey, counselor! I can hold him for questioning if I want to," Mills threatened.

"Gentlemen!" Burkes stepped between the two, who now almost touched noses. "Detective, I'm not trying to run your investigation. I just think it's in our best interest to let Ben get some rest while we gather more evidence and your people have time to give us more information."

"There are just too many unanswered questions here," Mills fumed. "Until we have a better understanding, I think we should all stick around."

"I'll take personal responsibility for Ben's whereabouts," Burkes replied.

Ben had composed himself enough to know he should be shocked by what he had just heard. He had finally won the respect and trust of John Burkes and now he was going to blow it by running. Maybe...just maybe, it wasn't his gun. But where was his gun? It wasn't on the dresser. Maybe the gun had fallen off somehow. Not a chance, he thought. The whole thing had looked like a frame-up from the beginning.... That was just another part of it. He couldn't imagine them getting his gun and then shooting his wife without him hearing them enter or anything. Randy was right—he had no choice but to run. It still seemed like a dream, but he had to pull himself together and quickly.

"I'm not going anywhere," Ben lied. "You need me, come get me.... I'll tell you anything I know. But I swear you know everything that I know about what happened here.... And I didn't have anything to do with it."

Mills didn't seem overjoyed but conceded to Ben's leaving.

Within moments, Randy and Ben were speeding across town toward President's Island. There was no conversation...just the silence of the night mixed with the low hum of the motor. Randy parked in front of the freight line entrance and called the security desk from his car phone to open the gate. The entire place was surrounded by a cyclone fence; a huge sign on the front gate read SEALS TRUCKING, INC.

The night security officer opened the gate and closed it immediately behind them as they drove through. After they parked, Randy led the way upstairs to his office. It was a simple layout and not very elegant since he seldom used it. His mother's office across the hall was more extravagant, as she ran the place.

Randy briskly entered the room and went straight to his desk drawer. Ben wandered into the office looking around at the computer terminal, filing cabinets, and pictures on the walls.

"Take this," Randy said thrusting a wad of cash at Ben. "I've got some more here in my wallet. Take this and let me get the rest."

"What now?" Ben asked.

"I'll drop you off at some sleazy hotel, and you lie low. Keep my pager, and I'll page you when I need you."

"Won't you need it?"

"This is my private pager, so to speak," Randy explained, smiling. "My women call me on this one."

"How do I know when it's you?"

"I'll put 911 after the seven-digit number to let you know it's me. When you get that on the readout, call me fast because it will be a secure phone, probably a pay phone. They'll be on me like a hawk to see if I have any contact with you. If it's your gun, it won't take them long to discover you're missing."

Ben looked more worried than ever. Randy tried to reassure him. "It's gonna work out. We'll get to the bottom of this together."

"Why me? Why Julie?" Ben teared up again. His crying became intense as he finally began to let it all go.

"We've got to go, Ben. Pull yourself together, for a while at least."

Ben nodded as if he understood.

"I know it's tough, but you've got to try and clear your head enough to save your own hide. Julie would have wanted you to look out for yourself in this situation."

Ben cried even harder.

"Come on, we gotta go." Randy led him back down to the car.

Randy drove Ben south toward the state line, looking for a cheap hotel full of truckers. The thought of truckers reminded him of a truckstop just over the state line that offered cots for the night at a nominal fee. His drivers from the freight line frequented the place for coffee.

Randy found the twenty-four–hour stop and parked inconspicuously at the side. He got out, told Ben to wait in the car, and went inside. He paid the five dollar fee and found the assigned cubicle. It was small but quaint...four walls made of office partitions. It was one of about ten or so in a line in the back of the truckstop. It would suit the purposes of keeping Ben out of sight for the time being. Randy returned to the car to find Ben wiping the tears from his face.

"Well, I got you a place for the night," Randy said. "Come on. Get out and let me give you this stuff."

Randy reached into the back seat and picked up a gym bag he kept workout clothes in.

Ben reached to take the bag from him. "So this is my life now. I'm down to a gym bag." He shook his head in disgust and disbelief.

"Hey, everything's going to be all right. Now you go straight to the third cubicle in the rear of this joint, back by the johns. Don't look at anybody up front and don't talk to anyone. I'll be in touch."

Ben couldn't have cared less about his surroundings at this point. His mind and body begged for rest. He threw the gym bag on the floor inside the cubicle and hit the waiting cot. He was beyond tired.... He had reached the point of wishing he were dead and figuring he would be better off that way. He tried to sleep, but visions of Julie and the blood and everything that had happened kept pounding his brain. He realized he must have drifted off to sleep when he woke with his first nightmare. By the time the fourth one awoke him, he gave up on the whole idea. He felt the time would soon come when he would take his own life.

Randy returned home to find his house still overrun with cops. He secluded himself in his bedroom and fell asleep. The sleep lasted only two short hours. At 6 a.m., he was awakened by a patrolman knocking on his door. The officer told Randy they were through and would need to secure the crime scene for the night. Randy left the place in their hands after quickly showering. He headed out for a quick breakfast and early entry into his law office.

He was sitting at his desk when his secretary, Shirley, arrived.

"I heard what happened," she said.

"Already?"

"Yes. Your mother called me this morning to see if I had heard from you. She said she was staying at a neighbor's and hadn't been able to reach you. Are you okay?

"Yeah, I'm fine. I had to get out of there early this morning so the cops could seal the place off until some more people from the crime lab could get down there today..."

"I'm sorry. I don't know what to say. Were you and your cousin close?"

"Well, not really in the past, but since he came up here this week, we've made the most of it."

"Why did this happen?"

"His wife had been fooling around with the wrong crowd for a long time. That's why he wound up here to begin with. It was probably inevitable..."

"The news didn't give any details."

"The news!"

"The radio. It was on the radio this morning, but they didn't give any details...just that a police officer's wife had been murdered in her sleep. "

"Great! That's all we need to hinder the real investigation...a bunch of reporters flocking around asking questions."

"The real investigation?"

"I mean—I just want to check things out on my own. It's not that I don't have confidence in the Memphis P.D., but...well, you know I don't."

Shirley backed up to the lounge chair near the door and took a seat. "Do you want to talk about it?"

"No."

"Well, what you want me to do?"

"I'll let you know. Right now, some juice would be nice."

"Sure." She left the room obviously dissatisfied that she had not found out all that she expected to.

Two hours later Shirley buzzed him on the intercom.

"There are detectives out here to see you," she stated.

"Send them on in."

Mills barged through the door first, followed by Burkes.

"Gentlemen." Randy didn't get up.

"Gentlemen, my ass!" Mills shouted. Randy looked out into the lobby where there were a number of uniformed officers. He leaned back in his chair with an arrogance all his own.

"How can I help you, gentlemen?"

"I'll tell you how!" Mills scowled. Burkes stood behind Mills and ignored the "I told you so" glances that Mills was giving him.

"You could start by telling us where that cousin of yours is." Mills' face was red and matted with a frown.

"Gentlemen, please!" Randy surveyed Burkes, who looked as though he had been dragged there and forced to stand at attention as some sort of punishment for bad behavior. "I don't think I like your attitude. Is there something I should know about?"

"As a matter of fact, there is, counselor!" Mills was leaning over Randy's desk now. "You'll find out soon enough."

"Well, actually, since he is my cousin, one of my partners will be representing him if he needs it. Of course, I would be involved in any pending investigation that involved a client of this firm."

"I don't give a damn! All of you can represent him. The fact still remains that the ATF trace came in on the firearm found at the scene. You'll never guess who it was registered to."

Randy shrugged his shoulders as if he had no clue. "You got me. Who?" he asked.

"Ben Seals! Ever heard of him?" Mills snorted.

"So they used his gun. Big deal!"

Mills laughed out loud. "You will be so kind as to tell us where he is, won't you?"

Burkes still had not spoken.

"Sure. I dropped him off at the 24/7 Motel on Lamar Avenue."

"Well then, we're headed that way right now. Why don't you come along? I'd hate for you to accidentally tip him off to our arrival." Mills glared right through Randy.

"Sure. I've got no problem with that. The sooner we get to the bottom of this, the sooner Ben will be cleared."

"Oh, yeah!" Mills scoffed. "We'll just see about that!"

The trio exited the office, startling Shirley, who had her ear to the door.

Randy sat uneasily in the back of the patrol car as it raced along

I-240 to the Perkins Road Exit. They were followed by two patrol cars with two uniformed officers in each. The cars pulled onto Perkins and headed south toward Lamar. The cars parked across the parking lot in front of a motel. Mills waved at the other cars to let them know he was going to the lobby.

Inside the lobby, he produced a warrant for Ben's arrest. He presented it to an Indian woman, dressed in a native gown, behind the counter. She apparently understood little English. Mills frantically tried to explain to her that he needed a room number. He wrote "Ben Seals" on a piece of paper so she could look it up. She took a quick glance at the guest register and shook her head, uttering something that meant "no." Mills mistook her to mean that she could not give out that information. He blew up. "Look, this is a court order. You understand? From a judge!"

The woman looked confused. The jewel in her forehead rose almost an inch when she raised her eyebrows. She babbled something at Mills that he didn't quite catch in his state of agitation.

"Lady, I can put you in jail for this!" he said, shoving a finger in front of her face.

She threw the guest register on the counter and pointed to the list. "See! See!" she panted.

Mills scanned the list in front of him. There was no Ben Seals. He must have used another name. He handed the list back to the lady without saying a word, turned and went outside, making a beeline for Randy's car door.

"What alias would he use?"

"Alias?" Randy acted surprised.

"You heard me. Ben Seals never checked in here. What other name might he have used? What was his wife's maiden name?"

"Chapman. I don't think he'd use an alias, though," Randy said.

"He must have. They've got no Ben Seals checked in here."

Burkes sat in the front seat quiet as a mouse. He turned to Randy with a look suggesting that maybe he knew Randy was lying, but he didn't care to help Mills.

Mills barged back into the motel office. He first checked the list for any Chapmans. No luck. Moments later Burkes was shaking his head as if he couldn't believe what he was seeing. Randy watched as Mills and the Indian woman came out the side door of the lobby. Mills motioned for the officers from the patrol cars to come. There was only one row of rooms in a U-shape around the lot. One officer stayed behind to secure the entrance and another went around to park in back in the event someone went out a window. Mills proceeded to knock on every door in the compound.

Burkes turned to Randy. "Please tell me I have no reason for standing guard with these idiots..."

Randy shifted in his seat, then said, "Ben wouldn't use a different name. Maybe he never checked in. I didn't actually see him go in. I just dropped him off here."

Burkes nodded his head as if he already knew. "That's what I thought." He opened his door.

"What are you going to do?" Randy asked.

Burkes thought for a moment. "I'm going to try to convince these geniuses that Ben just may have never checked in. I've got a feeling he didn't, don't you?"

Randy shrugged as if he didn't know anything.

Burkes headed Mills off after the second room. Randy could see Burkes yelling at Mills, and Mills yelling back. This lasted for a minute or so and then Burkes ambled back to the car and sat down in the front seat with his door open, feet propped up on the frame of the door. He sat sideways, eyeing Randy with a perturbed look.

"I don't know why you couldn't save us all a lot of time and trouble and just tell us that you don't know where he is. There must be sixty rooms here, and he's gonna go to every one that was rented last night, which is probably forty rooms.

"Well, this is where I left him," Randy said.

"Yeah, right. Maybe you did, but you knew damn well he wouldn't be here," Burkes scowled.

"Why? Do you know where he is? You crooked cops haven't killed Ben too, have you?" Randy asked in a halfway serious tone.

"Screw you!" Burkes never looked his way with the response. He merely thumped a cigarette that he was finishing onto the ground. "I don't want to know where he is, to be honest." He turned to Randy. "I just don't want to be wasting time out here on this giant circle jerk!"

"I don't know." Randy smiled. "I kinda like watching detectives at work."

Burkes shook his head.

Chapter 14

Ben spent the entire night upright on the cot leaning against the wall. He dozed five to ten minutes at a time and finally got up around six. He forced himself to eat at the McDonald's across the street as soon as it opened for business. He tried to find ways to pass time until Randy paged him. He feared that everything he did seemed suspicious. Everyone he saw looked familiar. He didn't know if his face had been on the news yet; if not, it would be soon. Around 8:30 a.m. he found himself wandering around a Kmart picking up a few items he would need...toothpaste and brush, a few T-shirts, underwear.

He had his eye on a pay phone just in case Randy called. He had already checked to make sure it was not out of order. Randy had told him to stay ready to return his call, and he was not about to screw that up. Until there was some word as to what was going on, Randy was his only connection to the world as he knew it. He was becoming impatient while waiting. He knew the call was sure to bring bad news, but he was ready for something to happen, good or bad. As it was, he could only dwell on Julie. His tears burst loose at regular intervals.

Terry Mills returned to the car to find Randy and John Burkes almost asleep. He flung Randy's door open and asked him to step outside. Burkes got out as well, not sure what Mills had in mind. Mills stood with his hands on his hips like a father about to pass judgment on a son. "You know what I think?" Mills asked Randy.

"Pray tell! No, I don't know what you think...at least I hope I don't. If I start thinking like you, God help me."

"Well, first of all, I think you're a smartass!" Mills gritted his teeth as if he were thinking of using physical force of some kind. "Second—"

"Oh, there's more?" Randy fired back.

"Second, I think you're lying. I think you've been lying all along. I don't think you ever brought him here, and I think you know where he is."

Burkes rolled his eyes. "Please tell me when you figured that out? Was it after you had searched forty rooms or before?" He spoke slowly as if talking to a small child who couldn't understand him.

"You know, I'm just about tired of your being so damn smart!" Mills shouted at Burkes. "You seem to forget that this is my case. This is a homicide—not a drug deal!"

"Hey! I'm just doing what the commissioner wants...and helping out to make sure no shame is brought to the Memphis P.D. by a cop in trouble."

"Well...maybe you and the commissioner would like to work the case together..."

"Gentlemen! Gentlemen!" Randy interjected. "I'd love to stay here and listen to the two of you butt heads, but I've got things to do."

"What are you saying? You don't know where he is?" Mills cocked his head to the side to wait on the answer. "Remember that you can be charged with obstructing justice if you lie, counselor."

"You remember that I've gotten more people off obstructing justice and contempt charges than you've ever charged." Randy adjusted his pinkie ring with confidence as if he were in a courtroom.

"We're gonna find him," Mills warned.

"I'm sure you will, and I'll do anything I can to help you," Randy answered. "But, right now, I'm ready to go back to my office. I'm sure he'll call me, and when he does, I'll convince him to come on in."

"You will call us if you hear from him, won't you?" Mills asked.

"But of course."

It was nearly noon, and Ben had become impatient to the point of becoming stir-crazy. The waiting was the hardest part. Finally the pager vibrated. He dialed the number from the McDonald's parking lot. Randy picked up on the other end.

"It's me," came the reply from his cousin.

"I didn't think you would ever call," Ben sighed over the phone.

"I don't think you want to hear this," Randy said.

"Oh, my God! It was my gun!"

"I thought you were prepared for that," Randy said.

"I am..." Ben said trying to pull himself back together. "I had just hoped...I don't know..."

"I'm sorry, man," Randy said. "We've gotta get you outta town."

"I thought you wanted me to help you investigate!"

"You gotta get out of here. I'll get to the bottom of this. Right now they have every cop in Memphis looking for you. You have to keep your mug out of sight."

"I don't think I want to leave."

"What do you mean? You can't stay here. You'll never get out of jail."

"I want to get these bastards if it kills me doing it." Ben sounded like a man obsessed and yet unsure of himself.

"No way. I'm already making arrangements for you to get out of town and stay low a while."

"I'm not leaving," Ben said emphatically. "I'm going to get these sons of bitches if it's the last thing I do."

"Ben, you're scaring me! Don't do anything. I'll call you in a little while. Lie low and let me figure something out. I'm on a pay phone in the lobby of my office building. I better get off now. I'll call you in a while. Just sit tight till then."

"You can't put yourself in jeopardy on my account, Randy. They'll bust you for helping me."

"Fine. If they take you, they may as well take me too."

Ben pondered the thought of going into hiding. For how long, he wondered...maybe forever. He couldn't do it. It wasn't his style. He couldn't let those bastards get away with ruining his life. He began to cry again thinking of Julie. He should have gone to work for her father when they first got married, and she would still be alive. He cried in pity for himself. No one was there for him. Nobody but Randy, and he could hardly have any contact with him. Someone walked up to use the pay phone he was leaning against. He wiped the tears from his eyes and swore vengeance on Gene McMasters. He walked away sheepishly, not knowing where to go or what to do, carrying only the articles he had purchased.

Ben tried to think amidst the tears. He had to disguise himself. He walked into a convenience store looking for baseball caps and sunglasses. He picked out a generic cap and some cheap shades. Having not shaved in twenty-four hours, his face was stubbled. He laid the cap and glasses on the counter so the young girl could ring up the sale. There was a small color television behind her. People were gathering inside the store on lunch break. Most of them were factory workers, judging by the name badges and hairnets most of them wore. Most were grabbing a piece of chicken or ribs from the glass-encased hot buffet. The girl rang up Ben's purchase. It was just over ten dollars. He fished a twenty from the wad Randy had given him. Suddenly the noonday news on the tube behind the girl caught Ben's ear. The anchor was giving the details on Julie's murder.

"She was fatally shot early this morning, and her husband, Memphis Police Officer Ben Seals, is the prime suspect..."

Ben fumbled her the money and slipped on the cap, trying not to act nervous. The place was full of people now. One guy listening to the broadcast punched his buddy. "Hey man, did you hear about that? It was on the radio this morning. They're saying that cop killed his own wife. I bet he was on the take and she threatened to tell on him."

Ben cringed, suppressing the urge to punch the know-it-all in the mouth. He collected his change just as he saw his picture on the TV screen.

"Officer Seals has been on the Memphis P.D. less than a week. This picture was obtained from his former employer, the Green County, Mississippi, Sheriff's Department. He is currently at large and is considered armed and dangerous. If you have contact with Officer Seals, please call the Memphis police, the Shelby County Sheriff's Department, or your local law enforcement authorities in the tri-state area."

Ben's heart raced. He tore the tags off the shades, pocketed his change and turned toward the door praying no one would recognize him.

One of the workers from the factory looked him dead in the eye through the shades. "Hey, man, ain't that something!" he said.

Ben froze. His heart had quit beating, he was sure of it. "That's a hell of a note," the guy continued, "when the damn cops are doing the murderin' and thievin'!" He either had not seen Ben's picture or had not recognized it. The picture did have Ben in full uniform. He recalled the photo, taken when he had received a citation for busting a large ring of pot growers almost singlehandedly.

"Yeah, that's a bitch," Ben agreed. He hustled past the guy and out the door.

Behind the building, he bent over in pain from an anxiety attack. The pressure was getting to him. He needed rest. The nightmare had to end. He thought about turning himself in and taking his story to the press. Yeah, why not? Better yet...stay in hiding but write a letter to the press. Fear gripped him. The fear of death row. The fear of McMasters getting away with all of it. Most of all, the fear of living his life without Julie. There must be revenge for that, he vowed. Surprise would be the key to his revenge, even though he did not yet know what that revenge would be. He hoped he would have the guts to back up what he felt he must do, for Julie's sake.

The pager vibrated again. It was Randy calling him from another phone. Ben didn't care so much about what Randy's plan was. He was beginning to feel the need to take care of himself. He had been trampled on enough. Maybe it was time to start fighting back on his own. He went to a pay phone and dailed the number on the pager.

"I'm sending someone to get you," Randy said.

"Don't bother," Ben said.

"Why?" Randy asked.

"You're gonna get yourself in trouble fooling with me. I'll take care of myself."

"You're out of your damn mind. I've been in tighter spots than this, and I will be again. I'll get you out of this mess, but you have to trust me!"

Silence.

"Are you there?"

"Yeah, I'm listening," Ben mumbled.

"Are you in the same place I left you?"

Silence.

"Ben...Ben!"

"Don't worry about me. I'll be okay." Ben hung up the phone.

"Dammit!" Randy slammed the phone down.

"He just slammed the phone down. I can't make...I can't tell anything about what he said. There was too much street noise."

"He's making contact with the subject," Mills said to the surveillance expert who was sitting across the street from Randy with binoculars and a high-powered microphone trying to hear what Randy was saying.

"He's leaving," the surveillance officer informed Mills.

"Unit two, follow him," Mills ordered over the radio. He sat comfortably back at communications running the surveillance over the radio and mobile phone. The officer following Randy carried a mobile phone to secure the connection from any police scanners. He had watched Randy through the windows of the law office even when he walked down the street to use the pay phone. From now on someone would be following Randy constantly.

Randy tried to page Ben again. No response. Then again. No response.

Ben sat on a curb trying to collect himself. He had to figure out a way to get the bastards without getting himself shot or busted first. The thought of getting killed hardly bothered him at this point. His life didn't mean anything anymore. He just wanted to live long enough to do some damage to this little empire set up by the scum of the earth, half of them professing themselves to be public servants.

He caught a cab back into the heart of the city, carrying all the items he had purchased in a paper sack along with some of the clothes Randy had given him. He wanted to travel light until he figured out what he would do. He was careful not to let the cab driver get a good look at him under his hat or glasses. Just a quick "keep the change" as he flipped the driver a twenty in front of a sports bar, and he was out.

The bar was dimly lit and very busy. He found a corner table and slid into the booth. He ordered a beer while he pored over the menu, never looking up at the waitress. The middle of town would be the last place they would expect him to be. They probably figured he was on his way to Mexico by now. Who knew what they thought? But he felt sure he was safest right up under their noses, yet disguised.

The beer was cold and soothing. Ben didn't really like to drink, but at this point he couldn't remember what he liked or didn't. He was a different man now. Life didn't hold the same value for him anymore. In fact, he couldn't see any value in it at all. He sucked down the beer thinking about Pookie and how he had been snuffed out like a match. He pondered how well Pookie's attack had been planned. He wished he had been in the room himself.

Ben cringed at the thoughts of Pookie's death. It now was occurring to him that Pookie could have been saved. There had been no need to keep him in Memphis overnight. He could have been sent straight to Knoxville or Nashville or anywhere. Burkes either blew it or he was tied in with the thugs just like Randy said. In fact, Burkes may have planned it for them.

Maybe B.J.'s people actually killed Julie. Could it really be that McMasters, B.J., Burkes, and all the rest of them were hooked up together? Burkes did have a sister in Greensburg. The D.A. in Memphis thought there was a leak on Burkes' team. Ben's heart pounded with anger. At least he was beginning to have emotions again...and retaliation was his utmost desire. He reasoned it would be easier to get to B.J. than to the cops. If he could just screw around with B.J.'s operations...and make it look like the cops were doing it.

It was coming together now. For the first time he thought he understood why B.J. had not been brought down. Burkes' having B.J. hauled in on Rose's murder charge had been a farce...a great big theatrical show for the D.A. and everybody else. B.J. knew all along that he would never face a grand jury. Ben couldn't help but smile. Burkes, B.J., and the others must have been laughing at the world as they played their games. He wondered how deep the coverups ran. How many towns besides Greensburg and Memphis had cops on the take stemming from this operation?

It was hard to believe that Steve Lyles, his own brother-in-law, may have been the supplier to the drug ring that ruined his life. How ironic! Then anger swelled inside him. Did Steve have anything to do with Julie's death? Surely not! he thought. But maybe...maybe this operation was so big that he would do the unthinkable to protect it. Ben pondered this thought for a moment, but in his heart he concluded that this was probably solely McMasters' work. This way he could keep Steve in the dark about his abuse of Julie. Gene probably got help from the Memphis gang—B.J. and the cops.

Ben sucked down another beer and mustered up the courage to go after B.J. first. That was his plan and not a very good one. The two beers had clouded his judgment. He was going after Memphis' own Al Capone, public enemy number one. Here he was, a country boy deputy sheriff, going after Goliath with a slingshot. Right now he didn't even have that. He would get it though. He knew just how. He knew nothing about the streets of Memphis, but he did know someone who could help. The problem would be convincing her to do it. He had been pitched a hard ball, and if he were going to have any success at all he would have to play hard himself. His plan was simple—try to get Tawana Griffin to help him. If she refused, he would use force. Pookie would turn over in his grave. But it was a crazy mixed-up world, and anybody or anything that could help him at this point was fair game. He was fighting for survival...and retaliation...nothing else.

He left a ten on the table after his third beer and headed for the door just as his pager buzzed. Randy was calling again. He debated for a moment about whether or not to call his cousin, who would surely be angered that he was still in town. He shuffled out the door and down the street to a pay phone beside a liquor store that was closing for the night.

"Where are you?" Randy asked frantically from the other end.

"Never mind. Can you get me a car?"

"Only if you promise to leave town."

"Of course, but I need a way out. Can you help me or not?"

"Yeah, I will. You know that."

"I need a gun too."

"No way. You'll just be asking for trouble."

"I'm not gonna use it! I'm just scared to death. I've carried one ever since I became a cop. Didn't go anywhere without one...and now that I'm a fugitive I'm even more scared."

"I'll have to get it from one of my security guards. He'll have to report it stolen or something.

"So I'll be in possession of stolen property. They can try me for that while I'm on death row."

"As long as you get far away and buy us some time," Randy said.

"ASAP!"

"I'll call you back with the arrangements."

"I'll be around."

Ben hung up and disappeared into the streets. He strolled down the sidewalk. He ditched the bag and clothes to avoid looking suspicious. Now half-drunk, he didn't concern himself with what he would do for clothes. He neared a diner with a canopy extending out onto the sidewalk. The doorman conversed with a police officer.

"Damn," Ben muttered under his breath. He had walked right upon one. Ben quickly snatched off the glasses he still wore and began rubbing his eyes so the cop couldn't see his face. It was too late.

"Hey! Hey, you!"

Ben sped up a little. The cop came out from under the canopy and began to follow Ben. "Hey, you!"

Ben turned the corner into the alley. He froze by a trash can, grabbing the top and holding the metal lid in his hand poised to strike, if necessary, but to the side as if he were looking into the can. The cop rounded the corner at that instant. Ben peered into the can as if he saw something. His heart was pounding.

"You looking for something?" the cop asked in a sarcastic tone.

"Yeah, I was here a minute ago, and I dropped something in the garbage that I didn't mean to." He was careful not to look him in the face.

"Maybe you're looking for this," the officer said.

Ben raised his head slowly, expecting a revolver to be pointed at him. The cop held his right hand out fully extended.

Ben focused in on what looked to be a bill.

"You dropped this back there. Ten bucks."

"Wow," Ben sighed, "it's nice to know there are some good cops left."

"Ha! There are still a few that haven't gone bad," the officer replied.

Ben didn't want to reach for the bill and give him a better look. "You keep it. You deserve it for being so honest."

"Hey, thanks."

"Don't mention it."

"Say...don't I know you?"

"Yeah, I used to...deliver pizza. As much as you cops eat, I'm sure I met you somewhere."

"Oh, yeah, you can see I've had my share." He slapped his belly. "You take care now."

"Sure, thanks again." Ben checked his pocket to see the wad of cash slowly creeping out. He pushed it deeper and scurried across the street.

John Burkes sat across from Bob Taylor, the D.A., looking at a spot on the carpet and waiting for him to hang up the phone.

"Thank you. I'll look into it. Well, I...I really can't talk right now, ah, someone is...with me. I'll call you back."

He hung up the phone and turned to Burkes. "Hi, John, sorry for the wait."

"That's okay."

"The reason I asked you here today is to discuss this whole B.J. White investigation.

"We-ll, you don't say!" Burkes raised his eyebrows as though this were real news, instead of the entity that had consumed his life.

"Actually, since your people blew the whole thing—"

"Now, hold on," Burkes interrupted him, "my people didn't blow a damn thing. Nothing that—"

"Just calm down a minute! I didn't mean it like that. What I mean is, there's still some investigating going on outside of Homicide's work on what happened to Pookie Jones."

"And that is?"

"My investigators are working on a possible link between B.J. White's group of thugs and the, shall we say, conspiracy to bribe police officers and then the actual bribes themselves."

"Are you still saying there's a leak on my team? I've got to tell you, I'm just about tired of hearing that. Right now, I'm tied up with this Seals situation. The last thing I need is to be worried about a leak among my people."

"That's exactly my point, John. I'm glad you brought that up about the Seals situation. You're right. You have too much going on. So much that I'm afraid you may not be able to see the forest for the trees."

"Your point, please? Sir?"

"John, how do you think those thugs knew to shoot Michael Rose before they even opened the door?"

"We already know. B.J. tipped them off. He probably had a spotter who recognized Rose."

"In a postal uniform?" Taylor asked.

"Well, I'm quite sure they knew we wouldn't come for them in dress blues, driving a patrol car. Every time they have something going on, they have spotters all over the neighborhood...just like we do."

"You don't think there's any chance that one of your people could have tipped them off?"

"No way!" John's voice rose to a shout.

"Well, how do you explain Pookie's murder?"

"Like I told you before, it's almost common knowledge where we keep witnesses. I've begged the commissioner to help us change that. I can't help the fact that they had a freakin' rocket!"

"How do you explain the fact that none of your officers got hurt?"

"Luck."

"How do you explain B.J. getting to Michael Rose's killer almost as soon as Pookie told it?"

"B.J. was scared when Pookie came up missing, and he figured Pookie might be singing. Or maybe he had already heard Pookie was in jail and figured he might sing. I don't know exactly."

"Well, I don't either, but it's an awful lot of coincidence. Especially when you consider how long we've been after this guy and can't nail him for anything. Now surely you've given this some consideration since I last mentioned it."

Burkes sat silent for a moment, then rubbed his chin. "Well, since you seem bent on prosecuting someone from within the police department, how far are you willing to take it?"

"What do you mean?"

"Well, Ben Seals....he has a wild story about corruption in the sheriff's office in Green County, Mississippi. He says there's a Memphis connection as well. Probably involving B.J. White and possibly someone from Memphis P.D."

"I know. Mills told me."

"That figures. Anyway, he says that's why he's here. They wanted to get rid of him, and things just kinda worked out so he could end up here. Even against my wishes, he was given the job."

"So?"

"I'm saying this guy, Seals, got busted back home on what should be a felony charge but doesn't get charged with anything. The next day he's working for me, and I don't even want him. Tried my best not to get him."

"If you didn't want him, why did you accept him?"

"I didn't at first. At least not until the commissioner explained how my job depended on it."

Taylor rocked back in his chair in disbelief.

Burkes continued. "That's why I asked you how far you're willing to go with your theory. This guy gets in trouble, then gets a job here. Then his wife gets murdered, and Mills thinks he did it. Now Seals is saying his wife knew all about this big drug ring. That's supposedly why she's murdered. I don't know.... He swears he was set up. I do know the commissioner gave him this job over everybody else, probably because he's so tight with Ben's cousin.... But, nevertheless, are you willing to follow the trail, even if it goes up through City Hall and the commissioner?"

Taylor gave him a searching look. "It sounds to me as though you've given this conspiracy idea a lot of thought."

"Not really. You're the one looking for blood, not me."

"I just want the truth!" Taylor slammed his fist on his desk.

"You want to be mayor and you know it!" Burkes shot back.

There was silence for a moment. "Let me consider all this and I'll be in touch," Taylor finally replied.

"Aye, aye, Captain," Burkes sarcastically saluted on his way out.

Ben awoke to the sound of cars rattling on a bridge over his head and the pager vibrating. He could only think about having a car and a gun. Ben looked at his surroundings. He was on an embankment of a small creek under the freeway across from a small shopping center. It was 5 a.m. He had wandered to this little hideaway during the night. He recalled the day before and the encounter with the cop. He realized for the first time that he would have hit the cop with the metal lid had it been necessary. It was so unlike him. He wondered how far he would have gone to remain free. He wondered if the cop ever placed his face.

He hurried down the embankment toward a little store near the off-ramp. There was a pay phone. Without warning someone's leg tripped him in the dark. He fell face first but quickly recovered.

"Hey! Hey! Leave me alone," came a cry. Evidently he had shared the pad of a homeless person.

He had no time to waste. He raced down the hill, fishing in his pocket for a quarter but finding nothing but a wad of cash left from what Randy had given him. Stores were closed. He had to have a quarter! He couldn't believe he hadn't thought of this sooner. His whole life was on hold because of a quarter, and he probably had over six hundred bucks in his pocket. He spotted another homeless guy leaning against the side of a store. The man with a scraggly beard and tattered clothes had a large plastic cup sitting beside him. A change cup, Ben thought. He approached the half-drunk, half-asleep man. The man arose slightly to see Ben.

"Here, I need a quarter. Five bucks is all I have." It was the smallest denomination he could find. "Take it and give me a quarter for the phone."

The man reached for the five, took it and pocketed it. Ben reached into the cup to grab a quarter. The outside lights of the store made for good visibility. Ben started to retrieve the quarter when the man grabbed his arm just below the elbow to prevent him retrieving the coin.

"What is it?" Ben snarled. The incoherent mumbling signaled that the guy was either drunk or mentally ill. Ben began to talk slowly, though he didn't know why.

"I-gave-you-five-dollars. I-need-a-quarter."

"N-n-n-" The guy wasn't interested. Ben didn't have time to argue, especially with someone who didn't understand him. He whacked the guy full force with the back of his hand, grabbed a quarter, and ran around the building to the phone. He picked up the receiver and dialed the number on the pager, all the while watching the corner to make sure the guy didn't come after him. He thought he had knocked him out, but he didn't have time to wait and see about him or even feel guilty for that matter.

There was an unfamiliar voice on the other end. "Ben?"

"Who's this?"

"I'm Joe. I work for Randy. I do security, maintenance, whatever he needs done. He trusts me. You can too."

"Have you got something for me?"

"Yeah, where can we meet?"

Ben looked around to get his bearings. "How about in front of the Sunflower Store in the North Square Shopping Center? It looks quiet. When can you be here?" Ben answered with a question to let this guy know he had no time for a conference.

"Ah, yeah, I know where you are. I'm supposed to drive you to Little Rock, then ride back with one of the freight line trucks tonight."

Damn! Ben thought. This was Randy's way of getting him out of town for his own safety! He appreciated his cousin's concern, but he had unfinished business here. There wasn't much way of getting revenge from Little Rock, Arkansas.

"Did you get me a gun?"

"You asked for one, didn't you?" Joe returned the sarcasm.

"Great! What about bullets?"

"I got you a .380 and several rounds of ammo."

"Is that all?"

"I can get you anything you want. Are you planning to be in a war?"

"Well, what can you get me?"

"You name it. I know some people."

"Well, some more ammo would be nice."

"Maybe later. I don't know what you have planned, but my orders are to take you to Little Rock. If you need something later, I'll get it for you."

"How long will it take you to get here?"

"Oh, about twenty-five minutes."

"The sun will be coming up soon. I'll see you in twenty."

"On my way, sir!" Joe hung up without waiting for a response.

Ben started across the street. He passed between the gas pumps in front of the store and heard footsteps. He wheeled to see the homeless guy ready to take a swing. Ben threw a quick right jab to the guy's nose. Blood burst from it as the man fell. Ben knew he would feel bad later. Right now he didn't have time to deal with any sideshows. He had his own full-length drama unfolding before his very eyes.

The shopping center was deserted at this hour. He strolled along the sidewalk looking in the shop windows. He had never cared much for shopping, much less window shopping. Julie had been one who loved to window shop. With his modest salary, that was about all she could ever afford to do. He knew how she had been accustomed to going to the mall on Saturday afternoons and blowing a thousand bucks. That had all ended when she married a cop. Occasionally she would have a garage sale and raise some shopping money.

He sometimes wondered how she could raise enough money to buy luxuries like a dishwasher, a top-of-the-line vacuum cleaner, and even a riding lawn mower. He knew some of the money was surely coming from her father. He never questioned it, though. Gabriel Chapman was the kind of guy who had a way of making you feel guilty about not taking his money. Like if you couldn't afford his daughter, then you shouldn't refuse his help. Julie never wanted to hurt Ben's feelings, and he never wanted to deprive her, so the subject was avoided altogether.

Now, staring into the shop windows, Ben wished he had gone shopping with her more. He thought of how nice it would be just to have the freedom to stroll down the streets of Greensburg, just to look. The simplest of things in life were magnified to him like never been before. He tried to fight back the tears that were now streaming.

Suddenly lights shone on the end of the shopping center. It was the spotlight from a police car doing a standard drive-by. He tried to suck up the tears. Had they seen him yet? He couldn't run, and it would look suspicious if he started to walk away. They would surely think he was a possible burglar and stop to question him.

Ben's thoughts raced as he tried desperately to decide what to do. The patrol car crept closer along the front of the shopping center. He took a deep breath and walked toward the car, tears in his eyes.

The officer driving was alone. That was good, Ben thought to himself. Finally he spotted Ben. He had been looking at the stores so intently, as his spotlight hit each door, that he hadn't even noticed Ben.

Damn! Ben thought. He probably could have turned the other way and walked out of there without being noticed, but it was too late now.

"Good morning, Officer!"

The light swung right into Ben's face. Perfect. That was exactly what Ben had hoped for. Now he could throw his arms over his face to shield his eyes and have an excuse for doing it.

"Oh-hh!" Ben yelled as the light hit his eyes. The cop quickly turned the light downward to beam into Ben's waist. Ben was quick to get the first word in. "You haven't seen a Dalmatian puppy running loose around here this morning, have you?"

"A Dalmatian?"

"Yeah, you know. Spotted dog. Only a puppy, his spots haven't turned black yet. They're still sort of brownish."

"You lost him?"

"Yeah, well, actually it's a her, not a him. We go walking about this time every morning, but today she had somehow gotten out of the back yard before I got up." Ben's years as a cop helped him to know exactly what was believable and what wasn't.

"Where do you live?"

Oh God, Ben thought. He didn't know any streets or neighborhoods to say.

"I live about a mile from here." It was best not to let him gain control of the conversation. "My wife dropped me off here, and she went on down a little ways to look. We've got to find that dog, Officer. It was a birthday present to my little girl. She's staying a few days with her grandparents, but if she comes home and that dog is gone, it'll break her heart!" Ben couldn't believe how good he sounded.

"Where else do you think we should look?"

Great, Ben thought. He bought it all.

"Well, we walk down this road every morning." Ben pointed at the road in front of the center. "I figure she's probably somewhere around here."

"Don't you think this road is rather unsafe to walk on. I mean with all the traffic you could get hit."

"Sir, if I get this dog back, I'll keep her at home from now on."

"If I see her, how do I get in touch with you? Give me your number."

Ben didn't know the prefixes for the area. "My pager is 673-9118. It's statewide. I can be reached anytime. Thank you, Officer."

The cop pulled away.

Ben waited for the longest twenty minutes he had ever felt until the white van pulled into the lot. It had seemed more like an hour as he paced on the edge of the parking lot in fear of the cop coming back by. He had tried to act as if he were looking in the tall grass at the end of the parking lot, but he could tell that his performance would not be very convincing if anyone were watching him.

"Hi, I'm Joe," a medium-framed, darkhaired, barely thirty-year-old said, stepping down from the van.

"Where's my piece?" Ben greeted him.

A small laugh and then a nod toward the van. "Get in. We're going to Little Rock."

"I'll drive. I'll drop you off wherever you want to go," Ben assured him.

"Sorry, I've got my orders. Randy said this might be your reaction. The best thing for you is to get out of town. Hop in."

Reluctantly Ben climbed in the passenger's seat of the van. As he had walked around, he saw that the truck had once belonged to a rental store. The logo had been painted over.

"Is this a company truck?" Ben asked. "I see rental markings used to be on the side."

"It's a repo. Randy had loaned some money to a rental store here in town. They failed to repay the notes, so he was forced to foreclose on their property."

"Really? I didn't know he was in the loan business, too."

Joe didn't answer.

The van sped away from the parking lot.

Joe smiled at Ben once they entered the expressway. "Speaking of loans, Randy sent you this." He shoved a paper sack at Ben. "It's a grand—small bills too."

"Thanks. What about ammo?"

Joe laughed. "I trust you're going to drop out of sight and won't need any. In the meantime, this is what you asked for." He reached under a blanket lying on the floor and handed Ben a Beretta .380 automatic. "It's fully loaded. There's a box under the blanket."

Ben locked the chamber to the rear, then released it, letting it fall forward and chamber the first round. Ben studied Joe, who had begun to sip coffee from a mug.

"Want some coffee?" Joe asked as he caught Ben's stare. "I brought a thermos for the trip."

"No," Ben answered emotionlessly. "The sun's coming up. Don't you hate this? You should still be in bed."

"Oh, I don't mind. I don't have any set hours. I just do what needs to be done."

Ben continued to stare. He noticed the pistol in Joe's boot. Joe caught his stare, again.

"I've got a permit for that," he said. "You'll have one too. We're getting you a fake I.D. and everything. Your name will be Tommy Lester."

"Where are you getting it?"

"I know some people. Don't worry about it. Unless you become a cop again...then you can bust me." He laughed.

Ben didn't. He just stared harder.

"Is something wrong?" Joe asked Ben.

Ben fished into the bag for a twenty to give Joe. "I need you to pull over and give me the van," he said. "Take this twenty and call a cab."

Joe rolled his head to the side. "I was sent here by your own cousin to help you. What are you going to do, shoot me?"

"Yeah, if I have to."

Joe shook his head and sped up. "Randy said you might be a little crazy right now."

Ben cocked the hammer and stuck the pistol in Joe's jaw. The flesh of his jaw pressed against his teeth. His head pressed against the van window.

"Oh, since you put it that way. I guess I could use a brisk early morning walk to get me going. Better than coffee anyday."

Ben nodded.

"I'll just park here." He pulled off the road. "Is this okay?"

"Fine."

"Good. We aim to please." Joe opened the door.

He sighed as Ben eased the hammer back into its original position.

"I'll be going now," Joe said.

Ben slid into the driver's seat.

Chapter 15

Ben realized that he was about to go to sleep when the first car pulled out of Tawana Griffin's sister's driveway. He had been sitting there for almost three hours. It was now eight o'clock. A black male in his early twenties was leaving the house. It looked like Tawana following him out to his car. Ben sat upright in the van seat to get a better look. He was almost a block away. He couldn't be sure it was her, but he was afraid to get too close to the house. The street had a small apartment complex at the end of it. It was only eight units, but it gave him a place to park without someone calling the cops. He decided to take a closer look. He eased down the street just as Tawana kissed the guy leaving her house. He got into his car and started backing out the driveway. Ben drove past just to make sure it was Tawana. It was. He wondered what Pookie would say if he could have witnessed the scene. He hadn't been covered with dirt yet, and she had another guy spending the night.

John Burkes sat behind his desk in preparation for a new day. He thumbed through some of the reports lying on his desk. They were being compiled for the commissioner and the mayor, who demanded full explanations for the events surrounding Pookie Jones' death in an attempt to justify the quarter million dollars worth of damage done to the hotel. He picked up the phone and called Bob Taylor. An hour later, the two met in the parking lot outside the precinct.

"You got anything for me yet?" Taylor got straight to it.

"Not yet. I'm working on a hunch. I need to go down to Greensburg, Mississippi. Can you call the D.A. down there and get him to help me?"

"Sure, but why? You're working on that Seals' case.

"Yeah, I'm afraid there may be some connection between all of this."

"I don't think so," Taylor reasoned. "I've thought about it. I appreciate the effort, but that seems a little too unbelievable for me. The sheriff down there may be involved with something, but I doubt it's B.J."

"I'm not so sure. I have some questions that I can't get out of my mind."

"Like what?"

"Well, don't you find it strange that the commissioner hired a cop for my task force against my wishes. A cop from Greensburg who was nothing more than a country hick."

"I thought you had decided Seals was doing a good job for you."

"He was...but there was no way anyone could have known that before he went to work here."

"Maybe the commissioner just had a hunch."

"No way. He knew I had a homicide detective from Birmingham and a vice cop from Nashville who wanted the job. If he wanted to hire an out-of-towner, he could have gotten any one of a number of people more qualified than some small-town deputy who had busted a few pot smokers and crackheads."

"Well, you know he only did it because he's buddies with Randy Seals, Besides, the city council had to approve it."

"They'll approve anything the commissioner wants. I don't understand...with all the heat to catch Michael Rose's killer, why would he go with such inexperience? He could have given Ben Seals a job anywhere in the department. Why on my team?"

"John, are you sure you're not just going to Greensburg to get away from all the heat?"

"The thought never crossed my mind."

"Yeah, right!" Taylor laughed. "I know things are hectic around here. I'm sure you're worried about keeping your place running the team too."

"Hey, they can't fire me if I'm not here," John chuckled.

"Right, but it does you no good to be somewhere else unless you really think you can find out something."

"It's just a hunch, but there may be something to it. Who knows?"

"Well, I certainly don't. I do know if you get transferred, there may be somebody put in your place that I can't trust."

"I know."

There was a moment of silence as the D.A. pondered the whole scenario. "If I set it up for you, I'll have to send a deputy D.A. with you."

"No problem."

"Do you really think you can find out anything?"

"I don't know what I'll find. The main thing, as I see it, is to go in on the pretense of finding out all we can about Ben Seals and to act as though he is already presumed guilty in our eyes. Then they'll be more inclined to trust us."

"Suppose we do find out something? Then what?"

"If part of Ben's story pans out, we'll have reasonable doubt about his guilt. Then I suspect the rest should be kept as top secret as possible. You can pick up the investigation from back here. There's no telling who all is involved if that becomes the case."

"As I said, if I do agree to this, I want to send someone with you."

"Fine."

"I've got this Johnson kid you've met before. He's sharp and needs all the investigation experience he can get. I'd like to send him."

"Sounds fine. I'd like to go this afternoon and maybe stay the night. Will your office cover our expenses?"

"I guess we'll have to. I'm sure you won't have any task force money left over by the time you pay for that freaking hotel." Taylor laughed.

"Oh, you're real funny!"

"Come by after lunch and pick up a credit card. I'll tell Johnson he's going with you. He'll be excited. He thinks you're some kind of legend."

"Why?"

"He sees you as a modern-day Elliot Ness who can bring in big-time drug dealers without stepping over the legal boundaries. But I'm afraid this whole ordeal with B.J. White is shaking his confidence in you." Taylor laughed again.

Burkes, in his most sarcastic tone, said, "Good, he can work with me for a couple of days and see that I'm just as human as he is."

"Yeah, maybe so, but hey...do me one favor."

"Yeah?"

"Don't blow anything up while you're down there!" Taylor bellowed.

Kiss my ass!"

Ben had waited all morning for the right moment to grab Tawana Griffin. If anyone knew how to get to B.J., it would be she. He followed her to the grocery store, to the car wash, and now to a beauty salon. She drove an older model Ninety-Eight Olds. It seemed that the guy leaving her sister's house that same morning was her new man. Probably one of B.J.'s boys. She was just passed from one to the other.

Now Ben sat in the van outside the Image Plus Hair Salon waiting for the right moment to grab her and hold her hostage until he got the information he wanted. His decision now was whether he would hit her in the head or simply put a gun to her and threaten to kill her if she didn't cooperate. He couldn't believe he was even contemplating such actions, but this was a matter of survival and revenge. He had seen the way Tawana acted when she was in custody along with Pookie. She was so wild and high-spirited that a blow to the head to render her unconscious seemed the best alternative

Three hours later Ben had grown impatient to the point of rage. Finally Tawana appeared. He had parked in the perfect spot this time. At the grocery and the car wash she had been in plain view of a number of people. This time she had parked on the side of the salon. Her car faced a brick wall along with at least three other cars. There was no one around. This was the perfect opportunity. Tawana rounded the corner and walked toward her car. Ben hustled around the side of the van and slid the side door open as if he were going to get something out. He had parked right beside her car. The open van door was adjacent to her door. She casually spoke, as did he. He apologized for being in the way without looking her in the eye. Gracefully he moved out of the way to allow her access to the door. She held a designer purse in one hand and her car keys in the other. As she stuck the keys in the car door, she turned her back to Ben. He reached under his shirt to produce the pistol. With all his force, he thrust the butt of the pistol against the back of her freshly styled head.

Thwack!

Her knees buckled and he feared for a moment that he might have killed her. The flow of adrenaline made it easy for him to pick her up and push her into the van. She began to moan softly as he jumped into the van and slammed the door shut. He quickly gagged her with a sock after he bound her hands tight with a lightweight extension cord from the van's toolbox. He then took the leftover cord and tied her hands to her feet. He knew when she came to, she would be a live wire.

John Burkes entered the D.A.'s office to pick up Marc Johnson, who was waiting eagerly.

"It's great to be working with you!" Marc asserted before Burkes could even say anything. "I'm Marc Johnson. I'm to be your traveling companion."

Without pausing for an answer, Johnson continued, "I met you before at the precinct. You might not remember. Of course, I didn't figure you would. You were so busy and all."

"I remember you," John lied. "Bob Taylor says you're really sharp."

"Oh, I don't know about that. I try hard!"

Ben drove to a deserted rural Mississippi Road, just across the state line. He parked the van and put the flashers on. Tawana was starting to make noises as if she were regaining her senses. Ben had elected to stop and talk to her but couldn't stay in one place long for fear that a constable or deputy might pass by and become suspicious. He stepped to the rear of the van where she lay. Removing the sock from her mouth he assured her that everything was okay and that she should not be frightened. He was amazed at how well she responded. He was expecting to see the wild woman he had seen back at the police precinct a few days before. Instead, she looked scared, yet calm. She had tears in her eyes when she said, "Why don't you just take my money?" She looked at her purse lying on the floor of the van, its contents partially spilled.

Ben took a quick glance toward her purse, then reached to retrieve it. He gently put back everything that had fallen out and put the purse down beside her. "I'm not interested in your money."

"Well," she stared at him, "are you going to untie my legs or just unzip your pants?"

"Excuse me?"

"You said you didn't want my money. There ain't but one other thing you could want. I can't hardly reach you lying here on my side, so you gotta do all the work or untie me or somethin'."

Ben couldn't believe how she was taking the idea of rape in stride. She was more street-hardened than Pookie.

"I don't want that either."

She looked bewildered. What could a white man want with her if he didn't want money or sex? Ben could see the fear beginning to swell in the young woman.

"Relax. I don't want to hurt you, but I will if you don't cooperate!"

"Hey! I know you! You're that cop on TV. The one they're looking for!"

Ben felt his face blush, but he had prepared for this. "Yeah, that's me," he frowned. "As you know by now, I killed my wife. She found out that I had been trafficking drugs on the side, and she was going to turn me in. I had to kill her." Ben had thought this out in detail. He had considered the implications that would follow after he released her. Once she told the cops that he had confessed to her that he had killed Julie, this would be used later in court should he be caught or turn himself in. He didn't figure that would matter at this point. He had no plans of being taken alive.

"I want to get in contact with B.J. White. I know you can help me."

"Why do you want to see B.J.?" Tawana's sarcasm was stronger than her fear.

"I've got a bunch of merchandise that I want to sell. I thought he might be interested. Maybe he can help me get outta town to someplace I can hide, too."

"Ha, ha," Tawana laughed as though her sides were about to split.

"You find that amusing, do you?"

"You want B.J. to buy dope from a cop?" She laughed even harder.

"I'm not exactly a cop anymore. I thought you knew that."

"That might be some kind of media trick the cops tryin' to play to get B.J. They can't get him no other way."

"I can assure you my wife is dead. This is no trick. I loved her very much, but I couldn't go to jail for her. Why are you laughing? You don't think I killed her?"

"I know for a fact you didn't kill her! Don't even try to play me like that!" She looked like a kid with her hand caught in proverbial cookie jar.

Ben was stone-faced. "How do you know I didn't? You know who did it, don't you?"

Silence.

"The only way you could know I didn't kill my wife is if you know who did." He cocked the pistol.

The trip to Greensburg was a quick one. Burkes insisted on driving and rarely stayed within the speed limit.

Upon reaching Greensburg, they checked into a local motel where Burkes called the precinct to touch base with Paul Crator. Even Crator didn't know the real reason for Burkes' visit. Burkes had said he was looking for clues that might help determine where Seals was hiding. Crator had tried to talk him into not going, saying it would be a waste of time. Burkes simply argued that the D.A. had insisted because he wanted Seals brought in. Crator naturally took charge of the task force until his return.

Seeing Burkes make an important call prompted the young D.A. to do the same. When Burkes hung up the phone, Marc Johnson picked it up and called the Shelby County D.A.'s office. He was put on hold momentarily until Bob Taylor was heard on the line.

"What is it, Johnson?" Taylor shouted. "What's wrong?"

"Nothing. I was just letting you know we made it here fine, and we've already checked in." Johnson glanced at Burkes to see if he was listening as he talked to his boss.

Taylor was flustered. "Then what the hell do you want?"

"N-nothing.... Just checking in."

"Johnson! I'm busy. Don't call me unless you have something important to tell me!"

"Yes sir!"

"Let me talk to Burkes," Taylor requested.

"Sir?"

"Let me talk to Burkes. Is he there?"

"Uh...yes sir." Johnson turned to Burkes. He wants to talk to you," he said, handing him the phone.

Burkes was on the phone briefly. After he hung up, he informed Johnson that they were supposed to go to the Green County D.A.'s office immediately.

Chapter 16

John Burkes parked at the address given to him for the Green County district attorney. The office appeared to be a recently converted fast-food joint. The duo was greeted in the lobby by a secretary and led to the rear of the building where the D.A. sat behind his desk on the phone.

"He's expecting you. Just have a seat, and he'll be right with you gentlemen," the secretary said.

They sat patiently listening to the D.A.'s conversation with what seemed to be a defense attorney.

"If you want to plead to simple assault and trespassing, that's fine. I won't take trespassing by itself. That's asking too damn much. Okay. Fine. I'll be in all day tomorrow. Call me."

He hung up the phone. "You must be Captain Burkes. I'm Manny Hampton." The D.A. extended his hand toward Burkes.

"It's good to know you," Burkes acknowledged as the two shook hands.

"Marc Johnson!" Marc jumped in to introduce himself. "Deputy D.A., Shelby County, Tennessee. I work primarily with homicide investigations. This is a little bit different for me."

The D.A. looked at him with a puzzled expression, as if he were supposed to care what this kid did. He then turned back to Burkes. "It's my understanding you want to see the files on Ben Seals' arrest."

"Come again?" Burkes raised his eyebrows.

"The Seals' files. We haven't even processed all of it yet, since it happened so recently. Normally I'd be hesitant to have somebody going through the files right now, but since it's a closed case, I guess it doesn't matter."

The D.A. wouldn't have been nearly so cooperative if he had known that they were trying to investigate the Green County Sheriff's Office. It just wasn't kosher to go around looking under the rugs of other law enforcement officials, and the D.A. would normally have a close relationship with the local sheriff's department.

"This is everything I have," Hampton said, reaching into a nearby filing cabinet. He handed Burkes a small stack of papers. "You can use my conference room to go through all this if you like."

"That would be great!" Burkes replied.

"There's coffee in there, and if there's anything else you need just let my secretary know. She'll be glad to help you."

"I see a number of assistants in the other offices here," Marc piped up. "Which one worked this case? In the event we have questions?"

"You're talking about a deputy sheriff arrested for drug trafficking," Hampton said. "Obviously, I handled it myself."

"Well, that makes sense," Marc responded.

Burkes smiled as they left the room. "Why don't you grab us some coffee, Marc?" he said.

Marc stopped and looked at Burkes, then mumbled something about being a go-fer as he walked across the conference room to the coffeemaker. He fixed a cup of coffee for Burkes and put it down on the conference table.

"That was a legitimate question, Marc. You've just got to remember that we're dealing with Mayberry, U.S.A. It's a big deal when a cop gets busted here."

"Tell me! Tell me right now!" Ben screamed.

Tawana looked frightened but did not answer. She gave just a slight shake of her head.

Ben produced the pistol he had struck her with and put it to her head. "Tell me now."

She didn't move. Then she tried to open her mouth. Ben awaited his answer.

"You ain't no killer."

He stared at her momentarily, then cocked the pistol and forced it into her mouth. She tried to scream but couldn't with the barrel of the pistol pressing against her tongue.

"Listen, lady." Ben's voice was now deep and gravelly. "I may not have killed my wife, but everybody thinks I did, so I may as well have. If you don't think I'll kill you, you're wrong. Or should I say...dead wrong. I only want to know who did it. If you're scared they'll kill you, you should worry about them later. Right now, you've got to worry about what I'll do to you. And if you lie to me, I'll kill you. I have nothing to lose. Do you understand?"

She nodded, trembling, the barrel of the gun moving with her head.

As John Burkes sifted through the case files given to him by Manny Hampton, Marc Johnson asked a question. "Say, don't you have family here? I thought Taylor said you had some kin here and that's how you knew your way around."

"I have a sister here. She owns an antique shop downtown. She and her husband went to Florida on vacation. The shop is closed until they return. It was probably best anyway. I sure don't have time to visit. We need to get back as soon as possible. I'd imagine I've been transferred to traffic detail by now the way things have been going lately."

"Do you really think they'd take the task force away from you?"

"Sure," Burkes responded. "There's been too much press about us, and none of it has been good. I'd do the same thing if I were in the commissioner's shoes."

"Do you think the commissioner is crooked?"

"That's a loaded question, Johnson. The walls may have ears."

"You wouldn't be here if you didn't think there was something to it."

"You're here. Does that mean you think he's guilty of something?"

"Maybe," Marc replied.

"Ha!" Burkes shook his head. "That's a lot easier for you to say, coming from the D.A.'s office. You forget who I work for. Besides, I think you've been around that power-hungry boss of yours too long.

"Either the commissioner is crooked or somebody close to him is. That's the only way Seals got that job."

"He got that job because of his cousin. Randy Seals gets anything he wants at City Hall."

The two busied themselves with the files until Burkes broke the forty-five minute silence.

"Marc, let me ask you something. If you were in Ben Seals' shoes and you had a load of illegal dope, why would you take it around this Mitch Williams, another deputy?" John asked, referring to the files in front of him.

Marc glanced at some of the sheets before them. " Mitch said Ben came by Carter's Store to shoot pool with him."

"Yeah, I read that," Burkes said, looking puzzled.

"He may have figured no one else would ever be suspicious of him," Marc said.

"Excellent point," Burkes agreed. "That's what bothers me."

"What?" Marc asked, seeming confused.

"Mitch said he found the dope when he walked out to Ben's patrol car to look for something. He says he had used Ben's patrol car the day before and had left something in the trunk."

"Yeah, yeah," Marc said, reading along with Burkes, who now sat beside him. "So?"

"So," Burkes repeated in disbelief, "Mitch found the dope snooping around in Ben's car. If you had a load of dope hidden in your car, would you give somebody the keys to your car?"

Marc couldn't believe he had not seen it for himself. "But even they know that's unbelievable. The sheriff's department may be crooked but they can't be that dumb."

Burkes laughed. "One: they probably didn't have time to make up a better story that would coincide with that of the other witnesses at the store. Two: if everybody on the department says the same thing, it's hard not to believe it."

"You're right," Marc stuttered. "I think you're onto something. There's only one thing."

"What's that?"

"Maybe things are different here, but in Memphis, if a cop gets busted the D.A. will prosecute him to the fullest extent as an example. Ben Seals' case was plea-bargained. That's ammo for the opponent at election time, valuable ammo, the kind that makes people not trust the system."

"Maybe he's not running," Burkes suggested as a recourse.

"I dunno. But it sure needs to be asked....even if we don't get a straight answer," Marc whispered.

Burkes and Johnson sifted through the files on Ben's arrest and plea bargain. Burkes was troubled by the plea bargain, especially when it seemed they had Ben so red-handed with witnesses at the small grocery store. It all seemed a little too much to believe—that the D.A., an elected official, would give in to such a deal. No matter how much pressure was applied by the sheriff's department to cut a quick deal, the D.A. would have the final authority.

Manny Hampton reentered the conference room unannounced. "Hey , guys, it's quittin' time around here. We're gonna knock off for the day. Do ya'll want to lock up?"

Johnson glanced at Burkes as if he should answer for them.

Burkes casually slid all the papers back into the file. "Let me ask you something."

"Shoot," Hampton said as he slipped on his jacket.

"Why is it that the Seals case was plea-bargained?" Burkes quizzed the D.A., watching his expression closely to detect anything that might tip him off that he was lying. His years of interrogating had taught him to read a person's emotions better than most polygraphs. Usually it was some street punk though, not a polished district attorney. He didn't know if he could tell anything about this guy or not.

Hampton looked annoyed for about two seconds, then decided it couldn't hurt to answer the question. "Because that's the way Gene wanted it."

"Gene? You mean Sheriff McMasters?"

"Right."

Burkes thought for a moment. Hampton could tell Burkes was not comfortable with the answer.

"Is something wrong, Captain? Maybe you disapprove?"

Burkes shook his head. "Oh, no, don't get me wrong. I don't pretend to be sticking my nose in where it doesn't belong..."

"Then don't!" Hampton cut him short.

Burkes laughed a sarcastic laugh. "I just wondered..."

"What, detective? What's bothering you?" Hampton asked.

"I can understand the high sheriff not wanting the bad publicity from having to bust one of his own deputies. I can't understand the D.A's office letting him off the hook so easily. I know you have to work closely with the sheriff, but come on." Burkes leaned forward onto the table propping his elbows up to study what Hampton had to say. "You could build an entire reelection campaign on just this case.... You could probably get reelected indefinitely just for trying the case. What was it? Was Ben Seals so popular down here that you didn't even want to try him?"

Manny's laugh echoed around the room. "Why do I feel like I'm in the police interrogation room?"

Burkes laughed with him for a moment, then abruptly transformed to a look of serious intent that would have rivaled the Mona Lisa. "I'm still wondering."

The D.A. adjusted the cuffs under his jacket. "Not that I have to answer, but I will."

"How many people live in metropolitan Memphis?" Hampton asked Burkes. "Just guess...your best guess."

"I don't know. About a mill or so."

"A million people," Hampton echoed in a boisterous voice.

"I'm not sure about that."

"It doesn't matter," Hampton cut him off. "Do you know how many live in Green County?"

"Not exactly," Burkes answered. He looked at Marc for help. Marc shrugged his shoulders.

"I'll tell you," Manny said. "Less than twenty-five thousand. I'm the D.A. for the adjacent county as well. It's hard to keep a constituency going in both counties without a little help. In Green County, Gene McMasters is a political machine. That's just a part of life that has to be accepted. He's been the sheriff here for a long time and will be for a long time to come. If he wants something, he usually gets it. He didn't want Ben Seals to do any time because he liked him. If I had tried to buck Gene I wouldn't have a snowball's chance in the next election. You see, people down here know each other..." He leaned over a chair to whisper, "This ain't Memphis! If Gene gets behind you, every farmer in the county is behind you. So is their money. If not, then you're dead in the water."

"Did Ben tell you he caught Gene in bed with his wife?"

Hampton turned a pale white. "Do what?"

John knew he had struck a nerve. "I said, did Ben tell you he had caught Gene sleeping with his wife?"

"Whose wife?"

"Ben's wife. Julie, I believe."

"No." Hampton looked confused himself.

"Are you saying Ben's attorney didn't mention it? We assumed that was the reason you were so quick to plea-bargain. The fallout from that might be rough for Gene."

"No," Hampton answered. "Randy Seals, Ben's cousin, was his attorney. He never said anything. He was probably saving it in case we went to trial."

Burkes raised his eyebrows. "You mean that's something that can be kept a secret in a town this size?"

Hampton was caught offguard by all of this. "I don't know. I tell you what.... Why don't you let me buy you gentlemen some dinner, and we can discuss this further."

Burkes and Marc followed the D.A. out of the conference room and into the hallway. When Hampton stepped into his office momentarily to pick up his coat, Burkes kept a watchful eye on him to see if he made a phone call.

The D.A. returned to the hallway with his coat over his arm. "Let's go," he said with a smile, as if he were suddenly looking forward to the conversation that would follow. The trio piled into Hampton's sedan and headed north to the edge of town. Hampton parked in front of a quaint little steakhouse and looked at the two Memphians with a smile. Burkes and Johnson surveyed the parking lot full of teenagers sitting around on the hoods of pickups and old cars. The lot was filled with laughter and joking among the boys and girls.

"C'mon, you'll love it!" Manny encouraged them. "They have the best barbecue in three counties."

"Barbecue?" Marc Johnson stammered. "It's not a steakhouse?"

"Well, yeah," Hampton explained, "it is. Well, it was. You see, Charlie Williams opened it as a steakhouse about six years ago. It wasn't long before he found out he wasn't that good with steaks, but he was a real genius at barbecue. He just left the name the same, but everybody knows his barbecue is king."

"Yeah," Burkes agreed, looking into the back seat at Marc. "You didn't know that?"

Marc smiled and shook his head.

Burkes and Marc had ordered barbecued chicken before Manny spoke up and said dinner was on the county. Then they changed their order to ribs. Hampton raised an eyebrow but didn't complain. The small talk was interrupted when the owner of the place walked over to their table.

Manny jumped to his feet with outstretched hands as if this were reelection year. "Charlie, how ya doin'?"

"Pretty good," Williams answered.

"Looks busy tonight."

"Yeah, a little bit. You brought me some new customers, I see." He peered behind the D.A. at Burkes and Marc.

"Yeah, this is Detective Burkes and his assistant from Memphis."

"I'm not his—" Marc started before Burkes grabbed the young attorney by the arm and under his breath whispered, "Just let it go." Marc choked his words, visibly annoyed.

"They're down here trying to find out more about Ben Seals. He was working for Officer Burkes when he killed Julie. They're finding out all they can about him. In fact, they'll be talking to Mitch and the rest of the sheriff's department tomorrow."

Charlie shook his head. "Yeah, Mitch said there were some cops from Memphis coming down here about Ben. He said ya'll were having trouble finding him."

Burkes cleared his throat trying to get the D.A's attention. He couldn't believe this guy's big mouth.

"It's a shame, I tell you, just a shame. A nice boy like that. I don't know what ever got into him to go bad all of a sudden," Charlie said.

Hampton turned to Burkes. "Charlie here has a nephew in the sheriff's department. You'll meet him tomorrow. He was one of the arresting officers when Ben was picked up here."

"Yeah, we saw that name on the arrest records."

"Mitch is right over there." Charlie motioned toward a jukebox in the corner.

"Hey, Mitch!" Hampton raised his voice just enough for the young deputy to hear him across the crowded room. "Come here."

Mitch lumbered across the room to their table. He wore jeans and cowboy boots and under his arm was a blonde who looked barely fifteen.

"Mitch, this is Detective Burkes and his assistant from Memphis."

Marc gritted his teeth and held his cool.

"You'll be talking with them tomorrow," Hampton said.

"Oh," Mitch said. "Ya'll are the suits from Memphis."

"Well, we're not exactly what you would call suits," Burkes corrected him. "I've been a cop for fourteen years."

"Yeah." Mitch shook his head. "All I can tell you is that Ben was bad to the bone. Rotten. Always was."

"That's funny," Burkes pointed out. "Your uncle was just telling us how nice Ben was."

"Shoot. He's just like all the old folks around here. They liked Ben because he played ball at LSU. Big deal!"

Burkes cleared his throat. "We'll see you tomorrow."

Mitch looked puzzled. He was being asked to leave but in a tactful way that almost went right over his redneck head.

"Okay, dudes. Tomorrow it is."

He left and the three sat back down. Hampton was speaking to several people at surrounding tables.

Burkes was furious. "Sir, with all due respect, I would greatly appreciate your not mentioning our business to anyone."

Hampton never took his eyes off the voters at the next table. He merely leaned back in his seat and said, "Relax, Burkes, I know the real reason you're here."

Burkes sat down the glass of water he was about to sip and glanced at Marc, who was two seats away. Burkes returned his focus to the D.A. "Suppose you tell me what it is you think I'm here for." His tone no longer diplomatic.

Hampton leaned way back in his chair as the waitress approached and asked for their drink order.

"Iced tea for me," Hampton smiled.

Burkes, still staring at him, didn't hear the question.

"Tea's fine for me," Marc said to break the silence.

Burkes wasn't as subtle. "Exactly what do you mean, counselor?"

His question was ignored again. "Make that three teas, please," Marc piped up.

The waitress sensed the emotions at the table and walked away to get the drinks.

"Relax, Detective," Hampton admonished.

"I think I have a genuine concern," Burkes defended himself. "I want to know what you think I'm doing here."

"It's a small town. Ben Seals was arrested in front of Carter's Grocery. That's a small country store on the edge of town.

Nevertheless, there were a lot of people around when Ben was arrested."

"I'm sorry," Burkes shrugged, "I don't follow you."

"People talk." Manny smiled at the detective. "You're not in Memphis. By these peoples' standards, you two would be considered Yankees."

Burkes looked blank.

"Look," Hampton said, "you said, or rather the Shelby County D.A. said, that you were coming here to find out what you could about Ben and his past. Maybe it could help you find out where he might be hiding now."

"That seems abnormal to you?" Burkes reasoned.

"No, but considering that the Tennessee State Police have been in constant contact with us, along with a Detective Mills from Memphis P.D., it seems strange to me that the head of the narcotics task force and an assistant D.A. would drive down here. I mean, we've already given them everything we have. So has the sheriff's department."

Burkes turned up his nose. "You obviously haven't spent that much time talking to Terry Mills. Don't worry, he confuses everybody."

"Oh, so you two aren't working together on this case? Mills gave me the impression that he was in charge of the whole investigation."

Burkes paused. "Uh, we're sorta working together."

"Well, it's a joint operation," Marc broke in. "Since Officer Seals had been assigned to Detective Burkes—"

"For two whole days!" Hampton interrupted. "I don't even know how he could have been given a job that quick."

Burkes responded, "The commissioner personally took care of the hiring of Ben."

"Regardless—" Marc tried to explain.

"Regardless of nothing..." Hampton fired back. "I told you this is a small town." He smiled at the two confused southern Yankees. "There were a lot of people who heard Ben yelling he was set up when he was arrested. There are still a lot of people around here who have known Ben Seals all his life and would probably vote for him if he ran for sheriff himself."

Burkes took a swallow of the tea now sitting in front of him. The food arrived at their table, and the conversation halted as they began to eat. The meal was great, but Burkes hardly tasted the food he consumed. Hampton insisted they eat and talk later. Burkes conceded to eat but his mind was stuck in fast-forward. His heart pounded a hundred-plus beats a minute, surpassed only by Marc's.

Everyone passed on dessert. Burkes eagerly picked up where he had left off. "Are you ready to tell me exactly what it is that you seem to be keeping from us? Since you obviously know more about this than we do?"

Hampton smiled a big smile. "You men say this is a joint operation, right?"

"I was trying to tell you that," Marc reminded Hampton.

The D.A. laughed. "Let me see, a joint operation between the Memphis P.D., the Tennessee Highway Patrol, and the Shelby County D.A.'s office. Yet you don't even have the information we gave to the highway patrol. Judging from your reaction, you didn't even know we had talked to the state police."

"We merely thought that if we got a full background analysis of him we could better guess what his moves might be."

Hampton sat motionless, as if he were trying to decide if Burkes were lying or not.

"That sounds like bullshit, Detective."

"Suppose you tell me some of this talk that you say you've heard in this small town."

Hampton bellowed with laughter. "You'd like that, wouldn't you? In fact, isn't that the real reason you're here?"

"There you go again." Burkes acted offended this time. "We don't know what talk you're referring to." Burkes turned to Marc with an expression that begged for help.

Marc said, "We don't even know what the hell you're talking about. You just informed us of some kind of rumors that Ben was set up. That's the first we've heard of it."

"Let's get out of here," Hampton said, handing the waitress his credit card.

"I trust we can continue this conversation?" Burkes asked, troubled that Hampton might be losing his eagerness to spill his guts.

"Sure, no problem," Hampton assured him.

Manny led the way up front, where he flagged down the waitress for the bill. He thanked her and said goodbye to Charlie Williams. The three headed back into town. The ride was silent with the exception of a few remarks made by Burkes as he pointed out things about the town that he had learned from his sister.

"May I make a suggestion?" Hampton asked.

Burkes glanced over his shoulder at Marc in the back seat and then back at Hampton. "Sure, what's on your mind?"

"Why don't we do this? Let me drop Johnson off at my office so he can pick up your vehicle, and I'll take you back to the hotel."

Marc was inflamed. "Why?" he barked.

John turned quickly toward Marc, whom he could barely see in the back seat amidst the dark night. "Marc is fully involved in this whole matter and is an outstanding prosecutor. He's also a team player. He'll be glad to, won't ya, Marc?"

Marc Johnson, who had scored in the twenty percent on the Tennessee bar exam, had been reared in a rough Memphis neighborhood compared with those of his law school buddies. He had been the first African-American to win the Warren Award for most outstanding law student in Tennessee. But all his life he had wanted to be a cop. Not just any cop, a super cop, somebody like John Burkes who really made a difference in a city like Memphis, or Chicago, or New Orleans. But his parents had insisted that he go to college and make something of himself...so he became a lawyer.... Still, his desire to pursue criminals was so strong he had joined the D.A.'s office.

Now he was working for the state, prosecuting the criminals that people like John Burkes got to bust, and was still living in South Memphis on his modest salary. His parents had mixed emotions about the whole thing. He had heard that his dad had told some of their relatives that the only reason Marc still lived in South Memphis was because most of the people he prosecuted were from there and it helped to be around that environment. Marc himself had no problem admitting that he made less money than some bank tellers, but his parents weren't so quick to admit it in public after they had worked extra jobs to help him get through law school.

Now he sat silently fuming until time to get out of the car.

John stepped out to speak to him for a moment. "Marc," he

whispered, checking to make sure Hampton wasn't getting out, "just play along. I'll tell you everything he says as soon as I get back. Let's play his little game until we can find out what he knows, okay?" He waited for Marc's reaction.

"Yeah, yeah, I'll wait up," Marc guaranteed John.

"Good boy," John said.

Marc winced.

Chapter 17

John Burkes sat patiently on the passenger's side of the vehicle as Manny Hampton drove through the streets of the quiet little town. Marc Johnson sat back at the hotel room kicking furniture.

Burkes had been as patient as long as he could stand it. As the car left the city limits heading east, he decided it was time to pry a little.

"So...you think there's a fly in the punch somewhere, huh?"

Hampton smiled. "I dunno. You tell me."

"Hey, I'm just a cop trying to do a job for extremely modest wages."

They laughed together, both feeling the awkwardness of the situation.

"My wife doesn't even know I'm out of town tonight. We've been working around the clock trying to catch up with Seals, and I haven't even talked to her in twenty-four hours."

"Do you wanna call from my cellular here?"

"Nah. She quit worrying after the first few years. Now she just expects me to be dead or something. That's why she doesn't have to divorce me for repeatedly breaking my promise to quit the force."

"I suspect it's pretty tough being married to a cop in a place like Memphis. There's so much goin' on all the time."

"Yeah, but apparently not anymore than there is down here."
John stared at Hampton, still waiting for him to spill his guts.

"Isn't it pretty out here at night?" Hampton changed the subject while turning off on a dirt road.

"All I see is...bushes," Burkes said squinting as limbs from trees popped the car windshield while they made their way down the old dirt road. "Oh, now I see what you mean," he continued as the brush ran out, and the car eased along the top of an old levee overlooking a small, oxbow lake lit by the moon and their headlights.

"Let's get out," Hampton said. "It's especially pretty at night. I brought you here to show some of our beauty so you'd have a good impression of our little community. Maybe you'll think more positively about us. Maybe you'll even pass that along to your sister.... I've been in her antique shop—it's nice. She and her husband seem like nice people." He lit up a cigarette.

Burkes was silent. Hampton was silent. Moments went by as they peered at the lake in the moonlight.

"Well?" Burkes shrugged his shoulders.

"I brought you here to see the beauty," Hampton said as he stamped out the cigarette. "I wanted you to see it...first...because....we've got enough ugliness around here."

Burkes' ears snapped to attention.

"As I'm sure you know by now..." Hampton was talking as he walked toward his car. He stopped at the front of the car and leaned against it to support himself.

"I assume you're talking about local law enforcement." Burkes tried putting words in his mouth.

"That's what I thought," Hampton chuckled. "You already know as much as I do, I'm sure."

Burkes just nodded with a slight smile on his face.

Hampton continued, "Yeah, I guess it's not really a secret. There's a lot that goes on in this county. Especially where the sheriff and his boys are concerned.... They cover all their tracks. It's futile to try and start something with them. The FBI camped out with them, you might say, for almost a month the year before last. What did they get? Nothing! Not one damn thing!"

"What were they looking for?"

"You name it.... There were reports that they were involved in extortion, prostitution, even selling drugs...unbelievable stuff!"

"You don't believe it?"

"Oh, I'd believe almost anything out of that bunch!" He shook his head. "People can't see anything but the good he does.... He's a master of perception, Gene that is. Vernon Myers runs the newspaper. When he gets through with a piece on a bust, you'd think the sheriff's department in Green County was the freakin' Miami vice or some shit. It's hilarious."

"You've never had anything you could nail him with?" Burkes asked.

"Are you kiddin'? They keep me in the dark more than anybody. If I did get something, who'd believe me? He's a legend around here." Hampton shook his head in disgust.

Burkes kicked the soft ground below his feet. "So why are you telling me?"

The D.A. smiled at the Memphis cop. "I'm waiting on you to come clean with me."

"In what way?"

"Well, I think it's obvious, isn't it?"

Burkes acted puzzled. "Fill in the blanks for me. I'm kinda slow sometimes."

"Come now, detective," Hampton looked out across the lake, "look across the water."

Burkes followed the man's index finger with his eyes.

"You see that pier on the other side?"

John could vaguely make out the outline of an old wooden pier.

"Do you see it?" Hampton repeated.

"Yeah," Burkes replied noncommittally.

"Well, that pier was built by Ben Seals and Willie Sanders. Willie's a black contractor who volunteered to help Ben. They did it in their spare time with the help of a few other people, but it was Ben's idea. He's the one who went before the board of supervisors to get permission to build it. Do you wanna know why they did it?"

Burkes sighed. "Why?"

"They did it for the kids who lived out in this part of the county. The summertime meant constant fighting and trouble out this way. Teenagers stayed in trouble, black and white. A local preacher called a group of teenagers and parents together to try to find some solutions. They deduced that there just wasn't enough for the kids to do around here when they weren't working...no recreational facilities whatsoever. Ben took it upon himself to start and finish that project as one way of giving the kids something to do...fish...swim...

whatever." Hampton turned to Burkes. "That's the kind of guy Ben Seals is. Now you're gonna tell me that he's selling drugs on the side and then kills his wife. I might would have learned to accept it eventually...if you had never shown up, Detective."

Burkes was silent, as if at a loss for words.

The D.A. went back on the offensive. "I told you before. I gave the Tennessee State Police everything I had. You know that...or at least you should.... I know you do. You're sharp.... I can tell."

Burkes stood speechless.

"Now, Detective, you don't really think Ben Seals killed his wife, do you?"

Burkes still said nothing.

"Course you don't.... That's why you're here. Or maybe it's just that you're looking out for him because he was one of your boys."

Burkes ignored the last remark. "The girl was killed by pros," he said. "They used a silencer and knew right where to hit Seals to knock him out in one lick without killing him. I believe McMasters was behind it, but his people weren't the ones."

"Then that would mean McMasters would have to have a Memphis connection to get that kind of job done so quickly," Manny remarked.

"Oh, he's got that. You can count on it!" Burkes said.

"How can you be so sure?"

"His name is B.J. White," Burkes mumbled.

"Who?" Hampton asked.

"My nemesis," Burkes muttered again. "The very reason I'm nearly fired." His voice faded as he wallowed in his own misery.

"I'm not sure I follow you," Hampton said with a strange look.

Burkes snapped out of his stupor for a moment. "Just a guy." He kicked the ground. "Just a lowlife sorry son of a bitch that I can't catch!"

"How do you know he's hooked up with McMasters?"

"Ben said McMasters is running drugs with his late wife's brother from New Orleans to Memphis. If they're going into Memphis, B.J.'s either allowing it or he'd be stopping it."

"You mean nobody in Memphis can ship drugs in without him?" Hampton asked in disbelief.

"No, but if it's a big operation, moving a lot, B.J. is involved. If you don't cut him in, he'll kill your operation or you."

Ben sat Tawana up a little so she could regain her composure after
he had scared the life out of her. He kept the pistol pointed at her
with the hammer still cocked and ready to fire.

"Please sir, please!" she cried through muffled tears.

"Lady, what happens to you from here on in is your decision."

She began babbling the names "Rico" and "Boojack."

"Rico and Boojack? How'd they get in the house? Did some cop
give them a copy of my key?"

She shrugged. "I don't know."

Ben held the pistol in his left hand and slapped her as hard as he
could with his right. "Don't screw around with me. I don't have
time for games."

"I don't know!" she screamed with her face mashed into the floor
sideways from the slap.

"You obviously know more than anyone else."

"Leroy told me they did it. That's all I know. I swear it, mister!"

"Leroy?" Ben glared at her.

"My man."

"Yeah, I saw you with him this morning," Ben said.

"You been followin' me all day?"

Ben didn't answer her question. "Where's Leroy? He's the one I
need to be talking to."

"Oh, no! Please, mister!" she cried. "You can't tell Leroy that I
told you. He'll kill me."

"Sorry!"

"No, mister, he don't know nothin' anyway. He found out about
it on the news when we watchin' TV, said he knew Rico and Boojack
did it. He don't know nothin' else, I swear it."

"I'm sorry, I've got to get Rico and Boojack, or whatever the
hell his name is."

"I'll take you to them. You just can't let anybody know I helped
you. B.J. will kill all of us if he finds out."

"You can take me to these guys?"

"They keep B.J.'s warehouse. They stay there and everything."

"What kind of warehouse?"

"Where he keeps all his stuff. I'm not sure what all it is. I know
he's got a lot of stuff."

"Like what?"

"I don't know...bombs or somethin'."

"Bombs?"

"I don't know for sure. I know he got a lot of stuff...weapons...stuff like that. Like that thing that blew up that hotel and kilt Pookie. Shit like that. They moved it there right after they kilt Pookie. They move it all around a lot in case the cops get suspicious or somethin'."

"Leroy told you about this?"

"No way. He said somethin' that let me know where it was."

Ben waited for her to continue.

"He said that Rico and Boojack was stayin' in this place. We was down by the river last night, and he went in to see Rico. He didn't know that I knew that they kept the explosives and stuff. Pookie had told me that a long time ago. Pookie said Boojack and Rico had busted out of some prison out west and couldn't go out in public that much...so B.J. gave them a job guardin' his stuff. They some bad boys. Don't mess around with them. They like to kill folks."

"You just let me worry about that. I'll expect you to show me the warehouse."

"Are you gonna let me go?"

"After I get to take care of my business with these two gentlemen."

"That won't take long."

"Why do you say that?"

"They gonna kill you if you come around them."

Ben laughed. "It's funny, you don't have much loyalty to B.J....telling me all this," Ben observed.

"I don't got shit for B.J. I'm just in with these boys for the ride. They all got money...not all the time...but when they run out, they know how to get more."

"Don't you ever want a life of your own?"

Ben was resorting to his old conservative self...trying to reason with a street person.

She ignored the question. " I'll have to do something after you go lookin' for Rico and Boojack. If they get you, they'll find out I told. If you get them, B.J. will find out I told. Either way I'm dead if I can't get out of town fast."

"They might not find out anything," Ben tried to reassure her.

"Yeah they will.... They can find out anything that happens in

Memphis. Please don't do it. Please, mister, just go away and let it be."

"Sorry, this has to be done."

"You gonna get killed."

"Probably." Ben stuck the now uncocked pistol back in his belt and crawled to the front of the van.

Ben took Tawana's directions toward a downtown warehouse where Rico and Boojack were supposed to be. He parked in an alley in the back and surveyed the place the best he could. It was old and rundown and seemingly devoid of activity. It was slightly red in color on the bottom half of the metal sides. The top consisted of glass windows from about five feet off the ground on up. Many of the windows were cracked or broken. The rest of the windows were tinted.

Ben noticed that someone had gone to great pains to seal a back door shut. It looked as if the seal had been made of heavy-gauge wire screen that was welded to the metal frame of the door. An old rundown warehouse sealed tight. Maybe he had hit upon something here after all. He left Tawana bound and gagged, tied to a handrail in the back of the van. It was near dusk, and Ben felt more at ease about exposing his face in the open. In the back of the building he found a tree that seemed to be growing into the building. It was tall and old. The limbs near the top were growing into the windows of the building. Some of the glass panes had broken from the tree's growth. With his heart racing, he climbed the tree and crawled onto a limb beside a window. The inside of the building was dark. Junk, such as old bicycles, appliances and a little bit of anything you might find in a warehouse, was piled along the sides of the walls.

Ben could see in the middle a mountain of crates of every size. That had to be it, Ben thought. Explosives, weapons and the like. He couldn't believe she had actually told him the truth. He tried to think, but his heart raced faster. Then he heard voices. One shadowy figure appeared in the distance across the warehouse. At the same moment a sliding door on the side of the building rolled up on its track as a burst of light poured into the old building.

Sweat popped up on Ben's forehead as he tried desperately to keep his heart in his chest. The figure who had opened the door was now driving a pickup in from the driveway. Ben's heart raced even faster. He was trying to see all he could. If these were the guys who had killed Julie, he wanted to shoot them on the spot. He had to keep himself alive long enough to get McMasters and maybe a few more along the way. One glimpse of him and these guys would surely shoot him at first sight. Another man had gone to the back of the truck. No one else seemed to be around. The men worked quickly unloading the truck. They grabbed either side of a crate and proceeded to pull it off the bed of the truck. One man pulled at the end of the truck bed. Before the crate reached the other end of the truck, the other man, who was much lighter, grabbed for the end to catch it before it fell. "Hey, muddafucka! Be careful! That's dyno-mite!" he admonished. His accent was Hispanic.

Dynamite! Ben thought. That's it. She wasn't lying. He studied the scene closely as the two carried the crate to the far edge of the building away from the other crates. They carefully placed it on the concrete floor by a side door, then gingerly covered it with a tarp and returned to the truck. Ben thought they would back the truck out of the building. Instead they merely rolled the sliding door down and began to walk to his side of the building. Ben ducked his head down and retreated to the van to make sure Tawana had not figured a way to work loose.

He hurried back to the van, where he was shocked to find that Tawana had not made any effort that he could see to try and free herself.

"Oh," he said, "I thought you would have at least tried to escape." He cranked the van and began to ease down the street.

"Are you crazy? If I move one muscle I'm gonna pee all over myself. You haven't let me go to the bathroom yet!"

"Oh, yeah, I'm sorry." Ben tried to think clearly but his lack of sleep was now taking its toll on his judgment. He couldn't seem to think of a solution to the problem.

"White boy, you gonna have to get me a cup or somethin'."

"Yeah, yeah, I will." Ben rubbed his eyes, his mind still trying to soak in all he had seen at the warehouse.

"Whatcha mean, 'I will'? I ain't peein' in no damn cup.... I wuz just B.S.in' about dat. I ain't peein' in no damn cup."

"Okay, okay, I'll figure something out."

"That's good. You figure something out, 'cause I ain't peein' in no damn cup. You can forget about that. Maybe you one of them freaks that gets off watching women using the bathroom or somethin', but I get paid for doin' somethin' like—"

"Shut the hell up!"

"Why you gettin' all mad? You ain't gotta pee. I gotta pee. Ain't no sense in you gettin' all upset."

Ben slammed the van in park right in the middle of the street. He jumped in the back with her, grabbed her by the hair, and snapped her head backward against the side of the van. "Listen to me!"

Fear returned to her eyes. She had gotten comfortable with Ben and was feeling bold again, until now. The glazed look in his eyes suggested something of a wild animal. He was tired, mad and confused, and he was going to nip this problem in the bud.

"Listen to me, bitch!" She was frozen. "Are you listening to me?"

Tawana nodded.

"Have I got your undivided attention?"

She was silent and motionless. He thrust his other hand under her throat and started to choke her. "I hope I have your attention, because I'm only going to say this once. I have absolutely nothing to lose. The cops and the world think I killed my wife. I have no proof to offer for my innocence. The only recourse I have is to get revenge on those who did this to my wife and to me. Therefore, I will commit murder. I promise you I will kill. Right now I have no intention of harming you, but so help me God, if you cause me any problem or do anything to get in my way, I will add your name to the list, and I will blow your freakin' brains out." Her eyes swelled in their sockets. "Do you think I give a damn about you? Do you?"

She shook her head. Ben let her go and moved back to the driver's seat.

"Never mind about the cup," her broken voice whimpered. Ben turned and saw that her jeans were wet in the crotch and legs.

John Burkes returned to the hotel room. Marc sat on his bed staring at the TV and didn't acknowledge Burkes' entrance. As Burkes stepped over the lamp in the middle of the floor, he said nothing to Marc.

Ben's night had been worse than Marc's. He'd stopped at an all-night truck stop to try and get some rest. This was after he had been forced to steal a nightgown off a clothesline to keep Tawana quiet. He had caught nothing but hell after making her urinate in her pants.

Finally he had found a place to stop. He pulled in beside the loud diesel engines that sat rumbling in the night as their drivers slept.

Tawana sat in the back of the van, hands tied, feet untied. She had been crying most of the night. Now she had dried up almost to a whimper. Ben parked the van and sat quietly with the radio playing softly, listening to Tawana sniffle and whine. He slouched over the steering wheel. How could his life have gone to hell so quickly? All he could do was fight for survival. He hoped the day would soon come when he was caught. He knew he would have to resist to the point of forcing the arresting officers to shoot him. He wanted to die. This was not worth it.

He listened as Tawana cried softly in the rear of the van. It was not her fault she had been dragged into this nightmare. She had probably done a lot of things in the past to warrant treatment worse than this, but this was not her fight. He hated himself for doing this to her. He was still trying to survive, and by some miracle, clear his good name. He was overcome with sudden rage...a wild desire to kill B.J., John Burkes, Gene McMasters, and anyone else behind all this. He grasped reality for a moment. How desperate had he become? This wasn't like him. No matter what had been done to him, he couldn't commit cold-blooded murder, could he?

He felt himself in another world drifting away. The sniffling broke his trance. He crawled to the rear of the van and sat across from the young woman. She eyed him cautiously between tears. He kept trying to say something but nothing would come out. He looked at her white eyes shining in the light that traveled from the neon sign across the parking lot.

"I just want you to know that I'm very sorry about all this," he finally said. "I don't want any harm to come to you, and I'm sorry for screwing up your world so suddenly. Please understand," Ben pleaded, "that I am fighting for my life here. I loved my wife—" His voice began to break. He recomposed himself. "I really loved my wife." Tawana had stopped her whimpering and was listening almost sympathetically.

"She did some terrible things. I mean, she really hurt me—bad! But I would never kill her. I loved her!"

Tawana now sat quietly staring at him as he broke down.

"The only thing I have left is avenging her death."

Tawana looked confused. "Killing somebody is gonna make you

feel better?"

Ben looked at her in wonder. It was the second time in less than five minutes that he had dealt with the thought of murdering someone, he realized. It was different thinking it and then hearing someone ask him that. It really hit home for the first time. Could he kill someone in cold blood? He asked himself the question again. He looked at the girl. "I set out to kill, but now..." his thoughts wandered for a moment, "if I can expose the crooked cops behind all this, maybe that would be revenge." He spoke his thoughts out loud. "Maybe...just maybe, I could clear my name. But..."

"But what?" she asked as if intrigued.

"But I've got a mountain to climb." His voice trailed off.

"I don't know about the cops, but B.J. will kill you if you go lookin' for him."

Ben sat staring straight ahead.

"What? You wanna die?" she asked.

Ben didn't answer.

"I'm sorry," Tawana quietly said.

"Not your problem," Ben said without looking at her.

"I'm sorry that everything is so bad for you right now."

"Oh, it's not your fault," Ben quietly assured her.

"B.J. has always been good to me. I won't help you do anything to him."

"Don't worry. I would never ask you to," Ben said. "If I want you to do something, I won't give you a choice in the matter!"

Ben sat with his knees bent, feet flat on the floor of the van, elbows propped up on his knees with his forehead in his hands.

"You really loved your wife, huh?" Tawana asked.

Ben never changed his expression. "She's the only woman I've ever been with," he solemnly stated.

"Do what?" she exclaimed.

"Those bastards took everything away—everything!" Ben's look became stern and vindictive. "And Gene McMasters will pay. One way or the other."

"Who?" Tawana asked. "Oh, never mind. Go back to what you said about your wife. What did you say?"

Ben didn't hear the question.

"I said, what did you say?" she practically yelled.

Ben was startled by her harshness. "What are you talking about?"

"What did you say?"

"When?" Ben asked.

"You said your wife was the only woman you had ever been with."

"Yeah, that's right."

"What do you mean 'been with'?"

"Just that. I've never really been with anybody else. I dated a few girls in high school but nothing serious."

"Oh, I thought you meant that's the only woman you ever done."

"You mean slept with?" Ben asked.

"Yeah." Tawana laughed.

"Well, that too," Ben acknowledged. He looked up to see Tawana's mouth open. Ben mustered a slight smile. "Yeah, I guess to somebody like you that seems impossible. But trust me, it happens more often than you think. Some people just find the right one."

"I'm sorry," Tawana confessed. "I didn't hear anything you said after you said you never slept with nobody else."

Ben saw a look come over the young girl's face like that of an animal stalking its prey. Her eyes were tuned to his. She licked her lips and scooted in his direction across the floor of the van. Ben tried to change the subject. Tawana ignored him. She had made her way to him. The nightgown rode up to her waist exposing her naked crotch. As Ben watched her in the dim light, a lump swelled in his throat. He couldn't speak. Slowly she eased her right leg around his waist and pulled herself up onto his legs. With her hands still bound behind her, she threw her left leg under Ben's right arm and hooked her foot behind the now helpless man's back, sliding her way up his legs as her bare bottom rubbed along his jeans until she stopped on his thighs.

"I hope I'm not too heavy."

Ben shook his head, still unable to speak.

"Well, what you waiting for?" She smiled a wicked smile. "I get up to two hundred bucks for what I'm giving you for free."

"What are you doing?" Ben heard himself say. He was sure his heart would soon jump right out of his chest.

"What does it look like I'm doing? I'm giving you what half the men in Memphis want."

"Why?" Ben asked, trying to stall as he admired how trim her body was.

"Because you got me so excited I can't hardly stand it," she sighed as she laid back on his legs. "You're almost a virgin."

"How do you figure that?" he asked, choking on his own words.

"Well, you said you've only been with one woman!" She was relaxed on his legs now with her bound hands at his crotch. "Push the gown up over my breasts!"

Slowly he ran his hands down her legs, over her knees to her crotch, where his thumbs protruded to where they almost met over her pubic area as she arched her back forcing her buttocks up so that her crotch would rub against his thumbs as they slid over her.

"Oh, God," she moaned.

Ben tightly grabbed her thighs and pushed her off him and back onto the floor of the van.

Her head snapped up. "What's wrong?"

He didn't answer.

"It's because I'm black, isn't it?"

Ben shook his head and looked at her with the solemnness of a man dying.

"You're a gorgeous woman, but I'm married."

"She's dead."

"But I'll always be married to her."

The sunlight through the hotel window heralded a new day in Greensburg. Burkes and Marc were off to an early start. They were sitting in their car in front of the courthouse when the sheriff arrived. Gene McMasters parked on the side of the courthouse and barreled his way down the sidewalk. His small office was located in a quiet corner in the rear of the courthouse basement. The office was level with the rear parking lot and was just a short stroll away from the county jail. John and Marc met the sheriff as he unlocked the door to his office.

"Sheriff McMasters," John spoke first.

McMasters never looked at the two but answered in a deep, gravelly voice. "You must be the boys from Memphis."

Burkes smiled, "I'm glad you were expecting me—us!"

"Manny said you'd be here early. You're lucky. I don't usually come in this early. You could have been waiting another couple of hours."

John accepted the elderly sheriff's method of establishing his authority with grace. "I'm glad it all worked out," Burkes said.

Inside, the sheriff led the two back to the interrogation room. "You can use this," McMasters explained. "Now, I kinda need to know just how long you expect to be 'round here. People get jumpy sometimes when they're being questioned by outsiders about a bad subject."

"I take it you consider Ben Seals a bad subject?" Burkes asked.

"That's exactly what I mean. In fact, I guess you may as well know, I wouldn't be in favor of this at all if the D.A. hadn't ordered it."

"Really?" Burkes acted surprised. "Why's that?"

"Because I hear this is part of an investigation on the premise that Ben Seals might not have killed his wife."

Burkes grinned. "Why, Sheriff, you act as if you know something we don't. If I didn't know better, I'd swear that you've already convicted a man who hasn't even been arrested yet. We just want to learn more about him so we can find him."

"He's guilty. You can bet the farm on that."

"He probably is, but he says he was framed. We wouldn't be doing our job if we didn't check out every angle, including his side of the story as well, now would we?"

The sheriff mumbled something incoherently as he entered the conference room ahead of the two who remained in the hallway.

"Well, I don't see what that has to do with my boys down here. Unless he said something about us."

That was what Burkes had been waiting to hear. All the while he was afraid that somebody, such as Terry Mills, may have slipped up and told McMasters of Ben's accusations. McMasters obviously didn't know what had been said and was fishing out of fear.

"I don't see where it's anybody's business," Marc said.

Burkes interrupted before he could elaborate. "Marc, we need to get set up before the deputies get here."

Burkes could see the tension coming back into Marc's face. He decided to smooth it over a little. "I mean, don't you think so, Marc?"

Marc didn't argue. He didn't even speak.

Gene headed for the door.

"Oh, Sheriff," Burkes stopped him at the door, "what makes you so sure Seals killed his wife?"

"He was bad news!" McMasters exclaimed. "Doing everything

on the side to make a fast buck. I think he was jealous of the money his wife had come from and wanted to get as much as he could as quickly as he could. He resented her for it."

"You think so?"

"I know so. He used to beat her all the time."

"Who told you that?"

"She did."

"Oh," Burkes was caught offguard.

Marc took a quick look over his shoulder at the sheriff. Was the sheriff about to confess to having an affair with her?

"Yeah," McMasters said, "she called down here several times wanting me to arrest him. I always smoothed things over between them."

"Really?" Burkes muttered. "That's interesting."

"Nah. Any sheriff or police chief worth his salt would do the same thing. You look out for your people. I run a real tight, close-knit house here. Seals never fit in. He was bad from the getgo. I gave him a job because he didn't have any family. I felt sorry for him. That was a mistake."

Mcmasters was still sadly shaking his head as he left the room.

Burkes and Marc set themselves up to begin the questioning of the deputies. While they were exchanging notes, Marc brought up McMasters. "I think he's lying."

"You mean the sheriff?" Burkes grinned.

"Yeah," Marc nodded.

"Yep. Like a dog."

Marc got excited. "Then you think we're on the right track?"

"I don't know what we're on, but we're definitely onto something...a monkey in the wrench...a fly in the soup...something."

"What are we gonna do if we think Seals' story is legit? There's a little problem of legality when it comes to a detective and an assistant D.A. testifying that we believe a suspect is innocent."

"Just keep your fingers crossed," Burkes said. "Something may shake loose."

During the night, Ben watched as the truck stop business slowed. He bound and gagged Tawana and slipped on the baseball cap. He had quietly and quickly eased back through the establishment to use their facilities and pick up a few snacks without ever making eye contact as he paid. The two ate in the rear of the van and slept the rest of the night.

The morning sunlight awoke the unlikely couple. Ben wasted no time getting on the road. The sleep had cleared his head. He was now convinced that B.J. and McMasters were in cahoots with someone on Memphis P.D. It all added up. Michael Rose's death, Pookie's untimely death, Michael Rose's murderer's death. The possibility that someone copied his condo key. Who would be the best cops to buy if you were trafficking dope? A narcotics task force. That's why Burkes didn't want him. He wanted to hand-pick somebody. It was like the Green County Sheriff's Department all over again. He steered the van downtown and found a parking space across the street from the precinct where he was still on payroll.

"Man, you crazy?" Tawana yelled. "There's cops everywhere!"

"I figured you'd want some cops to find you—to save you," he said.

"Man, they ain't gonna arrest you. They gonna shoot you. I don't want to be close to you when the caps start flying."

"Thanks, I appreciate the morale support."

"What are you doing here anyway?"

"Looking for somebody. He'll be here sooner or later."

Ben hopped out to put a quarter in the parking meter. He kept a close eye out for a traffic cop afoot who might be marking tires. Across the street in the parking lot a constant stream of people went in and out of the precinct. Through the cyclone fence, he could see several cars that resembled Burkes', but no sign of the detective.

Burkes and Marc Johnson had just gathered their notes and gotten their coffee when the sheriff sent in Deputy Johnny Greer, the first deputy to work that morning.

"The sheriff said you wanted to see me," Greer said.

"Come right on in," Burkes welcomed him.

"Please sit," Marc said.

The short deputy took a seat on the vacant side of the table. Burkes sat at one end while Marc sat across from the deputy.

"Why am I here? I want to know," Greer asked.

"We just want—" Burkes was cut off by a black man in civilian clothes entering the room. The sheriff trailed him.

"This is Officer Burse," the sheriff explained. "He's off duty today. I told him to come in and talk with you people. I didn't want you to think we were trying to hide anything."

"No, no, Sheriff," Burkes said as the sheriff was closing the door on his way out. Burkes sighed. This was a slick maneuver...to interrupt things to make it tougher on them...maybe to give Greer a chance to recompose himself if they had asked a tough question right off the bat.

"Officer Burse, is it?" Burkes asked.

"Mike Burse." The officer answered.

"My name is Burkes, John Burkes. We want to get your input, but we want to talk to everybody, one on one. If you don't mind, how about if we get to you next?"

"Well, I was going over to one of the casinos today. You know how long this will take?" Burse replied.

"Not long," Marc assured him. "If you could just wait outside, please. We'll be right with you."

He left, and the two refocused their attention on Johnny Greer.

Marc got up and locked the door. "Just so we don't have any more interruptions," he said.

"Officer Greer, what we're interested in knowing is whether or not Ben Seals ever discussed his wife at work." Burkes began.

"Nah, not at all. He was too caught up in his own thangs."

"Like what?"

"Oh, you know."

"No," Burkes said, "actually, we don't."

Marc backed Burkes up. "That's kinda why we wanted to talk to you. We heard you two were close," Marc lied as he fished around.

"I wouldn't say that," Greer replied.

"Well...I shouldn't say...close," Marc backtracked, realizing he was casting too deep. "What I meant or what I should have said was that we've been told that you two had high regard for each other, mutual respect," he lied again.

"Yeah, I would say so, but he never talked about his wife."

"What can you tell us about his wife?"

"Not much. She was pretty. Stayed at home all the time. She needed a good man, I think. Not somebody like Seals, who was worried about himself. But she was in love with him, so that's the way it goes sometimes."

"How do you know this?" Marc asked. "I mean, if Seals never

talked about her."

"He was a loser. I mean, I don't know. What I do know is mostly just bullshit rumors, I guess. You know how small towns are. I really don't know much at all. Just what I hear, which is the same as everybody else, I guess."

"I take it you didn't like Ben?" Burkes asked.

"He was okay as far as company, but he was a dirty cop. Everybody knew that. You know how things go on the force, though. You look out for one another."

"Yeah," Burkes agreed.

"You know he was dirty?" Marc asked.

"Yeah. I never saw what he did because he was slick. But word gets around. He was bad. You can count on it. Bad to the bone."

"Marc, that's all I have for Officer Greer. How about you?"

Johnny Greer got up and strolled to the door before being cut off by Burkes. "Oh, just one more thing, Officer."

"Yeah?"

"It's been rumored that Seals' wife was sleeping with another guy in the sheriff's department. You wouldn't happen to know who that might be, would you?"

"Hell, no. I hadn't even heard that."

"Thanks." Marc cut him short.

Greer's voice showed concern for the first time. "Who was supposed to be sleeping with her?"

"We don't know," Burkes answered.

"Oh, come on," Greer badgered them, "you heard something. I won't tell anyone. What's the scoop?"

"Thank you for your time," Marc answered.

Greer left the room, and the two smiled at one another. Quickly, Marc scribbled one word on a sheet of paper and passed it to Burkes. "Bingo," the note said. Burkes nodded in agreement. Marc scribbled again, "They're trying to hard to be cautious. They're tripping all over themselves." As Burkes again nodded his agreement, the door opened and Michael Burse entered again.

"The sheriff sent me on in."

Burkes scribbled a note back to Marc: "McMasters is trying to rush us. If you want to tell me something, just start writing. I'll slowly ask questions while you write."

Marc nodded.

"What have you gentlemen got on your minds?" the deputy asked as he seated himself and crossed his legs. He didn't even look at them as he crushed a pistachio nut and popped it into his mouth.

"Let's try to make this quick.... This is my day off."

Marc looked at Burkes. "I think I'm gonna let you handle this one."

Burkes nodded in agreement. "I just have one question. Do you think Ben Seals could have killed his own wife?"

"Damn right!" came the instant reply. "He was bad. There are good cops, bad cops, and then those that just straddle the fence. He was a bad cop...no two ways about it.... He was bad...bad to the bone."

Marc and Burkes again exchanged glances. This was beginning to sound like a broken record: Bad, bad to the bone. Like actors reading from the same script.

"Thank you. That's all I have," John said.

"Me too, " Marc acknowledged.

"What? You got me out of bed for something you could have called and asked me. Man, I oughta kick somebody's ass."

"There's the door," Burkes said without looking up from his notes.

The deputy looked at Marc, who was taking his own notes, then turned on his heel and left the room.

Before Marc could hand Burkes a note, the sheriff came bursting through the door.

"What in the hell do you think you're doing?"

"I'm sorry, Sheriff," Burkes said calmly. "Did we do something wrong?"

"Well, I don't know, but I've got a narcotics officer who's been on duty for a week straight. I finally get him a day off, and he has to come all the way up here to answer one damn question.... You tell me!"

"He told us it was his day off and he was in a hurry, so we cut it short. I'm sorry, Sheriff," Burkes said.

"Well, see that it goes better from here on out. Another thing, I told you Seals was a bad cop. You're asking everybody that. Do you think I'm lying?"

"Of course not!" Burkes exclaimed.

"Of course not!" Marc echoed.

"If you're working with the feds, I have a right to know. I may want legal counsel for my men."

Marc and Burkes exchanged glances.

"Heavens, no!" Marc said.

"Sheriff, we didn't mean any harm or to scare anyone. We're just asking routine questions—" Burkes was cut off by the sheriff.

"We're not scared. I was told you were trying to establish where Ben Seals might hang out!"

"We are," Burkes stalled.

"We've got to establish whether or not he may be suicidal first," Marc jumped in. "We need a profile of him. There are certain possibilities for him if he's suicidal and others if he's not."

The sheriff nodded as though that made sense to him. "I'll send the next one in. He just got here," he said in a more subdued voice as he left the room.

Burkes gave Marc a high-five and mouthed the word "Great!"

Marc swelled with pride.

The door swung open and a tall, lanky young man in a deputy's uniform appeared. His name was Marion Conner. He was as innocent and wholesome looking as a park ranger in a Lassie movie and appeared to be no more than twenty-eight. He shook hands with Marc and Burkes while holding his hat in his left hand. He took a seat and waited on the two to begin the questioning.

"Deputy Conner," Marc began.

"Yes?" the young deputy was listening intently.

"Ben Seals has escaped justice for the moment, as you well know. How well acquainted were you with Seals?'

"Oh, as well as anyone, I guess."

"Then it has to be your opinion that Ben Seals was a bad cop."

He shrugged, "I guess."

Burkes thought for a moment before continuing. "You guess? You guess he was a bad cop?"

The deputy just sat there, confused by their reaction, wondering if he had said something wrong.

They both continued looking at him until he finally spoke again. "Well...he was...I hear he was."

"But you don't really know for sure?" Marc put words into his mouth. "You never saw, or witnessed or heard him confess to doing anything illegal or unethical."

"Well...no."

"What about when you arrested him?" Burkes asked. "The police report says you were present when he was arrested."

"Yeah," the deputy answered quickly. "I was there and he did have a load of dope in his car that shouldn't have been there."

"You forgot about that just a minute ago, did you?" Burkes' tone had harshened.

"Well, no, of course not. I thought you meant other than that time. Everybody knows about that time," Conner justified himself.

"No," Marc said, "we just want to know if you think Seals was a bad cop. You implied that you were not entirely sure. So we'd like to know what would lead you to not be sure."

"Well, I mean, that's the only time I ever saw—"

Burkes cut him off. "Nevertheless, you were there. You assisted in arresting Seals that day. Now, did you people arrest him for committing a crime against the state of Mississippi?"

"Yes."

"Did you agree with the decision to arrest Ben Seals?"

"Yes."

"Then, it is justifiable to assume that you think Ben Seals was and is a bad cop. Right?"

Silence. Then: "Y-yes."

"Are you sure?" Marc asked.

"Sure."

Marc looked at Burkes, then back to the deputy. "And this assumption is based upon the arrest of Ben Seals for which you were present, and nothing else."

More silence. "Yeah...well...there were rumors."

"Did you believe them?"

"I don't know."

Burkes studied the deputy for a moment. "Do you enjoy your job?"

"Sure. Why? You got something open in Memphis?"

Burkes laughed. "Well, there's always something open. You can always apply."

"Well, when you do that, word gets around. You gave Seals a job overnight. Why not let me take his place?"

The less than subtle request caught Marc and Burkes completely offguard.

"Thank you for your time," Burkes said. "Do you have anything else, Marc?"

Marc shook his head.

"Is there something you would like to tell us?" John asked.

"No," Conner answered. He stood to leave. "Don't forget me if you need another hired gun up your way."

When he was comfortably outside, the two scribbled notes to one another. Marc to Burkes, "Do you think he's involved?"

Burkes' reply: "He's got to be—probably wants out and is scared."

When the door opened again, Mitch Williams appeared. He swaggered into the room and took a seat without being asked.

Marc stood to reach across the table and shake hands.

"Let's get on with it." Williams cut Marc's greeting short.

"For starters, let's talk about the day you arrested Ben Seals," Burkes said.

"I didn't arrest the guy."

"But you were there?" Burkes asked.

"Yeah. So what? The sheriff arrested the guy."

Burkes nodded. "Yeah, that's what we understand. We also understand that he came to you for help. That he thought he was in some kind of conflict with the sheriff and he turned to you, and then you turned him in."

"Bullshit, that's a lie!" Mitch shouted. He pushed his curly hair back on his forehead in a rage. "I was at Carter's Grocery, shootin' pool, and he showed up. He was askin' me to help him get rid of some stuff he had 'cause the sheriff was lookin' for him. I said 'What kinda stuff?' And he said it was 'kinda illegal,' so I said 'No way. I don't want any part of it at all.' "

"Wow! That's completely, totally different from the way Ben tells it," Burkes said.

"Well, what do you expect from a con on the run?" Mitch asked.

"Well, maybe so," Burkes grumbled.

"Maybe, my ass! That's what happened. Who you gonna believe...me or a guy who's been charged twice in the same week?

"Any idea why he would come to you and open up about something like that?" Burkes asked. "You two must have been close."

"No way!" Mitch emphatically insisted. "I guess because he was desperate. Desperate criminals do desperate things."

Burkes nodded in agreement as Marc handed him a note that read "Go for the kill."

Burkes looked Mitch square in the face. "Were you having sexual relations with Julie Seals?"

"Wha-at? I oughta kick your ass!"

"I'm sorry, but it's something we have to ask," Burkes said. "You see, some of the other deputies said the sheriff was having intercourse with her on a regular basis and that you may have been as well. Was it just the sheriff?"

Mitch was unable to answer as Gene McMasters burst through the door. "That's it, dammit! I've heard enough!"

"Why, Sheriff," Marc broke in, "were you eavesdropping?"

"Well...you can hear through...the damn door."

"You were listening?" Burkes asked.

"Boy, don't you worry about me! I'm telling you...this interview is over...finished! You tell that damn D.A. if he wants anything else he'll need a court order. This is bullshit, and I ain't gonna stand for it."

"But, Sheriff—" Marc tried to interrupt, grinning from ear to ear.

"Out! Both of ya, out! Carry yo' Yankee asses back to Memphis!"

As Burkes and Marc passed through the sheriff's office to leave, they ran into the deputies they had interviewed, as well as other deputies who had been waiting for an interview. They were all huddled on the sidewalk, smoking and talking. Burkes couldn't resist one parting shot: "We'll see you soon."

The two started across the parking lot. Burkes looked back at the deputies standing on the sidewalk. "They seem to be a real close-knit group, but I believe they're under a great deal of strain at the moment, thanks to us," he observed.

Marc agreed. "But how do we get them to crack?"

Burkes shook his head. "I doubt we can. The main thing is that we know, or rather we have reason to believe, that Seals may have been telling the truth. Maybe if nothing else, we can keep an innocent man from going to jail."

"Yeah," Marc agreed. "But I sure would like to bring these guys down."

They strolled toward their car. Burkes stopped momentarily to stare into McMasters' car parked on the edge of the lot. "What is it?" Marc called back to the seasoned detective while opening the door to their own car.

"Nothing," Burkes said glancing over his shoulder to acknowledge that he had an audience. "Just a thought I had! Let's go."

Chapter 18

Ben was still trying to get Tawana to shut up. She had been running her mouth for an hour now, and he was fed up. He was tired, hungry and confused, and this illiterate street girl was about to drive him crazy. He wondered if she got it from Pookie or he got it from her.

"I can't believe you sittin' right here up under the damn po-lice station. You gonna get shot, and I'm gonna get hit by a stray bullet, and then I'm gonna be pissed. You don't want to be around me when I gets pissed, no sir. You ain't seen pissed 'til I get pissed. I get so mad I could kick even Pookie Jones—God rest his soul—and you know he was one bad dude!"

"Will you please shut the hell up?" Ben screamed. "You know I figured this is where you would want to be more than anywhere else, right up under the cops. If somebody had kidnapped me, that's where I would want to be," Ben reasoned with her.

"You call this kidnapping? This ain't kidnapping. I been done a lot worse than this before. Kidnappin' is when they take you and tie you up for a couple of days and make you have sex with about five or six old men so they can soak them for cash, then they don't give you but a couple hundred bucks."

"Oh, you make it sound as if more money would make it okay," Ben laughed.

"Well, for a thousand a day I'll do all of em', unless they all white, then half of that will do. I love white men." She winked at

Ben. He shook his head and turned back around to once again ignore her. "Besides, they not gonna help me," she continued. "If they do find you they just gonna shoot this damn ole piece of van about five hundred times, and we'll both be worm food."

Ben gave her a searing look of disapproval, and snarled, "Will you shut up? You are so stupid!"

"You know it's true. They gonna shoot you, Ben Seals. You good as dead already. You ain't gotta take me down with you."

"Just shut up!" He pointed his finger in her face. "Just shut the hell up. I'm not gonna tell you again!" She had gotten to him. The fatigue, the stress, all of it was taking its toll on him. He feared he could not go much longer. He had to hold out long enough to exact his revenge against the perpetrators.

"Marc, I had a thought," Burkes said as the sedan rolled down Grand Avenue.

"Just one?" Marc laughed.

"A big one," Burkes said. "What do you think about driving into Vicksburg?"

"I thought we were going to the newspaper office."

"Vicksburg is only twenty minutes away. It won't take long."

"What about researching old newspaper clippings of the sheriff's department."

"The newspaper will be there. I've got a better idea. I noticed McMasters had a cellular phone in his car. I was thinking we might go to Delta Cellular in Vicksburg and look at his phone records. That's who his service was with, I noticed."

Marc started to laugh. "How do you propose we get those records? 'Hi! I'm Detective Burkes and this is Deputy D.A. Johnson. We're from Memphis and would like to see the phone records of Green County Sheriff Gene McMasters." Marc bellowed a loud laugh.

"Sure, why not?"

Marc continued to laugh before realizing Burkes was serious.

"You're kidding. They'll never let you touch those without a warrant and you'll never get that. We have trouble getting BellSouth records sometimes. You'll never get the cellular records of a sheriff. No judge would give that on what we've got. They'd laugh at us."

"I didn't plan to get a warrant. I was just going to ask for them."

"Ha, you are nuts. Why don't we just go down to the river and drop a hook in the water. Our chances are just as good.

Twenty-five minutes later the sedan parked in front of Delta Cellular Communications in Vicksburg, Mississippi.

"I can't believe we're doing this," Marc whined as they climbed the concrete steps to the building.

"Just be quiet and let me handle this," Burkes ordered the young assistant.

Marc gave the seasoned detective a scowling look but said nothing.

"Hi, I'm John Burkes, Memphis P.D. This is Marc Johnson, Shelby County District Attorney's office."

The young redhead behind the desk closed her fingernail polish. "Can I help you?" she asked, visibly irritated.

"We need to get some phone records."

"I'm sorry, we don't release any phone records, sir. Uh, that's just something—"

"Could I speak with your supervisor?" Burkes asked.

"Sir, that's something we don't do—I'm sorry."

Marc frowned at Burkes.

"Miss, if you could get your supervisor?"

"I'm sorry. He's on the phone. Would you like to wait? But I can tell you, you're wasting—"

"Get him."

"Excuse me! Are you ordering me?"

"You better believe I am."

"Sir, I think you should leave—"

"Listen lady, I've got a federal warrant." John produced a sheet of paper. "It gives me the right to search and seize anything, and I mean anything, in this building that I deem is evidence."

Marc's eyes were bulging from his head.

"So if you want a place to work, I suggest you get your supervisor before I close this place down."

Without saying a word, she stood and left the room with fear in her eyes.

Marc muffled his scream with a whisper. "What the hell is this? You didn't say we had a warrant—"

"Shut up! Read the judge's signature." John pushed the warrant toward him.

"It's not signed. This is an application. It's just a piece of paper."

"Just leave it to me." Burkes took the paper, seeing the girl walking up the hallway followed by a man.

"Oh my God," Marc mumbled under his breath. "I can't believe it. We're going to jail. We're going to jail. I know it. We're going to jail."

"Shut up!" Burkes whispered back.

"This is Mr. Vernon, our director."

"Good morning, I'm William Vernon." The geek in his mid-fifties combed the few strands of hair on his balding head with his hands.

There were no handshakes. Burkes merely handed the warrant application to the man. The bold heading on the paper stood out: Fifth District Federal Court Application for Warrant.

All the small writing absorbed William Vernon's attention.

Burkes banked on the layman not realizing the document was worthless.

"Mr. Vernon, we want to make this as easy as possible. We have every intention of seeing the cellular phone records for Sheriff Gene McMasters of Green County. The simplest way to accomplish this would be for you to just give us a printout on him for, say, the last three months."

The slim middle-aged executive perused the statement while sweat beads popped onto Marc's forehead.

"Well, I don't see where I have a lot of choice, do I?"

Marc sighed relief.

Burkes shrugged his shoulders. "That's up to you."

William Vernon left the room to get the printouts. There was an awkwardness as the two Memphians remained in the lobby with the secretary.

Marc's nerves were wearing thin. He moaned under his breath but loud enough for Burkes to hear, "I can't believe this. We're going to jail. I'm gonna be disbarred."

Will you shut up?" Burkes whispered back.

Marc leaned his head back and spoke to the ceiling, "I'll be brought up on ethics charges, fired, and be lucky if I'm not sent to the pen."

"Just shut up," Burkes whispered in a stronger voice. "You haven't done anything wrong. I take all responsibility."

Vernon returned to the lobby with the printouts. He gave Burkes the folded computer paper amidst a disapproving glare from Marc.

"I wouldn't do it if I were you," the secretary mumbled.

"Cindy, they have a court order. You can't disobey a court order. That's contempt," Vernon informed her.

"Thank you, sir," John said, reaching for the warrant application still in Vernon's hand. "This has to be returned to the judge. If you would just initial it on the top, we can be out of your way."

Marc patted his forehead with a handkerchief. "I can't believe this crap," he mumbled as Vernon initialed the paper.

Burkes gave him a scolding look and grabbed the paper. "Thank you, Mr. Vernon. I would like to remind you that this is official business of federal investigators. You will be in violation of a number of federal laws, including obstructing justice, if you discuss this matter with anyone, especially Sheriff McMasters or his attorney without approval from the fifth circuit court. Is that understood?"

Burkes had rattled the instructions off so fast it would be hard for anyone to guess he was embellishing. Except for Marc, who was now on the verge of fainting from nerves alone.

"Oh my God," he mumbled to the floor.

"Let's go, Mr. Johnson," Burkes ordered, turning for the door.

Somehow Marc's weak knees carried him to the car, where he fumbled with his keys.

"What's wrong with you?" Burkes asked from the other side of the sedan.

"What's wrong with me?" Marc asked, as he found the door key and sat down inside the hot interior. He unlocked Burkes' door and gathered his wits as Burkes sat beside him thumbing through the printouts. "What's wrong with me?"

"Yeah," Burkes said, without looking up from the computer sheets.

"Well, let's see," Marc said. "Maybe it was the fake warrant. No, no, I think it was impersonating federal agents."

"We didn't impersonate anybody!"

"You told them they would be violating a federal court order if they told anybody. I would say that would make us officers of a federal court if that's who we're supposed to be working for."

"Oh that. Well, maybe so." Burkes said, still never looking at Marc.

Marc shook his head as if he still could not believe what had just transpired. "Son-of-a-bitch! I can't believe it! Damn!"

"What is it now?" Burkes asked without looking up.

"What do you mean, what now? We just broke the law!" Marc screamed.

"Oh you're still on that," Burkes said, returning his eyes to the printout.

"Yeah…I'm still on that."

Burkes picked up the cell phone and dialed a number on the printout.

"Are you listening? Do you realize how much trouble we could get in for this?"

Burkes ignored him as the phone rang.

"If anybody ever finds out we did this…" Marc shook his head thinking about the consequences.

Burkes pressed the end button to cease the cellular transmission.

Marc rattled on as Burkes sat motionless with a blank stare. He said nothing.

Marc leaned toward him. "Well. What is it?"

Burkes looked at him but still said nothing.

"What is it?" Marc's voice began to break. The stress was now taking its toll on him .

Burkes just shook his head. "Look." He pointed to a number on the phone record. The prefix was 901.

"Memphis," Marc noted. "You think it's B.J. White's number?"

Burkes pressed the send button on the phone to redial the number. "You see for yourself. He called this number about a dozen times in just the last two months before he arrested Ben Seals, and that's just from his cellular. He may have called more from other phones."

Marc listened as the phone rang on the other end. The second ring produced a response. "Seals and Barrins, attorneys at law."

Marc's jaw dropped open. His eyes widened and he searched to find the end button to kill the call. "What the hell? I don't…I don't understand."

Burkes sat stunned. "I can't believe he was stupid enough to use his car phone. He must have felt they were invincible."

"You don't think Randy Seals and Gene McMasters are working together?"

"What else would you think?" Burkes asked. "It would explain a lot. Like how somebody broke into that condo, killed Julie Seals, locked Randy and his mom in their rooms, and never showed signs of entry or exit."

"Unbelievable!" Marc gasped.

"Randy and Michael Rose were best friends right up until Michael was murdered. In fact Randy sat beside Michael's mother at the funeral. I'll bet he picked Michael for information about task force operations. When Michael was killed, he lobbied his ass off to get Ben the job. He used all his influence with the commissioner and the mayor to get Ben on the narc team when there were other jobs in the P.D. he would have been better suited for. I wouldn't be surprised if B.J. and his boys didn't have pictures of my whole damn team hung up in hideouts for them to memorize."

"This is too much." Marc felt goose bumps all over.

Burkes looked at his young protege. "Now you tell me. Isn't it worth bending the law a little bit to keep an innocent man out of the gas chamber."

Marc didn't answer.

The ride back to Memphis was consumed by speculation on who all might be involved in what was turning out to be a major interstate drug ring. The phone calls to the other Memphis numbers were answered by the Seals' housekeeper and a secretary at Seals Trucking Company. All the interstate calls were to Randy Seals. Not even one call to B.J. or to a New Orleans connection. Burkes deduced that McMasters was working directly with Randy Seals as his mediator in the whole operation.

Marc called his boss to notify him that they were returning with extraordinary news. He agreed to meet them at the precinct where Burkes would pick up his car. No one could ever have guessed that Ben Seals was only yards away from the precinct awaiting Burkes' return.

The sedan rolled into the parking lot a few minutes past twelve. Burkes pulled up to Bob Taylor, who was standing there waiting for them.

"Gentlemen, I hope this is good," he said. "I've got high hopes resting on the two of you."

Marc was eager to look good in front of his boss. "I think you'll be pleased, sir." He handed Taylor the computer printout.

"What's this?"

"It suggests that Sheriff McMasters may have been involved in some extracurricular activity with someone in Memphis," Marc said.

"Ben Seals' story about the drug ring and there being a Memphis connection may have been right on the money."

"These are telephone records," Taylor observed. "How the hell did you get your hands on these without a warrant?"

Marc looked to Burkes to bail him out.

"I got them," Burkes spoke up while lighting a cigarette as if he didn't care whether Taylor liked it or not. "Don't ask how. You really don't want to know."

Marc cringed at the thought of what might be next.

"John!" Taylor barked, still looking at the phone records. He shook his head.

Marc spoke up quickly. "Sir, I know—"

"That's why I didn't stop you from going," Taylor interrupted. He gave John a wicked smile. "I knew it would take more than ordinary methods to retrieve this kind of information. Good work. I really appreciate it."

Marc nearly choked on his own saliva. Burkes merely lit a cigarette and nodded as if it was no big deal.

"Now suppose you two tell me what this means, because I see a bunch of calls you've highlighted to Memphis, but that could be anything, a girlfriend, accountant, anything."

Marc saw a chance to get back into the conversation. "They're all to Randy Seals," he said.

"What did you say?" Taylor asked as if he were hearing impaired.

"I thought you would like that," Burkes said. "Any defense attorney getting in trouble pleases a D.A. Especially a smartass like Randy Seals."

"You did say that, didn't you?" Taylor asked again, still dumbfounded.

Marc and Burkes nodded agreement.

"You mean to tell me that all these calls are to Randy Seals?"

"Yep," Marc boasted. "At one place or another. His office, home, trucking company. You can imagine what McMasters' home or office phone records might reveal."

"I figure they never thought they would be suspected, until Ben caught McMasters with his wife. That's why they were so bold," Burkes speculated. "You'll notice the calls seemed to stop recently. They're so nervous now they're lying low."

"You know this doesn't prove anything," Taylor said. "We don't know what was said in those phone calls. We don't know that he spoke directly to Randy. We don't even know that he made the calls himself."

"It may not prove Randy's guilt," Burkes said, "but it sure casts doubt as to Ben's guilt."

Taylor agreed.

"We need to move fast on this," Burkes said. "First I've got to catch my wife while she's at home on her lunch break and see if I'm still married. I never got a chance to tell her I was leaving town last night until I was already gone."

"I'm sure she'll forgive you," Taylor said.

"She did the first twenty times it happened," Burkes said. "The last twenty haven't been as good."

"Let's meet at my office around two," Taylor suggested.

"Great. That'll give me plenty of time," Burkes said. "Why don't you go ahead and call Terry Mills over at Homicide. I'm sure he'd rather find out this new info from the D.A. than from me."

Taylor frowned, then gave Marc a quick glance. Burkes picked up on the telepathy.

"You sons-of-bitches," Burkes scolded the two. "You're not gonna go to Homicide."

No one answered his accusations.

"You're going to keep it all in house. Do your own little investigation. Why? Since there'll be big players involved? That's good!" He shook his head in disgust. "That ought to put you in the mayor's chair for sure."

He looked at Marc. "You knew all along, didn't you?"

Marc didn't answer.

"You two lawyers want me to knowingly withhold evidence that could change the entire course of the investigation."

Marc defended his boss. "We don't know who might be involved. Even if you were asked to conceal evidence, I don't see what's so different from that and using a fake warrant."

"You're asking me to withhold evidence from a fellow police officer. One of my comrades."

"I thought you and Terry Mills hated each other." Taylor said sheepishly.

"We do," Burkes answered. "That's the only reason I'll go along with this."

Marc and the D.A. laughed in relief.

Burkes reached for the computer printouts Taylor still held. "I think I'll take these with me. I'd hate for them to make their way to Internal Affairs and me have to explain their origin."

Burkes got in his car and left, unaware that Ben had watched his every move from the back street of the precinct and was now following him onto Poplar Avenue.

Chapter 19

Poplar was especially clogged during the noon hour. Burkes weaved in and out of the busy lanes on his way home to his wife. He honked at a few people as he hurried along and came close to reaching under the seat for his blue light to plug in the cigarette lighter.

Ben stayed as close as the van would let him. Its immobility in the thick traffic combined with Tawana's whining had him completely unnerved. He had her bound to the back of the passenger's seat with her legs tucked under her to keep her immobile, but that had not shut her mouth. He made a mental note to gag the babbling girl before he got out of the van.

Swerving from lane to lane Ben tried desperately to keep up with Burkes, who unknowingly continued to put distance between the two.

Burkes reached a turnoff into a secluded residential area just off Poplar. Ben found himself in the wrong lane of traffic to turn off. He came to a complete stop in the middle of the road, backing traffic up. The nose of the van rested at an angle into the next lane.

It seemed everyone sat down on their horns to let him know of their disapproval. He was determined not to move until someone let him over in the lane so he could make the same turnoff as Burkes. Thoughts of being pulled over by a traffic cop raced through his mind as he caught a break and seized the opportunity to get over in the far right lane. He kicked the accelerator and raced down the street looking for Burkes.

He spotted the cop getting out of his car. A woman Ben assumed to be his wife stood with her arms folded under the garage. Ben sped by and made a U-turn in the cul de sac while trying to look back up the street to see if he was being watched. He watched as Burkes got out of his car and slowly waltzed up the drive. It looked to Ben as if Burkes was pleading with his wife about something.

Ben drove past the house again and parked the van on the curb three houses up from Burkes'. Sifting through a toolbox lying in the back of the van, he found a roll of black electrical tape. He would make a gag for Tawana using it and his handkerchief. It wasn't exactly what he was hoping to find. The van was used by maintenance workers at Seals Trucking. He thought there might be some heavier tape in the box but found only the thin tape. He compensated by wrapping the tape around the girl's head and handkerchief-filled mouth a number of times. When he was confident she couldn't cry for help, he returned his attention to Burkes.

Out of the rear window, he could see Burkes' wife leaving in her car with Burkes still trying to talk to her as she rolled her window up. He watched the detective wander almost aimlessly back up to the house as his wife left the neighborhood. Ben donned his baseball cap once again. He then paused to make sure Tawana was secure before quietly climbing out of the van.

Strolling briskly yet casually up the street, he could see that Burkes had closed only the screen door to the garage. The wood door remained open. He anticipated Burkes would soon be leaving again. Now was the time to make his move. His heart throbbed with fear and anticipation. Under the garage he drew the Beretta, pausing to lean against the brick wall to give the lump in his throat a chance to subside. Ten seconds later, the lump was bigger than ever. He must strike now! Creeping up to the screen door, he stopped to peer inside. Nothing. Burkes must be in the back of the house, he deduced.

"Come here!"

Ben crouched in the corner at the sound of Burkes' voice. The sweat from fear and the summer heat now drenched Ben's shirt. He could hear Burkes again. The noise sounded as though it was coming from behind the house. Ben peered through the screen again. This time he saw Burkes through the dining room window.

There he stood in a dog pen behind the house feeding some mutt.

The old screen door produced minor squeaks as Ben eased it shut behind him. Burkes' attention had not yet turned from the dog. Ben stepped lightly through the kitchen into the den. The back door stood open with the screen closed. He hid at the side of the door frame with his back against a brick fireplace. His ears strained to listen as Burkes closed the cyclone gate to the pen. Only seconds now separated the two.

Ben's head throbbed. His heart pulsated faster and faster. Enough time had passed. There was no Burkes. He feared looking around the corner. He tried to squat, but his nerves kept his body stiff. He could smell smoke from a cigarette.

Burkes must be just around the corner. He couldn't take it anymore. He had to make a move. Then Burkes stepped through the doorway.

Thwack!

The Beretta caught Burkes' head just behind the temple, knocking him staggering and falling into the kitchen. He stumbled sideways and twisted as he fell onto the hardwood floor. Ben followed and positioned himself over him as he hit the floor. Burkes grabbed his head and writhed in pain as Ben reached for his weapon, then his handcuffs on the other side of the holster. He threw Burkes' gun onto a countertop and grabbed him by the hands. Holding the Beretta in one hand and the handcuffs in the other, Ben managed to drag the bewildered detective three feet to the refrigerator. There he cuffed his hands together through the door handle.

Nearly a minute passed before Burkes' daze finally wore off enough to make out Ben's face.

"Jesus!" He tried to grab his head only to be hindered by the cuffs. "You've got a strange way of turning yourself in."

"I'm glad to see you taking this so well," Ben said. "Most men in this situation would be afraid for their very lives and rightfully so," he added without smiling.

"Any particular reason why you would choose to compound your problems by assaulting a police officer?" Burkes asked.

Ben started to laugh hysterically. "That's funny! That was good!
"

"Maybe you should clue me in on the joke," Burkes said.

The words had barely left Burkes' mouth when Ben jammed the barrel into his jaw. Ben's face turned blood red, his tone was that of a crazed man. "I have a warrant out against me for murder. Do you really think I give a damn whether or not I assault you or anybody else?"

"You're not like this," John muttered with the tip of the Beretta indenting his jaw. "They've gotten to you. You're not like this."

Thwack! The Beretta struck the side of Burkes' head again.

Ben's anger swelled as he thought of what this dirty cop represented. Everything that had happened to him was a result of Burkes and people like him. People the public trusted. Lowlife scumbags.

Burkes regained his composure through the pain. "What have they done to you? You're not like this, Ben. This is not you."

"Enough! Enough of your psychobabble! Just shut up!"

"Does the truth hurt?"

Thwack!

"Jesus!" screamed the detective. "I wish you would quit doing that."

Ben jerked the cop's head around to face him. The swelling on the side of Burkes' head was starting to show. "You know, I would think that if you really thought I killed my wife you would be a little more cautious about what you say. Hell, you might even try to get along with me. Wouldn't that be grand?" He smiled a crazy smile that signaled he was becoming more deranged by the second.

"I don't think you killed your wife."

There was silence as the two stared at each other.

Ben summed up the situation and decided Burkes would say or do anything at this point. Certainly, he would lie to save his own skin. "You make me sick," he said.

Thwack! This time to the other side of the face.

"I really wish you wouldn't do that." Burkes gritted his teeth and suffered the pain.

"You make me want to puke." Ben glared at his captive ."You tell me where I can find B.J."

"B.J.?"

"Where is he?"

The blows had caused a ringing in Burkes' ears. He wasn't sure he was hearing the question right. "You want to find B.J.? That's why you came here?"

"Don't play stupid with me," Ben warned the senior detective.

"How long did you think it would be before somebody figured it all out?"

"Figured out what?"

"I know you're into it up to your dirty little ears."

"You've got to be kidding," Burkes whispered, completely stunned. "You think I'm in it with B.J. My God, man. What have they done to you?"

"It's not hard to figure out," Ben informed him. "Not just Pookie getting killed while he was in your custody, but Michael Rose getting murdered on the job. I know the raid that Rose was killed in was mainly Crator's operation. I figure you tipped B.J. off at the last minute. If you'd had it your way there never would have been a raid to begin with."

John couldn't believe what he was hearing. "You're nuts!"

"Am I? Guess what else I know?"

Burkes shook his head. "I can't imagine."

"I know the D.A. thinks there's a leak on your team. I also know that my cousin's trucking company often delivers crates to you from your sister's antique shop in Greensburg. Right here to your house. Does your wife know there are drugs in those shipments?"

"You're not gonna believe how stupid you sound when this is all over," Burkes said.

"Really, Detective?" Ben smiled. "What about Michael Rose's killer? Nobody knew you were looking for him but Pookie and the cops. What happened to him? Dead. Fish bait, before you could even find him. You or your team is crooked. I believe you're in it all the way."

Burkes shook his head.

"You know what amazes me, Detective?" Ben asked.

"And what might that be?" Burkes became sarcastic for the first time.

"It just amazes me that in all these years, you can't put B.J. White away. No one can. Surely someone has suspected some hanky panky between him and the cops? Surely it didn't take little ole me to figure that one out."

Burkes thought while Ben stared.

"Are you going to give me what I want? Or am I going to have to shoot you?" Ben asked matter-of-factly.

"If you really feel that way you'll shoot me anyway."

Ben put his hand to his chin as if in deep thought. "Mmm. You're probably right. Well, I guess I'll just have to settle for the satisfaction of killing you without the information I came for." Ben smiled. "It doesn't really matter. I already know where B.J. has an arsenal of weapons stashed. Maybe I'll just burn it to the ground. That'll hurt him a little bit."

"How do you know something like that?"

"Scares you, doesn't it?" Ben smiled. "I might be infiltrating your little network."

"Seriously, we've known there had to be a place like that for a while." Burkes' voice was high with excitement from knowing someone might have information on a hideout of B.J.'s.

"I have my reliable sources," Ben laughed.

"Do you know for sure?" Burkes asked.

"Hell, I've seen it," Ben laughed louder this time. "Now I'm gonna burn it."

Burkes contemplated his next move. "I shouldn't be doing this. It's part of an ongoing investigation to clear you." Burkes winced at the thought of telling Ben of Randy's involvement. He feared Ben might try to warn Randy, thus ruining the secrecy of the investigation. Now he felt he had little choice under the circumstances. "Your cousin is who you want," Burkes said, relieved that he had gotten it out.

"What?"

"Your cousin, Randy. He's been working with McMasters all along, and I'm sure with B.J. as well. There's your Memphis connection. They're probably working with that brother-in-law of yours. That's how they all got hooked up together in the first place, behind your back. The D.A. and I feel like they're running drugs just like you said from New Orleans to Greensburg via the river, then disbursing them on up to Memphis or over to Birmingham, Shreveport, and the like." Burkes nodded, sad that he had to be the bearer of bad news.

Thwack!

"Jesus!" Burkes keeled over in pain. "I should have known that was coming." He moaned in agony.

Ben snatched the detective by the hair on his head, forcing him to look eye-to-eye. "I'm going to give you just about one more chance to cooperate." Ben's adrenaline-induced sweat now dripped onto Burkes' shirt.

Burkes thought of the phone bill in his shirt pocket proving Randy's involvement with McMasters. He resisted the temptation to give it to Ben. If Ben showed it to Randy, Burkes himself could wind up in jail. Right now jail seemed a viable alternative to his present situation.

Ben pulled at the very roots of Burkes' head, twisting it so he could easily stick the barrel of the Beretta into his mouth. "Well, if you're not going to come clean, you're no use to me," Ben said cocking the pistol.

"Mmm." Burkes' gurgling was that of a desperate man now realizing the severity of his situation. Ben removed the gun from Burkes' mouth. "Something you wanted to say to make your peace?"

"Yeah." Burkes' chest heaved a sigh, relieved to have thwarted an execution. "If I tell you anything, how do I know you're not going to kill me anyway?"

Ben pondered the question only momentarily. "You're right. I guess that leaves neither of us any options." He stuck the gun back into Burkes' throat.

"Mmm." Burkes moaned once again, and again was granted a stay of execution.

"Captain, this is the way things have to be. You're a crooked, lowlife scumbag snake who will never be caught, so it's my job to render judgment here and now. I hereby find you guilty and sentence you to death. Now open wide!"

"Wait! Wait!" Burkes begged. "Look in my shirt pocket."

Ben studied the detective, saw a piece of paper jutting from his shirt pocket and reached for it. Burkes' heart pounded as his captor unfolded the cellular bill.

"You cannot reveal this to your cousin—it will blow the entire investigation," Burkes warned Ben, who now could see the numbers and names of cities on the printout.

"What is this?"

"It's a copy of Gene McMasters' cellular bill for the last few months. The calls to Memphis are to your cousin. If you don't believe me, call yourself."

Ben raised his hand skyward to strike.

"Wait! Wait! Dammit!" Burkes flinched. "Why do you want to hit me? I didn't make him do it. I just caught him."

"It's a trick. Some kind of evil trick you're playing to save your own hide."

"Oh yeah. I just made all of it up because I figured you'd be waiting for me in my house when I got home." The detective shook his battered head in disgust. "You see McMasters' name on the printout. You can call the numbers, but I'm sure you probably recognize them anyway. It's your cousin—"

Burkes was interrupted by sniffling. Ben had slumped against the wall crying.

"God! Why are you doing this to me?" he bellowed.

The young man was broken. Burkes had to pounce now. "It's going to be okay. Everything's going to be okay."

Ben continued to sob.

"You need to try and get a hold of yourself enough to do the right thing."

Ben now bawled uncontrollably.

"You need to uncuff me and let me take you on in. This case is about to bust wide open. Your cousin will soon be arrested if we can keep a lid on this evidence long enough to obtain some more without him covering his tracks. I'm taking a big risk showing you that evidence anyway. Your cousin has no idea he's under investigation." Burkes didn't bother to mention that the evidence was worthless due to its illegal origin.

Ben tried to muffle the tears flowing from his face. "I just don't understand. I've always lived a good life. I've always tried to do the right things. How did all this happen to me? I just don't understand."

"It's all going to be alright. Just uncuff me."

"I loved her. I was loyal to Gene. I never did anything to Randy. Why do they all hate me so much?" Ben cried. His tears flowed like rain now.

"It's going to be alright. Just uncuff me. I'll help you."

Ben sucked up a few of the tears as he tried to read the printouts through foggy eyes.

"Ben, you've got to uncuff me. I can help you. You've got to let me."

Ben's sniffles subsided just enough for him to regroup and raise the barrel of the gun toward Burkes." You can help me, all right."

"Oh Jesus, I thought we'd been through that already." Burkes sank as if to give up.

Ben shook the gun at him. "Yeah. Yeah. You're right." The barrel dropped. "I've got a better plan for you."

Burkes' eyes searched the young man's face for an explanation.

"B.J.'s arsenal I told you about."

"Yeah?" Burkes hung on his words."

"Make a believer out of me."

" You name it." Burkes was ready to deal. '

"You raid the warehouse. There's enough stuff in that place to set B.J. back some serious cash. More importantly, it will convince me you're not involved. I'll be watching the news to make sure you fulfill your end of the deal, then I'll turn myself in. I wanna see live footage of the whole event so I'll know you're not fabricating some story for the media."

"You gonna clue me in as to where the warehouse might be? So I can find it?" Burkes asked.

"You take Main to Mina. It's just a little side street. Then you take Butler off of Mina. There's a field across from the old United warehouse. In the middle of that field sits a deserted building all boarded up. Looks like a barn. That's it. There are two armed guards, both of them convicted felons and fugitives."

"How do you know all this if you're not working with them?" Burkes queried. "How do I know this isn't a trick?"

"I"m holding Tawana Griffin hostage. She told me all this."

"Pookie's girlfriend?" John asked, flabbergasted.

"For now. If you don't hold up your end of the bargain, I'll kill her and write a letter to the *Commercial Appeal*."

"I didn't even know she was missing," Burkes said.

Ben exited the door he had come in through.

Chapter 20

Across town Ben felt his previously sporadic heartbeat begin to normalize. He made his way back downtown to the general area of the warehouse. He pulled into a parking lot full of cars where he felt reasonably concealed. Quickly he crawled into the back to untie Tawana just long enough for her to regain circulation in the extremities. He ungagged her only to be met by a nonstop nagging cry.

"Shut up! Please?" He begged of her.

"I've got to pee!"

Ben shook his head in disgust. "You're just going to have to wait. This should all be over in a little while."

"Are you gonna let me go?"

"If the cops keep their word," Ben assured her. "They're gonna raid your buddy's explosives depot."

"Oh my God, they'll find out who ratted them out. They'll start killin' folks till they got the right one. Man, why you doin' this to me?"

"It's a cruel world, Missy," Ben gruffed. "I suggest you move and find new friends."

She cried harder as Ben retied her after he felt she had regained circulation. "I've got to go now," he said.

"You just gonna leave me—" She was cut off by the gag shoved back into her throat.

"Don't worry. The cops will find you. They'll comb this entire area before the raid."

She groaned and shook her head as if she didn't believe him.

"Trust me," Ben tried to reassure her. "I know these things. I'm a cop."

There was grave concern back at the D.A.'s office as time passed and Burkes failed to show. Phone call after phone call were made to Burkes' residence and pager to no avail. He remained cuffed to the refrigerator until his wife returned home nearly three hours later.

Burkes calmed her down, then coaxed her into staying with a friend temporarily while insisting that there was no danger. His wife didn't believe a word but didn't question him further, as he once again promised her he would get a desk job, the same promise he had broken every year for the last fourteen years.

Burkes was met by a crowd at the D.A.'s office. The tale of his afternoon adventure with Memphis' now famous fugitive left jaws dropped and tongues silenced all over the office as the detective relayed the story to Bob Taylor and his key assistants. He had left out the part about the warehouse and Ben's demand for now.

"Sir, I think you and I need to speak in private for a moment," Burkes said while rubbing an icepack on his head.

There was momentary silence as everyone sat stunned about the revelation of current events. "Oh sure, sure," Taylor said. "Give us a minute everybody," he said, looking around the room.

The lawyers picked up their jaws and began to file out of the office offering amenities to the battered detective. Everyone left but Marc, who stood leaning against the wall as if he had not heard the instruction.

"What is it, Johnson?" Taylor asked.

Marc looked at his boss in disbelief. "I'm on the case too, sir."

"We'll call you back in a minute," Taylor said.

Burkes was still rubbing his head, having been unaware that Marc was still in the room until this conversation.

Marc huffed and sourly reached for the door.

"Johnson can stay," Burkes said.

Marc cut a quick look at Burkes, then at his boss. Taylor shrugged as if he didn't care either way. Marc swelled inside.

Bob Taylor laid to rest a pen he had been clicking for a few minutes while listening to Burkes' riveting tale. He leaned back in his chair, hands locked behind his head. "So what else could there possibly be?"

"Seals is willing to give himself up," Burkes said.

"Great. Let's set it up," Taylor said. "I want him to come to us, not Memphis P.D."

"Hold it. Just cool your heels for a minute and hear me out." Burkes held the icepack on his head. "He wants us to raid a warehouse."

"A warehouse?" Marc echoed.

"B.J.'s."

"Doesn't he know that we would have done that by now if we knew where B.J. had a warehouse," Taylor scoffed.

"Yeah, really," Marc agreed with his boss.

"Seals says he knows where B.J. has a major arsenal in a warehouse, and get this, in downtown Memphis. "

"No way!" Marc breathed.

Taylor said nothing.

"You go down Main to Mina. It's not two blocks off Main Street."

"You gotta be kiddin." Marc's eyes bulged in disbelief.

The D.A. still sat speechless.

"It's the perfect cover when you think about it. It's in an open field down by an old parking garage. No one would ever suspect something right up under our noses," Burkes commented.

Finally, Taylor voiced an opinion. "It also would lend more credibility to a Memphis P.D. connection. Maybe they cover for him."

"I knew you were gonna say that. You sound like Ben Seals." Burkes became irritated. "I can't vouch for Memphis P.D. But nobody on my team is involved with B.J. White, or that McMasters guy, or that guy from New Orleans, Lyles or whatever his name is. I'll stake my career on it. They're all good cops, not involved with those guys or anybody else in the underworld, and I'm just about tired of hearing that."

"So exactly what do you propose we do, John? Call up the commissioner and have him send S.W.A.T. in there on a raid?" Taylor asked sarcastically.

Burkes looked Taylor, then at Marc. "Sure. Why not?"

Taylor shook his head as if to say, "Out of the question," then said it: "Out of the question!"

"Sir, with all due respect—" Burkes was cut off.

"Out of the question. Out of the question. No way. It could be a setup. Seals may have been sent there by B.J."

"A setup? For what?" Burkes almost screamed. "You think B.J. wants to just kill a bunch of cops?"

"Maybe."

"No sir. You're wrong."

"How can you be sure?"

"Sir, I've hunted this guy throughout my entire career," Burkes said. "The last thing he wants is to fool around with cops. He tries to keep his nose as clean as possible by putting distance between himself and the crimes he perpetrates. If he's going to kill anybody, especially a cop, there's either money involved or he's trying to save his own hide. Even then, I don't think he would try to kill a cop. He certainly wouldn't have a reason to now. No sir. He's lying low. He's trying to let the heat die down. Seals is legit. I just know it. There's one more thing. He's holding Pookie Jones' girlfriend, the Griffin girl, hostage. He said he'd kill her if we didn't cooperate."

Taylor laughed. "Yeah, he sounds like a real standup guy."

"He's fighting for his life. He'd do anything, but he's looking for a way out. I believe him. I believe everything he says. I believe he's innocent, and I also believe he'll kill her if we don't cooperate."

Taylor sighed, not wanting to battle the detective seemingly entrenched in his theory. "What do you think, Johnson?"

Marc, unsure of what to think, changed the subject. "How is Seals supposed to know when the raid's been carried out?"

"He said he'd watch for news reports, and he wants to see live footage. I figure he'll be somewhere close by watching the whole event. We can probably scour the area and pick him up before going in. If we have to go in at all," Burkes surmised. "We need to go ahead and get a surveillance team set up to watch the place. Maybe get some high-powered scopes zoomed in on the building and see if we can see anything unusual. Do you want me to handle that?"

"No," Taylor said. "I'll take care of it."

Burkes bit his tongue to keep from lashing out at his superior. He couldn't resist a small stab, however. "You're afraid of letting anybody from my team get involved. You still think there may be a leak?"

"No, I don't think there's a leak on your team, not really. I just want to play it safe. No chances."

"What makes you think anybody else from Memphis P.D. is any more trustworthy than anybody I've got? Besides, this could be a big boost for me and my team. It might could get us out of the dog house."

"I don't want anybody from Memphis P.D. involved except you." Taylor said while buzzing his secretary on the intercom.

Burkes sat positively stunned. "Well, who you gonna get? Feds?"

"You'll see."

The secretary entered the room. "Yes sir?"

"Could you gentlemen excuse us for a minute?"

Marc stepped out of the room. Burkes remained in his seat, irritated and confused. "I know you're not gonna do something stupid like send a bunch of deputy D.A.'s in three-piece suits out there with automatic weapons."

"John, please. If you could excuse us for a little while," Taylor pleaded.

Burkes left the D.A.'s office to attend to personal business. He made a pass down by the now famous warehouse against the D.A.'s direct orders to stay clear of the property. There was no activity around the old building, but unbeknownst to him, Ben Seals was already inside.

Ben had parked the van in an alley just off Mina street. Tawana remained gagged and bound to the back of the passenger's seat. He knew the cops would soon find her as they combed the area checking vehicles and whatnot. Everything would soon come to a head, one way or another. He made sure she knew he was going in the building. This would guarantee that the cops raided the building. He bound her tight to restrict any movement. If she were to escape and somehow warn B.J., he would be dead within minutes. He hoped he had scared her enough to make her leave town. His bet was on the cops, though. Surely they would find her soon. He could only imagine the turmoil and confusion he must have stirred downtown.

Upon returning to the D.A.'s office, Burkes found Marc alone at his desk pecking away at his computer.

"You heard anything yet?" Burkes asked.

"We're all going down after a while to set up," Marc answered, never looking up from his PC.

"What are you working on? A warrant for the raid?"

"No. Somebody else is doing that." He continued to type.

Burkes leaned on the desk. "I'm nervous about this little expedition your boss has got us headed on. I hope he's well-prepared. These guys are more than just a bunch of two-bit pimps and hustlers."

"Tell me about it," Marc said, still intent on the screen in front of him.

Burkes leaned over to see what the young D.A. was so diligently involved in. His blood pressure rose as he yelled at his new friend, "You're drawing up papers against Ben Seals!"

"No, I'm not. The boss just wants me to make a summary of everything that we might have against Seals if he's brought in, just in case it should turn out that he is, you know, guilty."

"Guilty of what?"

"I don't know. I'm just summarizing the evidence."

Burkes fumed as Marc begged him to lower his voice.

"I don't know why I'm even needed around this dump!" Burkes tried to muffle his anger by lowering his tone.

Marc felt a strange sense of pride as if the seasoned veteran was becoming unraveled by something he had done this time. He decided to take the high road in the discussion, "Your years of experience are valuable to us at this juncture. We need—"

"My years of experience tell me one thing. Ben Seals is innocent." He slammed his fist down on the desk. An audience from around the room was forming, each from his or her own desk. Everyone's ears tuned in to what the detective was saying. Burkes couldn't have cared less. "He's innocent, Marc. I tell you, he's innocent! You talk about what you need. What you people need is my size 11 halfway up your butts. I just can't do that right now because everyone here has got their heads so far up there, there's no room for anything else!" He turned to walk away.

"John, don't you want justice?"

Burkes continued to walk, all eyes transfixed on him.

"Well, at least leave it up to a jury to weigh the evidence." Marc said.

Burkes froze in his tracks. Slowly he turned to face the deputy D.A. standing halfway across the now completely silent office.

"Oh, you've got the evidence, all right. Lots of it. And I'm sure you'll get a conviction. Not because of anything you did but because of the nifty job those thugs did of setting up an innocent man for murder. But when you go to sleep at night, you think about that man rotting away for a crime he didn't commit, and you be proud of yourself." Burkes turned and exited the room

Marc stood speechless and blushing while all eyes followed Burkes out the door, then circled back to him. "Damn!" he cursed under his breath while hanging his head so he wouldn't face his colleagues.

An hour passed before Burkes' return. He found the D.A.'s office crowded with prosecutors, including Marc. "Welcome, welcome, to the war room," Bob Taylor bellowed to Burkes as he entered the room.

Burkes surveyed the room. Everyone had a notepad out, pens armed and ready for Taylor's instructions. "I take it something important is about to happen."

"You might say that," Taylor grinned as he removed a cigar from his teeth. "This is Barry James, my senior investigator."

"I know Barry James—" Burkes interrupted the D.A.'s obviously proud speech.

"Well, it seems Pookie Jones' girlfriend was found tied up in an abandoned van. She said Ben Seals left her there while he went into the warehouse."

There was silence as every eye stared at Burkes. "Did you say in the warehouse?" he asked.

"That's r-i-g-h-t." Taylor puffed on the cigar. "It seems obvious to me that Seals is in kneedeep with B.J. White. He's just trying to rat them out so he can cop a deal, look good, that sort of thing."

"Don't you think he would cut a deal before giving up the warehouse? Think about that!" Burkes admonished the D.A. and everyone listening.

"Oh no," one of the assistant D.A.'s said. "This is just a preliminary to what he can do. He's showing us what he can give us. He'll give up the whole ring before it's over with. His cousin, his brother-in-law from New Orleans, B.J. All of them, in return for witness protection."

Burkes let the young man rattle on without saying a word. Obviously outnumbered in theory, he kept his objections to himself. Within the hour, he found himself riding with Marc to the soonto-be action scene that now gripped everybody's attention. Marc tried to make small talk the entire way. Burkes turned a deaf ear to the young

D.A.

"Please don't hold anything against me," Marc pleaded with the detective. "I'm just trying to do my job the best I can."

Burkes broke his silence. "Why are you even going down here? You're a lawyer, not an investigator. The D.A.'s office has plenty of investigators."

"I want to be there. I need to be there to help with the follow- up investigation."

Burkes sighed with sarcasm.

"Oh, I guess you figure I should just stay back at the office and wait for the real men to call me and tell me when it's safe to come down." Marc's voice seared with his anger.

Burkes chuckled. "All I can tell you is keep your head down."

"Don't worry, Captain, there are plenty of cops already there. Shelby County has at least a dozen or so deputies positioned in a parking garage across the street and more on the streets behind the warehouse. They're all plainclothes and out of sight, but rest assured the place is secure."

"Shelby County? "Burkes echoed, hoping he had misunderstood.
"Yeah."

"No feds?" Burkes asked.

"I didn't think you people cared too much for the feds," Marc jousted.

"Do you mean to tell me that the D.A.'s office is going to try and raid a warehouse that is known to contain an arsenal of weapons without even calling the ATF or somebody.?"

"I really don't think it's necessary," Marc speculated. "There's only supposed to be a couple of suspects in the building with the exception of Seals. Besides, you know how the feds like to take over a situation."

"Well I would hate for you to lose any press," Burkes scoffed.

""Hey, it's not my call. Don't blame me."

Burkes shook his head at what he deemed to be pure ignorance. "Do you have any idea what you could be walking into?"

"What do you mean?"

"Marc! These are not some punks...breaking into houses...or vandalizing cars or something." Burkes could hardly speak. "These guys will kill you."

"Oh, I know there are risks—" Marc tried to retaliate in his own defense before being slammed by Burkes again.

"You don't have a clue! Not a clue!" Burkes shook his head." I've watched B.J. White operate for years. I know what he and his people are capable of. They'll do anything. They may promise you they're going to come out peacefully and throw a grenade at you. They'll shoot you, cut you, burn you—they don't care. There's a man living in Germantown right now who stiffed one of B.J.'s prostitutes about six years ago, back when B.J. still worked his own ladies. Marc, the man has no testicles. They were mailed to his mom with a note that read, 'Your boy has been very bad.'"

Marc's mouth hung open as the images ran through his brain. He wheeled the car into a parking garage across the street from the warehouse.

As the car stopped, Burkes pleaded with young lawyer again. "All I'm saying to you is stay low, keep your head down."

A small crowd awaited Burkes and Marc on the fourth floor of the concrete structure. The garage had been out of use for a number of years, thanks to crime skyrocketing in that area of town. No businesses wanted to remain in that sector. The group now assembled was probably larger than all the traffic the garage had seen in a couple of years.

The D.A. greeted Burkes as he stepped out of the sedan.

"What's the game plan?" Burkes asked the chief prosecutor.

"We're going in at dusk. Sunset is 8:40 tonight. We're gonna try to go in around 8:33, if there are no problems before then. That gives us just a little over an hour to get ready if we aren't already. Burkes, I'd like for you to look around and make any suggestions."

"Where's your ordnance disposal team?" Burkes asked first.

A deputy listening to the conversation spoke up. "Captain Burkes?"

Burkes turned to his right to see a face he didn't recognize staring at him.

"I've heard a lot about you. I'm Deputy Cleveland Marrow, Shelby County S.O. I haven't met you yet. I just moved here a month ago from Little Rock. I understand it was your task force that came under attack at the Waltham Hotel last week."

"Yeah, yeah, that's us," Burkes said. "Where's your ordnance disposal unit?"

"Well, I personally have past experience with explosives—"

Cleveland Marrow began to say before being cut off by the D.A., who knew how unnerved Burkes was already.

"John, the sheriff's office doesn't have a bomb squad on hand. As you know, we felt it to be in the best interest of everyone to keep Memphis P.D. out of the picture, and there was no need to call in the feds," he said while evaluating Burkes' present state of mind. "Now John, I love having your help, your experience, and your advice, but I don't want you going around inciting people's fears. We can handle this."

Burkes' expressions remained unchanged. "R.V.'s?"

"What?"

"Have you got any R.V.'s, armored vehicles?"

"Don't need 'em," the D.A. said.

Cleveland Marrow interjected himself back into the conversation. "We're planning to use battering rams on the fronts of the S.O. Blazers. We have a couple of assault vehicles that are already equipped. That combined with the element of surprise is enough. They'll never know what hit them." Marrow smiled. "Don't forget, they're not expecting us."

Burkes laughed, crushed out a cigarette, and puffed. "I know they're not expecting you, Deputy, but don't you think they're ready for anything in there?"

Marrow shrugged as he pondered the question.

"John, if you've got something to say, just say it," Taylor said. "Go ahead and spit it out. Maybe then we can get on with the business at hand." The frustrated lawyer gave the detective a disapproving look.

Marc felt sympathy for Burkes because he knew the cop believed it was a dangerous mission being taken far too lightly. Taylor continued to scowl at the detective. "Now, I'm ready to go on with this thing. Go ahead and get it off your chest so we can be done with it."

Burkes took a drag on the cigarette but said nothing.

"Deputy Marrow," Taylor said with his eyes glaring right through Burkes, "let it be noted that Captain Burkes is diametrically opposed to our handling of this operation."

He stared at Burkes, who remained silent.

"Officer Burkes, any comment before we proceed?" Taylor asked with his hands placed firmly on his hips.

"Comment? No. No comment," Burkes replied. "But the word *Waco* does come to mind. Deputy Marrow, how many body bags did you bring?"

"Uh, well, there are only two, maybe three suspects in the warehouse, from what we understand."

"I don't mean for them." Burkes crushed the cigarette out on the ground. "For us!"

He walked away leaving the D.A. singed from his remarks.

Burkes walked to the edge of the garage to borrow a pair of binoculars from a deputy and look at the old warehouse for himself.

Marc and Taylor stayed behind in an effort to ignore Burkes. Marrow, on the other hand, couldn't let it go that easily. He followed Burkes to the edge of the parking garage. Burkes peered through the optical lenses at the building across the street.

"Officer Burkes, I want to take exception to your opinion of what we foresee happening here. I assure you we are in complete control of this situation, and the sheriff has assigned the very best people to carry out this mission."

"That's good," Burkes replied. "Real good."

The short answer only frustrated Marrow more. "Well, what would you do that is so different?"

Burkes smiled but continued to look through the binos. "What would I do differently? First of all, one of my closest friends is an ATF agent. I would call them. Then the FBI—"

Marrow cut him off short. "You know how the feds are…they just take over everything."

"You mean they take your press?" Burkes asked.

"You know what I mean."

"But the problem is—" Burkes paused while he adjusted the lenses to focus in on what he was seeing. "You may have a whole arsenal in there."

"But there are only a couple of guys in there. There's no need to bring in the feds. That would just be overkill." Marrow argued.

Burkes pulled the binos from his face and turned to face the deputy for the first time since they had met. "Overkill? You gotta be kidding. You've got a D.A., a freaking lawyer, heading up a raid on the most organized crime syndicate this town has ever seen. You have no idea what all might wait for you inside those walls. The suspects that you know about have probably killed more people than everyone here combined.

Deputy, that was my witness in that hotel room when an anti-tank missile fried the whole corner of the building. Please do not even try to insinuate that I might be overreacting. I've spent my entire career trying to bring down B.J. White. I know what he's capable of. If you did, we wouldn't be having this conversation." He shoved the binos into the deputy's hands and walked away.

Chapter 21

Inside the warehouse, Ben awoke from a brief nap. The minuscule amount of sleep had only made him feel worse. He felt numb from head to toe. His stomach ached with hunger pains. He was feverish. The combination of sleep deprivation, stress, hunger, and constipation resulted in a continuing stream of hot flashes. He was lucky enough to have found a nice resting spot at the rear of the warehouse under some empty crates. Nevertheless, it would take days of rest for his ailing body to recuperate. Burkes would soon bring his posse, though, and everything would come to a head.

He reflected on his plight for a moment. Could he go on? Where would he find the strength to continue his fight for survival? He remembered thinking those same thoughts on the hot practice fields at LSU. Surely having to battle the Louisiana sun during two-a-day workouts could never have made him this miserable. If he could just go back to those days and redo his life. He tried to block out the self-pity so he could focus on survival. He mustered the energy to crawl nearly fifty feet for a closer look. In the distance he could see two Hispanics in the center of the warehouse. They were sitting at what looked to be a card table, drinking beer and laughing.

Ben's heart began to pound with excitement. When would the cops show up? Would they show at all? They had to. Burkes now knew he was still in Memphis. They would have checked out the warehouse by now and surely found Tawana and the van. But where were they?

Another guy suddenly appeared from behind a truck parked in the middle of the warehouse. He had blond hair and carried a deck of cards. From the distance, Ben could not understand what the guy was saying as he threw the deck onto the table. Ben crawled through the narrow cracks in between the jumbled stacks of crates. He took each step slowly and deliberately, pausing only to feel for the .380. It was still tucked away in the small of his back.

He found his way through the maze until he was within earshot of the table. The criminals seemed to be having a good time drinking and were becoming more intense about the poker game at hand. Ben's neck ached as he strained to peer around the corner to watch the activity. Massaging the back of his neck, he noticed the stencil mark on the crate in front of him. The writing, though red in color, was difficult to read because of the building was so dark. Ben leaned closer to see: CAUTION: DYNAMITE.

Slowly raising the lid to the container, he peered into it. The crate was smaller than most of the crates in the building but its contents deadly. Plastic-sealed packages were neatly stacked in the crate. Ben slowly picked one up to see a bundle of dynamite wrapped tight by an elastic band. "My God," he whispered. He was nervous just being this close to the stuff. He couldn't imagine these guys living with it. He figured the warehouse was a temporary facility for illegal arms until B.J. could find a better place, maybe a holding place for new shipments. Nevertheless these guys were stuck with the job of babysitting what amounted to a Kmart for a third world army.

The crate had three compartments splitting it neatly into thirds. The middle compartments held remote devices for triggering the charges. The other compartment had spools of wire for rigging the explosives. Ben grabbed a remote and some wire, along with two bundles of dynamite. The more time that passed, the more Ben felt a quivering in his gut that something would go wrong. He was prepared to die, but not alone. If he had to die tonight, he would go out with a bang. He removed the contents from the crate, weaved his way back to where he had entered the building and left his newfound goodies against the rear wall.

It was nearly dark, and the sheriff had arrived at the parking garage. Because the D.A. and the sheriff were running the show, Burkes had not been assigned any duties. He now felt it was in his best interest to take his own advice and lie low.

He had just crushed out another cigarette on the ground when he saw the sheriff approaching. He tried to be evasive and get away as if he didn't see the sheriff at all.

"Captain Burkes," the sheriff called out. "I'm glad you're here."

"I wish I could say the same," Burkes said, reaching to shake the elected cop's hand.

The sheriff laughed. "Yeah, I heard you were against the whole operation."

"It's not that I'm against it. I just don't think we're fully prepared."

"You'd like us to call in the ATF? Maybe let them do like they did at Waco? Get a bunch of people killed?" The sheriff grinned.

"Call anybody," Burkes said, defending his position. "Call Bill Jensen, at the U.S. Marshall's office. I've got his home phone number. He could have a load of agents here by midnight."

"We don't have till midnight, Burkes. We need to move quickly while we still have some light. It's the only way we can seal the place off and make sure no civilians wonder into the area. Besides, you know how the feds are, they want to take over everything." The sheriff grinned. "I understand why you're jumpy. I'm sorry about your witness getting…well…you know…. Try to relax. This will go off without a hitch. We'll catch them by surprise and they'll never know what hit them." He walked away, leaving Burkes' ego bruised from the reference to Pookie.

With the raid only moments away, Deputy Marrow hounded the troops, ensuring that no civilians entered the area. Deputy Marrow dispatched a detail to make one last check behind garbage bins and whatnot. There had been high hopes that one of the suspects inside might leave the warehouse for something before the raid began, allowing the deputies to isolate, then apprehend him. As darkness drew near those hopes faded.

Burkes found Marc. Together the two walked down to the street, where they stood behind the parking garage watching as three deputies in an alley crouched low behind a garbage dumpster. These deputies would meet up with other trios once the raid began. A host of trios from every direction would sprint across the open field between the warehouse and surrounding buildings.

Simultaneously, two Blazers with battering rams would slam into the warehouse doors from both sides. The suspects would be so overpowered and overwhelmed, they would immediately surrender or be killed. All the deputies donned chemical masks and carried their own tear gas. Everyone was given strict orders to drop the tear gas only on the floor. No one would be allowed to throw the canisters because they sometimes created small sparks. The unknown nature of the explosives inside the building was the only variable that made Marrow's hair stiffen on his arm. Nevertheless, he was confident in his troops, as was the sheriff.

The time drew nigh. The deputies wore headsets and microphones. John and Marc found the D.A. and the sheriff huddled on the bottom floor of the parking garage listening to the two-way radio in the sheriff's car as the raid drew closer. Every squad leader had called in a "Go." The search teams had reported back "No civilians in the area."

"Let's roll!" came the cry from Marrow over the radio. Less than five seconds later, two Chevy Blazers from the Shelby County sheriff's office plowed into the warehouse from opposite sides.

"Police!" came the muffled screams through protective masks as the Blazers began their assault, pushing the boarded doors inward. The card table cleared, and the two Hispanics ran in the same direction, while the Caucasian was momentarily disoriented. He wasn't a regular at the warehouse and wasn't sure how to react. Quickly, he tried to recover himself and follow.

Ben heard the commotion from his vantage point at the rear of the building. He crawled behind several crates for safety and waited to be arrested. He was scared and relieved at the same time.

The Blazers struggled momentarily with the doors. The south door burst open first. The officer driving the first Blazer was lying almost in the floorboard as the door popped open. Quickly he threw the gear shift in reverse and sped back out into the open field he had just crossed. The night provided cover for the screaming shadows of the deputies running through the south entrance. The north door wasn't as easy to open. By the time it was finally ripped from its frame, the thugs had positioned themselves. The double doors sagged, clinging by only one hinge each, as the deputies ran through the hole and into a maze of rapid automatic fire. One deputy went down screaming, "My arm!" The protective vest did not cover his arms, legs, and extremities from the bullets now spraying the doorway.

There was complete silence at the sheriff's car as Burkes, Marrow, Taylor, the sheriff, and others listened to the deputies in the warehouse over the radio. There was an indescribable eeriness as the shots mixed with screams pierced the night air. Soon the warehouse filled with gunfire from both sides. The old metal building echoed with every shot. Ben's heart pounded as hard as everybody else's.

"There shouldn't be this much gunfire!" Marrow screamed as he turned the squelch on a loudspeaker that had been mounted on the second floor of the parking garage. "You are completely surrounded!" he yelled. "Throw down your weapons and come out with your hands up."

Inside, the thugs shot out the fluorescent lamps dangling from the ceiling and eliminated what little light there had been in the building. Marrow had not anticipated that. Now there was no way to see if someone did try to surrender. The leader on the ground had relayed the information back to Marrow, who now realized he might be losing control of the situation.

"Hold your positions!" he ordered the deputies over the radio. "Drop your gas canisters. Roll them in the direction of the gunfire. Use all your canisters. The gas will get them and they will run out."

Every deputy did as ordered. Even the wounded officer managed to fumble his canisters onto the floor, spewing their vapors. Neither Marrow nor the deputies inside had any way of knowing the thugs had their own chemical masks for just such an occasion.

Ramon, the shorter of the two thugs, crouched behind a stack of crates firing his AK47 aimlessly in the direction of the county employees. The other, Emilio, coughed and choked as he tried to get a good seal around his mask. Jimmy, the third card player, was simply making a delivery to the warehouse, so he had no mask. He fired his 9mm back in the direction of the deputies, coughing and choking as the gas reached him.

Ben crawled a few feet in the direction of the fire. He stayed belly to the ground. The bullets ripped the air above his head. It was too dark to make out anything that was going on. The gunfire became more rapid. Bullhorns screamed from the outside. Marrow ordered a cease-fire. Seconds after the deputies ceased fire, the suspects followed suit.

The bullhorns rang out in the night: "Throw down your weapons.

You are completely surrounded!" There was silence except for Jimmy coughing and the cops rustling around the general area positioning themselves where they thought the trio might be. The gas had not yet made it to the rear area of the building where Ben still lurked, but one officer had. Ben saw the shadow sprinting through the maze of crates bumping a few here and there and causing just enough noise for Ramon and Emilio to realize they were being moved on. They opened fire in that direction behind their little fortification. The mass of bullets burned through the night air. Three struck the deputy, two in his bulletproof vest, the other in the side of his head. He fell dead instantly.

Shots again filled the air from everywhere. Marrow barked over the radio, screaming for another cease-fire. Giant spotlights mounted atop nearby buildings now showed through the broken-down doors partially illuminating the inside. The deputies inside scurried to get away from the light avoiding exposure.

Jimmy's respiratory system had almost ceased all functions. The gas had infiltrated his sinuses and burned deep into his chest. He tried to mouth words to his preoccupied coworkers, but he couldn't muster a single syllable. He stumbled to his feet and staggered toward the light, hands in the air, to give himself up. He had been sent there on a delivery and hung around for a card game. He didn't understand the risk involved in guarding B.J. White's primary supply dump. It wasn't his job. It was a job meant for a couple of escapees doing multiple life terms in a Texas prison. He didn't know the rules. Ramon fired a single automatic burst riddling the Caucasian with holes. No one ratted out B.J., no one.

"Cease fire! Dammit! Cease fire!" Marrow screamed over the radio.

"We got one of them!" a squad leader yelled over the headset." He was trying to give up! Who fired that shot?"

"That came from them," someone answered.

"They wouldn't shoot their own people, would they?" the squad leader asked over the headset before being cut off by Marrow.

"Everybody shut up! It doesn't matter. We gotta get a hold here!"

John Burkes walked away from the squad car, not wanting to hear anymore.

Marrow ordered the officers with bullhorns outside the building to demand the surrender of the suspects again. The bullhorns echoed in the night, unaware the criminals were already on the move.

The two thugs had made their way to a predestined spot. A round cylinder-like object about three feet in diameter, made of tempered steel, and anchored to the concrete floor contained a remote wired to an array of explosives scattered around the premises. The two were unaware they had been spotted. An officer crawling through the maze of crates looking for the now dead officer had made out the figures of the two men moving through the shadows.

The adrenaline caused the cop to lose count of how many shots he had previously fired. Only three rounds remained in his extended clip. He fired at the two. One bullet slashed through the flesh and bone of Emilio's left leg, sending him wrenching in pain to the ground. The officer dropped to the floor from his kneeling position as his rifle clicked without firing. A wooden crate half-empty served as his only cover. He shuffled the clips in the dark inserting a full one as the spent magazine fell onto the floor.

Ramon fired back. Rat-tat-tat. Rat-tat-tat. Bullets ripped through the wooden crate killing the young deputy and father.

Emilio rolled on the ground grasping his leg and writhing in pain. Ben's nerve's were exploding inside his head. He was tired and scared to death as he sat in the dark at the very rear of the building. He had swiped the cap and police jacket from the first dead officer. He now wore Shelby County Sheriff's Department on his head and back. He hoped it would keep him from getting shot on sight. The fumes drifted more and more into his area. He had to move. Securing the dynamite and remote into the excess room of the jacket sleeves, he climbed out the window he had originally entered.

He had also taken the police headset from the dead officer and could hear the whole operation unfold around him.

"Pull back! Pull back!" Marrow ordered everyone.

The sheriff had ordered a retreat based on the radio conversations between the officers. Panic ensued when the two dead deputies failed to respond when called.

"Kill the lights!" Marrow yelled over the air. Instantly the once illuminated doorways became dim. The deputies began peeling out of the building without a single shot being fired. The deputies lined the outside of the building. Ben had exited the rear window and shimmied down the same tree he had climbed to enter the warehouse.

Even with the block completely surrounded, the darkness

concealed Ben's movements. While Marrow discussed with his squad leader via radio whether or not to go back in with night goggles, inside the building Ramon watched as the gas fumes burned into his partner's wound.

B.J.'s underground warehouse was to have been ready soon, and they would have been able to move. But it was too little too late. They couldn't go back. This time it would be death row with no possibility of escape. B.J. had been good to them. Their orders were strict. There could be no links to him in any way. Ramon popped the seal on the container over the tempered-steel plate, depressing the handle.

Vaaaa-boom! The very frame of the building started popping and blowing in all directions. Balls of fire lit up the night. Ben ran, nearly falling as the initial blast shook the ground below him and was followed closely by another. He didn't have time to think about the instability of the dynamite he carried. All he could do was run and run fast. Screams echoed in the night as deputies around the entrances were hit and burned by falling debris.

Fire shot from the building lighting up the night. Ammo stored inside the warehouse discharged randomly, creating a machine gun effect. Even Marrow and the sheriff hit the ground for cover at the sound.

Anyone who wasn't on fire and screaming or knocked unconscious by the blast or debris was on the ground taking cover. Everyone except Ben, who continued to run for all he was worth. He ran without breathing. He ran unnoticed through the perimeter of Shelby County Sheriff's Department cars that sealed the rear street. No one had a chance to see what Ben might be doing. Everyone was too busy ducking and sneaking peeks at the erupting volcano in front of them.

He ran without looking back. The explosion lit up the night behind him. Soon he put it at a distance, as if it was part of another world. A quarter-mile away, he ran out of room at the river. He stared aimlessly at the banks of the Mississippi. "Now what?" he asked of God. Gazing into the long stretch of brush and thickness that lay on the side of the hill separating him from the mighty river, he contemplated his next move.

The chaos Ben had left behind became more frantic with each passing second. The injured continued to scream, but now their screams were blended with everybody else's. People were running and yelling in every direction. Only two ambulances were on standby for the entire operation. Marrow was running in a number of directions and screaming almost incoherently. Burkes had lost the D.A. in the confusion. They spotted each other simultaneously. Taylor was screaming into his two-way radio at the investigators from his office who were scattered around the block.

"Don't start, John!" he paused to shout at the detective. Burkes didn't have a chance to respond. The police commissioner's voice rang out from behind him.

"What in God's name is going on?" the commissioner screamed from the top of his lungs at the sheriff, who was busy screaming at Marrow.

"Sheriff! I demand you tell me what's going on! I threatened to shoot one of your reserve deputies who wouldn't let me in."

"I'm busy, commissioner!" the sheriff tried to ignore the Memphis top cop amidst all the confusion.

"Sheriff! I've gotta dispatcher calling me at home telling me our patrol cars can't get through here because you're down here with a court order! I get down here and half a block is gone!"

The sirens and screams drowned the commissioner's pleas. The sheriff weaseled away, telling the commissioner to talk to the D.A. Bob Taylor spotted the commissioner coming his way.

"Now hold on!" he said, trying to head off the commissioner.

"I'll give you something to hold!"

Burkes leaned close to Taylor and spoke into his ear. "Now we do it my way!"

In a second he was gone. A minute later he was in his car when Marc Johnson ran to the driver's side and beat on the window.

"Let me go with you, please!" cried the deputy D.A. as Burkes rolled down the window.

"I'm sorry, Captain. I just had a job to do. Everybody should have listened to you," Marc begged. "Please!"

Burkes briefly surveyed the earnestness of the young lawyer. "You ready to do it my way?"

Marc answered with an affirmative nod.

"Get in."

Ben weaved his way along the banks off the Mississippi, unsure of exactly where he was. He knew it was best to turn himself in and take his chances with John Burkes and a public defender rescuing him from the mass conspiracy.

He would turn himself in. But first, there was one small piece of business that had to be dealt with. Randy had to be confronted. If what Burkes had said about Randy was true, then Ben would be risking his life again, but it had to be done. What an epitaph to a life with so much future. He should be in Memphis working as the offensive coordinator for the University of Memphis. But no, he had to fall in love in college, get married, and one day find himself walking the banks of the Mississippi contemplating the possible murder of his own cousin.

What a sad case he judged himself to be. He wormed his way along the waterfront in the unfamiliar surroundings until he spotted the famous Pyramid Sports arena nestled on the water's edge. He was only minutes away.

Chapter 22

Burkes and Marc had already been to the precinct, where Burkes had a private meeting with Bill Jensen from the U.S. Marshall's office.

The next order of business was to inform Randy Seals of his cousin's death. Marc badgered Burkes about what their plans were. He wanted to know why Burkes insisted on taking a police panel van instead of a car.

"Are there weapons in the back?" Marc asked, having not seen the contents of the van he was driving.

Burkes did not answer until 10:25 p.m. when Marc parked in front of Randy and Mary Seals' condo. "You said you were willing to do it my way."

"I am. I just want to know what we're doing."

Burkes took a quick glance at the condo sitting quietly in the night. "Would you agree with me that B.J. White is out of control. I mean, he's killed witnesses and now cops. He's gone too far, wouldn't you agree?"

"Yeah. I'd say that's a fair statement," Marc reluctantly agreed, as if not sure what all he might be agreeing to.

"Then we have to do something. He has to be stopped. Now! Kinda reminds me of those Malcolm X shirts you saw everywhere for a while. What was it Malcolm said? By any means necessary!"

Marc's face wrenched at John's words.

"John, I'm not willing to break the law. That would make us no better than them."

The detective smiled a wicked smile. "I wouldn't ask *you* to."

They got out of the van and walked to the front door, where they rang the buzzer. Randy answered the door with a cordless phone in his hand.

"Let me call you back, Susan," he said.

"Officer Burkes. I assume you're here with news about Ben. Have you found him?"

"Well, sorta. Could we come in, please?" Burkes asked politely.

Randy stepped aside to let the two law enforcement officials in.

"There's been a little accident," Burkes said.

"Oh my God. Is Ben okay?"

"Well, it's been a hectic night..." Burkes hesitated. "Marc will fill you in on what has transpired. If you don't mind, could I use your restroom?"

"Uh, sure. There's one upstairs on the right."

Marc was left behind, confused as to what he was supposed to do. "Well...let's see...um...just a couple of hours ago...we...uh. We believe Ben was hiding in a warehouse downtown. It belonged to B.J. White. There were a lot of explosives and ammunition and stuff in the place. There was an explosion."

Randy's expression never changed. "You don't know for sure that Ben's dead?" he asked.

"We're pretty sure. It's still a big mess down there." Marc fumbled along. "He just wanted to make sure B.J. got knocked down a couple of pegs. He planned to turn himself in after we raided the building."

"You talked to him?"

"Oh yeah. John did."

"When, for God's sake?" Randy shouted.

"Well...I...think...he followed John home. Uh...John! You want to get in here?"

Burkes reappeared from the stairwell. "He followed me home around noon today. Held me at gunpoint as a matter of fact. He had this crazy notion that I was working with B.J. White. Can you believe that? As a show of good faith, I was to raid B.J.'s primary arsenal. He provided the information and then was to wait and turn himself in after the fact."

Randy shook his head. "How could he possibly know where it was?"

"I don't know." Burkes kept Tawana's secret safe. "Anyway, things kinda went wrong and the place blew up."

The tears welled up in Randy's eyes. "I'll sue you! You...you...oh God!" He dropped onto the sofa crying. "How could you even be sure it was B.J. White's place. You probably just went in there on a whim."

Burkes had hoped for that reaction. Randy was more concerned about B.J. than Ben.

Quickly, Randy pulled himself together. "I'm sorry. It's not your fault. In a way it's probably for the best. All the hell he would have had to go through for killing Julie, even though she deserved it."

Marc and Burkes exchanged glances.

Burkes smiled. "You talk as if Ben really was guilty."

"You know he was," Randy answered through the tears that now gently rolled down his cheeks.

"You're taking a real gamble saying this now. What if we're wrong? What if he's still alive? You're a good attorney. If I didn't know better, I might think you didn't care whether he did time or not."

Randy was caught off guard by the veteran cop's intuition.

"Yeah, I guess you're right. I guess I'm just upset. Then again, if you do the crime, you should do the time."

"I certainly hope you remember that the next time we're on opposite sides in court." Burkes smiled."Is your mother here, Randy?"

"She's upstairs."

"Why don't you go break the news to her. We'll wait."

"Yeah, okay."

Randy sprinted up the stairs. Burkes made a beeline for the kitchen. Marc stood frozen and confused but didn't dare ask what his partner was doing for fear of the truth.

Burkes came back when he heard Randy's footsteps on the stairwell.

"My mother's not taking this too well. Could we just be alone now?"

"Sure. We'll get outta here. C'mon, Marc. Call us if you need anything."

As they walked down the sidewalk, Marc asked, "What are we doing?"

"Patience, my dear Johnson, patience," was Burkes' only reply.

Burkes directed Marc to a spot down the street. Marc steered the van into the parking lot of a small convenience store less than a block away.

"Get out!" Burkes ordered.

Marc obeyed out of fear and curiosity. The duo climbed in the back where there was an array of electronic circuitry.

"Oh no," Marc uttered in a low tone as Burkes played with a control panel. Slowly the detective tuned in one channel, then another. The sound of microphones in an empty room seemed to be all they could hear.

"You planted bugs all over the place! I knew it! You said we weren't gonna break the law!"

"I said I would never ask you to break the law," John corrected his young protege.

"We can't do this! It will never hold up in court."

"It doesn't have to. We just need to get an edge. Find out their next move so we can be ready for them."

"It's not right," Marc argued.

"They started this war!" Burkes' temper set in. "Would you rather them just go on killing whoever they want to? Shipping drugs in here? Peddling them off to kids! Huh?"

"It's just not—" Marc was cut off by the unmistakable sound of Randy Seals' voice saying, "I'll be back in a minute," followed by the slamming of a door.

"He's leaving!" Burkes deduced. "Get back up front! Quick!"

The two scurried back into the front of the van. This time Burkes took the wheel to ensure he didn't lose Seals wherever he went.

"He's got to come this way," Burkes said. "Unless he's going over to someone else's condo. Riverside Drive is blocked off at the back side of the condominiums for repair. Right now this street is the only entrance."

The two watched the Seals condo just a hundred yards away as Randy Seals pulled away from the curb in the town car.

"Get down," Burkes ordered.

Burkes peered ever so slightly over the wheel as the town car neared. He cranked the van but left it in park. The town car passed in front of the van. "Okay, let's roll," Burkes said, raising up out of the seat. "Watch it! Get back down!"

Randy had turned into the little store. Marc could see Randy from his side; Burkes could not.

"He's using a pay phone," Marc said.

"Damn! I've got something for that too, but it's in the back. I figured he'd have enough sense not to use his phone. He's got ten times the brains of Gene McMasters. A hundred to one says he's calling B.J. right now. I would hate to have to be in his shoes. I would imagine B.J. White is one pretty pissed-off gangster right now," Burkes said while throwing the van in drive and easing onto the street as inconspicuously as possible.

"Do you think he spotted us?" Marc's voice quivered as the excitement boiled.

"I hope not. He's probably too distracted right now."

Burkes eased down the street, made a loop and slowly worked their way back. Randy was off the phone, but standing beside it as if waiting for a call. Burkes pulled off on the side of the road a good distance from the all-night market.

Randy waited for nearly ten minutes, then picked up the receiver as if to answer a call. The conversation lasted only a couple of minutes, with Randy pausing once to look at his Rolex. Burkes guessed a meeting was being arranged for a certain time. Minutes later Randy had reparked in front of his condominium.

Burkes drove back up to the shoppette. This time he parked so they could pull away before Randy could get that far. The two settled in for what figured to be a long night of watching and waiting. Marc ignored the constant pages from the D.A. It was the first time he had ever stood up to his boss. In fact, it was the first time Marc ever remembered standing up to any form of authority. He wondered if too much John Burkes was beginning to rub off on him. It made him nervous. He volunteered to go for sodas and stepped out of the van.

"Hold it!" Burkes shouted.

"What is it?" Marc reached for the extra binos.

"Who the hell is this?" Burkes barked, trying to adjust one of the volume controls on the electronic receiver that transmitted signals from within the bugged condo.

"I don't see anything!" Marc said, adjusting his focus on the condo.

"Someone's beating on the back door," Burkes said, handing Marc an extra set of headphones to plug into the receiver.

"Who is it?" Marc asked.

"Shhhh." Burkes motioned for silence as he fine-tuned the controls.

"I can't believe it!" Randy said to his late-night visitor. "The cops were just here. They think you're dead! This is so incredible. Thank God!"

"No way!" Marc screamed.

"Shhhh." Burkes begged for silence.

Ben now stood inside Randy's kitchen. He was dirty, battered, scarred, and wearing a Shelby County Sheriff's Department jacket that caused Randy to bellow with laughter.

"Thank God you're alive! Mom's asleep. Let me get her."

"No, Randy don't bother her, please. I need to talk to you."

"I can't believe this!" Marc pounded his fist on the dash.

"Shhh. Listen," Burkes pleaded.

Ben adjusted the .380 in the small of his back so he could sit down. The explosives he had already dropped into the back of Randy's 4x4 Chevy truck parked behind the condo with a bass boat attached. He rested his body in the chair, trying his best to stay awake. Randy fixed him a cold drink.

"What are we gonna do?" Marc asked.

"Nothing," came Burkes' reply. "Just keep our mouths shut and we'll learn more right here than in all the years that I've known B.J. White."

Randy walked back to the table, put a cold soda in front of his cousin, and took a seat beside him. "Thank God you're alive."

Ben took a couple of gulps and gathered his nerve before questioning his next of kin. "Randy, I want to ask you something, and I want you to tell me the truth."

"Sure," Randy shrugged, somewhat surprised at Ben's tone.

"Explain to me exactly how you got me out of those drummed-up charges McMasters had me under down in Greensburg."

"What?"

"You heard me. Tell me how you did it."

"I just went in there and talked to McMasters. He said he had always liked you and hated to see anything bad happen to you. I worked out a deal with him and he took it to the D.A. No problem. What's the big deal?"

"Then explain why he would go and kill Julie."

"She would run her mouth. I'm sure he wasn't willing to take that chance," Randy laughed at his cousin's ignorance.

"He was willing to let me walk away, but he killed her."

Randy sat uneasily on the edge of his chair, concerned about his cousin's state of mind. "You didn't have anything on him except that he was sleeping with your wife. It might not get him reelected but it's not a crime." Randy forced himself to laugh again.

"When he had Julie killed he knew she had to have told me everything. He knew I would talk. Why not kill me too?"

"He didn't have to. He set you up where nobody would believe you. It looked liked you killed your own wife." Randy forced a laugh again. "Forget all this, man. We need to get you a new plan. You want to turn yourself in?"

"You spared my life, didn't you?" Ben demanded.

"What?"

"You told McMasters to let me go. You told his people to only kill Julie and to just set me up and let me become a fugitive. You couldn't bear to see your own cousin killed, but making me a fugitive was okay."

"Ben!" The blood rushed to Randy's face, showering him with a guilty blush. "Ben...I...I...don't know what's wrong with you, but—" Randy slid his chair away from the table and started to rise.

"Sit back down!" In one continuous move Ben retrieved and pointed the .380 at his cousin.

"Ben! My God! What are you doing?"

Ben nodded his head slowly. "Thank you for sparing my life. At least I know you did care about me. But I really wish you had let me die with my wife. I would have been better off."

"Ben, I...don't...know...what.... Put that gun away. Ben, this isn't funny!"

Burkes strained to hear every word coming from the kitchen nearly a hundred yards to the west. Marc's heart pounded the outer walls of his chest.

"I know, Randy. I know everything." Ben shook his head as if he still didn't believe it.

"Know what, Ben? What are you talking about, for God's sake?"

"I talked to John Burkes less than twenty-four hours ago."

"I know. He was here a while ago. He said he had talked to you. You were gonna turn yourself in after they raided a warehouse, but he thinks you're dead now."

"I know everything," Ben said, shaking his head.

"Well, tell me what you are talking about then, because I don't have a clue."

"Burkes has got a copy of Gene McMasters's cellular telephone bill. It seems he wasn't too discreet. He called you from his cellular."

Randy's face reddened a little more. "Yeah, if you must know, he called to check on you. Just to see how you were doing. I didn't know he was on his cellular. He called me before once or twice for some legal advice. I don't know whether he was at home or what. You know I've known Gene ever since I was a deputy D.A. in Green County years ago."

Ben cocked the pistol. "It wasn't just one cellular call. It was bunches, lots and lots of calls."

"He probably had been trying to call me and couldn't get me so he kept trying back—"

"No. These were before I was arrested. Burkes only had a couple of bills, but the calls lasted anywhere from five to thirty minutes. There were lots and lots of calls, over a dozen the month before I was arrested."

Randy sat in the chair beet red. "I don't remember talking…to… him…that much." Randy's voice drifted as he stared at the floor.

"It's over, Randy. It's over."

Randy gave Ben a blank stare.

"Burkes knows everything. He knows you're connected with B.J. and Steve Lyles. He knows everything."

Randy wiped perspiration from his forehead but said nothing.

"And to think my own cousin and step-brother-in-law and boss set me up. I was so naive to everything around me. I can't believe it. What did Steve Lyles have to say about the murder of his own step-sister? Did he okay it? Huh?"

Randy stared at the floor. "You don't understand," he mumbled.

"What's there to understand?"

"You don't know what you're doing. You haven't a clue of the kind of people you're fooling with."

"Maybe you can clue me in?"

"They're too big, too organized to stop." Randy's voice seemed aimless as if he was speaking to the air. He tried to refocus himself. "I can work you in. I'll bring you in, get you a new identity. You can make a fortune. The cops think you're dead anyway."

Ben acted as if he was toying with the notion. "Suppose I say okay. Then what?"

Randy pepped up at the glimmer of hope. "Everybody is meeting at the port in Greensburg at 4 a.m. Steve Lyles is having cash and explosives shipped upriver from a stash in Vicksburg to replace what you managed to destroy. We get B.J. settled down and we can introduce you. He'll tell Gene and Steve to keep their hands off, and everything will be okay. If the cops are after me too, you and I will get fake passports and go to South America. We can work on that end of the operation and live like kings in a tropical paradise. It'll be so much fun. You'll love it, Ben. I've got connections to take care of us forever. Whatta ya say?"

Ben smiled a deep satisfying smile. "You seem to be forgetting one thing. I'm a cop."

Randy stuttered as if unsure of what he was hearing. "A cop. Did you say a cop? You're a freakin' fugitive."

"I'll always be a cop."

Randy sat dazed.

Ben took a deep breath and bent his arm to point the Beretta toward the ceiling, keeping it cocked. "I came here...I think...to kill you. But after talking to you, I realize I really do believe in all those things that I've always stood for. Doing things the right way, the moral way. Justice will take care of you. I have faith."

"I never wanted to see you hurt. I'm the reason you're alive," Randy said. "You don't know what kind of risk I took allowing you to talk to the cops about Greensburg in the first place!" He shook his head. "You don't understand. You can't win unless you play along. The stakes are too high. The players are too big."

"You talk as if it's a game. It's not a game, Randy. It's real life."

"The hell it is! It's a game for high rollers only. Big people. Big names. Big bucks!"

"That's it to you. Just one great big crap shoot, huh?"

"If you want to call it that you can. One thing's for sure—you can never be a player without me."

"I don't want to be. This is one crap game I'm about to bust up!"

"Ha, ha, ha," Randy laughed at his country cousin. "You! You're gonna stop it! John Burkes and the Memphis P.D., the DEA, the New Orleans P.D., nobody has stopped it, and now you're going to?"

John Burkes felt goose bumps run up his back listening to the mockery and resisted the urge to drive up to the condo and fire off a couple of shots.

"You have absolutely no clue whatsoever!" Randy continued. "Even if you're successful in slowing things down—I mean you were able to put a little dent in the operation back at the warehouse— but there will always be more to follow. The only thing you'll accomplish is getting yourself killed. Sooner or later it will happen. You might be sitting in a restaurant in another state five years down the road and the waiter walks up to you with a menu and a submachine gun and splatters you right where you sit. You can't escape. You may as well join."

"Never! I may not have money, but I still have my principles. My morals. That's something we were both raised with and you lost somewhere along the way."

"Well, you can blame me, I guess. Seeing as how I raised him." Mary Seals' voice came from the other side of the kitchen where she stood with a .38 special in her hand, cocked and ready to kill her nephew.

Ben was aghast. Burkes and Marc adjusted their headphones, not sure if they were hearing correctly.

Mary gave her son instructions. "Get up and move away from the table. You should have had McMasters handle this from the very beginning."

Randy stood and looked at his cousin. "You couldn't stay dead, could you? You couldn't just go away. You had to come back here and try to screw everything up!"

"I see you've incorporated your mother into your little web. Aunt Mary, I can't believe you. I guess all of you are coke addicts or something, huh?" Ben looked at his aunt, who still clutched the revolver, pointed at his left side from nearly ten feet away.

"Lay the gun on the table," she commanded.

"Why? So you can shoot me and dump me in the river? Randy, just how does one go about involving his own mother into a drug ring?"

Randy smiled at the naive deputy. "Like you said, it's a crap shoot. Everyone loves a good crap game. Especially when you always win. When you're with me, every roll is a seven." He reached to take Ben's gun.

"The only reason you always win is because you cheat. You're always playing with loaded dice!"

Ben spun out of the chair just as Randy's hand touched the gun barrel. He hit the floor rolling. A slug from Mary's .38 discharged, striking the wood chair where Ben had been sitting. Even in his exhausted state, lying on the floor sideways, the young man from the backwoods of the Mississippi Delta had the poise to fire a perfect strike. In less than a second from the time Ben jumped out of his seat, his aunt lay on the floor dead from a gunshot to the cranium.

"Mama! Oh God! Mama!" Randy dove toward his mother and threw his arms around her.

Ben scurried across the floor to pick up the .38 lying on the floor.

"You bastard! Kill me too!" Randy begged his cousin between his tears. Ben clutched the .380 tight and pointed at his cousin while pondering the thought. "I can't kill somebody in cold blood." He turned to leave.

The police van headed up the street, peeling rubber to get to the condo.

"We can't go in there!" Marc screamed at the top of his lungs as the van slung him from side to side.

"People are being shot. We have to," Burkes screamed back.

"How will we explain what we're doing?" Marc shouted back as the van slid into the curb outside the condo.

"Worry about it later," the detective yelled, leaping from the van.

Marc jumped from the van panicked. "Jesus!" He slapped the top of his head with both hands. "Why did you get me into this?"

"Stay here!" Burkes said, running from the van only to be followed by the lawyer. Burkes ran to the shrubbery on the side of the porch with Marc on his heels.

"Give me your backup!" Marc begged Burkes.

"Are you sure?" Burkes asked as he handed Marc his backup .380.

Marc took the .380. "You take the front, I'll take the back."

Inside Ben turned to make his exit.

"You'll pay for this, you bastard!" His cousin screamed. "You should hear McMasters brag about screwing Julie!"

The words froze Ben. He faced his cousin and raised the pistol to kill the man who had provided him with the gun in the first place. Then he lowered it, unable to go through with it.

"They'd give her a couple hits of crack and then four or five deputies would take turns after McMasters. Sometimes, more than one at a time," Randy laughed a wicked laughed.

Pow! Pow! Pow! Pow! Pow! Pow! Click. Click. Click. Click.

The double-action weapon had expended its ammo into Randy Seals. Ben continued to click away.

"Police!" John Burkes shouted, kicking in the front door.

Ben shoved the .380 into his belt and ran for the back door gripping Mary's .38. He grabbed the keys to the 4x4 off the keyholder by the back door and ran to the truck.

"Freeze! Police!" Marc managed to get the nerve to shout from the darkness behind the condo.

Ben wheeled and fired one panicked shot from Mary's .38, striking the deputy D.A. in the chest. Burkes ran cautiously through the house to the back, where the shot had come from.

"Marc!" he yelled as he saw the tail end of the boat behind the 4x4, making its way around the side of the condo.

"Help me?" Burkes heard a moan in the dark.

He eased out the back door, peering into the darkness. "Oh my God! Marc!" He felt the lawyer's chest wound. It was severe. He had called for backup on the way up to the condo. There were sirens in the distance, but the wound couldn't wait. He had to get Marc to the hospital now. "Marc, I'm sorry. " He begged the young man for forgiveness as he tore open his shirt and filled the bullet hole with his own handkerchief. The close proximity of the hole to Marc's heart left him no chance for survival.

Marc's cries turned to light moans as the life faded from his body. Burkes reached to try and pick him up as a couple of neighbors showed up to investigate the shots in the night.

"Damn you Seals! Damn you!" Burkes screamed to the heavens. Marc tried to muster a breath as blood oozed from his lips. "I always...I always wanted to be a cop," Marc gasped.

Burkes struggled to hold back tears. "Be quiet. You're gonna make it."

"I guess...this...this is why...my parents didn't want me to... become...a cop." He faded off for good.

"Marc Johnson! Don't do this to me! Damn you! Damn you,

Seals!" Burkes wept.

"Police!" Two uniformed officers stood on either side of the house with their weapons drawn.

"Over here," Burkes cried out.

The officers moved in. "Stand up with your hands over your head where we can see them."

"Not me, fool! I'm John Burkes, Memphis P.D. We've got a triple homicide."

Seconds later the yard was full of cops and neighbors. Cops were pushing people off the yard and trying to get statements at the same time. Paramedics were running into cops who were trying to maintain the integrity of the crime scene.

Burkes tried to snap out of the daze that had come over him. He paged the D.A. and called Bill Jensen from the U.S. Marshall's office. The meeting Randy had scheduled for 4 a.m. at the Greensburg port was a chance to catch B.J. and the whole bunch red-handed. He couldn't blow this chance. The odds were in favor of Ben Seals showing up there as well. Burkes' plan was to bring down B.J. the right way, once and for all.

Burkes waited in the den for the Bob Taylor to show. He had to give some explanation for Marc's death. He blamed the murder on B.J.'s gang.

The D.A. showed up frazzled and confused, seemingly unable to cope with all the events of the night. Burkes tried to find words to explain what had transpired earlier. He omitted the parts about the illegal eavesdropping and the fact that Ben Seals was still alive. Deep in his heart he knew Ben was a good guy. This was just an unfortunate accident. If Taylor found out Ben Seals had killed Marc, he would probably have a lynch mob after him. There would be no trial. Just a bunch of cops with orders to shoot on sight.

He was trying to explain how Marc was just helping out when Terry Mills burst through the door. "What the hell is going on here? Burkes! I shoulda known you were here! I heard you were down at the subnuclear blast working with the D.A. here. You're making the rounds tonight."

Burkes saw Bill Jensen standing in the doorway. He ignored the homicide detective and pushed past him to talk to Jensen.

"Don't go anywhere, Burkes!" Mills scowled.

Burkes briefed Bill Jensen on everything that had taken place.

Jensen said they would take over from here. He would have to bring in the ATF and the FBI to have proper jurisdiction over the illegal arms shipments that were supposed to be taking place at Greensburg.

The D.A. burst out of the condo after gathering himself together enough to realize he had spotted a federal agent on the premises.

"John! Oh, John!"

Burkes stood in the street talking with Jensen, who was making notes to himself.

"John!" Taylor called out again.

"Yes?" Burkes answered, dreading the ensuing conversation.

"John." Taylor shook his head. "We have to find Marc's killer. I don't trust Homicide. We need to do this ourselves. We don't have time to stand around chit-chatting with the feds. No offense, Agent Jensen."

"None taken," Bill Jensen smiled at the district attorney he had dealt with in the past.

Burkes braced himself for the D.A.'s next reaction. "Sir, I'm bringing in the feds."

"Excuse me?"

"I said I'm bringing in the feds."

"On what authority?"

"There's something going down tonight across the state line. The feds are gonna have to come in."

Taylor's head swelled with anger. "You're screwing up, Burkes. You were gonna be a permanent transfer to my investigative team, if you wanted it. Now Memphis P.D. is gonna put you back at a desk job in a couple of weeks. You...you...you're screwin' up." He turned and stormed back toward the condo.

"Are you gonna be okay?"Jensen asked his friend.

"Sure, maybe a desk job will save my marriage," Burkes sighed with relief.

Jensen smiled. "I'll pick you up in an hour or so."

"Okay."

"By the way, John. I'll make up an official explanation for how we know about this gathering that's supposed to take place in Greensburg. But just for my own curiosity, how did you find out about it?"

John thought about an answer. "You don't want to know."

Chapter 23

Ben had no idea that Burkes had not revealed to anyone the fact that he was still alive. He couldn't understand why there weren't cops on his tail already, especially driving a four-wheel drive with a boat behind it. It wasn't as if he was hard to spot. Twenty minutes down Highway 61 he couldn't stand it anymore. He turned off on an old road that led back to the river and backed down an old boat ramp leading down to the swift currents of the mighty river. He tied the boat to a tree after sliding it off the trailer into the water, then parked in the deep brush and retrieved his dynamite and accessories. The 140 horses were soon fired up and pushing Ben down river toward Greensburg.

John Burkes was still the only person on earth who knew Ben was still alive. Burkes had gone home to shower and was now awaiting Bill Jensen's arrival. Jensen had already assembled a spurof-the-moment posse consisting of several agents from his own office, four ATF agents, three DEA special agents, and two representatives from the FBI. All were now working under the authority of a federal prosecutor who had been awakened in the middle of the night. Burkes was the only local or state officer asked to join the party.

The closer Ben got to Greensburg, the more his confidence grew. He was nervous about the possible encounter with the villains but more relaxed about his getaway from Memphis. He felt sure he would have a chance to launch an attack on those he held accountable for all that had happened to him.

He had his little batch of dynamite and materials on the seat beside him. The cool wind on the river in the dark of the night was comforting. Ben expected to die before the night was over. He used the serenity of the trip down river to make his peace with God and beg forgiveness on the people he had killed and those he was about to.

Small towns and communities lined the riverbanks. From the water they all seemed to look alike. He could only tell where he was by the signs on the various buildings and an occasional water tower. He still had plenty of time to reach his destination, but as he drew closer he became more and more nervous.

The feds, accompanied by John Burkes, also had plenty of time. The federal posse drove down in Blazers, with the exception of a couple of helicopter crews. The two birds were to be parked in Cohoma, the next county to the north, far away from McMasters reign. They would be brought in at the very last minute. The entire contingency was met by more agents from Mississippi who knew the layout of the land better. Counting John and two investigators from the federal prosecutor's office, there were a total of thirty-two officers making up the small army that would swarm down on the tiny town. Burkes worried that even more might be needed. At 2:10 a.m., two more agents arrived from Helena, Arkansas. They had obtained terrain maps from the Helena National Guard unit. Quickly plans were thrown together. People were assigned duties and issued fully automatic weapons. The time drew near.

Ben finally reached his destination. He rounded the big bend in the river and passed by the oxbow lake made by the natural flow of the river. There were two docks, one at the foot of the giant hill below the chemical plant and another downstream and across the river that was away from the lights of the chemical factory and hardly ever used. When Randy had said B.J. and Steve were meeting at the port in Greensburg, Ben knew that would be the one.

He silently trolled past the dock looking for any signs of activity. Everything was still quiet. He found a place to tie off the boat in the thick brush growing in the water. He grabbed the explosives and made the steep haul up the embankment through the thick brush. He rambled to the dock fighting stickers and limbs and stumbling over holes in the ground.

The whole dock was only forty yards long. It consisted of nothing more than an asphalt top on an embankment of dirt jutting into the river. He split the bundle of dynamite into two smaller bundles. Strategically he planted the two bundles on the dock to get the most effect and still be able to conceal their location. Using a stick he dug out little holes in the dirt on the edge of the dock. He envisioned Mitch Williams, or better yet Gene McMasters, standing close to one of the bundles and being ripped apart by the blast. A smile came over his face as he ran the wire from the dynamite caps back through the woods. He wouldn't be able to get all of them, but if he could get some he would be happy.

He found a small gully just the right size to hide in with the remote by his side. He wired the hot wire to the remote and checked his late aunt's .38, which had only four shots left. The extra ammo for the .380 was still in the van where he had left Tawana Griffin. Now he wished he hadn't wasted those extra bullets on Randy. After finding a good rock for a pillow, he lay back and unintentionally drifted off to sleep.

He awoke, startled that he had allowed himself to fall sound asleep. He meant only to doze for a few minutes. He pressed the illumination button on his sports watch: 3:28. He couldn't see anybody. The moonlight reflected a still-silent dock. He climbed the big hill to the main road. Lake Road had had another name at one time, but the people of Green County had called it Lake Road for so long the board of supervisors finally changed it.

It looked like home to Ben. Anything in Green County looked good to Ben, even in the dark. He was almost twenty yards from the road when a set of blue lights lit up the darkness. He tried to focus his eyes, but neither pupil seemed to cooperate. His heart palpitated as he knelt low to the ground and eased closer for a better look. He could barely make out what was going on.

Two deputies had turned on their lights to stop a couple on a date joyriding on the country roads. The deputies explained to the couple that Lake Road was temporarily sealed off. There were laughs between the two deputies about what the couple might be up to as they drove away. Unbeknownst to Ben and Gene McMasters' boys was the fact that the driver of the car was an FBI special agent. The woman posing as his date worked for the DEA.

"Damn!" Ben cursed himself under his breath. How could he have been so stupid? The pier at the lake. It was easy access from the river into the oxbow lake. It also provided perfect concealment for a rendezvous. He raced to the dock to retrieve the explosives. His time was short. A quarter-mile through the brush, he could see shadows looming by the pier.

The woods were filled with federal agents. The first hit was on the two deputies running the road block. They were quietly captured and arrested before they even knew they had company. The FBI agents had equipped most of the officers with night-vision goggles. John Burkes also carried a set of the four thousand dollar binos.

Ben watched in the tree line as a large boat entered the lake from the river. A "party barge," Ben deduced. Large enough to haul a number of people and yet fast like a ski boat. Ben could make it out from the lighted trim on the frame of the craft. A speed boat followed close behind. It was all but invisible in the dark. Steve Lyles waited on the dock with Gene McMasters and company as B.J. White neared the pier with his crew.

The river was a slow mode of transportation, but it was the only way to haul illegal weapons away from the highway patrol and other local law enforcement. Ben stumbled down the slope to the water a good twenty-five yards from the pier. He eased himself and the bundles into the waters. For the sake of his nerves, he kept telling himself this was no different from blowing up beaver dams around his old deer camp. He swam underwater using a sidestroke and carrying the bundles with one arm. The darkness provided him with cover. He found his way under the pier. The boats had docked . People climbed from the boats only a few feet from him.

"You! You muthaf—er! I oughta kill you right here!" B.J. White yelled at Gene McMasters.

"Yeah, you just try it!" the high sheriff retorted.

"Gentlemen! Please! We're here for business."

Ben recognized his brother-in-law's voice. Steve Lyles was trying to calm the two men.

Ben wrapped his feet around one of the posts anchoring the pier in the water to steady himself. The waves sloshing from the wake of the boat nearly drowned him, but they also served to camouflage the noises he made. He clung to the pier while tying the bundles with the wire that he would also run to the remote.

"Randy said his cousin led the cops straight to the warehouse.If you woulda handled things right from the beginning my f—ing warehouse never would have gotten blown up." B.J. yelled at the old sheriff.

"Your boys had a chance to kill Ben Seals when you killed his wife." McMasters retorted.

"If you hadn't been f—ing his wife in his bed, it never would have happened." B.J. screamed.

"That's my business!"

"You muthaf—er!" B.J. grabbed Gene's throat. The deputies drew their guns. B.J.'s boys slammed bolts forward on their automatic weapons.

"Jesus f—ing H. Christ! Would everybody relax!" Steve Lyles pleaded. "We're all in this together. I've got as much to lose as anybody if the cops trace back the offshore company that owned that warehouse and find out I'm connected to it."

Tensions eased momentarily. Ben swam away underwater dragging the wire in one hand and the remote in the other. The dynamite remained secured to the pier.

"B.J., we got some grenades for you, a couple of rocket launchers, and some car bombs for that armored truck job you wanted to do," Steve Lyles said. "I brought fifty thousand in cash and some fresh-cut Colombian you can sell to recoup some of your losses. There's at least a quartermil in street value in dope alone."

Ben struggled, trying to remain quiet while reaching for dry land. He pulled himself slowly from the water down onto the slope where he had entered the river.

John Burkes stood at the top of the hill scanning the riverbanks below in search of his former employee. There was no escaping the night-vision binos. He zoomed in on the figure exiting the murky waters below. He watched as Ben dried the tips of the wire and plugged them into the remote. Burkes raced down the hill toward him.

On the pier, one of the deputies called to McMasters to tell him the road lookouts were not responding to radio signals. Everyone on the pier sensed something was wrong. Before anyone could scramble away, Ben depressed the lever. By their own explosives, they would all meet their death. The dynamite blew in all directions igniting the other explosives Steve Lyles had brought to the pier. Bodies flew through the air. Both boats burst into flames. People screamed as they died. Ben smiled a venomous smile, then scampered up the hill.

The feds were stunned and had no plan for such contingency. Ben ran seemingly unnoticed up the hill until John Burkes cut through the woods at an angle to head him off. Ben had not seen anyone and had no idea anyone would be there. He heard the sound of a gun cock and a voice say, "I should shoot you and put you out of your misery."

He recognized the voice. Jesus! He couldn't believe it. Running uphill his head was close to the ground from the slope of the land. He leaned forward, placing his hands on the ground. He had almost made it.

Burkes spoke softly. "That was an assistant D.A. you whacked behind your cousin's condo. They'll crucify you for it."

"I don't care."

"You must've had getaway plans?" Burkes asked.

"Something like that," Ben mouthed without emotion, hands still firmly on the ground, head drooping downward.

"You could have waited. We were about to make a big bust here."

Ben shook his head. "But I have rendered justice."

Burkes nodded in agreement, still holding Ben at gunpoint. "Well, there are feds all over this hill to our right and a couple at the top of the hill. I'm a little preoccupied right now. The feds are all to the north and east. There are none to the south. You stay here till I get back. You're under arrest."

Burkes smiled and turned to walk away. "By the way, nobody else knows you're still alive." He walked into the dark woods in an easterly direction.

Ben disappeared into the night.